'Out of terrible personal circumstances, Matt Johnson has written a barnstormer of a book in *Wicked Game* – one that fans of Chris Ryan, Andy McNab and Peter James will drool over. His first-hand experience of police work and counter-terrorist operations gives this page-turner a chilling authenticity that few others in the genre can hope to rival. But despite his police pedigree, Johnson also gets inside the terrorists' heads to give them credible motivation. Nothing is clear-cut in a labyrinthine plot, which is gripping and which – despite thrills and spills aplenty – never falls short of believable. The ending is neatly tied up, but leaves the reader eager to follow lead character Robert Finlay's further adventures' David Young, author of *Stasi Child*

'The magic mix of jeopardy, emotion and action. I could *not* put it down' Louise Voss

'A book by an ex-cop and -soldier has the potential to go wrong and fall flat due to it being all about inside knowledge that is tough to decipher by the public. This book isn't like that. It is a genuine page-turner, very well written, and just flows from one scenario to the next. It is clear the author lived through these times and this is evident in knowledge and description. Excellent' Ian Patrick

'The Robert Finlay series is turning into something very exciting; I'll definitely be reading the next one' Jacob Reviews Books

'*Deadly Game* is a fantastic novel. It is a page-turning thriller but so much more. It really made me think about the world, not just terrorism, but the lengths the secret state will go to … I can't recommend this book enough and can't wait until the third instalment' The Crime Novel Reader

'For anybody wanting an action-packed, explosive read … *Deadly Game* should definitely be on their shopping list. In fact, it should be moved to the No.1 spot as that's where it deserves to be … I just hope there's more of Robert Finlay to come' Page Turner's Nook

'Whilst we all love a good edge-of-the-seat thriller, the kind of novels Matt writes are more in my ballpark; I want that emotive edge and that sense of genuine involvement. Proving that you can give multiple layers to the crime thriller genre and still not lose the thrill aspect (a thing that is not rare but is not common either), *Deadly Game* comes highly recommended by me … I simply can't wait for the next one, to see the bigger picture the author is creating here and because seriously, it's just a damned fine read. Don't miss it' Liz Loves Books

'I can't recommend this book enough. I think this is a PERFECT read for thriller fans. It has lots of thrilling moments but it also has lots of emotion at its core. Robert is desperately trying to protect his beloved family, he is suffering with PTSD *and* he is assigned to investigate the horrendous world of sex trafficking. There is so much going on in this book. I loved it. You'll see when you read it. Just the first chapter is enough to break your heart' Ronnie Turner

'Finlay desperately fought to save a colleague. But by the end of the book it felt like there had been a real shift in direction, particularly from where we first met Finlay and Jones, just weeks before, in *Wicked Game*. There is the promise of so many secrets yet to be revealed; of a story which is not ready to let the reader go just yet, and I for one can't wait to read more. A tension-filled and heroic deep-sea-diving five stars from me' Jen Meds Book Reviews

'I couldn't put it down! If anything, it slowed down my reading so I could really take in what was happening and as a result I was constantly being pulled further and further into this murky world where it is difficult to trust anyone. A brilliant, credible thriller with a tight, multi-layered, tension-filled plot that comes together brilliantly' Have Books Will Read

'Dealing with some extremely hard-hitting subjects, *Deadly Game* is not for the faint-hearted, but for those who can stomach the grittiest subjects in crime, this is definitely a book you need to add to your TBR pile, and you need to do it now!' Emma the Little Book Worm

'Johnson's writing style is tight, sharp and full of authenticity, based on his own personal history as a police officer. Finlay as a character was well developed and easily likable and the secondary characters were also richly developed, adding fantastic depth. The scariest part of the plot, for me, is that the sex-trade industry is really happening and the scenes with these poor young women were heartbreaking, shocking and harrowing' Novel Gossip

'Matt Johnson is an incredible writer, he writes such real, compelling books that deal with incredibly difficult subjects' Girls v Books

'Never dull and full of tension, I'm looking forward to the next instalment of Robert's story. In short: a nail-biting thriller and some great characters and serious issues' Books, Life & Everything

'Matt Johnson shows he's been there, done it and worn the T-shirt in his first novel. Entertaining and gripping throughout, it is authentic writing at its very best. His ability to overlap reality with the fictional characters, from both a soldier's and cop's perspective, is uncanny. Top-quality entertainment from a first-class writer' D.N. Ex-22SAS Regiment

'The human element of the book appealed to me the most – Finlay's reaction to events as opposed to gun-toting action; the horrific nature of human trafficking and the ripple effect of PTSD were all true to life and are what attracted me to this book. My head was spinning by the end of it and my paranoia levels were sky-high! This book is going to knock your socks off, blow your mind and have you reeling!' Chapter in My Life

'The plot in this book is absolutely five shining gold stars of brilliant, it really is. There is so much tension and suspense curled around the plot that the reader almost needs reminders to keep breathing. The complexities of the plot make this such a thrilling read, and quite terrifyingly realistic (in a good way!)' The Quiet Knitter

'I was quite blown away. As ever, you get the impression Johnson has been there, done it, and got the T-shirt – or scars! – to prove it. Again, there's no technical overload … Johnson makes a great hero, easygoing and funny. And wife Jenny's there again, with solid support. Can you tell I enjoyed it?' Crime Worm

'Johnson has created a gritty and current novel dealing with, sadly, very real issues. It is disturbing yet credible and has a real intelligence behind it. Days after finishing the book I still find myself worrying about one of the characters, demonstrating just how immersed you become in this book. I eagerly anticipate the next book in the series. Highly recommended, *Deadly Game* is tense, topical, exciting and gripping. More than just a detective novel, it really packs a punch and leaves you breathless!' Bloomin' Brilliant Books

'Having read both *Wicked Game* and *Deadly Game* I've found that the former was more action-packed whilst the latter was more suspenseful. Both are strong, credible thrillers. Through both darkly-lit novels, Finlay's character shines' Book Drunk

'This intelligent plot is amazingly well constructed with multiple layers. It doesn't just show the dark and disturbing world of criminals but also the games people in government and secret services play … Just like the first book, *Deadly Game* is gripping, compelling, authentic and highly realistic. It's a nail-biting ride of a thriller and if this was a movie, I'd be on the edge of my seat' Novel Delights

'A stunning thriller, a real page-turner, well researched and written by a brilliant storyteller' Atticus Finch

'What starts out slowly, soon explodes into a vibrant and Le Carré-esque read that had me on the edge of my seat from the first page' The Library Door

'Matt Johnson has once again produced a belting read. I loved the short chapters in the book. To begin with the scenes have a gentle build with them progressing to the more hardcore details much later on, some of which are very harrowing … A brilliant read again, so looking forward to a third book' Books From Dusk Till Dawn

'A former SAS officer finds himself a target of a terrorist cell years after he has left the forces, creating a fast-moving storyline. I was so gripped that I could not put it down. I loved the main protagonist, Robert Finlay, but I particularly loved his feisty wife, Jenny. I'll be looking out for the sequel' Segnalibro

'The writing is direct: facts and histories stated, not left for the reader to pick over: there isn't time to stop and sift the finer aspects of motivation – to do so would only slow the plot. Events cascade, ruthless killers spill into the open, and the agencies who should be tackling them are far less united and coherent than one might expect … You'll enjoy this book if you're into thriller and action: even if you think you're not, the pace of the writing will carry you away. Robert Finlay's not a man who gives up easily' Blue Book Balloon

'From the first page through to the last, the reader is completely hooked and drawn in by the writing and the descriptions; this is such an absorbing and thrilling read. The authenticity of the writing, and the knowledge of what happens in particular situations raises this above other thrillers. *Wicked Game* really does give you flash, bang, wallop, and, like bullets, no words are wasted, but hit the target every time' Library Thing

'A real cracker of a book and I have no hesitation to give it five stars. I look forward to reading more books from this gifted writer' Bookworm

'An action thriller of the highest order that deserves to be read widely. It is hard to believe such an accomplished work is a debut' Never Imitate

'Despite having read hundreds of thrillers, it's rare to find one with this level of authenticity and with some real passion behind the writing ... I would describe *Wicked Game* as a thriller with a heart, and the story behind it and Matt's own experiences are what makes it beat' Book Addict Shaun

'A gripping and quite frantic story of espionage, misplaced loyalties, revenge, retribution and double-crossing. With twists and turns, and red herrings at every corner, *Wicked Game* is an impressive debut' Random Things through My Letterbox

'*Wicked Game* is a tense, exciting thriller that presents Finlay's gigantic effort to keep his family safe, trying to rediscover physical and military skills long put to rest, and facing seemingly insurmountable odds. The ending is stunning!' For Winter Nights

'Talk about a kick-ass novel! From the very first page, I was shocked into holding my breath. It reads like an action movie, but with all the bubbling tension in between, some of it so quiet and subtle that Matt lulls you into a sense of false security. Then BANG, he thumps you, shocks you, jolts you into submission, before doing it all again' The Book Trail

'The sheer dogged determination of Robert Finlay provides one hell of an exhilarating ride, as he dodges bullets, explosives, and the shadows of his past in this *Wicked Game* of cat and mouse. Expect nothing less than a thrilling journey, where secrets and revenge are delivered with guts and precision and the stakes are as high as they get – Finlay gives new meaning to the SAS motto of "Who dares, wins"' Little Bookness Lane

'It's the first-hand experience of terrible events that really gives *Wicked Game* an unshakeable feeling of authenticity, which is woven deep into the fabric of the story' Espresso Coco

'I've always been a fan of thrillers, with the build-up of tension, the action-packed heroics and insane bravery. *Wicked Game* is a stonkingly accessible British thriller, with its roots firmly set in recent UK history and a strong sense of authenticity running through it' Northern Crime

'The story itself is a complex web that the police, security services and Finlay himself are all trying to untangle. It is never clear who can be trusted and what agendas they are trying to move forward, except for Finlay, whose fight for survival we follow most intimately through his own thoughts. The tension takes hold early on and never lets up as the danger gets closer to home and Finlay realises that only he can secure his family's safety as he is forced to face his past up close and personal' Live Many Lives

'Matt Johnson has a very real talent and gift for thriller writing. *Wicked Game* cracks along at a great pace, with plenty of gripping and original plot twists and turns, and a finale that wouldn't be out of place in a book with a protagonist called Reacher' Mumbling about…

'This is a breathtaking debut novel that will have you on the edge of your seat' Thrillers, Chillers & Killers

'With his first-hand real-life experience Johnson has an understanding of what was going on in the minds of his friends, superiors and even terrorists. This is translated into excellent psychological portraits of the main characters. Facts mixed with fiction and unclear boundaries between both are the basis for moving, authentic narration and brilliant storytelling' Crime Review

'*Wicked Game* is an absolutely brilliant new thriller, and the plot is fast-paced, twisted and exciting. Finlay is a man who is prepared to break all the rules to protect his family, but he is also very human and likable. I can't praise Matt Johnson and *Wicked Game* too highly' Promoting Crime Fiction

End Game

ABOUT THE AUTHOR

Matt Johnson served as a soldier and Metropolitan Police officer for twenty-five years. Blown off his feet at the London Baltic Exchange bombing in 1993, and one of the first police officers on the scene of the 1982 Regent's Park bombing, Matt was also at the Libyan People's Bureau shooting in 1984 where he escorted his mortally wounded friend and colleague, Yvonne Fletcher, to hospital.

Hidden wounds took their toll. In 1999, Matt was discharged from the police with Post Traumatic Stress Disorder. While undergoing treatment, he was encouraged by his counsellor to write about his career and his experience of murders, shootings and terrorism. One evening, Matt sat at his computer and started to weave these notes into a work of fiction that he described as having a tremendously cathartic effect on his own condition. His bestselling thriller, *Wicked Game*, which was shortlisted for the CWA John Creasey Dagger, was the result. *Deadly Game* and now *End Game*, the final book in the Robert Finlay series, also draw on Matt's experiences and drip with the same raw authenticity as their predecessors.

Follow Matt on Twitter *@Matt_Johnson_UK* and his website: *mattjohnsonauthor.com*.

End Game

Matt Johnson

**ORENDA
BOOKS**

Orenda Books
16 Carson Road
West Dulwich
London SE21 8HU
www.orendabooks.co.uk

First published in the United Kingdom by Orenda Books, 2018
Copyright © Matt Johnson 2018

Matt Johnson has asserted his moral right to be identified as the author of this
work in accordance with the Copyright, Designs and Patents Act, 1988.

A catalogue record for this book is available from the British Library.

ISBN 978-1-912374-09-0
eISBN 978-1-912374-10-6

Typeset in Arno by MacGuru Ltd
Printed and bound by CPI Group (UK) Ltd, Croydon CR0 4YY

For sales and distribution, please contact: *info@orendabooks.co.uk*

For all serving and retired members of the emergency services. Those first responders who, without hesitation, head toward the dangers from which we, the public, flee.

For WPC Yvonne Fletcher, killed on duty on 17th April 1984, a crime that remains the only unsolved murder of a UK police officer.

And with thanks to John Murray, whose tireless and dogged determination to see those responsible for Yvonne's murder brought to justice continues unabated.

'And maybe just remind the few, if ill of us they speak,
That we are all that stands between the monsters and the weak.'

—*Michael Marks*

Happy the man, and happy he alone,
He who can call today his own:
He who, secure within, can say,
Tomorrow do thy worst, for I have lived today.
Be fair or foul or rain or shine
The joys I have possessed, in spite of fate, are mine.
Not Heaven itself upon the past has power,
But what has been, has been, and I have had my hour.

—John Dryden (1631–1700)

Prologue

August 2002

Alone in his car, Grady cracked the knuckles of his free hand before answering the telephone call.

'Where the hell are you, Cathy?' He was angry. It was already ten o'clock. If the brief was correct, their target would soon be home.

'Sorry. You're on your own for this one, chum,' she answered. 'I'm on my way to Belgium.'

'Is Howard sending a clean-up team?'

'Negative. Instructions are to make it clean, remove the body and await further instructions.'

'On my own?'

'You're a big boy, Grady.'

He hung up. This wasn't the first time arrangements had changed at the last minute and he also knew Cathy wouldn't have let him down if she could have avoided it. If she had to go to Belgium there would be a reason and he knew better than to ask her why.

This job was one he'd been expecting, one he'd been told was in the offing some weeks previously. A laptop and manuscript needing to be recovered and the bearer terminated. It was just a question of where and when.

The street was quiet. Not surprising, he thought, considering the rural location. Earlier in the evening, the rain had forced him to raise the car window. The first few heavy, yet infrequent spots had lasted several minutes before giving way to a deluge that now crashed down on the car like an angry monster demanding entry. Rain and dark cloud would give him an additional edge – ensuring he wasn't seen or heard when the time came.

The rain was bouncing off the tarmac. Trees in the small gardens and along the street groaned in the wind and leaves in their thousands gave up their tenuous grip, covering the pavements in a soggy brown carpet.

Grady scowled. Cathy was right, of course. He could cope on his own. The female target was small in stature and easily bundled into the boot of his car. He would manage, as he always did.

Any passing cars were few and far between and it had now been nearly an hour since he had seen another human being – an old man walking his dog. With the arrival of the rain, the village had become quiet, the residents safe and cosy in their homes.

As the car windscreen started to mist over, he returned the mobile phone to one jacket pocket and from another pulled a handkerchief, which he used to slowly stroke the moisture from the glass surface. He was careful to avoid any attention-drawing movement. He disliked being in so public a place, but to fully cover the approach road, it was essential.

Improved vision secured, he flexed his fists and stretched his fingers, keeping the blood flowing and hands warm. Eyes still fixed on the street, he then reached for a small leather holdall beneath the passenger seat of the car. Opening it gently he felt the cold steel of a small semi-automatic Beretta Model 70. The Model 70 was a small calibre and not normally one he would have chosen, but the instructions had been quite clear: it was to be used and then returned to the officer who had sanctioned the operation. Grady didn't argue the point; at close range the weapon could be just as deadly as something larger.

Earlier, as he'd watched, vapour had begun to flow from the boiler exhaust in the wall of the target house: an internal thermostat must have reacted to the drop in temperature triggered by the rain. A few minutes later a light had come on in the hallway. For a fleeting moment he'd foreseen complications; it looked like someone might already be home. But no movement followed. The curtains remained open; rooms stayed dark. The hall light was on a timer, he concluded – to create the illusion someone was in.

He was looking for a BMW 5 series. The female, in her forties with blonde hair, would be smartly dressed and on her way home from some kind of event. She was the only occupier of the house and was reported to be unaccompanied.

Lights now appeared further along the street. He dropped a half-finished cigarette into the ashtray. As the car pulled up near to him he could see the rain in the headlights. He nodded as he recognised the familiar shape of a BMW.

The car pulled up outside the house and began to reverse into a parking space. He couldn't make out the driver but, from the number of attempts being made to get into the space, it appeared they were clearly struggling with the difficulty the rain was causing.

Finally, the car was parallel to the verge. The engine stopped and a few moments later, a folded umbrella edged over the top of the driver's door. It sprung open as a figure emerged. He saw dark clothes, trousers, a raincoat flapping in the wind, and then a briefcase. The head and upper body were obscured by the umbrella. It was impossible to be certain if the figure was female but it looked probable. Watching as the door to the car closed, he silently stepped out into the darkness.

The figure walked quickly across the footway and up the short path to the door of the house. He was now just a few yards behind. As the umbrella was placed carefully to one side, he could now see it was a woman, petite with fairly long blonde hair. It was the target. She seemed to be searching through her pockets for her door keys.

He approached, moving silently along the path behind her. Swapping the Beretta into his right hand, he pulled a small silencer from his left pocket and quickly attached it to the barrel. There was an almost inaudible click as it snapped into place. Rain trickled down the back of his neck. It was cold and uncomfortable, but it hid the sound of his feet on the path. He raised the gun.

The woman was distracted. He knew why. She couldn't get her key into the door lock. He had superglued it before settling down in the car to wait. Delayed entry to the house; long enough to make the kill.

A small key fell from the woman's wet hand. As it dropped to the ground, she bent over, seemingly desperate to retrieve it quickly.

Just as Grady fired.

The .22 calibre round ricocheted off the stone door surround at one side of the target's head, sparks flying off into the darkness. He cursed. The woman turned and looked up towards him, their eyes meeting as she saw the gun. She looked petrified; raised her empty hand towards him, the fingertips trembling. As he pulled the trigger for the second time she mouthed a word. He didn't hear it, the rain masked the sound, and this time he didn't miss. Two bullets struck home, just above her left eye. She crumpled and rolled heavily against the door.

He stood astride her for a moment. She lay on her side, eyes now closed, body curled up as if asleep, a trickle of blood running from her nose onto the wet porch area. Even though she displayed no sign of life, he aimed at her temple and squeezed the trigger again. Her head jerked slightly as the bullet entered her skull.

Before picking up the briefcase, he checked the path and street. All quiet. Satisfied he was safe, he scanned the ground carefully and recovered the spent cases ejected by the Beretta.

The lights of another car appeared further long the lane. He paused, staying still, gun in one hand, briefcase in the other, as he waited for it to pass by. But it looked like the driver was slowing down.

✝

'Come on … come on.' Grady breathed heavily from the exertion as he waited impatiently for the call to connect.

'What is it?' Howard was abrupt and angry, even though he would know Grady calling on a secure line could only mean something important.

'I hit a problem.'

'The target didn't turn up?'

'Oh, she turned up alright. Trouble was, just as I was about to put her in the boot of my car, she had a visitor.'

'What happened?'

'I had to take him out. No choice. Young bloke – not her type I wouldn't have thought – came up the drive.'

'You sure you had no choice?' Howard asked, anxiously.

'He clocked me. These things can happen when you don't have a look-out to work with.'

'OK, OK, point made. Where are you? Can you clean up the scene?'

'Don't worry, that's all taken care of. I'm well away from there now. I've done the best I can. I slung him back in his car and dumped it a couple of miles up the road in a lay-by.'

'A couple of miles away? How did you get back?'

'A long, wet run. Nothing I haven't done before.'

'So, this lad who saw you will be found there, eventually?'

'That's the plan. He had a baseball bat in his car so I laid him out as if he'd been in a fight and come off worse.'

'Good … good.' Howard seemed to be thinking as he spoke, weighing up options, making decisions. 'And what about the target?' he asked.

'I've got her. I'll bury her where you said.'

'Long drive, Grady. You'd best be on your way.'

'Roger that. You didn't want me for Belgium then?'

'Cathy can take care of it.'

'Without an oppo?'

'Drop it, Grady. You've made your point. I accept I should have sent both of you on this job.'

'And what about the two cops?'

Howard hesitated before replying. 'Leave it with me. Circumstances have changed, I need to give the issue some more thought.'

With the call ended, Grady flicked the windscreen wipers back on, lit a cigarette and pulled out onto the road. Like Howard said, it was going to be a long drive.

Chapter 1

London, late 2002

'*Chasing suspect…*'

I moved as quickly as I could. It was definitely Nina's voice on the radio, and it sounded like she was after our target.

The house had appeared empty. The SO19 firearms officers had declared it clear and we had moved in to start a more thorough search. We were looking for paperwork, documents – anything that might lead us further into the world of the trafficking gang we were investigating.

I was in the kitchen and had just unearthed some interesting passport-sized photographs of young women. Nina's voice was shrill, excited.

She was on the first floor checking the bedrooms so I headed that way. Just as I turned towards the hallway and stairs, I caught a sudden movement out of the corner of my eye. A figure falling from the flat roof extension into the rear garden: dark clothing, moving quickly.

'*Garden … garden. Male … dark jacket.*' It was Nina's voice again.

I reached the door to the back garden in time to see one of the German Shepherd dogs from the firearms support team launch head-long towards a man desperately trying to climb a fence. I heard screams of pain and guessed what had happened even before I saw it with my own eyes.

As I jogged across the garden I found the dog firmly locked onto the left calf muscle of Nina's fleeing suspect, who was trying to shake himself free of the animal's grip. His efforts were pointless and time was against him. On both sides of the fence I could see armour-clad cops closing in.

Nina appeared behind me. 'They got him?' she panted.

'Looks like it … at least the dog has. The Ninjas will have him cuffed in a tick.'

'Excellent. Good job we decided to use them. Bastard dropped out of the loft hatch and climbed through the window.'

Nina moved to push past me further into the garden.

'I wouldn't,' I said. 'Wait till they've got the dog back on its lead.'

'Ah … OK. Can I leave it with you? I left Matt upstairs on his own.'

I nodded, and Nina headed back to the first floor.

I watched her go. She moved smoothly, like an athlete. I had no doubt that, even with a head start, she would probably have caught our suspect without any help. I'd now known Nina Brasov for nearly a year. We were no longer Sergeant and Inspector, any conscious reference to rank was long since jettisoned. Matt was a Detective Inspector, a DI, the same as me. But to Nina, we were just Matt and Finlay. Two parts of the 'Three Degrees', as she called our team.

One of the SO19 lads – the Ninjas – gave me a thumbs-up as they lifted the injured suspect from the fence, checked the bite wound to his leg and slipped a set of ridged cuffs over his wrists. Satisfied the coast was clear, I walked over to them. The man Nina had described raised his head and turned towards me.

'Hello, Costas,' I said, smiling.

Costas Ioannidis curled his lip and snarled.

I ignored him and turned to the two dog handlers. 'Good effort, lads.'

Then, as our prisoner was led from the garden, I heard Nina call from an open window behind me.

'Was it him?' she asked.

'Yes,' I shouted. 'In the flesh.'

'Come upstairs, Finlay. We all need a good laugh, and you'll never believe what Matt has found.'

The first thing to hit me as I climbed the stairs was the smell. Stale ammonia. I was still puzzling as to the cause when I heard a squawk from behind one of the bedroom doors.

For a moment, I wondered what on earth they had discovered. Then, as I walked in, it became clear. The room was full of cages. Wall to wall parrots. African greys, to be exact.

Matt had counted them. There were eleven, he announced.

Nina produced a can of Easy-Start spray and shoved it towards my face. 'Have a sniff, Finlay.' She laughed at my puzzled expression. 'It contains ether. The junkies go into pet shops; one distracts the owner while another sprays the bird. Poor mister parrot keels over, which makes it easy to nick.'

'Seriously?' I asked.

'Damn right. These fetch over a grand a piece. Costas is the fence, he deals in stolen birds.'

It was my turn to laugh. 'So, what are we going to do with them?'

Matt interrupted as he brushed past me, heading towards the stairs. 'Nothing. Leave 'em where they are. I've already called the local CID. They've got loads to put to Mr Ioannidis. They knew someone was at it locally … it looks like we've found out who.'

Chapter 2

An hour later, with the arrest paperwork complete, we had handed Costas over to the local CID and were heading back to our office at New Scotland Yard. We'd wanted to talk to him about his alleged involvement with prostitution, but the evidence of his dealing in stolen goods had now taken priority. Our questions would have to wait.

I had the result of an important interview to think about, although Nina and Matt seemed more interested in talking about their discovery in Costas's upstairs bedroom. We'd been travelling for several miles before Nina noticed I wasn't joining in the conversation.

'Have you absolutely no idea if you passed the selection board, Finlay?' she asked as she swung the car into the offside lane and raced towards the junction. The traffic signal was just changing to amber and, as was typical of her style of driving, Nina was determined to beat the lights. We made it, just.

'None at all,' I said, as I started to breathe again. 'I even had a sneaky look through the boss's correspondence tray yesterday. There was nothing; no clue.'

Matt leaned over my shoulder from the back seat. 'It went well though, I heard. And it can't have done you any harm that you just completed the Hostage Negotiator course. Most people who do that training are earmarked for promotion.'

'True enough, but there aren't many spots for Chief Inspectors this year, and my time at Combat Stress won't have helped. So, to be honest, I'm not too hopeful.'

'It was a shame they held the board so close to you coming back to work,' said Nina. 'If there'd been a decent gap…'

'What's done is done,' I snapped, instantly regretting my lack of patience. Nina was being sympathetic, and I wasn't showing much appreciation.

'So, will they let you stay in the department as a DCI, or will you have to go back to being a wooden-top?' she asked calmly, having either not noticed or politely chosen to ignore my rudeness.

'I don't know that, either.'

'Jenny will be pleased … if you pass, I mean. Especially now you've an extra mouth to feed.'

I shrugged. Nina was right. The extra pay would help, especially as there was no chance Jenny would be going back to work any time soon. She was enjoying being a new mother again, and our daughter Becky loved having a little sister.

Nina interrupted my thoughts. 'Well, you've done your courses now. So, technically speaking you're a proper DI. And, if you don't mind me saying, you're not a bad one, either. I've worked with a lot worse, believe me.' She jabbed a thumb towards the rear seat and laughed.

'Bugger off, Nina,' said Matt, feigning anger. 'Fancy a job writing parking tickets do you?'

I didn't respond, but I appreciated Nina's words. It had been a tough year; one that I was glad was behind me. For now, all my thoughts were concerned with the result of the promotion board and what the implications would be if I had managed to scrape through.

I was certainly the oldest and, possibly, the least apprehensive of the applicants who assembled in the foyer of the interview rooms on the day of the selection board. The thought even crossed my mind that I'd been nominated so the Met couldn't be accused of excluding older officers. I saw a lot of female candidates, at least as many as the men, which didn't come as too much of a surprise given the effort the Met was making to put right its poor record on equal opportunities. We were all in best bib 'n' tucker – smart suits or full uniform, depending upon our current role. I'd felt quietly confident at that point, even as I'd walked through the door to the final interview room.

But now that I was due to see our new Superintendent to hear the result, I didn't really share Matt and Nina's faith in me. My lack of operational experience as an Inspector had generated quite a few questions from the three senior officers on the selection board. And I was asked the inevitable question – a tough one to answer: Did I think that spending several years guarding the Royal Family and just one year as a Detective Inspector was sufficient to prepare me for the demanding role of a Chief Inspector?

I had given as good an answer as I could, but it was clear to me that the question was posed to expose my Achilles heel. I'd done well on my CID courses, but I knew as well as the board did that I'd only been fast-tracked onto them due to my unusual situation. My interviewers didn't mention the six-week absence I'd taken to be treated for stress. But they knew about it – it was on my file – and I wasn't so naive as to think it wouldn't figure in their deliberations.

Our new Superintendent, Ron Cutts, was waiting as we arrived back at the office. He waved me over and, as I stepped into his office, he shut the door behind me and invited me to sit. My stomach felt hollow. Long in the tooth and with a long history of selection systems and examinations behind me, yet I still felt nervous.

He got straight to the point. 'How do you think the board went?'

I shrugged and screwed up my face a little. I was about to speak when he raised a hand to silence me.

'Sorry … not a lot of point in beating about the bush. That was a pointless question.'

'Not good news, then?' I asked.

'Not for you, no. I'll admit to some relief you'll be staying with us for a while longer, though.'

'Can't say I'm too surprised. I was the oldest by far and my CV kind of let me down.'

Cutts flicked through a file on his desk, appearing to re-read what had been said about me. 'Feedback was good: says if there had been more places you'd have been in with a shout. It suggests a posting where you can act up in the rank and then have another go.'

'I bet they say that to everyone who dips out. What do you think?'

He took a deep breath. 'If I'm honest, I think it's not just your age and length of service that work against you.'

'Something else?'

'Your history. Before I took command of this team, Mr Grahamslaw filled me in on what happened to you last year and how you ended up here.'

'You think that influenced the board?'

He closed the file and placed it in a drawer. 'I think you're a damn good cop, Finlay, and it's clear our Commander has your back. But, let's just say there are people in the job who thought you should have been prosecuted.'

There was little more to be said. I extended my thanks and headed back to the main office.

Nina and Matt were in the corridor grabbing coffee and a cake from the tea-lady's trolley.

Nina looked at me, expectantly. I guess my face told it all. 'No good, eh?' she asked.

'Better luck next time, I guess.' I did my best to look upbeat.

'Not a chance. I had to sleep with all three of the board to get them to turn you down!'

I laughed. Matt laughed. Even the tea-lady laughed.

'Well, at least you can enjoy the weekend,' said Matt. 'I've just had the DCI from Kilburn on the phone. They've been trying to catch up with Costas Ioannidis for months. Well pleased, he was, and he's agreed to take over the enquiry. We've got a weekend off to enjoy some down time.'

Chapter 3

Jenny's reception to my phone call came as something of a relief. She took the disappointing news well and was honest enough to admit that she hadn't really expected me to be successful. And, perhaps to soften the blow she'd anticipated, she'd arranged for us to have a drink that evening with my old friend Kevin Jones and his girlfriend, Sandi, so I had something to cheer me up.

Ron Cutts was right, of course, especially regarding the legality of some of the things Kevin and I had been involved in. The preceding year had been amongst the most difficult I'd ever known. Everything had changed the day I'd been at home with Jenny and had answered a telephone call from Nial Monaghan, my former CO at 22 SAS. I hadn't heard from Monaghan in many years and what he said to me that evening threw my life up in the air. And my family, having discovered I wasn't the ordinary former soldier they'd thought, had been drawn into a fight for survival so dangerous that I came very close to losing them.

And then, just when I'd thought the threat was at an end, I'd gone with Kevin to visit the widow of a former colleague murdered by the terrorists who'd been targeting us. On the face of it, we were simply helping her dispose of a trophy weapon, a pistol her husband had retained after leaving the army. But we'd been handed a document – the 'Al Anfal' report – which turned out to be so sensitive, so secret, that even knowledge of it placed a person at risk of being silenced by the Security Services. The report had been discovered by an ex-military team called Increment, who had been working in Afghanistan during the war with Russia. They had forwarded it to their MI6 controller but, before doing so, they'd photocopied it. Somehow, one or more of them must have realised its potential value and had tried to hawk it to the press. That decision had cost them their lives and our attempts to discover the significance of the document had very nearly resulted in us suffering a similar fate.

Our MI5 family liaison officer, Toni Fellowes, had uncovered the truth. Monaghan had been given the job of clearing up the leak and had set about it in the way he knew best. He'd then used the ruse of an official MI6 black op as an excuse to target Kevin and me in the mistaken belief we were both guilty of having had affairs with his late wife. It was a mistake that cost him his life.

✝

As was my habit, I picked up an evening paper and, on the underground journey up to Cockfosters, read it from cover to cover. I still found that crowded trains were a cause of some discomfort. The combination of noise, heat and the crush of people was an anxiety trigger I knew was best to avoid. Reading the paper was a coping strategy I'd learned. By immersing myself in newspaper articles, I could ignore my surroundings.

Today, one article in particular drew my attention. It was about a missing literary agent – Maggie Price, who I knew represented an author by the name of Chas Collins. About a year before, Collins had brought out a book called *Cyclone*. The book had caused a bit of a storm, especially when the author's claims about his work in the SAS Regiment had been exposed as lies. He'd since dropped out of circulation, but rumour had it he was working on a follow-up book.

Maggie Price had recently disappeared, and, when superglue had been discovered in the lock to the front door of her home, the papers had been full of the story, with some incredible conspiracy theories being aired. All kinds of 'experts' had come out of the woodwork, from former detectives through to supposed friends of both the agent and her author. All had different theories, from a random stalker to a hit by an assassin hired by an underworld crime syndicate. The truth was, nobody knew what had happened.

Maggie Price lived in rural Essex, so the Met had only been involved in a support role, helping to interview her friends and associates. With no ransom demand received and stumped as to how best to proceed, the Senior Investigating Officer had made an appeal on the BBC *Crimewatch* programme the previous night. I hadn't watched it, but several people at work had been talking about the case. The connection to the Collins book had been mentioned, as had the story that the author had gone into hiding in Belgium, fearing for his life. The SIO had made a public appeal for him to get in touch.

I had my own opinion on how successful that appeal was likely to be. Those of us who knew Collins of old also knew that if he didn't want to be found then he wouldn't be. Despite the false claims in his book, he'd still been a good soldier and would know how to look after himself.

The newspaper article, written by the reporter Max Tranter, and following up on the publicity caused by the *Crimewatch* appeal, was a good one. Tranter had been doing some digging of his own and had made a connection between the Price case and a murder that happened about two miles away from her home, the day before she was reported missing. A young man had been found shot dead on a quiet, country lane and Essex police were working on the premise that the killing was drugs related, the victim having possible connections to east London drug dealers. Max Tranter, however, had an alternative theory. He argued that it was too much of a coincidence that two major crimes could occur so close together without there being some kind of connection.

I wondered if he might be right. Maggie Price certainly had some shady connections. I'd met her the previous year at a wedding; the same event at which I'd last seen Chas Collins. The bride on that day was Marica Cristea, a young woman I'd met on holiday, and who'd been kind enough to invite Jenny and me to the ceremony. In different circumstances those facts might have been irrelevant, but in the weeks that followed I came to learn that the Cristea family were part of a gang of Eastern European criminals whose expertise extended from slave trafficking through to gun-running. That they could have been behind Maggie Price's disappearance was a distinct possibility.

What I'd learned about the Cristeas had helped me play a part in breaking up their sex-slave operation in the UK – one reason I wasn't likely to be on the family Christmas card list. In fact, I'd surmised a long time ago that I would be wise to avoid any further contact with them. They suspected I had attended the wedding as a police spy. And while they were wrong, my guess was that, if we ever met again, they were unlikely to listen to my explanation with much sympathy.

That said, the solution was simple. Make sure it never happened.

Chapter 4

Howard scanned the notes on his desk.

If there was one very important thing he had learned in his life with the Security Service, it was to be thorough. Be it the creation of a cover story, a fake identity, the logistics supporting an operation, even an answer to a parliamentary question; all warranted appropriate diligence.

And yet, he was troubled. The job was done, complete, and what had at first appeared to be a situation likely to threaten both the national and his own personal security had been averted. The irritant that was Chas Collins had been removed, his manuscript recovered and both he and his literary agent had been taken care of. But things hadn't gone as smoothly as they ought to have done. Grady had very nearly been compromised and the Belgium side of the clean-up had experienced unexpected delays when Collins had proved hard to locate. And now there was yet another problem.

As Howard sat back in his chair and arched his back in an attempt to ease the discomfort that had settled there during the last hour, the grey telephone on the desk rang twice and then stopped abruptly, interrupting his train of thought.

He waited. Five seconds later, the phone rang again. He picked up the receiver.

'Sir,' he began, having already guessed the identity of the caller.

'Do you have it?'

'We do. Both targets are black-bagged. And it was as we'd thought: Collins was trying to be clever by avoiding electronic back-ups. He and Mrs Price had the only hard copies and we have them both.'

'Very good. Your usual efficiency, Howard.'

'Thank you, sir.' *If only he knew*, Howard thought.

'Have you had a chance to look through the draft?'

'I have. Your decision proved correct, the book would have exposed a crucial aspect of our Islamic intelligence-gathering operation.'

'We can count ourselves lucky.'

'Indeed.' Howard took a deep breath. There was no time like the present; and it appeared the Director was in a good enough mood to handle the news. 'There is a new problem, however.'

'A related problem?'

'I'm not certain at this stage, but quite possibly,' Howard said, and heard a deep sigh at the other end of the line.

'Presumably, your mentioning it means it's something I need to know about?'

'I think it's best you do, yes,' Howard answered.

'Let's hear it then.'

'Very well. Someone has Googled the name. I had a notification from GCHQ a couple of days ago.'

'That's unfortunate. Do we have a source?'

'Not as yet. But I'm working on it.'

'I predicted this, you will recall. There really were too many potential leaks.'

'And I've always argued we needed to be proactive. Ask any decent surgeon – sometimes it's necessary to destroy good tissue to ensure the whole tumour is removed.'

'You're referring to the two policemen?' said the Director.

'Amongst others – all represent potential exposure risks.'

'We've had this debate before, Howard, I don't intend to repeat myself.'

'I understand. I'll keep you posted with regards to the Google search.'

The Director ended the call. Howard replaced the telephone receiver and then flicked through the scattered papers in front of him until he found what he was looking for. It was a photograph of a group of heavily armed soldiers in desert fatigues – some standing, some crouched – posing at the rear of a C-130 transport aircraft. He studied the photograph for a moment, mentally ticking off the names as he scanned the faces.

Finally, his gaze came to rest on one man. He half smiled as he muttered quietly to himself. 'Soon, old friend,' he promised. 'Very soon.'

Chapter 5

Arriving at the pub I looked in through a window and saw Kevin and his girlfriend, Sandi, talking to Jenny. My daughter Becky was perched on his left hip, her tiny arms on his shoulder as she looked up at him with her puppy-dog eyes.

As I walked in Becky dropped to the floor, ran to me and, as I bent down, did her usual trick of squeezing my neck so tight that I struggled to breathe. I swept her up and nibbled her ear.

'Urgh, Daddy. Stop that, it's disgusting,' she said, her tiny hand wiping away the evidence of my misdemeanour. I then sneaked a quick look into the crib sat on a table next to where I was standing. Our new daughter was sleeping soundly. Despite my promotion disappointment, I couldn't help but count myself a fortunate man.

✠

An hour later, I was outside enjoying a breath of fresh air when Kevin found me.

'Gutted at failing the board, boss?' he asked.

'Not really. It's the way it goes. And it's been great catching up with you and Sandi, by the way. I'm glad you could make it at such short notice.'

'Jenny can be very persuasive … There's another reason I came, though.'

'Oh?'

'We need to talk.' Kevin's face turned suddenly serious. There was an urgency in his words that immediately troubled me.

'Something up?' I asked. 'I noticed Sandi seems a bit distracted.'

From his jacket pocket, he removed what looked like a plastic button with a couple of wires hanging from it. He held it up in front of me. 'Know what this is?'

'I know what it looks like.'

'Sandi found it in a faulty plug socket, hard-wired into the mains. It's a listening device. Finding it has really shaken her up.'

'You're living together now?' I floundered a little, buying some thinking time as I grappled with the implications of what Kevin was saying.

'Not yet, but it's on the cards. What about this, though? It's a bug – someone has been keeping tabs on me.'

I glanced back into the pub. Jenny was back near the bar, chatting with Sandi, who I noticed was glancing nervously out towards us. 'Do you want me to check on it?' I asked. 'The tech lads up at the Yard will know exactly what it is.'

'I know what it fuckin' is, boss,' Kevin said, impatiently. 'What I want to know is what it was doing in my house and who was at the listening end.'

'Have you checked the rest of the house?'

'Not yet. I thought I'd ask you first. And maybe Toni Fellowes could have MI5 do a sweep.'

I thought about the idea. Toni was still, technically, our MI5 liaison officer, despite the enquiry into the attacks on Kevin and me having been wound down. In normal circumstances she would have been a good first call. But things were a little different now – Toni had moved on, been promoted to departmental head and was now based at the MI5 headquarters, Thames House.

'We're assuming, of course, that Toni Fellowes didn't plant it?' I suggested.

'I don't buy that,' he answered. 'A few weeks ago I came home and had this weird feeling someone had been in the house. One of the chairs in my dining room looked out of place – not where I thought it had been when I left. At the time, I kind of dismissed it, but now I'm wondering.'

'Careless if someone *was* planting surveillance kit, wasn't it?'

'Back in the day, we even photographed the insides of the target home to make sure everything went back as it was before we got there. If our Security Services were behind it, they were unusually sloppy.'

'Which is why you don't think it was Toni?' I asked.

'Correct. I was hoping we could ask her. If you're not happy with that, I'll ask her myself. Maybe you should get your place checked as well?'

'It was swept when we moved in as part of their routine checks, but I'll ask, yes. Can you leave it with me for now?'

Kevin nodded, his jaw tight. 'I'd prefer that, to be honest,' he said, quietly. 'You're better with words than me and I'd most likely go off on one, because I'm telling you now, I'm not going to be a sitting target this time, waiting around for whoever it is to do what they've got planned.'

'Are they likely to have heard anything we'd prefer them not to have done?' I said, trying to ease the tension.

He grinned, confusing me as he did so. 'What's so funny?' I asked.

'Well, if it's anything about the kit stashed under my allotment shed then, no. I don't talk to Sandi about that. But, well … let's just say that if someone was listening in they might have had an education in bedroom Olympics—'

'Enough!' I stopped Kevin in full flow. He'd hinted previously at the unusual games Sandi liked to play and I needed no details. 'One of these days one of her sons will catch you two and then you'll be sorry.'

I took the bug from Kevin's open palm and slipped it into my trouser pocket. 'Leave it with me. It'll have to wait until Monday, but I'll ask one of the geeks from the Technical Support Unit if they can give us any background on it. In the meantime, you could ask Hereford to do a sweep for you.'

Jenny appeared in the doorway. 'You two having a secret meeting?' she asked.

I turned to her and smiled. 'Surprising how much we had to catch up on. Kevin was telling me that Sandi and the boys are to move in with him soon.'

'Oh, that's lovely, Kevin.' Jenny put her free arm around his neck and kissed his cheek. 'I am sooo pleased for you.' Her left hand held a wine glass, now nearly empty. It was one of several that had passed her lips. Kevin raised an eyebrow as he turned back to me. If I read his thoughts correctly he was thinking we were lucky not to have been overheard and it was a good job I was the one driving home.

As we returned to the pub, it was clear it was time to leave. Becky looked tired, and I imagined that, along with the baby, both she and Jenny would be fast asleep as soon as their heads touched their pillows.

I was right. But, for me, it was nearly an hour after arriving home before I also felt able to turn in. What Kevin had said, and his idea about the listening device, were preying on my mind. Thinking a nightcap might help, I opened a bottle of whisky that Matt Miller had given me. It was one of his 'specials', a Welsh brand called Penderyn that hadn't yet gone into commercial production. He always kept a bottle in his bottom drawer and it had become something of an office favourite.

This time, the alcohol didn't soothe my busy mind though, and as I lay down, my head was still spinning with confused thoughts. A listening device in Kevin's house? Were MI5 secretly monitoring him? Were they also listening to me? And if so, why?

Too many questions.

Chapter 6

'Can I come, Daddy?'

I hesitated. Believing my family to still be asleep, I had crept downstairs quietly, donned my walking boots and was just opening the back door when Becky's voice startled me.

I looked around into the kitchen to see my little girl, still in her pyjamas. There was no way I could resist her.

'Shall we get you dressed then?' I whispered as I picked her up and cradled her tiny frame in my arms.

Ten minutes later, following much secretive giggling and exaggerated shushing of lips, I scribbled a quick note to Jenny on the back of an envelope and then quietly carried my daughter downstairs. 'Do you want to walk or ride on my back?' I asked.

Our daughter had become quite precocious, showing many of her mother's personality traits, and her vocabulary was growing almost as fast as her little frame. So, I wasn't at all surprised when, after having her dad slip her red *Postman Pat* wellingtons onto her feet, she strode off down the garden path, hands on hips, tossing her hair backwards with a flick of her head and calling back to me, 'I'll walk, thank you.'

I quickly followed. The early-morning sun was already quite warm. We headed to the stile at the end of the garden and climbed over into the neighbouring field. From here, a footpath headed off across the meadows in the direction of the local pub. Underfoot, the short grass was still damp.

We kept close to a hawthorn hedge, following the well-trodden track several dog walkers and ramblers had made. Becky kept several steps in front of me, pathfinder fashion.

'Where are we going, Daddy?'

'Just a walk, darling,' I answered. 'If you like we can have a go on the swing.'

'Oh, yesss…' Becky started to run, her tiny legs soon putting quite a distance between us. I watched her childish athleticism with a combination of pride and fascination.

She stopped and turned to face me. 'Will Charl … will?'

I laughed. 'Charlotte … it's Charlotte. But like your mummy told you, we can call her Charlie if that's easier?'

Becky was struggling with her sister's name. 'Yes, OK … will she be alright on her own with Mummy?'

'Yes, of course she will. Mummy did OK bringing you up, didn't she? And besides, she'll probably still be asleep when we get back.'

'I don't really remember being a baby. I'm nearly four now.'

I laughed and then made to rush past, pretending to race. Becky quickly took the bait and pushed in front of me. Soon we reached a huge oak that cast a shadow over the far end of the field. From one of the tree's mighty boughs, an old car tyre hung suspended by a rope. Both were covered in a thick layer of moss and lichen and looked to have been there for decades.

Becky dived onto the swing, oblivious to the dirt that immediately covered her trousers. Wrapping her tiny hands around the rope, she signalled for me to start pushing. I was happy to oblige. I was gentle, not too much swing and definitely not over the adjacent ditch. The ancient rope creaked, Becky giggled playfully and I soon started to forget the real reason I had headed out of the house to walk on my own.

I had been intending to formulate some ideas. Plans for who I was going to ask about the listening device Kevin had found and what we might do if we found out who had planted it. Plans that soon slipped to the back of my mind as I watched my daughter on the swing.

Ten minutes later we were heading back to the house.

As we approached I could see movement in the kitchen. It looked like Jenny was up. She was making tea for us and a feed for Charlotte.

Becky ran in through the open door. 'Mummy, we done swings,' she exclaimed.

Jenny winked at me. 'You two were up early.'

'I needed a little "me" time, make some plans now I know I'm not going to make Chief.'

Leaning forwards to kiss my cheek, Jenny was reassuring. 'To be honest, I don't think you had much more than an outside chance. When Kevin called to suggest the get-together, I knew it would be a good way of stopping you from stewing about how you were going to break the news. I just hope I didn't embarrass you.'

She hadn't, and I said so.

I was just about to sup at my tea when the telephone rang.

'That's early,' I said, my instincts already triggered. A call at such an hour wasn't going to be good news.

Chapter 7

Although the staff on the Negotiator course had warned me I would be available for call-out immediately, I hadn't expected it to be quite so soon.

The caller was Chief Superintendent John Southern from Kentish Town Police Station in Camden. I didn't recognise the name but John was certain he remembered me. As we spoke, a vague memory came back of an articulate and thoughtful detective who had been on the first National Hostage Negotiator course I'd attended back in 1980. I'd then been the token military attendee, a volunteer from the army, there to escape the drudgery of administration work as I recovered from an injury.

John explained there had been an incident in the communications room at the police station. Some underoccupied night-shift officers had taken it upon themselves to subject a new PC to an initiation ceremony. It was the kind of thing that went on in one form or another in all kinds of units, both military and police, and normally it was just harmless fun. But this time, things had gone badly wrong.

The PC chosen to be initiated had been jumped on by several of his colleagues as he walked in through the comms room door. Their plan had been to 'station-stamp' him, a potentially embarrassing but normally harmless procedure that involved pulling down the unfortunate victim's trousers and then using an official rubber stamp to place an ink mark on one exposed buttock.

The intended victim had reacted in a way none of his tormentors had expected. As they had attempted to hold him down, he'd flipped. What started as a game quickly turned into a violent struggle and then an all-out fight. A CS gas spray had been discharged and, in the melee, the unfortunate PC had grabbed hold of a bread knife that one of the others had been using to slice a birthday cake just a few minutes previously.

Two officers had been cut, not badly, but enough to require hospital treatment, and a third was now being held hostage in the men's toilets on the ground floor of the station.

Something very unusual had happened though, which was the reason I had been called. The victim, now hostage taker, had asked to speak to me personally. John didn't know why, but what he did know was that I was wanted there as soon as possible. He'd told me the PC's name – Doug Powell – but again it wasn't one I recognised. I figured that all would be revealed once I had the chance to speak to him.

I went upstairs to get changed, making sure to move quietly around our bedroom so as not to wake Charlotte. She was lying on her back fast asleep. I leaned into the cot, kissed my new-born daughter on the forehead and then headed downstairs.

It was as I was pulling on my jacket that I slipped my hand inside a pocket and found the tiny listening device Kevin had handed to me the previous evening. I decided to leave it where it was. If I was lucky, I might just bump into someone who could identify it.

Jenny and Becky were waiting for me in the hallway. I picked up my briefcase, gave them both a peck on the cheek and, just five minutes after picking up the telephone receiver to the call from London, I was in the car and on my way back into work.

But not in a direction I had ever driven before. On this morning I took an alternate route, via the local traffic police depot. They had a car waiting for me. It was blues-and-twos the whole way and in less than half an hour, I was being dropped off in the tiny yard at the rear of Kentish Town police station.

From the windows of the canteen overlooking the car park, I saw faces turn to stare. All eyes seemed to be on me, as if they had been awaiting my arrival. A young uniformed Inspector appeared as if from nowhere and opened the rear door of the police car. I stepped out.

'Mr Finlay?' he asked, hurriedly.

'That's me.'

'I've been asked to take you straight up to the Divisional Commander's office. Mr Southern is waiting for you with some people from the Hostage Negotiation team.'

'I had the impression that Mr Southern is the lead negotiator?'

'No … he's our local Chief Superintendent. Now, if you'd follow me, sir?'

'It's not sir, I'm the same rank as you.'

He didn't respond but, as we strode across the yard to where a PC was holding a door open for us, he did reveal that two senior officers from CIB, the Met's Complaint Investigation Branch, were also waiting to see me. In the canteen a specialist firearms team and a dog handler were on stand-by in case they were needed. Every contingency seemed to have been covered.

John Southern was the first face I saw as his office door was opened for me. He was sat behind a large desk and, although it had been more than twenty years, he was familiar. With somewhat boyish looks, he had aged well, even if, on this particular morning, I could see he looked tired, his face drawn and grey.

I was taken aback by the number of people crowded into the small office. Most of those present were standing and the majority were in suits – detectives by the look; amongst them I guessed would be the head-hunters from CIB. There was an air of tension in the room, and the smell of nervous sweat – the kind men exude when under pressure. In the far corner I noticed an Inspector in black kit and body armour – SO19 firearms – and an older, scruffily dressed man I recognised as one of the Met techies. I made a mental note to get his name; he would be a good contact once this was all over, to ask about the bug Kevin had found.

'Come in, Inspector.' Southern said.

One of the suits, who had been sat with his back to me opposite the Chief Superintendent's desk, stood up. Southern indicated for me to take his place.

'Thanks for coming so quickly. I'll start with the introductions.'

I was impressed to learn how Southern knew every name. With the exception of three – the techie, Peter Hesp, and the Chief Negotiator, Mike Rogers – I hadn't met any of them before.

I'd been right about the CIB presence. A Superintendent and a Sergeant. The Superintendent's name was familiar: Jim Mellor. His reputation was well known amongst ordinary coppers. Mellor had been investigating complaints for many years and had made that many enemies, rumour had it that it proved impossible to end his period of tenure and transfer him back to a divisional posting. Nobody would have him, so CIB were compelled to keep him in post. Most believed that suited Jim Mellor quite nicely.

My eyes rested on his face for slightly longer than the others present. He looked a hard man – rugged face, strong jaw and deep-set eyes. The suit he wore looked expensive, a departmental tie neatly knotted over a crisp, white shirt. As John Southern introduced him he didn't so much as raise an eyebrow.

Formalities over, the situation and the reason for my presence was quickly explained to me. The hostage-taker, PC Doug Powell, had demanded to speak to me as a condition for the release of the single hostage he was holding. Her name was Carole, and she had been the officer intent on 'station-stamping' Doug Powell's exposed buttocks when things had kicked off.

'Why did Powell ask for me?' I asked.

'We were hoping you'd be able to tell us that yourself, Mr Finlay.' The comment, or question, if that's what it was, came from behind me. I didn't have to guess whose gruff voice it was.

I remained facing forwards and addressed my response direct to

Southern. 'At the moment, I have no idea. I don't know the name Doug Powell. Have you checked to see if I've ever worked with him?'

'We've been talking about little else for the last hour. Let me bring you up to speed.'

I listened as the Chief Superintendent read from some notes, seemingly for the benefit of all present. Powell had only been in the Met for three years. He'd completed a two-year probationary period at Ruislip, a quiet division in west London. As soon as permitted, he had requested a move to a busier station. He'd arrived at Kentish Town about a month before and had settled in quickly. His shift Inspector reported that he was hard working, fit and popular with the lads. He was also ex-army.

Mellor spoke up again. 'It's apparent that he either knows you or knows of you. You're confident you've never worked with him, Inspector? Maybe you know him socially, perhaps?'

I shook my head, again without turning. 'Do we have a photograph?'

Southern's expression was pensive as he opened a buff folder and turned it around so I could see the picture clipped to the top. The face wasn't familiar.

'No … I don't know him,' I said.

'We wondered if he might know you from the army?' the Chief Superintendent asked.

'What regiment was he?'

'Royal Scots. Served from 1986 until three years ago.'

'I was already in this job in '86,' I replied. 'Perhaps the best thing is for me to ask him?'

'I agree. Go with Mike Rogers, he's today's Negotiation Coordinator. He'll get you briefed on the layout of the room and the strategy we're adopting. You'll be assigned to the negotiator who's talking to him at the moment. Take your lead from her.'

I heard the door behind me open.

'We'll be able to hear everything, Finlay. Just make sure this ends with nobody badly hurt, please.'

I nodded, stood up and then followed the same Inspector who had met me in the yard. I could feel all eleven sets of eyes in the room boring into the back of my skull as I headed into the corridor. I wondered what they must be thinking. Who is this man? What is his connection to the hostage taker? And exactly what had made a relatively harmless prank escalate into such a dangerous scenario? Within a few minutes, I hoped to have some answers for them.

But there was one major issue troubling me, something none of us had prepared for and certainly hadn't been covered during the training course I'd only recently attended. This time the hostage-taker was a fellow cop.

Chapter 8

'So, what do you remember from your course?' Mike Rogers smiled reassuringly as he tucked the aerial from the earpiece behind my ear.

My mouth felt dry. 'My name's Dave and I'm here to help?' I answered, raising my eyebrows. 'It's over twenty years since I first did the training and I've still never been involved in a live one.'

'Except for the Iranian Embassy, of course?'

'You know about that?'

'Yes. Don't forget John Southern was also on that first course you did. He remembers you.'

'I wasn't part of the negotiating team though, just an observer.'

'No matter. Sue Corfield is lead today, she's talking to the PC right now and she knows you're coming.'

Mike walked across to the opposite side of the room and stood adjacent to a large notice board bearing handwritten, dry-wipe pen entries. Notes, comments, names and other data – a 'situation board'. The volume of information it contained would grow with the negotiation: important data and other key knowledge, such as the names of members of the suspect's family, sometimes picked up by the lead negotiator and at other times by listeners and researchers.

To the right of the situation was the 'PPA' board – positive police actions – reminders of ideas to use and things to say in case the hostage-taker expressed concern about what was being done to help him. On the wall, a series of flip-chart pages had been attached with masking tape. They were blank except for the headings: 'Hostage'; 'Suspect'; 'Delivery Plan'; 'Coming-Out Plan'. The last one was labelled 'SITREP', and would contain the latest situation report to be used by anyone who wanted a quick update on developments.

Mike saw me looking at them. 'We're just about to update them. The Yard are having Powell's army file faxed over and should have it with us shortly.'

'And the hostage?' I asked.

'WPC, twelve years' service, all at this nick and all on the same shift. She's well liked it seems.'

Mike whispered into a microphone on the desk in front of the two boards. His voice came through clearly in my right ear.

'This normal?' I asked. 'For a negotiator to get an earpiece?'

'Not really, no. This is because you're newly trained and we're using you as an intermediary. Take your lead from Sue. We'll be able to hear you, and with your earpiece in place we can feed anything we need to you. Sue doesn't have one. It's plausible deniability – if you don't know it's happening, you don't have to tell lies about it and you can maintain your credibility with the hostage-taker.'

I nodded to indicate that I understood.

'Right,' he continued. 'Let's set some ground rules. Number one, Commanders command, negotiators negotiate. You don't offer any deals, any way out, any solution without authority, clear?'

'I remember. The golden rule.'

'That's it. Well at least that's one thing we have straight. You have no control over tactics and options. You are a conduit, a source of information so that others can make decisions, OK?'

'I get it. So, who is going to do the talking, Sue or me?'

'To start with, it will be Sue. She will introduce you and then the two of you can take it from there. Our last sitrep had both PC and WPC inside a toilet cubicle. He seems to be sitting on the john; she is standing with her back to him, up against the door with her hands on the top of the door.'

'And he still has the knife?'

'Apparently … against her back.'

'So, he has control, as we can't see him or the weapon?'

'Exactly.'

I pictured the scene in my mind's eye: a trembling, tearful WPC, face to a closed door, unable to see her assailant and fearful that any moment might be her last. She might be trying to keep her abductor talking, trying to build up a friendship, empathy, any kind of relationship that would reduce the possibility of him wanting to end her life.

'Doug has promised to release Carole as soon as you enter the toilet area and he gets to speak to you,' Mike continued. 'If he's true to his word then a decision will be made at that point whether to go in hard or to try and talk him out.'

'Is Doug what I call him?'

'That's what we've agreed so far. We've kept it informal and he seems fine with it.'

'Is there a concern he might top himself after he lets the WPC go?'

'It had occurred to us, yes. Somebody upstairs suggested he might want you there to witness him commit suicide.'

'But you decided it was worth the risk?'

'We concluded that, as he doesn't seem to actually know you, suicide probably isn't his reason for wanting your presence.'

'But it could be?'

Mike scowled. 'That won't happen on my watch, trust me. If he has the means to end his life then we keep him talking until this all ends peacefully. Nobody dies. Not him, not Carole, not anyone. OK … you ready?'

My stomach felt tight as I walked the short distance to the toilet door. I tapped gently and pushed. It opened smoothly, quietly. In my ear a calm voice spoke. *'Good luck, Finlay.'*

I took a step. On the floor, secured with duct tape, I noticed a thin cable. A microphone, I guessed. So the decision-makers could listen in to what was taking place. A second door opened as easily as the first.

The toilet was quiet. Edging forwards, I started to get a better view of the room. To my left were the wash basins, four of them, with a large mirror behind. On the far wall, two hand dryers. I leaned in. To my right, there were three cubicles, the first two with doors open, the third closed. I could just see beneath it a pair of the soft cushion-soled shoes popular with women officers. As Mike had suggested, the position of the feet put the owner standing with her face against the cubicle door.

The toilet was surprisingly chilly and smelled fresh, as if it had been recently cleaned.

I caught sight of two more feet contained in what looked like light-weight walking boots. It looked like their owner was sat, leaning against the wall near the urinals which, I surmised, were off to my right. I shuffled further into the room.

Sue had her back to the wall. In her hand she held a small notepad. There was writing on it and as she held it up to me I could see the words 'Leave the talking to me'.

I nodded.

She turned toward the closed cubicle door. 'Doug, we've been joined by one more person. In a moment I'm going to ask him to speak to you. It's the man you've been asking to see. But before we go any further, can I ask you if Carole is still OK?'

A croaky male voice spoke from inside the toilet cubicle. 'The bitch is fine … as I'm sure she will tell you.'

'I'm fine, I'm fine.' It was Carole, also from behind the door. Her voice was quavering; she sounded scared.

'And can we confirm what we agreed would happen when Mr Finlay arrived to speak to you, Doug?'

'I said I'd let this bitch go and I meant it. That you, boss? I would nae trust these shites not to send an imposter.'

Sue nodded to me.

'Yes, I'm Bob Finlay,' I said.

'Well that's dandy. But I'll be needing you to prove that.' Doug's accent was strong, possibly Glaswegian, I thought.

I did my best to pull a questioning face at Sue, raising my hands and extending my open palms to indicate my need for advice. She scribbled quickly on her notepad and, once more, held it up to me: *'Ask him how.'*

'How can I do that, Doug?' I asked.

'You'll know my brother – you served with him. Mac Powell; remember him?'

I did. Powell had been a Sergeant on the same squadron as me, a long time ago. He'd been on a different troop but we'd worked together. That was until the day he decided to take on three bouncers at a nightclub in Hereford and had ended up being returned to his home unit, the Royal Scots.

'I remember him, Doug. Good soldier he was.'

'Aye … a good soldier. He was that. And he thought a lot of you. He lost his place in the SAS for fighting, but it was you that stopped him getting charged and taken to the civil court.'

'It was self-defence. He was attacked – three against one…'

'You went out on a limb for him when others turned their backs.'

'I do remember him saying he had a kid brother,' I lied, and immediately regretted breaking another of the golden negotiator rules – don't lie, unless you have to; and then don't tell a lie that is easily exposed. I cringed, even as the words came from my mouth.

'My brother's mate told me you can be trusted. You're OK, he said. If I ever needed help I should go to you.'

'Your brother's mate?' I asked, in search of a name.

'Brian McNeil. You worked with him too. My brother and him went back a long ways.'

For a moment I was silent, grateful the earpiece I wore wasn't able to pick up my increased heart rate. Brian McNeil. The missing Increment soldier Toni Fellowes had been so keen to trace after discovering the real reason for the murders of his friends. He and Chris Grady were the last surviving members of the Increment patrol responsible for the appearance of the Al Anfal document.

'McNeil?' I asked. 'I thought he'd been killed.'

'Unless it was his ghost who visited me a few weeks ago I'd say he's very much alive.'

A few weeks ago. So, McNeil was alive and, not only that, he was in the UK. My mind raced. Although I now knew why Doug Powell had asked for me, I had a huge new problem. I needed to find a way to contact McNeil – to warn him what had happened to the others, and to get some answers to questions that still worried me over what had really been going on when he and his friends had tried to sell the document to the newspapers.

Right now, though, I had to keep Powell talking. And then I had to find a way to speak to him out of earshot of the Negotiation control room.

'So how do I prove this is me, Doug?' I asked. 'You've managed to get me here … and it is me, I assure you.'

'Tell me how my brother was killed.'

I frowned. Sue scribbled another note: *'Be honest – if you can!'*

'I don't know how he died, Doug. When did it happen?'

'1988. Lisburn. You remember that?'

'I was out of the army by then, Doug. I joined the Met in '85. I moved on, didn't really stay in touch.'

'I didn't know that … thought you'd have known. I heard about the attacks last year … Brian told me it was the same man my brother and he had worked with. They really rated you, you know. When this shit happened you were the first person I thought of. I guess I'll just have to take the risk.'

'How do you think I can help you, Doug?'

'Hoped you of all people might understand. I'm in deep shit, I know that. I just want people to understand.'

'Will you let Carole go before we start to talk, Doug? I promise you, I'm not going anywhere. Then we can chat, if that's OK?'

There was a deep sigh from behind the door then a click; it sounded as if the lock had been released.

It had. Carole's feet shuffled backwards as the door started to open.

Sue was scribbling furiously. I glanced across to her. *'Keep calm. I'll take C. Keep talking. Tell D I'll be back soon.'*

I nodded to show I understood. By now, Carole had been in the cubicle for a considerable time. Throughout the whole awful experience, she must have been in fear for her life. Now Sue wanted her out of the way, and quickly.

A small hand appeared around the cubicle door as it started to open.

'Promise me there's nobody waiting to rush me, boss,' said Doug, quietly. He sounded subdued, defeated.

'It's just me and Sue out here, mate. Sue is going to take Carole outside and then she'll be back in a minute.'

'OK … Don't let me down now, boss.'

'You have my word, Doug.'

Carole's face appeared. Her eyes were bloodshot. Lines of dried black mascara ran down her pale cheeks. I beckoned her towards me.

As she squeezed around the partially open door, I saw her hands were shaking. I knew the thoughts that would be going through her mind: Will he change his mind at the last moment? Will they try and rush him? Will he hurt me?

She edged forwards, her face full of anguish, taking tiny, shuffling steps as her feet slid on the floor. Her shoes left a damp trail from where raw fear had over-ridden her ability to retain control of her bladder.

She stopped. I held out my hand. The message was clear, I hoped: *Come to me.*

Carole reached out, her fingers trembling. Her message was also clear: *Help me.*

I was about to move forwards when Sue spoke.

'Doug, it's me, Sue. I'm just going to step forwards to help Carole, if that's OK?' She held up a hand to me – a 'stop' sign – telling me, in no uncertain terms, to keep still and stay where I was. There was no reply from the cubicle. The door inched further open and, realising she had enough space, Carole started to squeeze through the gap.

Sue silently mouthed a word to her: *'Slowly.'*

Carole either didn't recognise the instruction or chose to ignore it.

As soon as she manoeuvred around the cubicle door she bolted for the exit. The door flew open – enough for me to glimpse a male figure in police uniform sat on the toilet seat – and then slammed shut again.

Sue went after her and, as she did so, she raised two fingers to me and mouthed the words, *'Two minutes.'*

I nodded. The door to the outside corridor closed noisily behind Sue.

Silence returned.

I glanced once more at the cable and microphone that would be relaying every word spoken to the control room no more than ten seconds' walk away. The cable had been slightly dislodged by Carole's rapid exit, but, to my frustration, it seemed intact. I still had no way of asking Doug about McNeil without being overheard.

I looked around the room, trying to decide where I should sit or stand as I continued the conversation. Sue had seemed quite comfortable sat with her back to the wall near the urinals. I guessed that had been her plan, to relax the situation, lower the tension and secure a passive resolution. So far, it had worked. We just needed to get Doug to surrender quietly.

I decided to stand, although I moved away from the door in case a decision was made elsewhere to make a rapid entry. I doubted that would happen. Even though Doug only had a small knife, he could do immense harm to himself in the few seconds it would take to cross the floor, force open the cubicle and then immobilise him.

It looked like, for now, it was down to me. I took a deep breath. 'Just the two of us now, Doug.' I was just about to continue when a voice sounded in my earpiece: *'Stand clear of the door. Entry in five minutes.'*

They were coming in hard. The decision puzzled me, but then I wasn't the expert. My job was to keep Doug alive and keep him talking.

'Cat got your tongue, boss?' Doug asked.

I heard the toilet seat creak and a movement from behind the door that suggested he was standing up.

'Is it a bit cramped in there?' I asked.

'It is, but I'm not so green as I am cabbage-looking. Soon as I step out this door they'll be in here, I'll be decked and we won't get a chance to talk.'

'What was it you wanted to talk to me about, Doug ... to understand?'

'Ireland,' he answered.

'Ireland?'

'Yes, that's right, Ireland. It's what you and me have in common and why I needed to talk to you.'

Chapter 9

'What about Ireland?' I asked.

'Where were you in March '88, boss?'

I smiled to myself. 'Well, funnily enough, I was here ... in this very nick. I'd been in the Met a couple of years and I was here working on the crime squad. Why do you ask?'

'March 1988 is the reason I'm in the shit now.' There was another creaking sound from the cubicle. Doug had returned to his sitting position. I figured I had about four minutes to find out what it was he wanted me to understand.

'Something happened to you?' I asked.

Doug laughed, but not in humour, more a mixture of scorn and irony. 'You could say that. But it could have been worse. I wasn't beaten to a pulp by a mob and then shot in cold blood.'

The penny dropped. March 1988: a month and an event burned into the memory of every British soldier. Andersonstown, Belfast: the murder of two Corporals who had inadvertently strayed into the path of the funeral of IRA member, Kevin Brady. Television news teams in attendance had recorded and described a scene of unspeakable horror as the soldiers had been dragged from their car, tortured and then shot with their own weapons. Never before had the British public witnessed such an event. Not that that provided any consolation to the Corporals' families and friends, but many believed it changed public opinion to such an extent that it acted as a trigger to commence the Northern Ireland peace process.

'You were at Andersonstown?' I asked.

'I hope you're prepared to listen … to try and understand. I'm not stupid, Mr Finlay. I know they're probably recording this and I know this might be my one and only chance to explain what happened last night. I also know that any minute now, SO19 will come bursting through the door behind you.'

As Doug spoke and as my own personal memories of that day returned to me, I shuffled across the room and placed my back against the exit door.

'I'm standing against the door, Doug,' I said. 'They'll have to come through me.'

Video footage from Andersonstown had been on television the day it happened and, such was the public horror, for a long time afterwards I'd tuned into every channel I could, so obsessed was I with understanding what had happened.

Eight years prior to the murders I had been ambushed by the IRA while returning to my squadron base from a meeting in Castlederg. I had made similar mistakes to the two Corporals, I'd been armed with just a pistol, hadn't checked my route and I'd nearly paid the ultimate price. I'd been very fortunate. When the firefight was over, three of my attackers were dead and another was on the run. I'd been shot in the foot and had just one round left in my magazine. I'd often wondered whether I would have had the courage to use it on myself. The way the murders at Andersonstown had taken place had triggered nightmares, repeated and frequent. In them I would be ambushed and find myself held down by a tangle of hands that stopped me from moving or escaping. It never ended well. I would see the barrel of my own pistol turned on me, be unable to resist and realise I was about to die. And at that point, I would wake up, soaked in sweat, shivering and with my heart pounding, grateful that, in my case, it was only a dream.

And now, I found myself wanting to hear what Doug had to say.

I knew that by standing next to the door and by telling the listening negotiators where I was and why, I was sending a message the decision-makers were not going to like. But this had now become personal. Doug Powell knew things, things that I wanted to know, and I wasn't planning on our dialogue ending before he had the chance to tell me what they were.

I wondered what was taking Sue so long. 'You were there?' I asked again.

'I was, but that's only part of it. I was Royal Scots. We were on QRF that day – the Quick Reaction Force. One of our lads was observer on the Lynx helicopter that was doing the eye-in-the-sky job. The crew saw what was going down and called it into the Ops room at Lisburn. We all thought it was another attack by the protestants, nobody realised they were army.'

'That's what I heard, Doug. They accidentally strayed into an area that had been declared out of bounds. There was nothing you could have done, really.'

'It was only down the road from Milltown Cemetery, for Christ's sake. The RUC managed to save a terrorist that attacked that funeral, why not our guys?'

'I know,' I replied. 'I think everybody at the funeral thought it was another attack like the one in the cemetery, too … So is that behind what happened with you last night?'

The earpiece voice spoke again: *'Get away from the door, Finlay.'*

Where was Sue? I thought again. I ignored the voice. 'So, what happened last night?' I asked again, trying to change the subject from the Irish murders.

'I lost it. I knew it would happen one day, I just knew it. I lost it at home once when the kids were roughhousing with me. We were wrestling over the remote for the TV. They jumped on me and I had a panic, threw them off, broke the TV screen. The missus went crazy.'

'You have children?'

'Yeah, two – a boy and a girl.'

'Two girls for me.'

Doug laughed. 'Stronger sperm, boss. That's what they say, good seed produces girls.'

I laughed too. And I hoped the control room were listening. As things stood, Doug and I were chatting and building a rapport. Given time, the negotiating team knew that I would try and move the dialogue onto the here and now, the situation that we found ourselves in and how we might peacefully resolve it. Whoever it was speaking in my earpiece just needed to listen … and to back off.

'So you get the picture?' said Doug.

'I think so. When they tried the station stamp stunt on you it triggered a reaction.'

'They don't know how close we came, how close I came to going the same way as those two lads.'

'Last night, you mean.'

'No, no, no … not then! I mean back in Ireland. Now listen…'

I listened. I listened while another soldier-turned-cop explained how he had faced death at the hands of a mob. He explained how, just three days after the Andersonstown murders he had been called with his mates from the Royal Scots as back-up to support some lads who were under attack by rioters in the Enniskillen area. About a hundred youths were throwing rocks and petrol bombs and had managed to set an RUC Land Rover ablaze. The soldiers had been well armed – all carrying the SLR – the .762 calibre self-loading rifle – but their rules of engagement prevented them from opening fire. None of them wanted to be facing a murder charge for shooting a petrol bomber.

With the smoke from the burning Land Rover and numerous other small fires blocking their vision, Doug and five other young squaddies had become separated from their main force. The rioters had spotted the opportunity, upped the volume of missiles and had eventually driven the small group of soldiers into a cul-de-sac, a blocked off street with no escape route other than straight through the missile throwers.

The soldiers were isolated and frightened. They faced being burned, hit by a rock, or worse, if a gunman should target them. They pointed their weapons at the youths but were met by jeers and an increasing level of missiles as the crowd drew closer. Doug then described what had happened next.

'We panicked. I don't mind telling you, I was fuckin' bricking it. They were kids, just like us. We were scared of them and scared of opening up on them. I kept thinking, *this isn't happening; it's some kind of crazy nightmare.* One of the lads got burning petrol on his legs. Just as we're trying to put it out one of the scum tried to grab his SLR. Fuck me, it all kicked off then. I had my safety off and was gonna shoot the fucker when, out of nowhere, an armoured RUC truck came up behind the rioters. They legged it.'

'Nick of time.'

'Exactly. But we were kids, Mr Finlay. We'd all heard stories about what the IRA did to people they captured, and we'd all seen what happened to the two signallers. We thought we were goners. My mouth was dry as sandpaper; I couldn't even talk about it for ages after.'

'What happened to the lad that was on fire?'

'Ah, he was OK. The flames didn't touch his skin. He got pissed up like the rest of us, but that was no cure. Now it seems that every time I get crowded in, memories of that day just blot everything else out. I lose it … just lose it, and woe betide anyone close to me.'

'So, why did you need me to hear you out?'

'Like I said. McNeil says you are a top bloke and that you were someone the lads knew they could turn to if they were in the shit.'

'But that was twenty-odd years ago?'

'I know, I'm sorry. I should have explained. I heard what happened to you last year when the Real IRA tried to blow you up. Rumour was that a copper who'd been SAS had been the target. I asked McNeil, he made a call to Hereford and in no time, we knew it was you. I'm kinda hoping that you'll put in a good word for me. I'm finished in the job, I know that, but I've still got a family and responsibilities. If I go down for this, if they stick me in prison, they'll be the ones that suffer.'

'It would help if you came out now, surrendered straight away.' That would give me two minutes, I thought. Enough time to ask him where I could find McNeil.

'Only if you promise to speak up for me, to explain. It's only people like you and me understand, boss.'

Giving such an undertaking wasn't going to be too difficult. The bigger question was whether it would have any effect. I was mulling things over in my mind when an object slid across the floor from beneath the cubicle door. It came to a stop right between my feet. I looked down. It was a small knife, maybe a four-inch blade, stainless steel and with a black handle. There was a dark stain on the blade that looked like blood.

'Doug,' I said. 'Your knife ended up right between my feet. Can I assume this means that you're coming out?'

I spoke clearly, aware that my words were being intently listened to. The control room would now know that the weapon was secure and that a peaceful resolution was within my grasp.

'Entry team stand down.' The words in my earpiece were clear. The door behind me wasn't about to burst open. I might just get the chance I needed.

I leaned down, deftly picked up the knife by the tip of the handle and, with my free hand, opened the door behind me. Sue was on the other side. She held out a clear-plastic weapons tube. I dropped the knife in and turned back towards the room.

'Doug, I've just given the knife to someone in the corridor and I can confirm that it's safe for you to come out.'

The cubicle door creaked further opened. A figure emerged.

Doug Powell looked dead beat. He was in shirt sleeves, his clip-on tie tucked through an epaulette over his left shoulder. His white shirt was splattered with blood and bore all the tell-tale creases and dirt marks of the scuffle that had caused his violent reaction. He half smiled and then did something that caught me completely by surprise. He held out his right hand.

I held back for a moment, unsure whether I was being tricked or whether the greeting was genuine. I nodded and winked at him. As I held out my own hand, I trusted that my message was clear.

Whatever I could do to help, I would.

Chapter 10

Doug walked out in front of me. I had one opportunity. The small area between the inner and outer doors to the toilets might give me the seconds I needed.

But, no sooner had we reached the narrow corridor than Doug was jumped by two PCs from the firearms response team. They bundled him into the corridor and threw him against the far wall where they spread his arms and legs before searching him thoroughly. I cursed under my breath. One of the firearms officers handed what looked like a wallet and some car keys to a figure standing just out of my line of sight.

I couldn't see who it was, but as soon as I heard the man speak, I knew. It was Jim Mellor.

The Superintendent was intent on telling Doug who he was, as if he expected the stunned and now-silent PC to have heard of him. Doug kept quiet, remaining passive as he allowed the two firearms lads to finish their search.

'He's clear, guv,' said the officer nearest to me, who I could now see from the rank insignia on his chest was a Sergeant.

Mellor ordered the group to follow him. The firearms PC took Doug's arm. I followed behind with the Sergeant in the hope I may yet have a final chance. There was no sign of Sue Corfield or any of the divisional senior officers.

We passed the room that the negotiating team had taken over. The door was closed, the only evidence of its use being the wire that trailed along the floor from the toilet. They would be waiting to debrief me, I expected. Every negotiation team followed the same procedure, together with an analysis and a report. Lessons learned, that kind of thing.

As Mellor started to tell Doug that he was under arrest and to caution him, I seized the opportunity to lean into the Sergeant and whisper into his ear.

'Go easy on him,' I said.

The Sergeant turned to me and winked. 'No worries, guv. Our Inspector heard everything that happened in there and relayed it to us. One of our lads was also in Ireland at the time and knew all about it.' He nodded towards where Superintendent Mellor was opening the door into the station yard and then lowered his voice as he whispered in my ear. 'He's the one you want to worry about. He ordered the rapid entry. There's been an almighty bust-up upstairs between him and the local Chief.'

Mellor stopped outside the door, preventing us from continuing the conversation without being overheard. After a few seconds, two more men in suits appeared. They placed themselves either side of Doug and, as the firearms officer stood to one side, took hold of his arms.

'With us, PC Powell,' one said.

With that, they walked briskly out into the sunlight that now filled the yard. I made to follow them when a hand was placed firmly on my chest.

It was Mellor. 'My prisoner I believe, Inspector Finlay.'

I stopped, taken aback by the forcefulness of Mellor's manner. He clearly didn't want me anywhere near Doug Powell. And then, as my fists tensed and I experienced a surge of heat flush upwards from my chest, I felt the red-mist of temper rising.

Mellor saw it. He leaned in close to me. 'I fuckin' dare you, *Inspector*,' he said, his tone threatening, taunting.

I stepped back. And, before I could react further, the yard door was closed firmly in my face. I turned to the SO19 Sergeant. 'I think I see what you mean. He doesn't do discussion, does he?'

'Legend in his own mind, guv, and a bad man to cross.'

'I'll remember that.'

'If that had been me, I'd have clocked him, Superintendent or no.'

I nodded, took a slow breath and turned back into the corridor. Mike Rogers was emerging from the negotiation control room. He saw me.

'Debrief in ten, Finlay. You OK? The Chief Super wants us upstairs.'

'I'm fine,' I said. 'All of us?' I pointed to the lads from the firearms team who were just behind me.

'No, just you and me. Full debrief will be in the parade room afterwards.'

I was still shaking. And although the surge of uncontrolled anger was easing, I was shocked at how close I had come to losing control. It wasn't like me. I couldn't remember the last time I had felt that desire to really batter another human being. I shrugged and followed Mike to the stairs. John Southern was waiting for us in his office, alone. Mike walked straight in, indicated for me to sit and closed the door behind us.

Southern must have read the confused look on my face. 'Bit unusual I know, Finlay, but I wanted to have a quick word before we head across to the parade room.'

'About what, specifically?' I asked.

'Well, first things first, you did a great job. We heard everything. You handled it well, kept PC Powell calm and achieved an outcome as good as we could have hoped for.'

'Thanks.'

'Mike tells me that you've not been involved in any live negotiation since we were on our course back in 1980?'

'Not really, no. The course was useful, mind. Made me think about how to handle things and came in very handy over the years.'

'In the army?'

'Mostly, and a couple of times since.'

'That's good … but that's not really why I wanted to speak to you now.'

Southern stood up from behind his desk, and walked to the window of his office. It looked out onto Holmes Road, a narrow street off the main drag through Kentish Town. Hands shoved hard into his trouser pockets, he faced away from me as he continued. 'There's been a few problems,' he began.

I turned to where Mike was sitting beside me and scowled. He didn't comment, just raised his eyebrows.

'What kind of problems?' I asked.

'Nothing you did or didn't do, Finlay. But I thought it only right that you should know.' Southern turned around to face us. 'Do you mind if I ask if you've ever met Superintendent Mellor before?'

'I haven't.'

'That's interesting ... because he clearly seems to know you, or know of you. Did you hear the rapid entry plan on your earpiece?'

'I did. And I hope you don't mind me saying, I thought the timing wasn't good. Did you catch my reaction? I stood against the door and made sure you knew I was there. That was supposed to tell you to back off.'

'We heard it ... we all heard it. What you need to know was that it was Mellor's decision to go in hard to effect arrest, it wasn't mine, and it didn't come from the negotiation team.'

'So who was in charge then, who got to make the final decision?'

'Mellor did. As Powell is subject of a criminal investigation now, complaints branch were effectively in charge.'

'Even though he's one of yours?'

'Yes, even then. Mellor was extremely angry when he heard your reaction to the command to prepare for a forced entry.' Southern turned to face Mike Rogers. 'I might even use the word livid, wouldn't you, Mike?'

The Negotiation Coordinator nodded, his hands clasped firmly together on his lap. 'Livid, yes,' he said. 'So much so, he let slip something he probably shouldn't have.'

'Like what?' I asked.

As Southern continued, I turned back to face him. 'Look, Finlay, it's common knowledge these days that you were once in the SAS Regiment. Any idea you had of keeping it quiet is long gone. What Mellor said shows he is clearly someone who thought you should have been either prosecuted or disciplined for something that happened last year during the IRA attacks.'

'Did he say that?' I asked, as I thought about what had just happened in the ground-floor corridor and the way Mellor had pushed his hand into my chest, almost as if he had intended to goad me.

'Not in as many words, but it was clear that's what he meant,' Southern replied.

'And you think I should know I'm on his radar?'

'Mellor is the kind of man who won't just leave it at that. He'll be gunning for you.'

'And you think that influenced his decision to go in hard today, before I'd had a chance to resolve things peacefully?'

'I do. He wanted to deny you the chance to do well.'

'Nice man,' I said.

'He's not. I've known Jim Mellor for years. In fact, we go back a long way to a time when he was an Inspector here at this very nick and I was one of his PCs.'

'You have some history, then?'

'You could say that. One night shift we had a disagreement over something petty. For the life of me, I can't recall what it was, but the upshot was that he offered me outside. He wanted to resolve the argument in a fist fight.'

I was stunned for a moment. It wasn't uncommon for disputes to be settled by soldiers in such a way, but I'd never heard of it in police circles. And for an Inspector – the equivalent of a commissioned officer – to square up to a PC was virtually unthinkable.

'What happened?' I enquired.

'I walked off, but it really affected me. And I don't mind telling you, he scared me as well. I put in for a transfer the very next day.'

'And now he's junior to you?'

'He is, but men like Mellor don't let little things like rank bother them.'

'No,' I said, as I recalled the proximity of the Superintendent's face to mine, the heat of his breath on my face, the way he'd dared me to react to him. 'No, I guess they don't.'

Chapter 11

An hour later, with the formal debrief concluded, I headed back to the negotiation control room. No further mention was made of Superintendent Mellor's decision to use a rapid entry while negotiation was still ongoing. The advice from John Southern was timely and went some way to making me feel better about what had happened.

I was hoping to find Peter Hesp from the Technical Support Unit before he finished packing up ready to head back to Scotland Yard. I was in luck. He was sealing the last of his kit into plastic crates as I walked through the door.

'Cometh the man, cometh the hour eh, Finlay?' Peter teased.

I glanced around. We were alone. 'At least we got a result and nobody was hurt,' I said.

'Not much of a result for that poor PC though. And I reckon the girl he was holding will have a few nightmares after today.'

'You were listening in then?'

'Always. In case there's a comms issue, that kind of thing.' He started stacking the crates, ready for loading into his van, I assumed.

'So, how did I do?' I asked.

'Pretty good, I reckon, especially as it was your first call-out. And from the thumbs-up and looks that went around the office, I reckon the old hands approved.'

'Did you hear the argument between the divisional lads and the CIB Superintendent?' I was curious, and it was useful small talk as I worked out if Peter was likely to be receptive to my real reason for seeking him out.

'Nah,' he said. 'That happened offline, in an upstairs office. Got pretty heated from what I heard.'

'That's what I was told too.' I reached in my pocket and gently took hold of the device from Kevin's house. 'Peter,' I asked. 'I wonder if I could beg a favour?'

He peered towards me, a look of curiosity on his face which was

soon replaced by a smile. 'If you want me to put a bug in that Superintendent's office, forget it,' he said, grinning from ear to ear.

'Nothing like that. But I do need you to give me some private advice,
something I'd prefer was just between us.'

The smile turned to a frown. 'I work in a world of secrecy, Mr Finlay.
You'd probably be surprised, maybe horrified, to know the kind of
things that I keep shtum about.'

I held out my hand, the tiny device and attached wire now clear for
him to see.

He stepped forwards, reached into his trouser pocket and pulled
out a grubby pair of spectacles. After wiping them clean on a handkerchief that looked like it doubled in function as a rag used to check
the oil on his car, he slipped them over his nose and leaned over my
open hand.

'May I?' he held out his hand, indicating that I should pass the device
to him. I placed it carefully on his palm.

He studied it for a moment, turning it over, seemingly looking for an
identifying mark. 'Where did you get this?' he asked, finally.

I rubbed at the stubble on my chin. Peter then raised a hand, his
smile enigmatic. He was effectively calling a halt to any need for me to
lie. 'No worries,' he said. 'I should know better than to ask. But, I would
be interested to know. It's a device of the kind that our budget normally
doesn't run to. State of the art, great range and uses the power of the
mains system so it can last almost indefinitely.'

'It's a listening device?' I demanded.

'A Bowland Technics A700X.'

'That's pretty specific.'

'It should be. I put in a requisition for a few of these babies not too
long ago. It was turned down on account of their cost.'

'Expensive?'

'Very. So much so that they aren't commonly used. You can get
much cheaper products that do the same job, well nearly. Like I said,
these have a great range, fantastic sound quality and they don't rely on
battery power.'

'So whoever planted it … they're not from the Met?'

'I wouldn't have thought so.' Peter shrugged and shook his head. 'We've had similar devices on trial occasionally but, to the best of my knowledge, only the Arabs and the Yanks use these. Not even our intelligence services can justify the cost.'

'Intelligence services? You mean it isn't a police-used device?'

'Smart money would be on the CIA or similar.' He hesitated for a moment, frowning. 'That said, there were a few sent out as samples to MI5 and Six. But like I said, after field tests, I think they decided not to buy them. The Met may have looked at them but we don't use them.'

'So … say for argument's sake it was found in a house here in the capital, it's possible it might be someone within our own Security Services who planted it?'

He smirked. 'You'd have to ask them, Finlay. It has a serial number but you'll need better eyes than mine to read it. Trouble is, as soon as you start asking where it came from, sure as eggs are eggs the department that placed it will be tipped off.'

'How come?'

'MI5 operate like us in many ways. They have stores, logistics, admin … just like any large organisation.' He handed the tiny device back to me. 'Expensive stuff like this has to be accounted for. There'll be a record of who it's booked out to … or there should be.'

'Unless someone reported it as lost or destroyed,' I said, wryly.

The door opened. It was Mike Rogers and Sue was with him. Carefully, making sure that my hand was hidden by my body, I slipped the bug back into my jacket pocket and pulled myself together.

'Did we miss something?' Mike asked.

I didn't answer. Peter turned away and, with Mike's help, continued his work. I was going to have to make a couple of calls to see what I could find out about the listening device. The first would be to an old friend, Toni Fellowes.

'You did a great job,' said Sue, extending her hand to me.

Mike raised an eyebrow and winked at me. I offered my thanks and headed for the control room. It was time to see about arranging a lift

home and to give some thought as to how I might be able to help Doug
Powell.

Chapter 12

I secured a lift back to Hertfordshire courtesy of an early-turn PC
who had ended his shift and was heading home to Stevenage. We
chatted briefly about what had happened but, as he didn't really know
Doug Powell and I couldn't say much about the negotiation, our conversation soon dried up.

By the time we reached my car, the weather had changed for the
worse with heavy rain and a squally wind. It put paid to any thoughts I
might have had to take Becky out on another walk.

As soon as I arrived home, I rang Kevin to update him on my news
about the listening device. Not surprisingly, he hadn't wasted any time
getting in touch with Hereford. They'd put him in touch with one of
the lads, now retired, who ran a London-based security company. He'd
been happy to help Kevin straight away. His house had already been
swept for any lurking devices and had been declared clear. The bug had
been a one-off.

Which was a little surprising. Not that I was particularly experienced
at covert surveillance, but even I knew that one device wasn't enough to
make that kind of operation effective. I'd done some work in Northern
Ireland with Special Branch and one thing all such operations seemed to
have in common was the placement of multiple sources of listening data.
Bedrooms were a favourite but many an informal conversation around
the dinner table had resulted in valuable information being overheard.

The expert who checked Kevin's home had a couple of theories
and, in the absence of any better ideas, we thought them quite feasible.
Either the team tasked with installing the hardware had been disturbed
before completing the job – which might also explain the chair out of

place; or the surveillance was low key, perhaps speculative, to be followed up if the device revealed anything interesting. But that still didn't explain who had installed it or why.

✝

On the Monday, I rose early, beat the rush hour, and was at my desk by seven-thirty. The office was quiet. Most people would start to drift in from about eight.

I knew Toni Fellowes was normally an early starter and was just about to lift the telephone to tell her the news about Brian McNeil when Bill Grahamslaw popped his head through the open door. It wasn't often that the Commander of the Anti-Terrorist Squad ventured into our corridor, and I guessed he might be looking for me.

I was right. 'Got a minute, Finlay?' he asked.

'Always,' I smiled. Despite being many ranks above me, Grahamslaw had become a friend. We didn't socialise together – I'd heard he always kept his work and home life separate – but within the working environment we always got along extremely well. I was in his debt over what had happened a year previously. He knew it but he had never laboured the point. As John Southern had mentioned at Kentish Town, there were some who would have happily seen me and Kevin prosecuted, even sent to prison, but Grahamslaw had stuck to his word, going out on a limb to make sure that didn't happen.

Perched on the end of my desk, on the small and only available space clear of my usual clutter of papers, pens and mugs of half-consumed tea, the Commander looked around the office. Satisfied we were alone, he grunted reassuringly. 'Looks like we're the early birds today,' he said.

I checked my watch. 'Not for long. Most of us are in before eight these days. Nobody likes the tube trains, especially on a Monday.'

'True enough. How are you coping with the journey? You used to have some problems with the crowds, I recall?'

I sat back in my chair and must have given my thoughts away through my screwed-up face.

'No better then?' he said.

'Not perfect, no. But much better than it was a few months ago. I try to avoid the major rush and, if there's a full carriage, I tend to wait for the next train or try and find one with more space.'

Grahamslaw folded his arms, gently sucking his teeth. He was building up to something, I sensed it. 'I don't blame you. I hate the bloody things and I haven't had half the problems you've had.'

'Can I make you a brew?' I asked.

He laughed briefly, nodding his head towards the collection of mugs that adorned my desk. 'Do you ever finish one?'

I smiled. 'Family trait. I like my tea hot, as it cools down I tend to abandon it.'

'Likewise … but I didn't come here to talk about how we like our tea. Before anyone else comes in, I want a quick chat about what happened at Kentish Town over the weekend.'

I'd guessed right. 'That reached you quickly,' I said. 'What can I tell you?'

'Well, I'm not going to beat around the bush so here it is. I've had two reports about you land on my desk this morning. One is from the local Chief Super, and it couldn't be more glowing. Says you responded promptly to a call-out from home and that you did a fantastic job persuading the hostage-taker to surrender.'

'Did he tell you what happened … and that the hostage-taker was a PC?' I asked.

'He did … and he also explained the circumstances. From what he says, you'll no doubt be in line for a commendation of some kind.'

'I'd rather see the PC getting help for his problems. What's in the second report?'

'It's from Complaints Branch. One of their Superintendents claims you were obstructive and that you deliberately blocked a rapid entry he had authorised.'

'If recognising that the PC was about to surrender and standing in front of the door to prevent an almighty cock-up is being obstructive, then I guess I'm guilty. But I'd be more than happy to discuss it with Mr Mellor, if that's what he wants?'

'You know Jim Mellor, then?'

'Not really. Saturday was the first time we've crossed paths. But there were several at the scene who seemed quite keen to warn me about him.'

'Well, you can add me to that list, Finlay. Mellor is one of a kind, a man with no friends to speak of and with a single-minded determination to do what he thinks is right.'

'You know him better than me then.'

From the corridor, I heard the lift doors opening. Grahamslaw paused for a moment, glancing over his shoulder to see if we were about to be disturbed. From some distance away, we heard a door open and close. We had a few moments more.

'I do … and you can trust me when I say that his report will be filed in my office, never to see the light of day again. I can deal with the likes of Jim Mellor. But a word to the wise: be careful of him and, if you can, try and keep off his radar. He's like a dog with a bone if he has it in for you.'

'From what I was told at Kentish Town, I think it's too late. He said something about last year, along the lines that Kevin Jones and I should have been hung out to dry.'

Grahamslaw scowled. 'Did he now? Well, that kind of explains his report and how it found its way to my desk so quickly.'

'I nearly lost it with him.'

'How do you mean?'

'We had a bit of an altercation in the corridor when I tried to speak to him about the PC who'd taken the hostage.'

'What happened?'

'In hindsight, I think he was trying to provoke me. It very nearly worked. I had a rush of red mist and, well, let's just say I nearly did something I would have regretted.'

'I can guess,' he replied. 'So, how do you feel now?'

'A bit bleak, to be honest. It unsettled me to think I might have a more sensitive trigger than when I was younger.'

'We all have a temper, Finlay, and we all have our buttons. Maybe Mellor pressed one of yours?'

'Yes, perhaps he did.' I stood up, moved to the door and poked my head out into the corridor. All clear. Closing the door, I then reached into my jacket pocket.

'There's nothing I can do now about Mellor, but I appreciate the warning. In the meantime, can I show you something?'

'Sure.'

I held out my hand, now open with the listening device resting on my palm.

'Kevin found this in his house last week.'

He took a deep breath, but made no attempt to take the bug. 'You realise what that is?'

'I do … I asked one of the geeks at Kentish Town on Saturday if he could shed any light on it. It's an expensive type that he thinks MI5 and the Met might have trialled some while ago but didn't buy.'

'Someone's listening in on Kevin Jones, you figure?'

'No other conclusion, really,' I said.

'And you'd like to know who?'

'And why, of course.'

'Would you like me to make some calls … see if I can help? There'd be a risk with that, though. Whoever placed it would likely realise you were trying to identify them.'

'Would that be an issue?'

Grahamslaw thought for a moment before replying. 'Depends who that person is, or what department. It might well be the Security Services.'

'Keeping an eye on us, you mean?'

'It's possible. It's the kind of thing I might do in the circumstances. You could ask Ms Fellowes, possibly? As your MI5 liaison, she ought to know if someone in her service is monitoring Kevin.'

'What you're saying means you think MI5 might also be keeping a watching brief on me as well?'

'It's likely. Like I said, it's what I might do if I were them. Do you want me to ask her?'

'Would you?' I asked.

'I could, but it might come better from you. Maybe an informal, friendly approach might work better than going through official channels?'

I thought for a moment, and as I did so, the narrow window alongside the office door revealed another figure walking quickly along the corridor.

'I agree, it might.'

Grahamslaw was just about to respond when the door opened. It was Nina Brasov. The Commander and I both looked towards her.

He turned back to me. 'Anyway ... as I was saying ... great work. The lead negotiator was well impressed and has suggested you put your name forward to do the International Hostage Course. I'm happy to go along with that if you are.'

Nina said nothing, just winked at me and then headed across the office to hang up her coat.

'I'll have a think,' I said.

'It would help for the next promotion board.'

'What can I say?' I turned to where Nina was pulling a chair up to her desk.

'Go for it,' she said. 'You get to travel to places where British subjects get themselves kidnapped.'

'Sounds wonderful,' I said, sarcastically.

'He'll do it, guv,' she said to our Commander.

'OK,' he replied. 'That's confirmed then. I'll put you down for the next available course ... and email me the details of that car part. I'll see if I can find a stockist.'

Chapter 13

Some considerable time had now passed since I'd last ventured into the small suite Toni Fellowes occupied with her team. Her promotion meant spending more time at the Security Services headquarters at Thames House, but her open-plan office at New Scotland Yard appeared to remain her favoured workplace. We'd crossed paths a couple of times in the lifts and on several occasions I had seen her arriving at or leaving Bill Grahamslaw's office, but we'd not spoken for some time. So, it was with some trepidation that I pressed the buzzer that would allow me entry to one of the most secure sections of the New Scotland Yard corridors. Once inside, I had a question to ask. Did keeping an eye on me and Kevin include spying on us?

The door opened, Toni's assistant, Nell, waved hello from her desk, and I waited patiently while her boss finished a telephone call.

A few moments later Toni hung up the phone, swung around in her chair and indicated that I should use the seat next to her.

'I think I've found someone you were looking for earlier this year,' I said.

She glanced across at Nell, who was, once again, busy at her keyboard. 'You can speak freely, Finlay.'

'OK, if you're sure. I picked up a lead on Brian McNeil, one of the missing Increment members.'

'How so?'

'Weirdest thing. I did a hostage negotiation over the weekend. The perp had asked for me and said it was because of a recent recommendation by McNeil.'

'A recommendation?'

'Yes,' I said. 'He had told the lad to ask for me if he ever got into bother.'

'Really? How recent?'

'A couple of weeks.'

'He's resurfaced?'

'Looks that way. I hoped to find out where he is but the negotiation was being recorded.'

'You did the right thing,' Toni paused, as if mulling things over in her mind. 'What do you think, Nell?' she added, without turning away from me.

Nell stopped typing. 'He ought to be warned, probably. Your call.'

I turned to Toni. 'I thought you said the hounds were called off once the Al Anfal document was destroyed?'

'That's right,' she said. 'What Nell's saying is we should make sure this McNeil character doesn't change that situation.'

'So what do we do?'

'*We* don't do anything, Finlay. I'll take care of it. Just leave me a note with everything you know and I'll follow it up.'

I nodded in agreement and reached into my pocket for the listening device. 'Can I ask you about this?' I said, as I held it out for her to see.

'It's a surveillance bug,' she replied, almost dismissively.

'It was in Kevin's house.'

'And your point is?'

'We'd like to know how it got there.'

'And you expect me to find out?'

For a moment, I was taken aback by the apparent scorn in Toni's voice. Across the opposite side of the office, I noticed Nell raise her eyebrows and then turn away from us as she slipped a set of headphones over her ears.

I placed the bug on the desk. 'Sorry, Toni,' I said. 'I wasn't suggesting it was you that planted it. I just wanted to know if you knew anything.'

'What bloody difference does that make, Finlay? You coppers are all the same, suspicious to the core. It's perfectly clear you either think I had it planted or that I knew it was there.'

I took a deep breath. I'd been clumsy, I knew it. But I also knew there could be another explanation. I'd seen the kind of reaction Toni was showing on many occasions when a suspect is unexpectedly confronted with evidence that appears to implicate them. Angry denial – emphasising a sense of grievance – is actually a mask to hide guilt. In Toni's case, I still wasn't sure, but for now I was prepared to give her the benefit of the doubt.

'OK, I'm sorry. I didn't mean it to sound that way.' I glanced down at the desk to where the listening device sat untouched. 'Kevin said himself he doesn't think it was you. Anyway, if we did, do you think I'd be asking you now?'

'I have no reason whatsoever to be bugging Kevin's home, Finlay, none at all.'

'I know, I know. I'm sorry if it sounded like an accusation. Kevin also said some furniture was moved and we thought that a wee bit sloppy for any branch of the Security Service.'

Toni raised her hands, closed her eyes momentarily, and in a moment regained her composition. 'No, *I'm* sorry, Finlay,' she answered. 'You didn't deserve that, especially after all you've been through. You say Kevin found it in his house?'

I picked up the bug and handed it to her. 'Hard-wired inside a plug socket. I've had the Geek Squad look at it and they tell me it's a type that was on trial in the Met and MI5 but proved to be too expensive. We only wondered if you might be able to track its serial number to see who this one might have been sold or loaned to.'

'I am busy, you know,' was the sharp response. 'Can't your own people do some checks? I'd start with the techie stores, see who booked it out or who had it on trial.'

'I was going to do that until it was pointed out to me that whoever that was might get tipped off if I started asking questions.'

'You asked me, for goodness sake.'

'I trust you … and I trust Nell.' I saw the researcher smile. Clearly the headphones were a ruse; she was listening to every word we were saying.

Toni twisted the bug between her thumb and first finger. 'Can you leave it with me? I'll need to ask Nell to see what she can do. I'm not promising, mind. We might only find out what country it was exported to – some of these devices soon drop off the radar.'

'Anything is better than nothing,' I said. 'Do you think we should do a sweep on my home again?'

'Would it make you feel better if we did?'

'It might give me some reassurance. I'm not sure how Jenny would react to it though.'

'We could do it with a drive-by to check for a transmitter and I could ask Nell to check the phones. We wouldn't need to go into the house.'

'That would be great. Maybe soon?'

'I'll see what I can do.'

'So, nothing's changed with regard to Howard Green then?'

'Nothing,' Toni replied. 'As I told you several months ago, Howard was told in no uncertain terms that you and Kevin are not to be touched. Any ideas he may have had about including you in the clean-up operation were quashed.'

'That's good to hear. I really don't want to spend the rest of my life looking over my shoulder.'

'How's the new baby? A little girl, I heard.'

Normal service resumed, I thought, as Toni changed the tack of the conversation.

'That's right,' I said, slowly. 'We've called her Charlotte.'

She laughed. 'My mother's name. She'll be Charlie before you know it.'

'She already is.'

'And what about the promotion board? How did that go?'

I shrugged. 'No joy. Bit too old, I reckon.'

'Well, Nina Brasov will be pleased. I heard her saying to someone in the canteen queue not long ago that she had only just licked you into shape and now it looked like she was going to lose you.'

It was my turn to laugh. Toni handed the bug to Nell and undertook to get back to me as soon as she had any news. I pressed her for a faster response but all she would promise was that she would be as quick as she could. Sensing that I was beginning to outstay my welcome, I headed for the door and made my way back to my squad offices. I had some calls to make.

Chapter 14

'Don't you think you were a little hard on him?' Nell stared hard at her Section Head, her face expressionless.

Toni was reaching for her coat, her thoughts elsewhere as she prepared to head back to Thames House. 'Where's Stuart?' she asked.

'With Special Branch upstairs, I think. He said something about a meeting.'

'How's he settling in?'

'Pretty good, really. Things aren't quite the same since you were promoted, but he seems to be enjoying the extra responsibility.'

'Good. And yes, you're right. I did overreact a bit. But I didn't like the inference from Finlay suggesting we'd been spying on him and his friend.'

Nell nodded and then paused, as if gathering her thoughts. 'Can I speak plainly?'

'Of course.'

'Do you think the reappearance of Brian McNeil may have unsettled you a bit?'

'It wasn't the best news I've had recently. So far as I was concerned that Al Anfal business was dead and buried.'

'And it most probably is. I also think we may need to take a step back. I'm not sure Finlay is concerned so much about *who* has been listening in on Kevin Jones so much as *why*.'

'Don't you think that hadn't occurred to me?' Toni answered impatiently. 'Fact is, it wasn't us. But to start digging and asking questions about it could make waves. It really is bloody annoying that someone is targeting Jones, but should we really be surprised after what has happened earlier in the year?'

'It has to be Howard Green,' said Nell. 'He's being careful, double-checking what the Director told him. Making sure, like you said, that neither of them were part of the plan to sell secrets to the newspapers.'

'Could we check?'

'I could try and find out quietly, if that might help? Without making any ripples.'

'Electronically, you mean?'

'Yes, and I'll make sure there's no trail back to here. If you leave the device with me, I'll see what I can find out about it. If I can see who it was issued to that might tell us what we need to know.'

It was Toni's turn to reflect. Perhaps she could be more accommodating? There was little to lose and, if Nell could be discreet, it would be useful to know and might help Finlay answer his concerns.

'OK,' she answered finally. 'I'll be back at Thames House in about an hour. Ping me an email if you find anything. But keep it to yourself, don't mention it to Stuart for the time being.'

'I will. But I have to confess to being very concerned.'

'About what, exactly?'

Nell leaned forwards, a look of concern on her face. 'That call I had from Kevin Jones a few weeks ago, surely you haven't forgotten it? And now McNeil surfaces. There seems to be lots of moving parts going on here. We don't know them all; we don't have the facts. It seems to me that somebody is pulling strings and we don't even know what those strings are or why.'

'You think there might be a connection between that call and Howard being behind the deaths of the soldiers?'

'Don't you? We established that Kevin Jones had an issue with Howard Green because something happened between them in Afghan.'

'When Howard nearly got him killed?'

'Exactly. And because of that I agreed with your decision only to tell Finlay that Howard had been behind the operation.'

'If Jones had been told, he would have gone after Howard. It was best he be kept in the dark.'

'And I'm not saying now that was the wrong decision. But Jones calling me asking about an Arabic translator – which is exactly what Finlay did when he first got hold of that secret Al Anfal document – and now McNeil … and a listening device turns up in Jones's home … I know coincidence isn't causality, but surely it's odds-on Howard

Green or our Director may be behind it somewhere? They were last time, after all?'

Toni knew Nell was right, and that she was doing what she always did: avoiding the irrelevant distraction and focussing on the real issue. Toni took a deep breath. Could they have intercepted the call from Jones and then decided to start surveillance on him?

'I was assured the operation was over,' she said. 'I had that from the Director himself.'

Nell simply raised her eyebrows; she didn't need to say a word.

As she headed out to the street, Toni was still thinking about her conversation with Nell. As she so often did, her former researcher had hit the nail on the head. But looking into the origins of the listening device would very likely open a can of worms. It was possible that Howard Green's operation was still live. He would want to be absolutely sure that Finlay and Jones weren't a risk; bugging their homes would be one way of doing that. And, as much as the prospect annoyed her, it was quite possible the Director may have lied to her in order to try and make sure she stayed out of the way.

And what of Kevin and his question? Why had he been asking for a translator? Had he secured access to a copy of the Al Anfal document? Was McNeil's reappearance a coincidence or not? A shiver ran down her spine as she exited the building and began the long walk back to her office. She hoped she was wrong, that his request and the appearance of the listening device were just a coincidence. But, in her heart of hearts she doubted it was and, should her fears prove to be right, the probability was that he was heading towards a heap of trouble.

Chapter 15

Grahamslaw left the door to his office open as he went through the mound of paperwork on his desk.

Top of the pile was a letter from Omar Shabat, the Housing Minister. He had requested some information and data on people trafficking. Nina Brasov had put together a report and was to attend Shabat's offices to discuss it with him.

Pinned to the file was a handwritten note from Assistant Commissioner, George Mason. It read simply, 'Speak to me before you talk to Shabat.'

No time like the present.

Grahamslaw picked up the telephone and dialled Mason's direct number.

The AC answered immediately, and got straight to the point.

'Who are you sending to see the Housing Minister to discuss his questions?'

'Nina Brasov. She knows more about the subject than any of us.'

'Send Superintendent Cutts with her, or someone else of rank. We can't have his Private Secretary complaining we've only sent a bloody Sergeant.'

'I'll do that.'

Abrupt as always, Mason ended the call.

Grahamslaw replaced the receiver, just as Mick Parratt walked past his office door.

'Perfect timing, Mick,' Grahamslaw called out.

From the corridor, his number two leaned around the door frame, a beaming smile across his lips. 'You spotted me, guv.'

'Come in and close the door, will you? Now, the AC just told me he wants Ron Cutts to go with Nina to see the Housing Minister,' continued Grahamslaw as Parratt took a seat.

'Ron's on annual. Do you want me to go instead?'

'Ah, damn. I forgot. No, I'll send Bob Finlay. He could do with a morning sat drinking tea and exchanging small-talk with a politician.' As Grahamslaw spoke he reached into his jacket pocket and pulled out a white envelope.

'What's that?' asked Parratt.

The Commander paused. 'Something I need your advice on,' he said, finally.

'Sounds ominous. Is it personal?'

'Ha … you know me too well. Yes, it's personal … something I need to talk over … to try and get my head around.'

Grahamslaw paused and closed his eyes for a moment before continuing.

'I've had a letter from my wife's solicitors,' he began. 'It's divorce.'

'She give a reason?'

'Adultery.'

Parratt sighed deeply. 'Meaning she knows. She knew about Emma and she knows you've got another squeeze on the go.'

'She thinks…'

'She *knows*, guv. She ain't stupid. If I've sussed you splashing on the Old Spice and digging out your best suit every time you head off for a meeting with a certain MI5 officer, you can bet your wife's spotted it as well.'

Grahamslaw leaned hard back in his chair, the legs creaking under the strain. His friend was right. 'Does anyone else know?' he asked, quietly.

'If they do, then it hasn't reached my ears. Liz in the squad office made a crack about the aftershave a few weeks ago, but even she hasn't a clue who it is.'

'They know there's someone though?'

'They're not blind, guv. Most of the times you've been picked up from the flat it's been clocked there was someone with you.'

'I thought I'd been discreet.'

The Superintendent's lips curled upwards into a warm smile. 'We're coppers, guv. People know what we're like.'

Chapter 16

If I walked along Grahamslaw's corridor once in the hope of finding his office door open, I must have done it half a dozen times. Each visit produced the same result: door closed and Grahamslaw deep in conversation with his Superintendent, Mick Parratt.

Eventually, I struck lucky. The door was open, Parratt was nowhere to be seen but, as was often the case, the Commander was on the telephone.

My presence in the doorway must have registered, as he beckoned me in with an almost regal wave of his free hand. I took a seat and waited. It didn't sound like the call was ending any time soon.

Given that Bill Grahamslaw held one of the most prestigious commands in the policing world, the size and décor of his office must have come as quite a surprise to those that called on him. It wasn't large, more than needed for one person but smaller than you might have expected for a Commander. And it was untidy, unusually so. In one corner, several pictures were on the floor, stacked together against the wall. It looked like they were intended for display but, for one reason or another, it had never happened.

Two glass-fronted book cases contained what looked like copies of old case files and a surprising number of novels. On each occasion I had previously sat in his visitor's seat, I tried to spot the new titles. Grahamslaw's reading habits were similar to mine, in that he only found time, he'd said, to read while travelling on the tube. Although my preference was for a decent newspaper, we agreed that being transported into another world by a good writer was a useful way to make underground commutes more tolerable. Our tastes differed though; I preferred thrillers whereas Grahamslaw was a science-fiction fan. Alongside his collection of weighty legal almanacs that included the latest *Stone's Justices' Manual* and *Cox's Criminal Law Cases*, I noted several well-known sci-fi titles.

Grahamslaw slammed the receiver down. 'Bastards!' he exclaimed.

Although distracted during my study of our surroundings, I'd heard enough of the conversation to work out that it was a discussion about manpower. 'Not a good time?' I asked.

'No. Sorry, Finlay. Actually, your timing is perfect for once. That was HR playing silly buggers with the transfer dates of some detectives we've selected to fill vacancies in the office. I sometimes wonder if our new breed of human resource managers actually realise the kind of pressure we're under these days and that the numbers they see on paper are actually real people.'

'Rather than resources?'

'Exactly.' The Commander leaned back in his chair. 'But that isn't what you're here to see me about, I guess?'

'I was wondering if you had any news for me.'

'On that complaint from Jim Mellor? Yes. It's canned. Mellor can take a hike as far as I'm concerned. But, like I said in your office, be careful of him in future.'

'I've met people like him, even before I joined the Met. The army investigation branch had its fair share of awkward bastards. Before this job I always had a policy of not trusting men in suits.'

Grahamslaw laughed. 'And now you're wearing one? How times change.'

'I guess.'

'Now, about your other question. I got your email, thanks, and I did some checking. The device is one of a type the Met trialled but decided not to buy.'

'So, we're no closer to knowing who planted it?'

'We're not. I've had lads on discipline boards for using official listening devices to check on their wives when they think they're having an affair. A lot cheaper than employing a private detective and a good reason to hide that it's booked out to you.'

'But this one turned up in Kevin Jones's house,' I said. 'So, unless his girlfriend's ex-husband is spying on him, that's not going to be the reason.'

'Is he in the job?'

'Actually … yes.'

'Best you check him out then, before we start jumping to conclusions. Simplest answers are often the right ones.'

I couldn't recall the name of Sandi's ex but I did remember Kevin saying he was a uniform Sergeant somewhere. And although I accepted that a quick phone call might place him as a suspect or eliminate him, I doubted he could have had access to the device. That said, I still had to check. I thanked the Commander for his effort and was just about to head back to my office when he called me back. He had a job for me – accompanying Nina to see a Housing Minister where she was to present him with some data on people trafficking. 'Make sure the Minister knows you're a senior officer,' he said. 'And make sure you're both on your best behaviour.'

The trafficking office was empty as I returned. I checked my watch – lunchtime. I guessed Matt and Nina had popped out for a sandwich. I closed the office door, sat down at my desk and tried Kevin's phone. Three attempts, each time cutting through to his answerphone. I gave up and left a message for him to contact me.

Stomach rumbling, I grabbed my jacket and headed for the canteen.

☩

I was deep in thought, having just polished off a large bacon sandwich, when my musings were disturbed by one of the last people I expected to see. I'd picked a quieter end of the canteen, far from the servery area and near the window, somewhere I could watch who came and went.

At the counter, I noticed the familiar figure of Nell Mahoney – the MI5 researcher who worked with Toni Fellows – as she paid for a meal. Nell, I'd learned, had Asperger's and tended to keep herself to herself. So, in normal circumstances, I wouldn't have expected her to head towards me. We weren't friends and, although we had spoken several times, I had noticed she only ever had a light snack and tended to spend just a few minutes eating it alone before heading back to her office. On this occasion, she came in my direction and sat down opposite me at my table.

'Will you be here long, Mr Finlay?' she asked, immediately tucking into her food.

I smiled to myself as I saw what she was eating for her late breakfast – a large pile of chips with plenty of tomato sauce and a pint of cold milk – but then I knew Nell wasn't a woman who bowed to conventional behaviour. 'I was about to head back, to be honest,' I replied. 'How are you?'

Nell shovelled a handful of chips between her lips and smiled as she began to chew. 'I'm good, thanks, keeping busy like you do. I've got some news for you.'

It looked like this was no chance encounter. 'From Toni, you mean?'

Half a fairly large glass of milk disappeared in one go, leaving a white circle around Nell's mouth which she swiftly removed with the back of her sleeve. 'Not exactly, no,' she answered, between mouthfuls. 'This is what you coppers might call off-the-record.'

I scowled. 'Does Toni know you're speaking to me?'

'No … so don't go mentioning it, will you?'

'OK,' I said, slowly. I was trying hard not to show my confusion, but from the uncertainty in my voice, it must have been quite apparent. This was by far the longest conversation we'd ever had and it seemed Nell was about to go out on a limb to tell me about something. 'Mum's the word, Nell.'

She half smiled, forking another chip into her mouth before checking over her shoulder as if looking to see if anyone was watching us. It was clear Nell's table manners weren't quite in line with the fastidious and ordered way in which she maintained her office space. Leaning towards me, she spoke quietly. 'The bug. It's one of yours.'

'One of mine … What do you mean, one of mine?'

'One of yours … the Met. It's a police bug. It was one of a few of them that you had on trial.'

'I already heard that, Nell.'

'You knew it for definite?'

'Well, I know it's a type we trialled, yes.'

'I can tell you for definite. I checked the serial number. It was sent to the Met for evaluation and never returned to the manufacturer.'

'Really? That's great, thanks. But what I really need to know is *who* planted it in Kevin's home.'

'*You* did,' she answered.

'Sorry?'

Another chip, another slurp of milk. 'The Met did. It was your own people that put it there.'

I shook my head. 'I'm sorry, Nell. Can't you be a bit more specific? There are a hell of a lot of people in this building alone, without including all the others out on division.'

'Ah … OK. I get you. You wanna know who authorised it being placed in the house?'

'If that's not too much trouble, yes.'

'Can't say.'

'Can't or won't?'

'Can't. Give me more time and I might.'

'So, we're no closer to knowing?' I asked.

'You'd need to break into the police stores to find out any more.'

I sighed.

'Not the end of the world though,' Nell continued.

'Why's that?'

'It was broken. Internal circuits were fried, so I guess whoever was listening didn't learn very much.'

'Unless there was more than one bug?' I suggested.

'True. Didn't think of that. Not many surveillance ops use just one device. Probably a fisherman.'

'A fisherman?'

'Yep. A single bug that someone installs cos they are fishing … you know, looking for something concrete before they go for an official placement authorised by a Commander.'

'So, if that was the case, there wouldn't be a record.'

Nell belched slightly, and then smiled in apparent embarrassment before answering my question. 'Unlikely,' she said. 'Best you have a think about who might be fishing for something on your friend.'

I went to stand up. 'Thanks, Nell…'

'Haven't finished,' she added.

'I'm sorry?' I said, returning to my seat.

'Haven't finished. Something else I need to tell you.'

'Like what?' I leaned forwards again, anxious not to miss what Nell was saying.

But she remained silent. I thought she had perhaps changed her mind about continuing when, just as I was about to prompt her, a uniform WPC walked past us, close enough to have overheard what was being said. Only when the officer had moved out of earshot, did Nell speak.

'Al Anfal,' she said quietly, lowering her face close to mine as she said the words.

'What about it, Nell?' I asked.

'Not it … them.'

'Them? I'm not following you. And how do you know about it anyway?'

'Toni had me research it. Most of what she knows is down to me. She was interested … until someone warned her off.'

'Warned her off?'

'Yep. One minute she's dead keen on learning everything about Al Anfal. Next minute, drop everything. We're told never to mention it again.'

'Someone put pressure on her?'

'Sure as eggs are eggs.' Nell laughed and then used the last chip on her plate to mop up the remaining tomato sauce. 'Eggs are eggs, good one that. Being as everyone knows eggs are eggs, I mean they can't exactly be jumbo jets can they?'

We were wandering off track. 'So what did you have to tell me about it … or them?'

'She said not to tell you – *he* said I should.'

'Who's she … and who is *he* for that matter?' I'd heard Nell could be difficult to work with, at the moment she was being exasperating.

'Toni, of course. She gives the orders … always orders. But Stuart said I should tell you.'

Stuart Anderson. Toni's assistant. 'I see. Tell me what, exactly?'

Nell took a deep breath, a huffy breath, as if I wasn't getting something she considered blindingly obvious. 'Tell you about Al Anfal.'

'The document?'

'Not a document. An organisation. Secret … very secret. People died; your people. That's why Stuart says I should tell you.'

'That it's an organisation?'

'Yes. And everyone who knows about it ends up dead. All except you, Jones, and McNeil and Grady. All dead. All murdered. Which is why we thought it best to warn you. Best heed Toni's advice. Maybe time to tell Kevin Jones?'

'Did Toni send you?' I asked.

Nell looked confused, and I quickly dismissed the idea. If Toni had wanted to repeat her warning to me, she could have done it herself. 'Do we know any more about McNeil now?' I asked.

'Private military contractor, McNeil.' Nell was now speaking much faster, as if she was rushing, either to get things over with or, possibly, excited at what she was illicitly revealing.

'What do you know about him, Nell?' I reached out, touched her hand. I needed to know what she knew.

'He's the missing link, the only survivor of the team that found the Al Anfal document. Don't mention I told you, will you? But he's the only survivor other than Grady. And that man is a ghost.'

'I don't follow; you mean Chris Grady?'

'Yes, him … dead maybe. Not sure … maybe disappeared. Very odd … couldn't find him. No records, no pension, no nothing. Just gone … like that Maggie Price.'

Chapter 17

The conversation with Nell had left me with more questions than answers. I was already aware that possessing any knowledge of Al Anfal was a risk. Nearly a year had now passed since Toni had explained the fate of the men from the Afghan Increment patrol who'd first discovered the Al Anfal document. But I was more than a little curious as to why Nell had seen fit to tell me herself, and why now? Was it simply because she and Stuart had decided I ought to know? Did they really think it was time to warn Kevin off now that McNeil was out there somewhere?

A phone was ringing as I walked back into the office. There was still no sign of Nina and, with Matt engaged on another call, I picked up the receiver.

'Finlay? Thought it was you I saw in the foyer. How did the promotion board go?'

I recognised the voice immediately. There weren't many men I knew who spoke with such depth and power as Rupert Reid. I hadn't spoken to the barrel-chested bomb disposal officer in several months.

'How did you know I was up for it?' I asked.

'Word gets around, you know. So, how did it go? Are we going to see your imminent promotion in notices soon?'

'Afraid not. Boss gave me the bad news a few days ago. Not that I'm complaining, but I guess I'm stuck with these two miscreants for the time being.' I smiled at Matt as he finished his call.

'That's a pity. The job needs a few people with your type of character to shake it up a bit.'

'My kind of character?' I asked.

'I'm sure you know what I mean, Finlay. The senior ranks are attracting far too many politically correct butterflies who flit from one job to another as they climb up the ladder.'

'Without any real experience anywhere, you mean?'

'Exactly.'

'A bit like me with less than a year in a detective role and now I'm a DI?'

Rupert coughed. 'Er … yes. Anyway, that's not really why I called. Do you have a minute to pop over to my office? Something I need to discuss.'

'Right now you mean?'

'If you can, yes.'

I agreed and put down the phone.

'Have you done that Misper report for the boss?' Matt asked, as I headed to the door. 'He was asking for it earlier.'

'On it,' I said, although that wasn't actually true. I'd been neglecting the day job, I knew that. But my head was elsewhere, and at that moment, talking to Rupert sounded like a priority.

Conversations with my old friend tended to quickly focus on the old days in Northern Ireland, how things had been then and how the Met had changed – in his opinion not for the better.

Rupert was waiting for me. As I walked in through the door to his office, he was already pouring coffee from a percolator. 'Black, if I remember correctly, and no sugar?' he said as he handed me a mug.

The office was empty, something that surprised me. 'Nobody else at work today?' I asked.

'A few are down at Chattenden on a training day, the rest are in the canteen. Having the office to myself gave me an ideal opportunity to speak to you about something that's been troubling me.'

'You're still using Chattenden then?'

'For the time being. Word is that the MOD wants to sell off both Lodge Hill and Chattenden training areas for housing developments. Bloody disgrace if you ask me. The only thing that seems to be holding them up has nothing to do with military expedience – it's a population of nightingales living in the woodland.'

'You're still a twitcher?'

'When I can, yes. I've spent many a happy hour at Lodge Hill, I can tell you. Do you know that small wood is home to one percent of the entire UK population of nightingales?'

'I didn't.'

'Bloody heathen you are, Finlay. I bet you wouldn't even recognise a nightingale song if you heard it.'

'Possibly not,' I said. 'But I didn't come here to talk birds. You said something's been troubling you?'

Rupert indicated I should take a seat at a set of four adjacent desks near the coffee machine. Each of them bore the hallmarks of recent occupation – stacked files, glossy photographs and mugs filled with chewed pens. Polystyrene coffee cups, most of which looked pretty ancient, in which grew a variety of multi-coloured mould colonies.

'I've had your friend Jones on the phone,' Rupert said, as I made myself comfortable.

'What did he want?' I asked.

'Remember when you came to see me at the end of last year with that Arabic document?'

'Of course,' I replied. Immediately, I felt my heart rate accelerate in response to yet another mention of the Al Anfal text. If Kevin was still asking questions about it, that could cause problems.

'Well, it seems your friend has it.'

'It was destroyed,' I said, a little too quickly. Again, alarm bells were sounding as I recalled Nell's warning and her mention of Brian McNeil. And I wondered for a moment if Julian Armstrong, the translator, had gone back on his word to burn the document.

'Was it?' said Rupert. 'Well, I guess your friend has another copy. He asked the same questions as you did – about its meaning and the content. As I knew I couldn't help him, I referred him on, as I did for you.'

'To Dr Armstrong? He agreed to look at it again?'

'Yes, he did.'

I was a little taken aback at the news. Given what Julian Armstrong had told me about the Al Anfal text, I would have expected him to want to give it a wide berth. 'Was this call from Kevin today?' I asked.

'No, no. It must have been a couple of weeks ago, probably more. It was only when I spotted you in the foyer just now that it reminded me I ought to tell you about it.'

'The copy I had was destroyed,' I repeated. 'Dr Armstrong reckoned it was so sensitive we would be in deep shit explaining where it came from and how come we'd laid hands on it.'

'Seems pragmatic if it was that sensitive,' Rupert replied. 'We're assuming, of course, that it is the same document, or a copy of it?'

'Bit of a coincidence otherwise…' I said.

'I suppose so. Anyway, I thought you should know, just in case it was important.'

'Yes, thanks.' I sipped at the coffee. It was still too hot to drink and, I had the feeling that by some unholy coincidence, Rupert may just have answered the question as to why Nell had suggested I speak to Kevin. I stood up to leave.

'In a hurry?' Rupert asked.

'Sorry, yes. I need to call Kevin, find out what's going on.'

☩

Having thanked Rupert for his help, I headed back in the direction of my own office. I didn't want Matt to overhear the call I was about to make, so as soon as I reached the lift stairwell, I called Kevin from my mobile. He answered after just two rings.

'I've just left a meeting with Rupert Reid,' I began.

'Ah … I wondered how long it would take before that news reached you.'

'What the hell are you up to?' I demanded.

There was a pause. 'Are you busy?'

'How do you mean?'

'Well, I've kinda been expecting your call, boss.'

'Do you want to explain to me what's going on?'

'Not on the phone. I'm meeting with Sandi this afternoon so, if you're free, how about right away?'

I thought for a moment. If we met halfway, I could slip out and my absence would hardly be noticed. No time like the present, I figured.

Chapter 18

Howard closed his office door, his mobile telephone held tight to his ear. 'It's a go for today, Grady,' he said, calmly.

'As planned?'

Howard glanced down at the transcript of the text-message exchange before answering. 'Yes. Get to the woman's house for 1300 hours. She'll be waiting for him in the bedroom; the front door will be unlocked. Make sure no one sees you.'

'Roger that. And has Petre confirmed?'

'Yes, he'll be taking care of the delay. Target two won't reach the plot until about 1315 hours. You'll have more than enough time.'

'OK. Just to check, you want her dead on the bed, him to look like the killer? But if things go tits up and we're unable to arrange the scene as required, Petre will remove both bodies covertly at 1330 hours?'

'Confirmed. You know all this – so why the questions? I'm relying on you to get this right, Grady.'

There was a pause. 'Cathy thinks it's too elaborate.'

'I have my reasons and I don't need to explain myself to her,' Howard snapped. Grady didn't respond. '1300 hours today,' he continued. 'Call me at 1400 with confirmation. And Grady – don't fuck this one up. This can't come back to bite us on the arse. It has to look like suicide.'

The line went dead.

Howard returned to his office chair, inhaling deeply as he sank into it. To be fair to Cathy, she was right. The arrangements had been rushed and were a little complex, but, given that his original plan to ensure a clean, deniable operation had failed thanks to the selected agent not being up to the task, the new arrangement was a reasonable alternative.

Exactly what he would do about the disappointing response from the agent would have to wait, but of the need to do something, he was certain. Sometimes, people needed to be reminded just how much they owed.

Chapter 19

An hour after my brief conversation with Kevin, I was in the waiting room at Canning Town tube station, watching for the arrival of a west-bound train. It was a perfect spot to meet.

In the sealed environment of a railway waiting room, there was virtually no possibility of us being overheard. Even outside the closed doors, the background noise generated by central London at its busiest served to drown out all but the loudest of voices. Inside, we could easily speak freely. Which was just as well, considering the subject I was about to raise.

Kevin kept me waiting for a few minutes and appeared just as a train from the Docklands Light Railway was pulling into one of the platforms.

'It looks like there's no shadow on you,' he said, as he sat on the plastic seat immediately next to me. He leaned forwards, talking quietly so we wouldn't be overheard, even though there were no other passengers in the waiting room.

'You thought there might be?' I replied.

'After finding that bug in the house I reckon anything's possible.'

Through the grey-stained windows, I spotted a suited commuter walking along the platform. He glanced at me, as if checking whether the waiting room was free of undesirable types. He was genuine – no surveillance operative would risk making eye contact – and, presumably, having decided Kevin and I weren't the kind of people he wanted to share a waiting room with, he moved on.

'You've no doubt guessed what Rupert told me?' I began. 'You've been calling people trying to find a translator for a copy of that Arabic document. Do you want to tell me where you got it from?'

'I can't say.'

'You don't have to, Kev,' I said, angrily. 'Brian McNeil is the answer.'

'How the fuck?'

'I know he's surfaced and he's the last known member of that patrol. I put two and two together. You've been helping him.'

Kevin was silent for a moment before replying. 'I'm sorry ... I should have said something at the pub, but we'd already put the wheels in motion. Truth is, McNeil already has things sorted.'

'Using the same translator, Dr Armstrong?'

'Yes.'

I didn't reply, as I weighed up my options and the warnings Toni and Armstrong had given me. 'So, what happened when you contacted the Doctor?' I asked.

'McNeil said he would do the job, but he said it was a waste of time if it was the same thing he'd looked at before.'

'He's scared.'

'Why's that, then?'

'Something I should have shared with you at the time ... but we never figured another copy of the document would ever surface.'

'Something? Like what?'

'I told you at the time that it was valueless. Well, that wasn't exactly what he said to me. He said that possession of it was a poison chalice, a curse – whoever had it would have to explain how he came by it.'

'I'm not following. "Cursed" – was does that mean?'

I half smiled. 'No, not in that way. It's a highly secret document that our Security Services either have already or are likely to be looking for. Anyone even knowing about it is at risk; and actual possession of a copy would be a curse. Al Anfal, or whoever they are, plus Al Q'aeda, MI5, Six, the CIA – they'll all be looking for it, and Armstrong was quite certain they would be prepared to eliminate whoever got in their way.'

Kevin was stunned into silence. 'So, I'm not the only one who's been keeping secrets, boss ... that's why all our lads were killed, isn't it? Someone making sure it stays secret.'

'That was Armstrong's conclusion, yes.'

'And it's potentially valuable?'

I sighed. 'Sometimes I wonder about you, Kev. Are you not listening? Yes, it has some value, but that's not the point. You can't sell it. Nobody with any sense would touch it and, as soon as you try to find a buyer, you'd make yourself a target.'

'We could be careful, use an intermediary? Highest bidder gets it?'

'Are you serious?'

'I'm not sure,' he replied, more thoughtfully now. 'Something McNeil said to me. Like he already had some idea what it is. He said it was called Al Anfal.'

'That is its name, yes, and, likely as not, he does know what it is and he only wanted your help because he thought you could help sell it. Why do you think the others on the Increment patrol were keeping copies? They already had an idea what it was.'

'So what happened to the copy you took to the translator?'

'He burned it … and with my approval. It's from a world way beyond our understanding, Kev.'

'Probably explains why, when McNeil first called him, he said he had no idea what he was talking about. He might think his phone is bugged as well.'

'He told me that if you Googled the name "Al Anfal", GCHQ would pick that up and the Security Services would soon be knocking on your door.'

'Really?'

'Where is McNeil?'

'He's laying low.'

I shook my head. The day was going from bad to worse. 'So, where is his copy of the document at the moment?'

'Armstrong still has it. But I guess that's the least of my worries.'

'How do you mean?'

'Google. I already searched the name.'

Chapter 20

Sandi checked the clock on her dressing table. It had gone one, Kevin was late.

Whenever he came on one of his daytime visits, she felt a mixed sense of anticipation and a delicious excitement. The last months had been an awakening. No man she had met had excited her the way he did, and no man had ever suggested they try the things she now enjoyed so much. And no man could have persuaded her to be waiting in her house alone, dressed as she was now.

It had started slowly. In hospital, as he recovered from a bullet wound, they had started talking. He was chatting her up, she knew that, but unlike with the other overly amorous patients in the men's ward, she had been flattered by his attentions. There was something special about him, something mysterious that she found enticing. There were stories on the ward – confirmed as she got to know him – that he was a soldier-turned-cop who'd only just survived a terrorist attack. After exchanging phone numbers, she'd sent him a text. Nothing too forward, just a hello, first contact. It was an hour before he responded. An hour during which she must have checked her phone a hundred times.

His first, uncertain, messages were nice, polite. He apologised for being so familiar, for teasing her, and for risking getting her in trouble with the hospital authorities. Soon, they arranged to meet.

In the days that followed she had been unable to concentrate at work or think of anything else, frequently checking her phone and finding reasons to text him. She felt as if she was regressing into a love-sick teenager, constantly thinking about Kevin. Even her two boys – her darling teenage sons – had commented that she'd seemed distracted.

When she and Kevin finally met in a car park near the hospital they had talked incessantly and only when the time had come to part had they kissed.

The next day was her day off. It was also the first time he came to the house. Living in a suburban close, most people were out at work. Even so, he parked in a nearby street and then walked the rest of the way.

With the boys at school, she'd spent hours tidying, getting the bedroom just perfect so he wouldn't think her a slob. She even experimented with different light bulbs, trying to create the right mood lighting. Her hands had been shaking as she'd hit the switch to judge the impact, such was her excitement. That first time they didn't make it upstairs. She made coffee and, as she passed him his mug, her excitement had made her clumsy and she spilt it. He took her hand, held it gently and kissed her. He was tender, and to her surprise, it was she who leaned into him, held him closer and began to deepen the kiss. They made love there, in the sitting room – on the sofa and then the floor. Even with his injuries so fresh, Sandi was aware of his hard muscles and exciting strength.

As the weeks passed they met more frequently. She introduced him to the boys, cooked for him, even helped him with his own house. They became very much a couple.

One day, just as an experiment, she had dressed up for him. It was a surprise, a treat – something spicy to give him pleasure. She'd been nervous, but she'd remembered how he reacted to her teasing him in hospital. Not having the confidence to risk a face-to-face encounter – or God forbid an actual conversation with a shop assistant – she had performed a discreet Google search and then maintained her secret as she waited for the specialist lingerie to be delivered.

It worked and, for the two of them, it opened up a whole new world. They tried new things and she found just how much being tied up excited her. At first he was hesitant, checking with her frequently, but as their trust in each other grew he experimented. He would bind her to a chair, to the bed, anywhere he could take her at a time when she was his captive. It excited him, and it almost shocked her how arousing she found it. Now they had reached a point where he would text her in the middle of the day, when she was in the house alone, tell her what to wear and how to place herself ready for his visit. Sometimes he would have her stand over the bed and blindfold herself, other times she would lie on the bed waiting. She had to leave the front door unlocked. She would hear him arrive, climb the stairs and then he would take her. On some occasions he wouldn't even undress.

He had sent her such a text today. She was to be laid face up on the bed, dressed and blindfolded, with her wrists secured to the headboard.

The bedroom was now ready and so was she. She'd showered and perfumed her skin, and then dressed very slowly, savouring the anticipation that grew with every minute. She'd picked one of his favourite basques together with sheer black stockings and high heels. As per his instructions, she tied ropes to the headboard, knotted so she could easily insert her hands and give the appearance of restraint they both enjoyed.

She listened carefully for the sound of the front door and, when it came, she shuddered. One day, she feared, that sound would be her son arriving home early. Not today though, her eldest boy didn't finish school until after three, so there was plenty of time.

She heard the door close. Sliding the eye mask on, she lay back and slipped her wrists into the ropes. There were footsteps on the stairs, the familiar heavy creak of the fourth tread. It was him. Her nerves eased, neither of the boys was heavy enough to make a sound that loud. The bedroom door swung open and a gentle draft teased her already erect nipples. Squeezing her thighs together, she shuddered with excitement. She sensed, rather than felt him. He was close. Something – a hand – stroked her knee, her leg, pulled gently at her suspender. He was teasing her.

Something touched her face. A glove? No, a hood, maybe plastic of some kind. He was pulling a hood over her head. A new toy, she mused, as she gave way to the anticipation of what was to come.

Then something took hold of her feet. It was tight and felt like hands but no, it couldn't be, he was still pulling the hood around her neck. What was it? As the hood tightened around her neck, the grip on her ankles hurt and breathing became harder. A first sensation of panic hit her. She tried to twist her mouth away from the hood, tried to call out, but it was too tight. She couldn't speak, couldn't breathe. The grip around her legs was now unmistakeable. There were two pairs of hands. There were definitely two people.

She tried to scream but the hand on her face held tight. He was hurting her. What on earth did he think he was doing? She felt sick, giddy.

For Christ's sake, Kevin, she tried to say, *stop…*

Chapter 21

'Come on, Finlay, or we'll be late,' Nina shouted from the corridor.

I hurriedly restored the papers on my desk into some form of order, grabbed my coat from the back of the chair and marched quickly to catch up with her. 'Sorry, didn't realise the time,' I replied.

'You alright?' she asked, as we waited at the lift. 'You seem a bit distracted.'

'Yeah, a few things on my mind.'

The lift alarm pinged to indicate its arrival.

'Best put it behind you, there's always next year's board.'

'Do you know the route?' I asked. 'I had a look on the street atlas in the office. I reckon we could take the back streets through to Horseferry Road and then turn into Marsham Street.'

'I know where it is. The Ministry offices are on the corner at number two.'

As we exited the building and set off along Dacre Street, Nina began to chat about the reason for the Minister's request. Apparently, he had come in for some criticism in the House of Commons when he was unable to answer questions on the number of council-owned properties where victims of trafficking had been discovered and the use of those properties as brothels. She ran me through the results of her research, which was embarrassingly limited given that no UK force seemed to record information that would fully answer the question. We only broke away from the subject once, when we passed a news vendor where the advertising billboard displayed a headline concerning news that a mass roadblock had been set up in Hampshire following the discovery of the body of a young girl missing in the area since March.

'She'll be amongst those misper reports on your desk,' said Nina, indicating the billboard. 'How are you getting on with that report?'

'Slowly,' I said. 'Too many distractions.'

'Well, if you need some help, just ask, eh? Does that kind of thing worry you more now that you have kids?' she asked.

'It does, yes. They've confirmed it's Millie Dowler then?'

'Apparently so. I did hear the dental records have provided a match.'

I let out a sigh. 'Every parent's nightmare, losing a child. Not a cop in the country who wouldn't give his eye teeth to find the bastard that did that.'

Nina didn't reply and I didn't continue with the conversation. I struggled to even imagine the trauma the Dowlers were going through at that very moment.

We pushed on and, as we arrived at the huge glass-fronted ministry building at 2, Marsham Street, I asked Nina what she knew about Shabat, the Minister we were due to meet.

'Very little,' she answered. 'He's had a charmed career, one of the new wave of politicians who were born elsewhere, immigrated here and worked their way up the ladder very quickly. From what I've been able to learn he's a Shia Muslim from Iraq who came here in the early nineties with his family to escape the regime in that country.'

'A Muslim?'

'Yes. The boss said I wasn't to try and shake his hand and should wait to see what he does. You'd probably best do the same.'

The automated glass door to the reception area swung open. The security guards were expecting us and after checking our warrant cards, we were joined by a civil servant who led the way through the building to a corridor that overlooked an internal courtyard. It was deserted for the time being but, from the layout of the narrow gravel paths, the benches and the shrubbery, it looked to be designed as somewhere to relax, a place where hard-pressed staff could unwind for a few minutes.

The civil servant indicated we should wait and make use of a row of seats positioned near to a large double-width wooden door through which he headed. To me, the pale timber looked like oak, expensive. In fact, the whole appearance of the entrance to the Minister's offices was one of plush, if not ostentatious, comfort. Privilege of office, I assumed.

As the double door closed, I glanced around me, and upwards towards a ceiling that was surprisingly ornate for what I had thought to be a fairly modern building. The corridor was quiet and every other door I could see was closed. A pale-green carpet lay along the centre with what looked like polished parquet timber down each side. Several large portraits of long-dead politicians adorned the walls. One or two I thought I recognised, the majority not.

'That looks ominous,' Nina said, pointing to the empty seat next to me. Several dark spots had stained the upholstery. 'Looks like blood splashes,' she commented.

I pulled a small handkerchief from my pocket and moistened a corner with my tongue. Dabbing one of the spots, the white material turned pink as it made contact with one of the dark stains. 'Could be,' I said. 'Do housing ministers make it a routine to torture their visitors?'

She laughed, just as the oak door swung open from the inside. Omar Shabat extended a hand towards his office. 'Please, come in.'

The Minister wore an expensive-looking, grey two-piece suit. A heavy gold watch adorned his wrist. As we followed him into the large office I saw that his civil servant had disappeared. Two closed doors in one wall suggested where he may have gone. Near the window I noticed a large desk that appeared to be completely covered in documents, document boxes and folders in all manner of different colours. He indicated we should join him at an informal setting of chairs near the far wall where tea and coffee had been laid out on a small table.

As we sat, Shabat addressed his first question to Nina. 'I didn't expect you to have someone with you, Ms Brasov,' he said, almost quizzically, glancing towards me as he spoke.

'Inspector Finlay is my line manager, sir. He may well be able to help with any questions you have.'

Our host turned fully towards me and, for the first time, I noticed a slight ruffling of his composure. It was slight, hardly perceptible, but it was there. Something about my presence or my name had registered with him. As I accepted his hand in greeting, I noticed how gentle his touch was, almost as if he were attempting to ensure I didn't notice the moistness of his skin. 'Finlay?' he asked. 'And what is your first name, Mr Finlay?'

An unusual question, I thought, and assuming the Minister was being polite I told him. It was as I answered the question that I registered a flicker of concern in his eyes. I also noticed, as Nina had predicted, that he only shook my hand, not hers. With dark coffee poured from an aluminium thermos jug, we soon returned to the purpose of the meeting. Shabat got straight to the point, asking Nina a series of questions. He seemed pleased with the answers she provided.

Ten minutes later, Shabat was the only one of us to have emptied his cup. As Nina concluded her final answer to a question on trafficking trends, he turned to me.

'And what exactly is it you do at Scotland Yard, Mr Finlay, apart from being Ms Brasov's manager that is?'

'We're both part of a small team investigating trafficking, sir, mostly focussed on sex workers. We've been on task for about a year now.'

'That is very interesting. I have read in the newspapers and reports I have seen that the Met has been taking the problem more seriously of late.'

'We're doing our best, sir.'

'Are you familiar, possibly, with organisations in the Middle East who consider slavery to be a perfectly acceptable practice?'

It was an unusual question, and not one I had expected, given the purpose of our visit. I wondered if the Minister was testing me, to see if I was really Nina's boss.

'I'm aware, yes,' I said, 'but I wouldn't describe myself as being as expert as Sergeant Brasov.'

He appeared interested by my reply. 'You have heard of the Muslim Brotherhood … and, perhaps, of Al Anfal?'

If it was a test, it was a good one. A sucker punch, and very cleverly slipped beneath my guard to see if I reacted. Just as the Minister had shown a response to me telling him my full name, I knew my facial muscles had shown a similar, just perceptible reaction to the term 'Al Anfal'.

I decided to ignore it and carry on as normal. 'The names are vaguely familiar, yes,' I said, keeping my voice as matter-of-fact as I could. 'But our main focus is on Eastern-European gangs trafficking people into the UK.'

'Yes, of course. A prevalent problem, I'm sure.'

'"We will conquer your Rome, break your crosses, and enslave your women,"' said Nina, as if sensing a slightly increased tension in the room needed defusing.

'For the benefit of our new friend, Sergeant Brasov,' said Shabat. 'Do explain that quote.'

Nina continued. 'There are factions within the Muslim community who favour a return to ancient ideologies where Shia Muslims such as the Minister here are *persona non grata*. To their minds, becoming part of a system that involves being voted into power is a sin, and any Muslim who does so is declared apostate.'

'Meaning what, in layman's terms?' I asked.

'It means that people like the Minister are, to the minds of such people, sinners, and they should be killed. Others, like you and me, as non-Muslims, are spared death provided we agree to be subjugated. Then, we would be taken as slaves.'

'And that's a way of life they wish to see come back?'

'Some, yes,' said Shabat, interrupting. 'And for some the notion has never gone away. Thankfully, such extreme views are still in the minority.' He stood, and it looked like our visit was at an end. 'What were you doing as I opened the door earlier?' he asked. 'On the chair with your handkerchief.'

'Once a cop, always a cop,' I said. 'I spotted what looked like spots of blood.'

'Ah, yes. I know where you mean now. I had forgotten to ask for it to be cleaned. A previous visitor with a most unfortunate habit chewing the ends of his fingers in a way that makes them bleed.'

'Dermatophagia,' said Nina. 'Compulsive nail-biting.'

'Yes … as you say. I will ask the cleaners to attend to it.'

We bade the Minister goodbye and, with the oak doors closed behind us, headed back towards reception and the exit to the street.

As we reached a point in the corridor out of ear-shot of any potential listener, Nina leaned in close to me. 'That was interesting,' she said.

'Which part in particular?' I asked.

'All of it, really. But especially the bit when he wanted to talk to you about slavery. Did you get the impression he might know who you are? And what was that question about those Islamic groups I'd never heard of?'

'I wasn't quite sure,' I said. 'He did seem a bit ruffled when you introduced me. I wondered if it was simply because you'd brought someone along and he was testing me to see if I was who you'd said.'

Nina shrugged without answering.

But she was right, it was odd, and I thought at that moment I was going to have to wait and ask Toni Fellowes to see if she could throw some light on the subject.

However, as we arrived back at the reception desk, one of the security officers called out my name.

He had a message: the Minister wanted me to return – just me. He wished to speak to me again.

Chapter 22

Shabat was waiting in the corridor leading to his office.

On seeing me he turned and pushed open a door to a stairwell, quietly murmuring an instruction to follow him. We climbed four flights of stairs, exited through a similar door and then crossed the passageway through an open entrance into what looked like a small recording room. Inside, in the centre, there was one small desk, two chairs with a set of headphones on each, what appeared to be some type of recording equipment and a television on the far wall. The single window to the corridor was made of very thick perspex material and on the walls and ceiling were tiles that resembled egg boxes. To me, it looked like some kind of sound booth.

Shabat closed the door behind us. 'Please, take a seat, Inspector. We cannot be overheard in here.'

'Is this an interview room?' I asked.

'Yes, for radio and television. The measures you see are more to prevent outside noises from interfering with live transmissions, but they have the advantage that this room can be used to talk privately.'

'Handy,' I said. 'Why just me, though?'

'I think you and I both know why I asked you to return.'

I shrugged, feigning ignorance as I eased myself onto one of the seats. Shabat leaned back against the door. At first I thought he was trying to appear casual but then I realised, in that part of the room, he wouldn't be seen from the corridor – wouldn't be seen talking to me.

'You have me at a clear disadvantage, Minister.'

Shabat breathed in deeply. 'Very well, but please don't take me for a fool, Mr Finlay. When Sergeant Brasov introduced you, I recognised your name. I heard it first quite some time ago.'

I made to reply, but was met with a raised hand. 'Please, allow me to continue,' he said. 'I recognised your name from a meeting with a member of our Security Services in which you were mentioned.'

'Can I ask by who and why?'

'Who? No, of course I cannot divulge such information. But the context I will explain.'

'Sounds good to me, sir.'

'Good. Firstly, I asked you if you had heard of Muslim Brotherhood.'

'And I explained that my knowledge is more European based.'

'Yes, I'm sure. I also asked you about another group, and I saw your reaction to the name. That reaction confirmed to me that you were almost certainly the same Inspector Finlay who had been mentioned to me previously.'

'Al Anfal, you mean?' I replied, as I wondered where this was heading, especially given my recent conversation with Kevin.

'What do you know of them?'

'Well, my recollection is a bit sketchy but, as I recall, they were a group similar in nature to Al Q'aeda but they preceded them. I think they were effectively replaced by that new group.'

'You believe Al Anfal is a group of terrorists?'

'From what I remember, yes.'

'And how did you learn of them? From a police briefing?'

'Before that. I was a soldier before joining the police. During the Russian invasion of Afghanistan, I ran some training programmes for Mujahideen fighters. Amongst other things, they told us about Al Anfal.'

'Mujahideen fighters, you say? So, you have known about the group for a very long time?'

'Yes.'

'Not something you learned recently from a document that fell into your hands.'

I frowned as a pit formed in my stomach, anxious my face shouldn't again give away my true thoughts. Why on earth was a government minister asking me about something Dr Armstrong had warned me was so sensitive?

'Not at all,' I said. 'Do you mind if I ask your reason for asking?'

For a few moments, Shabat studied me without speaking. If it was a ploy, it worked, as I immediately felt uncomfortable. 'What do you think of Muslims, Inspector?' he asked, finally.

It was a left-field question, of the kind I'd been taught about on a recent interview skills course at Hendon, the police training college. I answered in the way the training staff had taught us.

'In relation to what?' I said, remembering the lesson to answer a question with a question, to throw the interrogator off track.

It didn't work. Shabat came back at me without hesitation. 'Do you, for example, think that Islamic terrorism is the greatest threat in the world at the moment? More than, say, North Korea, for example?'

'That's very deep, sir. Not something that people of my rank give a lot of thought to.'

'But as a person, you must have an opinion, surely?' He smiled knowingly.

Just where was this leading? I wondered.

'To be honest, sir, I have little sympathy for anyone who uses religion to justify violence, regardless of what that religion is. So, although I might understand how it can happen, I would never condone it.'

'So, you understand what drives men of strong beliefs to act in such ways?'

'I've studied it a little during my time as an army officer. It was part of the syllabus.'

'That's very interesting. Some might conclude you to be better informed than many in your position.'

'They might,' I said.

Shabat paused and glanced again through the observation window to the corridor before continuing. 'Do you think others might see that as a threat, possibly? The fact that you have such knowledge?'

I knew now where this was heading. Toni Fellowes' words came back to me: *'Mere knowledge of this document, of this group places a person at great risk.'*

'Not really,' I said. 'There's nothing I know that isn't in the public domain now. Things like that may have been secret back in the 1980s, but like Al Q'aeda, I believe they're pretty common knowledge now.'

'You knew of Al Q'aeda back then?'

'No, what I'm saying is their existence might have been a secret in those days, but it isn't now.'

'I see. Tell me, would you like to know more about Al Anfal?'

Check. Like a skilled chess master, Shabat had lured me into a corner. If I said no, that would seem unnatural. Yes was the logical answer, yet if I knew the risks of such knowledge; he knew that would cause me some anxiety. I had to at least pretend to be interested.

'Do we have long enough?' I said, buying time to think. 'I imagine you're very busy.'

'Everything has its moment, Mr Finlay. We have time, if you are interested?' Check again; my move.

'Fire away, if you're sure,' I replied.

He paused again, and this time moved away from the door to make use of the empty seat beside me. I pushed back slightly, conscious of wanting to maintain a personal space between us.

'Good. Islam, as you will know, is a religion steeped in great history. Within this, and spreading its wings across all the opinions, is Al Anfal.'

'I'm not sure I follow?' I said.

'You will, I'm sure. Al Q'aeda sees terror as a means to create a cali- phate – a place where the ways of Islam are perfectly adhered to. But even with that group there are differing opinions on how this can be achieved. Some, for example, foresee a great battle in which Islam will conquer Rome, break the infidel crosses and enslave their women.'

'Conquer Rome?'

'These are ancient beliefs, Mr Finlay. It was foretold that in the ancient town of Dabiq, the forces of Rome would finally be defeated. In modern-day parlance, this would be taken to mean the forces of the West. Al Anfal is a philosophy; some refer to it as "The Project" – a long- term plan to create a caliphate where Islam can exist in peace.'

'Peace is something we would all welcome, sir.'

'Quite so. Within that plan, there are, of course, many differing opin- ions. But what they do share is a vision – a vision of the future.'

'So, if peace is the goal, why is it that Sunni and Shia Muslims seem to be at each other's throats?'

'Ah, an easy question for me to answer as I am Shia, so I understand this very well. To some, Shia beliefs are regarded as new and innovative. And to innovate on the Koran is to deny its initial perfection.'

'Well, that's all very interesting,' I said politely, but I was beginning to tire of the philosophical lecture and wanted to get to what I hoped would be the real reason Shabat had summoned me. 'But it strikes me you wouldn't ask me to return and then bring us to a sound-proof booth so we could discuss Islamic history and politics.'

The Minister looked down at his feet, as if contemplating his next move. I waited three, four, five seconds, and was just reaching the point of thinking the conversation was over when he raised his gaze towards the corridor window.

'Please be patient, Mr Finlay. I wish you to understand these aspects of Islam so you will appreciate the context of what I am about to tell you.'

So, he *was* building up to something. 'OK,' I replied.

'Very good. What I want you understand is that Al Anfal is not so much an organisation as a philosophy.'

'You mentioned a project.'

'Yes, some call it that. Al Anfal is something I personally subscribe to and follow.'

'I'm sorry,' I interrupted. 'Are you saying you want to confess to being a member of a terrorist organisation?'

He remained patient. 'Not at all. Al Anfal does not support violence as a means to achieve objectives.'

'Which are what, exactly?'

'As I said, to further the spread of Islam throughout the world, something that people here in the West are not at all comfortable with.'

I was confused again, not quite gaining a handle on what he seemed to be telling me. 'Are you saying you're part of an organisation working inside the West to eventually take over?'

Shabat sighed, and although he remained composed, I had the feeling my feigned ignorance was trying his patience. 'No, that is not what I am saying, although given your limited understanding of Islam, I can understand how many in your position might draw that conclusion.'

'Perhaps it's not an unreasonable one in the circumstances?' I asked.

'No, and it is a conclusion that others within the Services in this country have come to. And it is how I come to find myself talking to you now.'

'Please go on, sir.'

'You may be aware I first came to this country from Iraq?'

'Yes, sir. I was told about that.'

'Were you told that I tried to warn your people that Saddam Hussein was planning attacks on the West in response to the Gulf War?'

'I wasn't, no.'

'No matter,' he replied. 'You know now. At that time, myself and others who follow Al Anfal believed this to be a serious error, so we decided to warn of Saddam's plans. It was then that I met an MI6 officer who helped me to resettle here in the UK and to start a new life. As the years passed, he arranged for me to improve my education and he smoothed my path. At his suggestion, I entered into politics.'

'I've a feeling I know where this might be leading.'

'I doubt that, but we will see. What you might have guessed is, as I owe this officer a great deal and he knows a lot about me, once I had achieved some status he began to ask favours.'

'Do you mind if I ask what kind of favours?'

'I don't, no. He would ask me to provide him with background information on certain political activists, on who they associated with, whether they had any weaknesses or secrets that could be exploited, that kind of thing.'

'Normal Secret Services stuff, then?'

'Yes, I'm sure. Quite normal for them. In recent times I have not heard much from him, but a while ago he came to see me again. In fact, that is his blood you saw on the seat outside my office door. He bites his fingers raw, quite unpleasant.'

'I'm sure it is. Am I allowed to ask what this man wanted?' I didn't ask for a name, but I was already running through a very short list of MI6 operatives I had met over the years, wondering if it might be one of them. One name figured highly in my thoughts.

'The reason for his visit is the same reason I asked you to return, Mr Finlay. He came to demand I do something for him, something he said was essential to maintain my position and the sanctity of Al Anfal.'

'What was it?'

'He asked me to arrange the deaths of two people, Mr Finlay.'

'Deaths? He wanted you to have two people killed?'

'To ensure the continued security of my position, he said.'

'So what did you do?'

'I refused. I am not an animal and I will not be involved in bloodshed.'

'So you risked him turning on you?'

'That risk is why I now need your help.'

'You need me to persuade an MI6 officer to back off and leave you alone? How on earth would I achieve that? I don't have that kind of influence.'

'I would leave the how to you.'

'Well, I think I now understand why you wanted to talk in this booth, but what on earth makes you think I'm somebody who could help you?'

'Incentive, Mr Finlay. The two men this officer asked me to take care of? One of them is you.'

Chapter 23

Nina had left a message for me in reception explaining she'd had to head back to the office.

I headed out into the street, dipped into my jacket pocket for my phone and was about to ring Kevin when I noticed an old text message from him was already on the screen: *Have news from BM. Call me.*

Good timing, I thought. Unfortunately, my return call went straight through to voicemail. I hung up, and then tapped in a response text: *Tried mate. No answer.*

My next call was to the one person I thought could help, the only person available who might have some idea what I should do in response to what Omar Shabat had just told me – Toni Fellowes.

She answered immediately. I explained that I needed to talk about 'our friends on the coast'. It was code, something she had insisted on upon using if I needed her urgently.

'Where are you?' she demanded, brusquely. It appeared she wasn't too impressed at my request.

'Marsham Street.'

'What are you doing there, Finlay?'

'That's what I need to talk to you about.'

The line went quiet for a moment. 'St John's Gardens. There's a

bench opposite the Royal Veterinary College. Wait there and I'll see
you in about five minutes.'

✝

I walked as quickly as I could along Horseferry Road, passed a long
line of parked coaches and soon found what I assumed to be the
bench Toni was referring to. To my frustration, it was occupied by
an elderly woman holding a large, brown paper bag from which she
scattered handfuls of seed to an ever-increasing audience of pigeons.
Every time her arm swung from the bag, the flock took to the air, startled but still focussed on the growing supply of food building up on
the path.

Anxious not to move too far away lest Toni miss me, I turned back
the way I had come and walked along the wide pavement adjacent
to some black metal railings that marked the edge of a small park. I
found a spot about thirty or so yards from the elderly pigeon feeder and
leaned against a stone pillar. It supported an arched metal gate providing access to a heavily shaded oasis that looked to be popular with local
office workers. I spotted several more benches inside, also occupied,
and quite a number of people strolling around, most of whom seemed
to be deeply engrossed in telephone calls.

I stood for a while, gazing into the park, lost in a world of my own.
I wasn't certain whether to feel angry or anxious, fearful or dismissive.

Although I owed it to Kevin to tell him, I first needed to talk with
Toni before the feelings of anxiety I was experiencing began to affect
me. To my mind, there was only one possible connection – one man
who I knew might want to bug Kevin and who would be minded to
force someone he had a hold over to do a dirty job for him – Howard
Green.

'Walk with me, Finlay.' A female voice disturbed my thoughts. I
turned to see Toni had joined me.

As she walked purposefully through the entrance to the gardens and
along the nearest path, I followed just behind her. She kept going until

we reached a fountain that sprinkled gently into a small raised pond. There, she stopped.

I stood to her left, about an arm's length between us. As she said something, she faced toward the water jets. I couldn't make her words out. Shuffling a little closer I raised my voice slightly to ask what she'd just said.

'Nothing important. I just wanted to make sure you couldn't hear me.'

'That I *couldn't* hear you?' I asked, quizzically.

'Talk towards the water, Finlay. It drowns out and absorbs sound very effectively – we want to avoid all possibility that our conversation is overheard.'

'You think we may have been followed?'

'No, I don't think that at all. But you are definitely what we might call a "person of interest", so it's within the realms of possibility you could be watched, if not all the time, then as and when.'

'I see. Err … do you come here often?'

'Not really, at least not for work. I used to grab a sandwich and a Starbucks to spend some time here on one of the benches. But it's becoming too popular now they've finished building the fountain.'

'It's new?'

'Completed this year. Would you believe this was once a cemetery … where we are standing?'

'It has that quiet feel about it.' I kept polite, played the conversation game, but I was becoming impatient. I had things I needed to discuss, questions I needed answered.

'That's the trees,' Toni continued. 'Another good reason for meeting here. Apparently the local teaching hospitals used to pay people to rob the graves for research and so the surgeons could practise their dissection skills. Anyway … that's not why we're here, is it? You look edgy. There's been a development, I presume?'

'Yes, there has.' I replied, relieved the small talk was at an end. I explained about the request to accompany Nina to see the Housing Minister, Omar Shabat, and of the revelation – to me – that he had been an MI6 agent. I then concluded by summarising the conversation that had taken place when Shabat had called me back in to the building.

Toni listened intently and didn't speak until after I'd mentioned my intention to warn Kevin about what might be a renewed threat. 'Well, I can tell you who the MI6 officer is,' she said.

'You can? You knew about all this?'

'No. But there's only one man I know who has been in this up to his neck from the day it all started in Afghanistan … and he also chews the ends of his fingers until they bleed.'

'Who's that?' I asked, already guessing at the name.

'Someone I asked you about nearly a year ago, when this all came out. Howard Green.'

I was right. 'So, what is it with him?' I demanded. 'Why ask an agent to take out Kevin and me rather than the same people he used for the others?'

'Plausible deniability. You and Kevin were never part of the clean-up operation but you came up on his radar. Before the Director shut him down he had every intention of taking you out of the game. He may have had a reason for wanting to use an agent rather than one of his team. We sometimes do things like that if we want to make sure things don't come back to bite us in the arse.'

'But Shabat said no.'

'Which may well have bought you some time, during which the Director learned of Howard's intentions and ordered him to back off.'

'Why do you think the Minister would wait until now to speak to me,' I asked.

'My guess is he's allowed it to fester and this chance meeting with you created an opportunity to finally get Green off his back.'

'And he thinks I could do that?'

'He comes from a country and a culture where such things happen. He thinks that by making it look like your life is under threat you will be prepared to help him. He doesn't realise it's old news and no longer a problem.'

'You're sure? I mean really sure? Don't guess or assess here, Toni. This is my life we're talking about.'

'Trust me, I'm in that loop now and I can tell you unequivocally that Howard has been ordered to stay away from you and Kevin.'

'You don't think that bug Kevin found in his home was from MI6 then?'

She shrugged. 'Not impossible. He's the kind to keep a watching brief on you, just in case things change, but the latest I heard was that Nell had it as being a Met device.'

In case things change, I pondered. Like Brian McNeil emerging from the woodwork with a copy of the very document Green had been at pains to keep secret, or like Kevin being stupid enough to Google the name of that document. I wondered whether to tell her what I'd learned from Kevin but decided to hold back. It was still within the realms of possibility that I could persuade both my friend and Brian McNeil to abandon their idea, then recover the new copy of the Al Anfal document and to have it destroyed before the shit hit the fan.

'Is it possible Howard Green could use a bug given to the Met?' I asked.

'Not in normal circumstances. And why would he? MI6 have plenty of their own.'

I decided to try something. 'OK,' I said. 'Is it alright to mention all this to Kevin?'

'Kevin?' Toni hesitated as she appeared to weigh up the pros and cons of my suggestion. 'Err … best not. Let me think. How are Jenny and the girls?' she asked, as she turned away from the fountain and headed back towards the street.

'Pretty good,' I said, confused as to why Toni was changing the subject so abruptly. 'Becky loves having a sister and they're all doing fine. So, what do I do about the Minister?'

'Let me give that some thought,' she said, letting out a small sigh. 'He clearly has no intention of doing what was asked of him but it would be useful to know exactly when he was asked. My first thought is that you should go and see him, tell him you know it's Howard. That should be enough to satisfy him. It might be better coming from me, but if Shabat told Howard I'd done that, it could prove awkward. Like I said, let me think about it.'

'OK, I will. But soon, please. I want this over with.' A beep from my jacket pocket told me a text message had arrived. I apologised to Toni as I checked it. It was from Grahamslaw, asking me to contact him ASAP.

'Grahamslaw wants me,' I said.

'Have you spoken to him today?'

'I haven't, no. But, getting back to what we were saying, I'd appreciate some help on this. Truth is, Toni, I think my judgement is shot to pieces. Sometimes I just can't think straight.'

'I thought your stay with the Combat Stress charity addressed those issues?'

I shrugged. 'I'm not denying I was better after that – I was. But PTSD isn't something that goes away easily, Toni. You have to learn to live with it, to manage it so that it doesn't get the better of you. I thought I had it all under control. But Kevin finding the bug … and now this thing with Shabat – it's like it's starting all over again.'

'At the risk of repeating myself, it isn't. So, Grahamslaw hasn't called you, then?' There was an emphasis in her tone, an urgency that revealed a feeling of concern.

I felt my stomach lurch. 'Something up?' I asked.

She didn't reply until we reached the gate onto the street, where she stopped walking. 'You'd best make him your first port of call when you get back to the Yard.' She looked straight ahead as she spoke.

'What's happened?' I demanded, now feeling confused at her evasiveness. 'I don't understand. Has something happened?'

'I'm sorry.'

'Sorry? Why? What's going on? You don't seem to be getting this. I've had people trying to kill me and my family for reasons I don't really understand, and now I seem to be heading back into the position of being a patsy, a pawn, and all you can say is you're sorry. I mean, if Howard Green is listening-in on Kevin, that means he's looking for a reason to target us, surely?'

Toni turned as if in a hurry to get away. 'I can't say much Finlay, but please do believe me when I say there is no credible evidence suggesting Howard has you in his sights again. What's happened has nothing to do with MI6, I'm sure.'

'So, what's this big thing you're keeping from me?'

'I'm sorry, Finlay, but I promised Grahamslaw to leave it to him. Just make sure you see him without delay.'

'But what ... what is it?' My voice was raised now, my anxiety clear.

I only just heard Toni's final words as she walked away, all the time avoiding eye contact. 'I'm sorry,' she said. 'It was wrong of me to have mentioned it. Just make sure you call Commander Grahamslaw.'

Chapter 24

'Mick.' Grahamslaw called loudly to his Superintendent through the open office door. He'd just caught a glimpse of his number two heading towards the main squad office.

A moment later, Parratt leaned his bulky form around the door post. 'You rang, m'lord?'

'Come in and shut the door, will you?'

Parratt did as ordered. 'Developments?' he enquired.

'You first. What's the latest from the hospital?'

'He's still unconscious. According to Mellor, he's swallowed ketamine. If the son hadn't found him, he may well have died.'

'And Complaints Branch are certain it's a domestic?'

'A bit early to say, but it looks that way. Does Finlay know yet?'

'That's why I called you in. He's on his way up right now.'

A loud knock on the door interrupted the conversation. Parratt turned towards the sound. 'Want me to stay?' he asked.

Grahamslaw lowered his voice. 'Best you do. This is gonna be a toughie. They go back a long way.'

Parratt opened the door, called the Inspector in and then closed it again behind him.

The Commander indicated they should both sit down. Finlay was sweating and looked flustered, as if he'd been rushing, or even running. 'Can I get you a brew, Inspector?' he asked, trying to create a sense of calm.

Finlay took a deep breath. 'Perhaps later, if you don't mind, sir. I was out at a meeting when I got your text.'

'OK … well, I've been mulling over how to break this to you for the last hour and I haven't come up with a good way. So, I'm just going to tell you straight. There's been an incident involving Kevin Jones.'

'What kind of incident?'

'A bad one. Yesterday afternoon a lad arrived home from school to find his mother dead and her boyfriend unconscious on the living-room floor having taken a drug overdose. The woman I believe you know. Her name is Sandra Beattie. The suspect is your mate, Kevin.'

Finlay sat stony-faced for several seconds, before turning his gaze towards the window. It wasn't the response Grahamslaw had expected.

Parratt came to the rescue. 'Kevin is alive, Inspector,' he said, his tone kind and warm, as reassuring as seemed appropriate. 'Mrs Beattie's son arrived home from school early and found them. He called an ambulance and they managed to get Kevin to hospital in time.'

'Can I see him?' Finlay said, his voice quavering as he continued staring out the window.

'He's in custody, under arrest. I doubt if he'll be allowed visits just yet.'

'What happened?'

Parratt continued. 'It's all a wee bit sketchy at the moment due to Complaints Branch having taken over supervision of the enquiry.'

'Is that normal?'

'Yes. The immediate criminal investigation will be conducted by the local Major Investigation team, but CIB will have a big say in decisions.'

'So, what do we know?'

'It seems to have been some kind of sex-game gone wrong. Jones was unconscious near the front door. Mrs Beattie was found upstairs in the main bedroom and from the fact that she was tied to the bed wearing just her underwear, it looks like Kevin might have … killed her…'

'He wouldn't do that … not Kev.'

'All aspects have to be looked at, as I'm sure you know, Finlay. And all possibilities explored. It's quite possible it was an accident, but, even then, Kevin could be facing a manslaughter charge.'

Finlay stood up, the legs of his chair rubbing noisily on the carpet. 'I need to make some calls,' he said, quietly.

'I'm sorry you had to wait to hear this,' said Grahamslaw. 'But, I thought it best you got the news from me. I'll get Mr Parratt here to find out as much as we can and we'll be in touch.'

'I just came back from seeing Toni Fellowes. I thought her reaction was odd when I said I was going to ring Kevin. Now I know why.'

As the door closed behind the departing Inspector, both men exhaled, but neither spoke.

No words seemed suitable.

Chapter 25

'How did he take the news?' Toni said from the kitchen.

As she watched, Bill leaned forwards from the settee to rest his mug on the coffee table. Toni was in the tiny kitchen of the flat preparing omelettes as he flicked through the *Evening Standard*. He appeared to guess immediately what she was referring to. Putting the newspaper to one side, he stood up and came to join her.

As he entered the hallway, she pointed towards the drawers next to the sink. 'Want to put the eating irons out? Even police commanders have to help you know.'

Bill returned her smile. 'He didn't look too good, to be honest. On the surface he seemed composed but he was tense and I got the feeling that, behind those blue eyes, his brain was working ten to the dozen.'

'Not every day you find out one of your best mates has been arrested for murder.'

'True. That listening device Jones found is bothering me. It may be a coincidence, of course, but …' Bill walked back into the living room and began laying the dining table.

'Nell's been doing some digging but nothing's come up so far. Like you say, it may simply be a coincidence.'

'Keep me posted will you? Having a PC find a listening device in his home is something I really should be investigating, especially given what's happened. I'm happy to leave it to you for now but the moment you find out who's behind it, I want to know.'

'I will, I promise. Do you think Finlay will keep away from the enquiry?'

'Finlay? Not a bloody chance. Here … put this somewhere safe.' He handed her a small card bearing a mobile telephone number.

'What's this for?' she said. 'A secret number to contact you on? Don't tell me Mick Parratt suspects?' She grinned mischievously, as she followed him with their food.

'Mick Parratt probably knows,' he replied, sniffing gently at her neck as she eased past him. 'I'd trust that man with my life, though.'

'Careful, you'll knock the plates over and, even if I say so myself, these are damn good omelettes. So what's the number for?'

Bill sat beside her. 'Smells good,' he said, as he ran his eyes over her cooking efforts. 'It's a phone I plan to give Finlay as soon as I get a chance. The Complaints Superintendent is someone who's had it in for him and Jones since the Home Secretary gave them immunity from prosecution. I wouldn't be too surprised if he comes looking to stick him with a disciplinary charge if he so much as sniffs the same air as the Murder Squad are breathing. I'll tell Finlay to transfer all his numbers onto that phone and to keep it somewhere nobody will find it. If the shit hits the fan and CIB seize his work phone, you'll have a way of keeping in touch with him.'

'You think it's that serious for Finlay as well, then?'

'I do, yes. There's this particular Superintendent in CIB who seems to be on a mission to get something he can pin on both him and Jones.'

'This Superintendent have a name?' said Toni.

'Jim Mellor. He's the one I expect will want Finlay's phone.'

'Well, in that case I can probably go one better for him. I'll get him a burner.'

'You sure?' Bill asked, tucking in with enthusiasm.

'I am. It'll have the advantage that we can use it to keep tabs on him as well. Are we staying tonight? I brought a change of clothes in case.'

'I'd like that, if you can? Going home to an empty house isn't much fun, as you know.'

'You've heard nothing more from your wife since the divorce request then?'

He shook his head.

It was only as they finished eating that Toni noticed how the conversation had dried up, and only then because Bill asked her if something was wrong.

'How do you mean?' she asked.

'You're very quiet, like you've got something on your mind. Not having any regrets about us are you?'

Toni smiled and reached a hand out to his. 'No, it's nothing like that. I'm having trouble putting some threads together.'

'Because of what's happened to Kevin Jones?'

'Yes … Can I be straight with you?'

Bill nodded as he piled the plates together and started to clear the table. 'Of course,' he replied. 'That was delicious, by the way.'

Toni nodded her thanks. 'I've never had anyone I could really talk to about work. Sometimes I think it's important to have a sounding board, someone to brainstorm with. You know what I mean?'

'A bit difficult to discuss national security matters with a parent or sibling, you mean?'

'Yes, exactly. I just have a feeling I'm missing a trick. I could do with an objective view.'

'Where do you want to start?'

'It's all to do with Finlay, of course, and what's been happening.'

'OK, fire away.' Bill put down the plates. 'Shall I open some wine?'

'It might help. The main issue as I see it is someone being behind the listening device in Kevin's home and the fact that he really should have been dead if that drug overdose had worked.'

'You don't buy the manslaughter-suicide idea then?'

'Call it a gut feeling, but I don't.'

'I call it instinct,' Bill said, wryly. 'A copper's nose to smell when something's not right. So, what are you thinking?'

'That someone is behind it?'

'Do you have a suspect?' Bill said as he opened a bottle and placed it carefully on the table. 'You pour.'

Toni did as he asked. It was a Malbec, one of her favourites. Bill's ability to remember such details was something she found comforting. 'Howard Green, of course,' she replied. 'His fingers seem to be all over it. I just can't see him being so determined to take out Kevin Jones that he would risk going against the direct orders of an MI5 Director.'

'You're suggesting he may have set Kevin up? Seems a bit far-fetched. Why would he do that?'

'Kevin called Nell a couple of weeks back asking if we knew of an Arab translator. I wondered if he's laid his hands on another copy of that document Howard Green was working so hard to keep secret?'

'Think about what happened to the other people involved in that. I thought you told me Finlay and Jones were safe because, so far as Howard was concerned, they knew nothing about it?'

'That's right.'

Bill sipped thoughtfully at his wine. 'So, if Kevin became a security risk, Howard could simply secure authority to have him killed – terminated like all the others … whatever the term is people like that use.'

'That's true, yes, and it's a clean-up.'

'So, when did Howard first appear as part of this investigation?'

'Last year. When he pulled me in after I sent Finlay to Egypt on holiday to try and locate that author, Chas Collins – the one who'd exposed the CIA operation in Afghanistan. Not my finest hour, I know. Anyway, Finlay met some people, and that resulted in Howard getting in touch to warn me not to get involved with the hunt for Collins.'

'So, what did Howard actually say?' Bill asked.

'He told me to leave it to him. I concluded at the time that he wanted the kudos for himself.'

'We're talking about the same author whose agent is now missing and who the newspapers are suggesting has been abducted or maybe killed?'

Toni nodded. 'The very same, yes.'

'How did Howard find out Finlay was in Egypt?'

'From the Cristea family ... it was only later I found out that they aren't just a publishing company.'

'So, one of them got a message to Howard. Seems an unusual connection, a Romania-based family who are involved in sex-trafficking and a London-based MI6 officer?'

'The Cristeas used to run drugs and weapons into and out of Afghanistan before they switched to trafficking people.'

'And I remember you telling me that Afghanistan is where Finlay and Jones knew Howard Green from. Green supposedly made an enemy of Jones during some kind of incident where Jones was nearly killed I recall...'

'That's right,' said Toni. 'That was why I agreed with Finlay not to tell Jones who had been behind the deaths of their friends.'

Bill stood up, and headed to the window. He seemed deep in thought. 'What are you thinking?' she asked.

'Have you looked into the connection between the Cristeas and Howard Green?'

'We have, yes. Nell found out last year that Gheorghe Cristea has a PF, a personal file that Howard created. He's been keeping tabs on the family for years.'

'Have you looked deeper than that? Maybe explored the possibility that the connection to the Cristeas may go deeper than simple monitoring?'

'In what way?' Toni sat up, intrigued at how Bill's investigative mind was working.

'The Cristeas appear to operate with some impunity,' he replied. 'Is it possible they have an arrangement with Howard?'

'A deal, you mean? But how would that have any relevance to what's happening here and now with Kevin Jones?'

'Motive, Toni, motive. What if he had another reason, more pressing to him than the national security question over Al Anfal? What if he has own personal reasons for wanting Jones – and maybe Finlay – out of the picture?'

'Which is why he went to Shabat? He wants Finlay and Jones taken care of in a way that doesn't lead back to him?' Toni sat up, it was as if a light had been turned on.

'And Shabat said no. And then Jones supposedly kills his girlfriend and then tries to kill himself.'

'And our Director has no cause to believe Howard has gone against his orders?'

'Exactly. You'd better start digging to see if it's more than just a theory.'

Later that evening, Bill returned to the kitchen to wash the dishes as she watched the late news. It was part of their routine, a tacit agreement that met both their expectations. In fact, it wasn't too dissimilar to their relationship, which also seemed to fulfil mutual needs. The affair – if she dared call it that – had started slowly at first and, given their age difference, with some reluctance on both their parts. But the more they had found the time to meet outside work, the more they accepted they each had something the other could offer. Within a few months, they started dating frequently and it didn't take too long before the difference in their ages became irrelevant.

They'd continued to discuss her concerns and, at one point he had drawn a mind map, a visual aid to help focus her thoughts. It produced exactly the same as their initial, less structured discussion. A series of facts, events, theories and ideas, and at the centre of them all sat one man, Howard Green.

As Bill was returning crockery to the kitchen cupboards, his mobile telephone began to ring.

Toni glanced across from her seat in front of the television as he returned to the sitting room and then nodded his way through a short conversation, all the while making notes on a small pad he habitually kept near the front door. As he ended the call, she saw the concerned expression on his face. She turned the TV off and swung around in her seat towards him.

'Work?' she asked.

'It was. Shit's hit the fan a bit quicker than I expected. That was Jim Mellor. He wants to interview Finlay tomorrow – in my office.'

'He's already been poking his nose in?'

'No, much worse. They want to ask him about a loaded Glock pistol their search team just found in the boot of Kevin Jones's car.'

Chapter 26

Howard was feeling angry as he waited for the call.

He was also very tired. It was late and he was desperate to get some sleep. Shuffling up and down the floor of his study, he glanced frequently at the telephone sat silently in the corner near the window. The time had finally come for him to get to grips with this clusterfuck of an operation.

As he walked, he chewed his fingers. Not just the nails, but the skin, the end of his fingers and, even the knuckles. It was an annoying habit that had started in his childhood and continued throughout the whole of his life. He had tried all kinds of remedies, from covering the ends of his fingers in plasters through to sucking a sweet every time the urge overwhelmed him. Nothing seemed to work, particularly as he often failed to notice the damage he was causing until it was too late.

Now, as he waited for Grady to call, he stared at the raw, bleeding tip of his left index finger. Pulling a handkerchief from his trouser pocket, he wrapped the cloth tightly around the now-tender flesh.

The phone rang. He waited. After four rings, it cut off.

Twenty seconds later, it rang again. With his free hand, Howard picked up the receiver. 'Grady?' he demanded, angrily.

'I rang as soon as I got your message. Is there a problem?'

'You could say that. Jones is alive.'

There was a pause. 'How come? We gave him enough ket to kill a horse,' Grady replied, his tone one of puzzlement, almost exasperation.

'One of the woman's kids came home early from school and found him. A paramedic saved his life.'

'He's a lucky bastard. If you recall, Cathy did say it was a chancy operation.'

'Don't fucking lecture me,' Howard snapped.

'Not my intention, boss, sorry. So, where is Jones now?'

'In custody. The police are convinced he killed the woman and then tried to end his own life.'

'Well, at least that part worked.'

'But he knows the truth,' said Howard.

'He has no idea what happened. Cathy took him out with a taser before he even saw us.'

'It's still a loose end. He knows someone else killed his girlfriend.'

'No one will believe him,' Grady said, confidently.

'Finlay will.'

'I thought you had a plan to deal with him?'

'Had a plan, Grady, had a plan,' said Howard. 'We now need a rethink.'

'I could take Jones out.'

'I know, but it's not that simple. I have an idea, but it will need the three of you to mobilise with just an hour's notice.'

'We can do that.'

'OK. And Grady…'

'What?'

'This is the last time I'll say this: No more mistakes.'

Howard placed the telephone receiver on its cradle and turned towards the hallway door.

The house was quiet. Upstairs, his wife would be reading in bed.

He headed up the stairs quietly, switching off the light as he reached the landing.

His heart was racing, and he understood why. A great many years had passed since he'd been out in the field, and he'd missed it. Now, if this unholy mess was going to get sorted, he was going to have to become a lot more 'hands on'.

The prospect was something he found very exciting.

Chapter 27

Grahamslaw waited as Mellor began the formal introductions before starting the interview.

The room they sat in was small and windowless. There were four seats, two each side of a narrow wooden desk. At one end of the desk sat a twin tape deck. The room was left over from the days when the Complaints Unit used to occupy offices in the main building at New Scotland Yard, so it currently saw little use. Nowadays, CIB had their own offices, well away from the people they were tasked with investigating. Security had been the acceptable and public argument for the move, but many within the service accepted that the infamy and reputation of the branch suggested it was a sensible move to place them well away from the mainstream.

'My name is Superintendent James Mellor; with me is Detective Sergeant Ian Bishop. Also present is...'

'William Grahamslaw. Commander, Specialist Operations Directorate.'

The Complaints Superintendent then introduced Robert Finlay, who was sat alongside his Commander, much in the way a solicitor might sit with his client. Finlay spoke his name in response to Mellor's prompt.

Mellor then outlined the purpose of the interview – that he was investigating the involvement of Police Constable Kevin Jones in criminal activities, including murder and the possession of firearms. He continued with the formal caution that they were all familiar with, to let Finlay know he wasn't under arrest, he wasn't obliged to remain in the interview and answer questions, and that he was entitled, at any time, to break off and obtain legal advice.

Finlay answered 'yes' when asked if he understood his rights. The Commander had done his level best to prepare his Inspector for what was to come but, he'd made it clear that, once the questioning started, Finlay was on his own.

Mellor opened a file. 'OK, let's make a start, Inspector. First things first: how long have you known PC Kevin Jones?'

Finlay sat upright in his chair, his back straight, his gaze steady. He'd kept his jacket on and looked smart, if perhaps a little uncomfortable. Grahamslaw knew that his work phone was in his pocket, turned off. The Commander had suggested Finlay put it there because he figured Mellor would want to seize it. Also on the desk in front of them sat Finlay's work diary. It was a log that every detective was expected to keep, and showed the hours and days he'd been working as well as what he'd been doing and when.

'I've known him for a little over twenty years, sir,' came the reply.

'And how did you first meet?'

Finlay glanced across at the Commander before answering. 'He was a member of 22 SAS Directing Staff overseeing selection for the Regiment. I first met him when I was doing that selection.'

Grahamslaw remained impassive as he listened. He'd recommended Finlay was open about the Special Air Service and his army experience. They'd agreed that, to avoid appearing to be evasive, he would answer as honestly as he could.

'So, you were soldiers together?'

'Not exactly together. I was applying to become an officer in the

Regiment. Jones was a Corporal at the time and was on a different squadron to me. Our paths didn't cross for some time after that first meeting.'

'Until when, if you can tell us?'

'Until he joined my squadron on promotion to Sergeant. That would have been in … early 1980.'

'You have a good memory for dates, Inspector.'

'Not especially, sir. I remember because I was injured in a firefight in the January of that year, which resulted in my doing a course with the Met while I recovered. It was that experience that started my interest in becoming a police officer.'

'And, of course, as well we all know, a large number of your fellow soldiers were involved in the Iranian Embassy siege in the April of that year.'

'Correct.'

'Were you and Jones both on that siege, Inspector?'

'I'm sorry, sir. As I believe Mr Grahamslaw can confirm, I cannot disclose the identity of any soldier who took part in that operation.'

Mellor turned to the Commander who simply nodded in response.

The Superintendent took a deep breath and exhaled slowly. 'Very well, I understand – although, given the number of men who have written about Operation Nimrod, I don't think it would have caused any particular conflict. Right, let's move on … and try to relax a little, Inspector.'

Mellor probed about the length and strength of the friendship that had developed between an officer and one of his sergeants. He suggested, and Finlay agreed, that it was unusual but not unheard of.

'You were in touch quite a lot in late August and early September 2001, would that be fair to say?'

'We were. We'd not seen each other for a while and had drifted apart to some extent. As you're probably aware, we were both the subject of an attempt by people from our past to have us killed.'

'The IRA?'

'Correct.'

'And you've heard the reports of two soldier-types abseiling onto a block of flats called Alma House in Hackney and giving our SO19 boys a bit of a licking?'

Finlay didn't answer. The pause was deliberate.

Grahamslaw recognised the signal to cut in. 'The Inspector has been instructed by Director MI5 not to speak about events of that period, I'm afraid. Shall we move on?'

Mellor scowled. 'So, you wouldn't be able to tell me if PC Jones was one of the men on the roof of Alma House?'

Again, Finlay remained silent and poker-faced.

'And what about the reports of a helicopter being heard in the fields near the house you lived in at the time? A large helicopter of the kind used at the Hackney flats? I suppose you can't answer anything about that, either?' Mellor raised his voice as he leaned forwards in his chair.

Grahamslaw recognised the tactic. It was a ploy designed to unsettle. The Superintendent was too experienced to allow his temper to show, he was hoping to gradually unnerve Finlay, by revealing some things he knew and others that he might hint at knowing.

It didn't work.

'I understand enquiries made at the time with the RAF confirmed that to be one of their flights at low level, sir,' Finlay replied.

Grahamslaw stifled a smile. 'That's correct,' he added.

'Yes ... all rather convenient,' Mellor scoffed. He stared hard at Finlay, who shifted his gaze towards the Sergeant making notes on a small pad.

'Do you mind if I ask a question?' Finlay asked.

'This is my interview, Inspector. If you have any comments or questions we can deal with them at the end. Is that clear?'

Finlay didn't reply.

Mellor cleared his throat before continuing. 'What have you been doing workwise since the attacks on you in late 2001, Mr Finlay?'

'I'm sure you're aware, Mr Mellor. After a period of leave, I returned to work here at the Yard, working on the anti-trafficking team.'

'And have you had much contact with PC Jones in the last year?'

'A fair bit, yes. My wife and I used to visit him in hospital and when he was discharged, and we've met socially on quite a number of occasions.'

'You'd describe him as a close friend, then?'

'Certainly, which is why I find it almost impossible to believe the allegations I've heard concerning him.'

'Which are?'

'That he's in hospital having taken an overdose and that Sandi, his girlfriend, died at his hands.'

'What did you know about their sex life? Did he discuss it with you, for example?'

'Is that relevant?'

'Just answer the question, please.'

Finlay shrugged. 'He didn't discuss it with me.'

'So, if he said he *had* discussed it with you, he'd be lying?'

Nice move, thought Grahamslaw. Create doubt. But Finlay wasn't that wet behind the ears.

'I'd say he might remember something I've forgotten,' he said.

Good reply. The Commander fought hard not to revel in the frustration he knew Mellor would be feeling.

'Indeed,' said the Superintendent. 'When did you last see him?'

'Last week. We had a drink with him and Sandi at my local pub.'

'Mrs Beattie was with him?'

'Yes.'

'How did they seem together?'

'They seemed to be getting along fine. I had the impression they were very fond of each other.'

'Did either of them mention to you that they liked to use recreational drugs?'

'Kevin doesn't take drugs.'

'And what about Mrs Beattie?' Mellor demanded.

'I saw nothing to suggest it, no.'

Grahamslaw noticed a slight edge to Finlay's response, a hint of anger, or possibly frustration. Beneath the calm exterior, something was definitely bothering him.

Mellor continued. 'You've no idea why PC Jones might decide to kill Mrs Beattie?'

'Like I said a moment ago, sir. I find it hard to believe he did.'

'Yes … as you say.' Mellor glanced towards his Sergeant, who reached into a briefcase on the floor and then placed an A4-sized brown envelope on the desk between the Superintendent and Finlay.

Grahamslaw glanced at it. Although open at one end, the contents were concealed. He had a feeling he knew what was coming. The revelation that a gun had been found in the boot of Jones's car was something he had kept from Finlay. It wasn't that he wanted to give the Complaints Branch an edge, more a sense of wanting to know the truth. Finlay was a good cop, of that there was no doubt, but all police officers knew they must act within the law, so if the Inspector knew something, now was the time to find out.

Mellor fingered the envelope, as if teasing his interviewee with the fact he knew its contents and his opponent didn't. 'Tell me what you understand by the term "trophy weapon", Mr Finlay?'

'A memento of battle, sir. Like an *assegai* brought home from the Zulu wars, or a German bayonet kept by a Tommy as a keepsake memory from World War Two.'

'And what about the rights and wrongs of doing so? We all know that lots of soldiers do it; even journalists have been known to bring back trophies. What do *you* think?'

'You want my opinion, sir?'

'Indulge me a moment, yes. I'm sure that members of the SAS have quite a collection.'

'There's a process to deal with trophies and, to the best of my knowledge, it is stuck to. Museums throughout the country would be somewhat bare if it wasn't for such things, don't you think?'

'That's as maybe, Inspector. With regard to PC Jones, are you aware of his having kept any weapon or equipment after leaving the armed services?'

'I am not, sir.'

Grahamslaw again watched Finlay closely for any sign of discomfort. That there were none didn't come as too much of a surprise. Although it was many years since the Inspector had undergone training in how to resist interrogation, he had only recently attended CID training courses where his memory and skills would have been refreshed, albeit from the approach of the interrogator rather than the suspect. He was lying, of course – of that the Commander was certain, but it didn't show.

'What about you?' Mellor continued. 'Did you decide to keep anything as a memory keepsake of your time in the army?'

'Just a few bits and bobs. Badges, hats, that kind of thing.'

'Nothing illegal, then?'

'No, nothing illegal.'

'No … of course not,' Mellor replied, his expression tight-lipped.

Grahamslaw recognised the cynicism and when the Superintendent raised his eyebrows and turned towards him in what appeared to be an attempt to secure a degree of empathy, he was careful not to react.

'So, you would have no idea where PC Jones might have obtained a Glock 9mm pistol, I assume?' Mellor continued.

'Not as a trophy weapon, certainly.'

'What makes you say that?'

'When Kevin and I left the services, we were using the Browning. The Glock only became popular many years later.'

'My information is that the Glock was in use as early as 1982. So, it's quite possible PC Jones could have obtained one before leaving the army.'

Finlay raised an eyebrow. 'Are we discussing a theory, or a specific weapon? If it's a theory, I'd have to accept you could be right. If it's a specific weapon you're referring to then the first thing I would do is check when it was manufactured.'

Mellor paused, and the Commander wondered if Finlay's response had given him a new line of enquiry to follow up on. After a moment, Mellor turned to his Sergeant, who slid the envelope across the table towards him. Slowly, and deliberately he removed a series of medium-sized photographs, which he placed face down on the desk. 'What car does PC Jones drive, Inspector?'

'A blue Peugeot.'

'Would you recognise it? Do you recall the registration number, for example?'

Finlay shifted in his seat and gazed to where the fingers of Mellor's right hand were teasing at the edge of the uppermost photograph. As the Superintendent turned it over, Grahamslaw noticed a slight flicker in the Inspector's eyes.

Mellor simply smiled.

Chapter 28

'Can I thank you for your cooperation, sir?' Mellor handed Finlay's mobile telephone to his Sergeant, who placed it carefully into an open evidence bag. With the interview concluded, the Superintendent had requested they return to the Commander's office to discuss developments.

'How long will you need it for?' asked Grahamslaw as he sat down behind his desk. 'We don't exactly have a large number of spares these days.'

'If it's clean, just a few days. If it reveals anything we need to speak to Mr Finlay about, then I couldn't say.'

'Very well. I thought you might have been a little more helpful when he asked about that PC from Kentish Town, the one who held the WPC at knifepoint.'

'None of his business, with respect, sir. That officer will face charges and get everything due to him. People like that have no place in this job and shouldn't be any concern to us.'

Grahamslaw bit his tongue as, for just a second, he felt a rush of temper. 'Finlay made him some promises,' he said, firmly.

'As part of the negotiation to secure the release of a hostage and sur-render of a weapon. He did that job fairly well until his insubordinate response at the point where I had ordered an immediate arrest.'

'Which he pointed out was unnecessary,' Grahamslaw replied, tersely.

'In his opinion. Finlay might do well to remember we have a rank structure in the police service.'

'Yes … as should we all, Superintendent. Your report did reach me by the way.'

'And you canned it, I heard.'

'I discussed it with your Commander. We were both of the opinion that your publicly expressed opinion on the decision last year not to prosecute Finlay may have influenced the impartiality of your conclusions.'

Mellor huffed just as a tap on the door indicated that Mick Parratt had returned. He walked straight in. 'Here's the charger,' he said, placing the device on the desk in front of Mellor. 'I've told him to take the rest of the day off.'

Mellor handed it to his sergeant.

'Can you give us a minute, Mick?' said Grahamslaw.

Parratt didn't reply. He nodded and, ignoring the two complaints unit detectives, left the room, closing the door behind him.

'Thank you,' said Mellor. 'But my opinion on that decision is most unlikely to change.'

'I'm aware of that, Jim. I didn't ask Mick to step out for your benefit. I want to know what else you have on Kevin Jones.'

'Only what was mentioned in interview, so far. He's regained con-sciousness but we have yet to talk to him formally. The gun we found in the boot of his car has gone off to the lab for analysis. All I can say for certain at this time is that it looks like a case of either murder-suicide or manslaughter-suicide. Jones killed his girlfriend and then decided to end it all.'

'Cause of death?'

'Looks to be a ligature around the neck. Either they were indulging in a bit of autoerotic asphyxiation to heighten the sexual experience and he killed her accidentally, or he did it deliberately for reasons we have yet to establish.'

'She was suffocated?'

'Post-mortem will confirm that, I expect.'

'Tidy that he had a supply of horse tranquilisers at hand, don't you think?' Grahamslaw commented.

'Don't think we hadn't considered that, sir. We'll ask him what he was doing with those when we question him, but we're aware that ketamine can be used as a recreational drug as well as being a powerful sedative.'

'I'd also be asking myself why he didn't shoot himself when he had that gun available.'

'Again, that's something we plan to put to him. Now, with your leave, we'll be heading back to Barkingside.'

'Is that where they've based the murder squad?'

'It is.'

Grahamslaw shook hands with the two detectives before they left and, with his office vacated, telephoned Parratt.

In less than a minute, his Superintendent was at the door with Robert Finlay.

'Come in, both of you … and shut the bloody door.'

As the Inspector sat in front of him, he loosened his collar.

'You OK, Finlay?' Grahamslaw asked.

'Never better,' he said, although the irony in his voice was crystal clear.

'They want you suspended from duty.'

'On what grounds, guv?' Parratt interjected.

'Material witness to a murder? Maybe as a suspect? I've known people suspended for a lot less. I told them to fuck off and come back when they had something more than guesswork and theory.'

'Thanks,' Finlay responded weakly.

'You're not out of the woods yet,' Grahamslaw answered as he turned to him. 'Mellor clearly wants your scalp and he thinks he's close. He's trying to rattle your cage to see what drops out.'

'Did you find out any more about what's happened to Kevin?'

'He's back in the world of the living, if that's what you mean. But Mellor hasn't had clearance to interview him yet. That won't be long coming, mind. Later today, possibly.'

'No way he killed Sandi.'

'Maybe not deliberately, no. But from what I'm hearing, it sounds like a sex game gone wrong.'

'I still can't believe it.'

'Well, for now that doesn't matter. All that does matter is you keep your fuckin' nose out of the enquiry.'

'He's a mate, and if he needs help…'

'Then he'll get it from a solicitor, not you. And I'll tell you this: if your mate has been keeping trophy weapons then no solicitor on this earth is going to be able to help him. He'll be going away for a fuckin' long stretch. Any – and I repeat, *any* – cop caught doing that kind of thing would be for the high jump, understood?'

Finlay nodded, and Grahamslaw hoped the message got through to him.

'Right, now leave Mr Parratt and me to get on with what we're supposed to be doing.'

Finlay stood and was just opening the office door to the corridor as Grahamslaw spoke again. 'Don't forget what I said about Jim Mellor, he's like a dog with a bone. You've made an enemy you'd be wise to treat with respect.'

The Inspector paused for a moment before replying.

'I know that, guv. I know that.'

Chapter 29

I made my way back to the trafficking office where I signed 'off duty' in my diary. My hands trembled as I wrote. Fortunately, the office was empty as I certainly wasn't in the mood to answer the questions Matt and Nina would no doubt have been itching to ask.

In all my days as both a soldier and policeman, I don't think I'd ever felt quite so angry, or experienced such hatred for another human being. Jim Mellor had really managed to get under my skin. It wasn't the fact he was investigating a suspicious death that a friend of mine appeared responsible for; it was his complete indifference that stunned me. The interview had progressed as Grahamslaw had predicted, save for the surprise concerning the pistol found in Kevin's car.

Right at the end, Mellor had let rip into me for what he referred to as my 'insubordinate behaviour' and made it perfectly clear if I went anywhere near the investigation into Kevin, he would have me immediately suspended pending disciplinary action. My protests met with the stonewall indifference of an individual who was clearly used to getting his own way. And as he spoke, he also used verbal and facial expressions that I knew the tape couldn't pick up and which seemed designed to wind me up. It worked, I bit. And it was only thanks to Grahamslaw's interjection that the interview didn't descend into a full-on row.

They say that every man has his trigger point. For some, even simple arguments over a pint in the pub can see that red mist descend. For others, it takes a great deal more. But this was my friend we were talking about, and, as I waited for the lift, I knew my personal buttons had been pushed so much I'd had to work hard to maintain control. Mellor had made me angry. He was clearly the kind of cop who made up his mind about a crime and then looked for the evidence to support his view. But he was wrong – so wrong. Somehow I had to make him see that. But I also wondered if I'd been wrong myself when I'd lied about whether or not Kevin had told me about his sex life. He had, and I knew the direction it had taken. So it hadn't surprised me to learn what he had been heading off to after we'd parted. But Kevin wasn't an idiot, he wouldn't do anything to put Sandi at risk and he definitely didn't do drugs. That meant there had to be another explanation for what had happened.

My heart was still racing several minutes afterwards, and in the relative silence of the lift cubicle I could actually hear the sound of blood rushing near my inner ear. I flexed my fingers, paced my breathing and took deep gulps of air to try and maintain composure. Exiting the building provided some relief. As the cooler air entered my lungs and I headed towards the train, I felt my core temperature lowering and, slowly, normal breathing resumed. Beneath my jacket, I felt cold and damp, my back tacky where beads of sweat had stuck to my skin before evaporating.

I hardly noticed my tube journey, made the changes between trains without conscious thought, and by the time I arrived at Cockfosters to collect my car from the station car park, I had lost all track of time. I probably shouldn't have driven in my distracted, emotional state, but the Citroen started reliably as always and, before I knew it, I was pulling into the driveway of our home.

Jenny was waiting at the door. Grahamslaw had telephoned, warning her to expect me. 'You've been sweating,' she said, as we embraced.

I was starting to shiver. 'Not a good morning,' I muttered.

'And you look like shit.'

'Where are the girls?'

'Charlie is sleeping, Becky's at play school. I mean what I said. You look really tired. Why don't you have a sit down and I'll make tea?'

I wasn't about to argue.

I slipped off my jacket and slumped into the soft chair I liked to use when watching the television. Closing my eyes, I tried to relax. I knew Jenny was going to be asking a lot of questions in a few moments and I needed to prepare what I was going to say. The news about Kevin was going to be particularly hard to explain, especially the part about the gun.

Within moments, I was asleep.

Chapter 30

I woke to find a mug of cold tea on the table next to me.

Jenny was giving the girls their tea. As I appeared in the kitchen door she took one look at me and then sent me upstairs to take a bath.

An hour later, feeling a lot more human, I joined her in front of the television. She turned it off. 'I'll open a bottle of wine,' she said. 'And I think we should chat.'

I agreed, and waited on the sofa in the living room until Jenny appeared with two glasses.

'Do you want to start at the beginning?' she said, as she poured.

I wasn't sure where to start and, to begin with I didn't make a lot of sense. But, the more we talked, the more focussed the conversation became. Jenny listened as I talked, asked questions and joined in with ideas and suggestions when I seemed to be either stuck for the right words or lacking the means to describe how I felt. She took the news of Sandi's death quite badly and for several minutes I found that it was me comforting her.

'She was lovely, I can't believe she's gone,' she said, as she held me tight.

I couldn't either.

'We need you back, Robert,' Jenny then said, unexpectedly, as she pulled away from me. 'Looking after your girls.'

I was confused. 'I've not been anywhere.'

'Not in the physical sense, no. But you've been away in a different world, especially over the last couple of days. I've lost count of the number of times I've spoken to you and you haven't even heard me.'

'I'm sorry … I didn't realise,' I said.

'I know. That's why I don't make a fuss about it. But it's not easy, I'm telling you.'

'Kevin's in trouble, Jen. If what I'm saying is right, somebody has fitted him up.'

'Is that likely? I mean *really* likely?'

'How do you mean?'

'I mean, isn't the most obvious answer likely to be the right one? That they were having some fun and something went badly wrong.'

'I refuse to believe that Jen,' I said. 'But I guess you're right, I'll only know for sure when I get the chance to ask him myself.'

'And God only knows what he was doing with that gun in his car,' she said.

'He has some kit stashed, you know that as well as I do. But he lost the Browning he'd kept from the old days when that terrorist attacked him last year. And the Superintendent from CIB said it was a Glock they found. He's never had a Glock so far as I know.'

'And that's the point – only as far as you know.' Jenny leaned towards me, her hand resting on my knee. 'Look, it doesn't look good for him, I accept. But I'm sure he'll get the best of help from the Police Federation. All you should do is be there to support him.'

'We go back a long way.'

'There are some things that even you don't have the power to achieve, Robert. If he needs your help, he'll ask for it.'

'I'll have to go and see him.'

'When the time is right, I know. But he'll have the best legal support possible, I'm sure.'

Jenny's suggestion of opening a bottle of wine turned out to be a good one. I wasn't sure that alcohol fell within any recommendation likely to be offered by a doctor, but it worked for me. I relaxed, we talked more and by nine o'clock we were already talking about heading to bed.

I was washing up the wine glasses when Nina phoned. She was at home and wanted to offer sympathies regarding Kevin. Bill Grahamslaw had let my Superintendent know what had been going on and why I had been told to head home early. He, in turn, had told Nina and Matt Miller.

'Mellor will get his, one day,' she said.

'He has a job to do,' I replied in as noncommittal a tone as I could muster. I wanted there to be no clue, no inkling at all I was hoping to stop Mellor doing just that.

'He's a bully, nothing more, nothing less. And my experience of people like him is they all have something they need to keep hidden, some little skeleton in their past that will one day appear to bite them on the arse.'

I laughed quietly. 'Wouldn't we all like to be a fly on the wall when that happens?'

'Too bloody right. Do you want me to keep you updated on what happens to your friend?'

'Could you do that?'

'Easy. An old girlfriend of mine is on the enquiry. She won't be in on the interviews and such, but I'll be able to find out if they decide to charge him or possibly any significant developments.'

'Mellor seemed to be suggesting it's inevitable he'll be charged.'

'He doesn't have the final say – the CPS do. And if the Crown Prosecution decision is no, even Mellor can't overrule it.'

'What's your gut feeling?'

Nina hesitated. 'At the end of the day a woman is dead and justice has to be seen to be done. So, be prepared for the worst, Finlay. Even if the case is weak, prosecutions like this really have to go in front of a jury otherwise we get accused of looking after our own.'

'What if he's not fit to be interviewed … if the hospital keep him in?'

'All that would have happened then is the detention clock goes on hold until he's back in the cells. But that's irrelevant now … I thought you knew? He's already at Barkingside nick.'

'Really? That was quick.'

'Possibly. Anyway, my guess is they will have a prelim interview with him this evening and then give him an overnighter in the cells ready to get stuck in tomorrow morning.'

'And then?'

'Knowing Mellor, he'll work by the book. He might apply to a court to extend Kevin's detention period or they can charge him and then it would probably be a remand in custody. Whichever way it goes, he'll be appearing at court within a couple of days, I'd say.'

As we ended the call, Nina suggested I take the next day off and give myself the space to do some thinking.

I agreed with her, and as I saw Jenny nod her head in response, I figured she did too.

Chapter 31

I slept surprisingly well that night. Not that I felt particularly calm or rested, quite the opposite in fact, but some good hot food and several glasses of my favourite red and I was soon drifting off into the land of nod. I only opened my eyes as the curtains were pulled back and, a moment later, a familiar hand squeezed my shoulder.

'How are you feeling now?' Jenny asked, her voice still showing concern.

'OK … it's almost like yesterday was all a bit of a dream,' I mumbled in response.

'You snored all night, nearly,' she smiled as she handed me a large mug of tea.

Dazzled by the morning light, I focussed hard on the clock near the bed. It was already nine o'clock. 'Anything on the news about Kevin?' I asked.

'And you talked in your sleep as well,' Jenny replied, tapping my nose playfully. 'Just as well it was his name you were calling out and not some woman's.'

'What was I saying?' I sipped at the hot liquid, enjoying the sense of relief as it eased the dryness in my throat.

'Nothing I could make out apart from the name Kevin. What have you got planned for today?'

'I haven't really. But, after yesterday, I guess I'll just take it easy. So, what about the news? Anything being said?'

'Nothing at all. And, if you're going to be home, you can drive me to the shops. Make a nice change to have someone carry Charlie while I load up the trolley.'

I showered while Jenny drove Becky to the pre-school group she now went to every weekday morning. I could hear our second daughter stirring as I emerged from the bathroom and, as I opened her bedroom door to check on her, a recognisable smell hit my nostrils.

I suppose it's just a question of practice, but if you're like me and will do virtually anything to avoid changing a nappy, those occasions when it's impossible to duck the responsibility become all the more challenging. Ten minutes later, a very amused baby girl – who had no idea as to the meaning of the strange four-letter words her father had been uttering – giggled and smiled, now cosily wrapped up in a clean babygro. I sat back exhausted, wondering how on earth her mother managed to do the job so often and with such speed and dexterity. As I gazed into the deep-blue eyes of my second child, I forgot for a moment all the problems, issues and niggles that had been so dominating my thoughts.

'None of it matters to you does it, Charlie?' I said, as I watched her face light up in response to my gently tweaking her nose. And it didn't. Just as her elder sister had demonstrated at a similar age, all my little girl cared about was being warm, well fed and cared for. In many ways, I envied her.

Jenny was soon back and, after a quick slice of toast, we loaded up the car and headed into the local town. After finding a parking space, I stood still as Jenny attached the baby carrier to me, adjusted the buckles and then popped Charlie against my chest. As I took in that unique, delicious scent of new baby, our daughter promptly closed her eyes and fell asleep.

We had just collected one of the trolleys outside the supermarket and were heading in through the entrance when Jenny's phone rang. It was Toni Fellowes.

After a few moments, she passed the phone to me.

Toni got straight to the point. 'Will you be in the office tomorrow? We need to speak about Kevin's arrest.'

'Yes,' I said quietly, careful not to wake Charlie. 'I expect so. Is it something urgent? I've been given a strong warning to keep away from the enquiry team.'

'Nothing that can't wait until the morning. I'll be at the Yard at about nine, if that suits?'

'Sure, see you then.'

As I ended the call, Jenny was dropping a milk container into the trolley. 'More problems?' she asked.

'Story of my life at the moment. She wants to talk about Kevin.'

Chapter 32

At nine the following morning, I headed toward the same quiet table in the corner of the canteen where I'd met up with Nell Mahoney. I still hadn't decided whether to mention to Toni about Kevin's recent renewed interest in the Al Anfal document. Given what had happened, it now seemed less relevant.

Toni was one step ahead of me. As I walked in and passed the rows of similar tables, I could see she was already waiting and was on her telephone. First thing I noticed were the lines across her furrowed brow. There was no smile, no greeting as I sat down.

I noticed a small box she was cradling on her lap. 'Is that for me?' I asked, as the call ended.

Finally, she smiled. 'All in good time, Finlay. I've made some checks regarding Mr Shabat's claims. Like I suggested, it looks like ancient history. I'm as sure as I can be that Shabat's handler is Howard Green, so that would be consistent with the threat having been lifted. I think, if I were you, I really wouldn't be inclined to worry about it.'

Toni was doing her best to sound reassuring, I could sense that from her voice. But the question remained: exactly when had Shabat been approached?

'Do you still want me to find out from him when he was asked?' I said.

'If it helps put your mind at rest, yes,' she replied.

'Is that the only reason you wanted to see me?'

'No … I'm afraid that's just a part of the reason. There's been a very unusual development regarding Kevin Jones.'

'What, even more than getting arrested for killing his girlfriend during a sex game?'

'Sorry,' she continued. 'Sensitive subject, I know.'

'So, what is it?'

She paused, as if struggling to find the right words.

'Well, I hope it's good news.' I did my best to force a smile.

She took a deep breath. 'No … it isn't. Quite the opposite, in fact. It's about the gun that was found in the boot of Kevin's car.'

'Don't tell me. His prints were on it?'

'No, actually they weren't. And it's still the subject of DNA testing so no tie-up from that. No, what I'm referring to is the ballistics results from the lab.'

'So far as I know, Kevin never had access to a Glock. I told Mellor that.'

'Mellor from CIB?' Toni asked.

'That's him.'

'Commander Grahamslaw told me about him. And from what I'm told, he dismissed the point. To be honest, I can't really blame him. As we both know, Kevin would probably have been killed last year if it hadn't been for an illicitly held weapon, so let's not pretend he couldn't have had access to another pistol.'

She was right, and it was a fair point. The IRA man who'd tried to murder Kevin had only been overcome thanks to the Browning Kevin had kept hidden.

'What I'm talking about is far worse than that,' she continued. 'Do you recall the case of Maggie Price, the literary agent that's gone missing?'

'Of course,' I answered. 'Chas Collins' agent. It was only in the papers a few weeks ago. From what I hear, the author is missing as well.'

'Yes … yes, that's right. And did you read that on the same night there was a shooting a couple of miles away from the Price home?'

'Yes, I read that. That journalist, Max Tranter, was trying to link a drug-dealer killing to the Price disappearance.'

'That's the one. Well, Kevin had a copy of the book Maggie Price's author brought out last year at his house,' Toni said. 'Mellor's team found a circled reference to Maggie Price inside it.'

'He bought a copy to check if it compromised any of our friends from the Afghan operation Chas Collins wrote about.'

'Well, Mellor's team have made the connection so they're having ballistic tests done to see if it's the murder weapon.'

'So, Kevin is in the frame for that as well?' I asked.

'It's taken things into a whole different sphere. The Service is also involved in the hunt for Maggie Price.'

'Do you think she's dead?'

'We've no doubt. Since the day she disappeared there's been no indication of life whatsoever.'

'And you think Collins is involved?'

'Or a victim as well. The trail for him went cold several months ago. Kevin has never come up on our radar as a suspect.'

'He wouldn't, would he … no way is he involved,' I said, adamantly.

'There's the obvious answer, of course.'

'Which is?' Toni asked.

'Howard Green and the need to keep Collins quiet about the Al Anfal organisation. Maybe Price was collateral damage?'

'Maybe … and maybe your friend Kevin is actually a hired gun?'

'For God's sake, Toni. There's not a chance,' I exclaimed.

But I'd now realised I was going to have to take Toni into my confidence over what Kevin had told me about the copy of the Al Anfal document McNeil had brought to him. I turned and checked around the canteen. Although many of the tables were occupied, those nearest to us remained empty. It was safe to speak. I took a deep breath, leaned forwards to speak quietly and, having secured her attention, I began. She listened attentively as I summarised what I knew. It didn't take long, there wasn't much to tell.

'So, Kevin and Brian McNeil *have* been making arrangements to have it translated in the same way you did?' she asked.

'That's about the sum of it,' I said, slightly taken aback by the lack of surprise in her response.

'That confirms it, then?'

'Confirms what?'

'Kevin called Nell some while ago asking if she could help him with finding an Arab translator. He told her it was just a letter he needed help with. Do we know where this new copy of the document is now?'

'I think they've given it to Dr Armstrong.'

'We'll need to find out. You never told Kevin about Howard Green and the mop-up of the Increment men then?' As she spoke, her gaze switched nervously between me and checking over my shoulder.

'Just as we agreed. Some things are best left untold. Do you think the odd circumstances of the arrest and this gun appearing are connected to that?'

'I have no idea, Finlay.' She focussed on me, her voice now sounding angry and impatient. 'What I do know is that we need to speak to him, and urgently.'

'To what end, exactly?'

'To answer some questions. And when I say *we*, I mean you. I can't get involved at this point.' Her hand moved from her lap and placed the small, brown box on the table in front of me. 'Kind of makes this all the more relevant.'

'What is it?' I asked.

'A mobile phone. Bill Grahamslaw told me what happened to your work phone. CIB will return it and when they do I want you to take it to Nell to give it a once-over.'

'Why exactly?'

'To see if they've chipped it,' Toni answered. 'Which they most likely will have. You're probably not aware of it yet but the Met has been trialling a tracking system called "Stingray". When Commander Grahamslaw queried why they wanted your phone, it occurred to me that might be what they were up to. Stingray inserts software onto the phone that will send details of your calls, texts and location to whoever is monitoring you.'

'A bug in my pocket?' I said. 'Kind of reminds me of the device Kevin found at his home.'

'Which still remains something of a mystery, I'm afraid. Nell hasn't been able to find who might have planted it.'

I pulled the small box towards me and opened it. 'Is it an ordinary phone?' I asked. 'Or does it mean you can listen in to me as well.'

'It's called a burner phone. It operates via a South African network on an unregistered SIM card. Expensive to run on pay-as-you-go but almost impossible to trace. I've programmed it with my numbers and your home number. I suggest you only use it when you really need to do so. Hopefully the first occasion will be when you call to tell me what Kevin has to say.'

'You expect me to go and see him?'

Toni passed me a small slip of paper across the table. 'I'd be surprised if you didn't,' she said.

I looked down to see that the note contained a long series of numbers.

'Memorise them,' she continued. 'It's your new phone number. And make sure you give the number to Kevin. But, whatever you do, destroy that note and tell him not to record it either.'

'Understood.'

'And one other thing.' Her eyes again flicked upwards towards the far end of the canteen. 'It has a help facility. Dial treble eight and it will transmit a "come find me" signal via GCHQ.'

'A locator beacon?'

'You're familiar with them?'

'I had one in Northern Ireland, fitted to the car we used. Came in handy once.'

Toni's facial expression suddenly changed. She smiled, warmly. 'Looks like there's some news,' she exclaimed, as she focussed on someone behind me.

A moment later, Nina Brasov sat down with us. She looked worried and was slightly out of breath, as if she'd been running. 'I've been trying to find you everywhere, Finlay,' she said as she nodded a very brief acknowledgement towards Toni. 'It's Kevin. He's being produced at court this afternoon where they're going to be asking for a warrant of further detention to keep him in for additional questioning. I thought you'd want to know.'

Chapter 33

A warrant of further detention. That meant an additional thirty-six hours in the police cells for Kevin. Plenty of time for Mellor to have the pistol forensically tested and then interrogate him about it.

And Nina knew, as I did, that getting the warrant would also involve a court appearance, a public outing, and a short period in the court cells waiting for the Magistrate to hear the application. For a few hours, possibly, Kevin would be somewhere I could get to speak to him.

Not that it would be easy. Secure transport from the police station would be followed by equally impregnable conditions in the court cells. Most courts held prisoners in a basement cell area, with internal security doors and corridors providing access to a secure 'dock', where the accused would stand while the case was heard. To my mind, there would be one opportunity to speak to Kevin, and one only – as he waited in the court cell prior to the hearing. At that time, only police officers, prison escort staff and solicitors could expect to be allowed access.

I rang Barkingside court. The hearing was scheduled for noon, just enough time. My next call was a tough one and required a great deal of persistence before I was finally put through to Omar Shabat. I explained that I needed to speak to him again and he readily accepted my offer of two o'clock that afternoon.

✝

The court building appeared quiet as I arrived. I parked my car and headed up the steps towards the heavy glass front doors. Immediately inside, two uniformed security guards were supervising a walk-through metal detector. I dropped my car keys, the burner phone and some small change from my pocket into a tray and stepped through.

'DI Finlay,' I said to the first guard, as I recovered my possessions. 'There's a cop called Jones being produced here in about half an hour. Do you know who is representing him?'

The guard scanned a sheet of A4 paper. 'That'll be Mr Marshall from Kemeys Solicitors. He's just gone down to the cells to see his client.'

I offered my thanks. 'I'm new here,' I continued. 'Can you point me towards the cell area?'

'Door in the corner. Press the buzzer and wait for it to be opened – and have your warrant card ready. They're a bit twitchy today for some reason.'

I looked in the direction where the guard had tilted his head and saw a grey security door with a red light above it. 'Are the other detectives here?'

'All in Court One with the Crown Prosecutor.'

I scanned the public area for anyone I recognised. It would be all I needed to bump into Mellor at this point. I doubted very much whether my reasons for wanting to see Kevin would cut much ice with him. There were a couple of people sitting on benches reading news-papers, a suited solicitor in deep conversation with a man in equally smart attire and a uniform officer standing with his back to one of the entrances to the courts that I guessed was probably Court One. It looked to be a quiet morning. What the guard had suggested regarding the detectives already being in Court One made sense. With the court security team now responsible for bringing prisoners up from the cells, Mellor and his team would have joined the CPS solicitor to talk over the warrant application and make sure he or she was fully briefed. Kevin was entitled to a private consultation with his solicitor, an oppor-tunity I planned to exploit.

I pressed the buzzer to the cell-block door and waited.

A few moments later a face appeared at the small grilled window in the centre of the door. I held up my warrant card. There was a click and then the door swung open towards me.

'I need to see the solicitor that just came in,' I said to the guard. 'Mr Marshall.'

'Follow me.'

I stood to one side to allow the door to be closed and then followed my guide down two flights of narrow stairs. The smell of stale urine grew with every step and, as the stairs opened out into the cell reception area, the air became heavy and unpleasant. With detention periods limited to court appearances, those that had built the cell area had seen no need for modern ventilation or air-conditioning.

Behind a heavy wooden counter, an overweight guard was hunched over some paperwork.

'Fred, this bloke wants to see Mr Marshall,' said the guard with me.

Fred stopped what he was doing. 'He's in cell four with his client. Take a seat and I'll get someone to let him know you're here.' With his pen, he pointed towards a small bench against the opposite wall.

'I'd prefer to see Mr Marshall with his client, if that's OK,' I said.

'Who are you guv', part of the enquiry team?'

'DI Finlay. I just need to have a few words with them.'

Fred shrugged, and didn't seem minded to protest. I guessed he was used to cops occasionally appearing in the cell area and didn't consider my request to be that unusual.

My guide produced a large set of keys from a belt clip and opened a grilled gate that controlled entry to the cell corridor. I followed him through. At cell four he inserted another key into the brass lock and pulled the heavy door open.

A familiar face looked up from the plastic bench on the opposite side of the cell.

Chapter 34

As I walked in, Kevin stood up quickly and thrust his hand into mine.

'How the hell did you get in here?' he asked, warmly. He looked tired, drawn, his eyes lacking their usual spark. And he appeared to have aged several years in the two days since we had last met.

A grey-haired man in a dark pin-striped suit who had been sitting on the opposite end of the bunk also got to his feet.

'You'd be Mr Marshall?' I asked.

He nodded. 'And I presume you to be Inspector Finlay? Kevin and I were just discussing you.'

'Not all bad, I hope. I need a few minutes with your client if that's possible?'

'No worries,' said Kevin. 'We're just about done, aren't we Tom?'

Marshall gathered up some papers and placed them carefully into a leather briefcase. 'Yes, I'll make your case as we've discussed, but warrant applications like this tend to go through on the nod ... wouldn't you say, Mr Finlay?'

'That's true, Kev.'

Kevin nodded and shrugged. 'We'll see.'

'Do you want me to leave the door open?' asked the guard.

'I'm done here,' the solicitor answered, as he closed his case.

'OK, sir. If you'd like to come with me? I'll be at the reception area, Inspector. Just call as soon as you're finished.'

I nodded to indicate I understood and then waited until I heard the gate at the end of the corridor close. Only then did I turn towards Kevin and press a finger against my lips to indicate he should be quiet. I beckoned him towards the sink in the corner of the cell and then turned on the tap. 'Something I recently learned from Toni,' I said, quietly.

'You think we might be overheard?' Kevin replied.

'After finding that bug in your house, do you want to take the chance?'

He sighed. 'Well, I hope you're wrong.'

'Why's that?'

'Nothing, really. Anyway, I wasn't expecting to see you here. You're taking a bloody chance coming to see me.'

'A chance?' I said. 'Kev, if it hadn't escaped your attention you've been nicked for murdering Sandi. There's no way I wasn't going to find a way to get to you.'

'The lead investigator tried to suggest you were prepared to give evidence against me.'

'He's a bloody liar. That's just the kind of trick he'd use to rattle you. So, do you want to tell me what the hell is going on?'

'I'm being stitched up, that's what.'

'I knew you wouldn't have killed Sandi, not even accidentally.'

'I wondered whether to tell them about the bug … try and get them to think something might be going on, but they just seem totally set on building a case against me. I … I really appreciate you coming, boss.'

'Let's hope you're worth it.' I reached in my pocket and pulled out the tiny piece of paper Toni had given me containing the number of the burner phone. I showed it to Kevin. 'Before we talk any more, read it back to me,' I said.

He did as asked.

'Now, remember it. It's the only way you'll have of contacting me.'

He took a moment to reread the number a couple of times before continuing. 'Doesn't look like any number I've ever seen?' he asked.

'It's a special MI5 phone Toni gave me. Now what's the number?'

He repeated it correctly.

I smiled. 'Great. Now don't forget it. You're in deep shit, Kev, and you need help. I was thinking of getting in touch with Harry Mac from B Squadron. He's a barrister now.'

'No need. It's all taken care of. Is that what you came about?'

'Just part. And how do you mean, it's taken care of?'

'Tom Marshall used to be in the army legal department. He knows who to talk to so I get the best.'

'You trust him?' I asked as Kevin raised a hand. There was a noise from outside. I stepped gingerly across the cell to the door to confirm we were still unheard. I nodded to him and gave a thumbs-up as I saw the corridor was empty.

'For now, or until proved otherwise,' he continued. 'Don't imagine you're the only one who's been trying to work out what the fuck is going on here. I Google the bloody Al Anfal words, then I get bugged, and then I'm knocked out with enough ketamine to kill me … and when I come round I find that some bastard from Complaints is stitching me up for murder. Someone is behind this.'

'Enough to kill you?'

'Sandi's eldest boy came home from school early. He found me on the floor and called an ambulance.'

'He found his mum as well?' I said, imagining the horrific sight the poor boy must have seen.

Kevin lowered his gaze. 'Yes … poor kid.'

'So, if the boy hadn't found you, you'd be dead?'

'As the proverbial dodo,' he replied.

'Do you have any ideas?'

'Not at the moment, but Tom has a couple of lads working on it.'

'So, does he think he can get you out on bail?' I asked.

'I'm a cop, fixed address, that kind of thing. He thinks I have a chance. Surrendering my passport might help he says.'

'It might, yes.' I paused. 'Kev, I've some things I need to tell you and some things I need to ask of you.'

'Like what?' he demanded.

I held up my hand to encourage my friend to stay where he was and again walked the short distance across the cell to the door. The guard had left it slightly ajar. I peered through the gap and could see that Fred was still busy at his desk.

'OK, let's start at the beginning. What the hell happened at Sandi's house?'

Kevin scowled. 'You tell me. Sandi and me were meeting up for a little fun. She loves dressing up and getting me to call round. Anyway, this time I called and the front door was open. I thought it was one of her games. Next thing, I'm hit by some massive electric shock and when I wake up I'm in the hospital ward having had my stomach pumped, and with an armed uniform lad watching over me. I'm sitting there, wondering what the fuck is going on when in strolls a dick in a suit acting like he's some kind of friggin' god … and then he nicks me for Sandi's murder. That's it in a nutshell, really.'

'The dick was Mellor from Complaints?'

'You know him? He's not a friend of yours is he?'

'Met him. He's not what you'd call a mate. Did they question you about the overdose?' I asked.

'They did, and I'm telling you I never swallowed no horse tranquillisers. Like I've kept telling them, I thought I'd been knocked out by a faulty light switch or something. I never even saw Sandi. And, do you know what? They're telling me she was strangled in some kind of weird sex game. Some bastard killed her and then knocked me out and, I'm telling you now…'

'Now you have to prove it wasn't you, Kev.'

'I'll bloody do for them, that's what I'm saying. Have you heard anything about Sandi's boys? They're good lads. I don't want them blaming me for what happened to their mother.'

'I've not heard. But I'll see if I can find out.'

'I need to set things right with them. I just wish I knew how.'

'Have they told you about the Glock found in your car?'

'Yep, that bastard Mellor was very smug when he told me I was also being nicked for it. It's not mine, that I can tell you. And before you ask, I've got no idea how it got into my car.'

'So, is your kit hide still intact?'

'As far as I know, yes. But I'll need your help to relocate it before it's discovered.'

'OK, I can do that. It gets worse, though. Mellor found your copy of Chas Collins' book with the name of his missing agent circled. As a result he thinks the Glock may be linked to other murders.'

Kevin threw his head back. 'Ah … this is getting ridiculous.'

'Which is why I think we need to get you the best legal brains on side … and why you must tell me everything about the Al Anfal document Brian McNeil came to you with.'

'Why?' Kevin demanded. 'Are you saying that might be linked to all this as well?'

'Don't you remember, we talked about it at the DLR station waiting room?'

'I forget … things have been a tad confused these last couple of days. So, you think there's a link?'

'I'm not jumping to any conclusions at the moment. Just checking under every stone.'

'Well, with all that's going on, I'm surprised they're not trying to stitch me up with that as well.'

'With what?' I asked.

'I guess you haven't heard? Well, I suppose you wouldn't have. You know McNeil took it to the same translator that Rupert Reid recommended to you – Dr Armstrong?'

'That's what you told me.'

'OK, well, a couple of days ago Armstrong only went and topped himself, didn't he. When McNeil went to visit him to see how the job was going, the house was crawling with local coppers. I sent you a text to call me so I could tell you.'

'I got it, but by the time I called you back I guess you were already in hospital. So … Armstrong's dead is he?'

'Hung himself from a tree in his garden, apparently. Anyway, there was no chance of recovering the document so McNeil had to leave it there.'

I was silent, momentarily stunned by the revelation. Kevin was right, unless the death had made the TV news channels, I probably wouldn't have heard about it.

'So the document is still at Armstrong's house, so far as you know?' I asked.

'Unless the local lads found it, yes.' The scowl on my friend's face faded to be replaced by a look of hope. 'What's the chance you could try and get it back?' he asked.

'From Armstrong's home you mean? I'd have thought it would have been seized.'

'Why would they? McNeil said he had loads of stuff about the Middle East so they maybe wouldn't have paid it any particular attention.'

I thought about what Kevin was saying. He might be right. There was no reason that a particular set of papers would stick out from all the other documents in Armstrong's home.

'It's early days,' Kevin continued. 'With any luck, his relatives won't have had the place emptied yet. You could have a look and see if he left it there.'

I heard keys in the door at the end of the corridor. Turning the tap off, I made as if I'd been washing my hands. 'I'll have to go now, Kev. Mellor is up in court waiting and if he sees me he won't be impressed. But I'll think about what you said and, well, I'm not making any promises.'

'But you'll try.'

'I'll try. Now, repeat that phone number for me.'

The cell door swung open before he could speak. 'Times up, I'm afraid, gents. The magistrate is ready.'

'Good luck, mate,' I said, patting Kevin gently on the back. He forced a grim smile.

'She's dead, boss,' he said quietly, his shoulders slumped.

And, in that moment I realised how thoughtless I had been. So focussed was I on helping my friend achieve justice that I had forgotten that the woman he stood accused of killing meant a great deal to him.

'We're with you, mate,' I said, struggling to think what best to say.

Kevin looked up and appeared to be about to reply just as the guard interjected. It was time for me to go.

Heading out into the fresh air, I felt powerless to help. As a cop, Kevin would need to be protected from the general prison population and, while he could look after himself, he was no superman. Eventually, caught with his guard down or taken by surprise, he would fall like any man.

His only hope lay with securing the services of a damn good lawyer, and that was going to cost. I couldn't afford it, neither could he. And, given the nature of the charges he would be facing, there was little possibility the Police Federation would fund his legal defence. Kevin needed funds and, ironically, the document that had been such a danger to us previously now seemed to represent his best hope; what he had been hoping could provide for his retirement now looked like being his stay-out-of-jail card.

And he was relying on me to make it happen.

Chapter 35

Toni checked her watch as she exited the lift. Ten to nine. Finlay would be here in a few minutes. He'd made his first use of the burner phone to request another chat.

With Nell also wanting to talk, she'd arranged meetings with both in the office at New Scotland Yard. The security door lock clicked open as she approached. She smiled broadly at the new CCTV camera overseeing her approach and through which Nell must have seen her arrival.

Stuart was waiting inside the door. 'Morning ma'am,' he said, warmly. 'Will it be the usual?'

'White, no sugar, please,' she said.

'On its way.'

'And try and make it a clean mug this time will you?' she called as Stuart disappeared into the small lobby where they kept the kettle.

Nell was at her work station, her fingers a speeding blur across her keyboard, eyes glued to the screen.

'How's things?' Toni asked, not really expecting a reply.

'OK,' Nell answered. 'I did what you asked.'

'And Finlay was convinced you were sharing something with him without me knowing?'

'I believe so. Do you know what a nonce is, Toni?'

Nell's question was unexpected and unusually aggressive. Toni felt quite taken aback. 'Of course, why do you ask?' she replied.

'Do you know where the expression comes from?'

'It's what prison inmates call the sex offenders.'

Nell huffed slightly as she stopped typing. 'It stands for "Not On Normal Courtyard Exercise" and is an acronym for prisoners who cannot mix with the normal prison population.'

'If any of that population might be described as normal, Nell.'

'My point is that Kevin Jones will be a nonce. We're supposed to have been keeping a watching brief on him and now the poor man is going to end up behind bars … and we all know what happens to policemen in those situations.'

'Ah, I was wondering when you might mention him.'

'He was in touch with us only a fortnight ago. We should have followed that up.'

Stuart appeared with two mugs, placing one on the desk next to Toni. 'Inspector Finlay should be here in a minute,' he said.

'Thanks.' Toni eased herself onto an empty chair while she thought how best to deal with Nell's question. 'Nell,' she began, and then paused as her former researcher appeared distracted by a movement on her display. A moment later, as her assistant turned back, she finished what she wanted to say. 'Easy with hindsight is an expression that comes to mind.'

Nell wasn't persuaded. 'We hadn't heard from him for months. Are you telling me it's a complete coincidence that he calls up wanting to speak to us about translating an Arabic letter and then soon afterwards he's arrested?'

'For murder, Nell. The death of his girlfriend had nothing to do with his wanting to speak with us.'

'And now they're trying to link him to the drug-dealer murder?'

'OK, OK, I agree, it doesn't look good for him. But, as we've discussed before, there's no direct evidence to link that shooting to Maggie Price going missing.'

'And, like I keep saying, it's too much of a coincidence. What if the cops link the gun from Kevin's car to that shooting? And I'd bet you a month's pay the two incidents are connected.'

'As you keep saying, yes, I know.' Toni did her best not to sound frustrated.

Stuart coughed and, as she turned toward him, she followed his eyes in the direction of the CCTV monitor. Finlay was in the lift area outside.

She turned back to Nell. 'We'll continue this conversation after I've spoken with Finlay. In the meantime, try to keep quiet and do not – I repeat *do not* – mention what you just said to me.'

Nell simply nodded in response.

Stuart pressed the door release just as the camera showed Finlay's hand about to press the entry buzzer.

Toni clocked a slight smile as she saw the policeman jump. 'You two are due a break, I believe,' she said as the door swung open.

'I'm fine,' said Nell.

Stuart was more receptive to the motive behind the suggestion. 'Come on, Nell,' he said, as he gently took hold of her arm. 'Coffees are on me.'

A few moments later, Finlay accepted Toni's suggestion he have Stuart's untouched tea. He had been breathing heavily as he'd entered the office but now seemed more composed.

'There's no sugar in it,' she added, as he sipped.

He raised the mug slightly, as if making a toast. 'Thanks for that,' he said. 'Sorry I'm a bit late. I gave up waiting for the lift and decided to run up the stairs. Six floors wasn't quite the breeze it was when I was younger.'

She smiled sympathetically. 'There's many your age wouldn't have even tried it.'

'I guess, and thanks for giving Stuart and Nell a break. Having just the two of us here will make things a lot easier.'

'OK. So, you worked out how to use the burner phone then?'

'And how to add a few more essential numbers to its contact list. I had to tell Jenny about it though, in case she needs to get hold of me.'

'Ah, yes. Well, make sure you brief her not to say anything to anyone about it. And, in terms of use, I should have told you to make sure it's kept turned on. That way I can get hold of you anytime.'

'You might want to do that then?'

'I might. How did you get on with Minister Shabat?'

'Before we come to that,' Finlay paused, as if searching for the right words. 'I went to see Kevin.'

'Good. Did you have any problems?'

'None,' he replied. 'But he told me he'd been in touch with you recently.'

'That's correct, yes.'

'What did he say?'

'I thought I'd already mentioned this? He spoke to Nell, said he needed a translator. When she asked him why he ended the conversation.'

'So, you didn't help him?'

'No, we didn't,' Toni replied. 'I might suggest you ask Rupert Reid, the bomb disposal officer who you first went to.'

'I already did that, and, yes, Kevin did follow that route. He ended up giving the document to the same translator I used.' Finlay said.

'Dr Armstrong?'

Finlay nodded.

Toni hesitated for a moment before continuing. 'I see ... OK ... I guess I can share this with you, it will be public knowledge in a few days anyway. Your translator friend is no more. A couple of days ago he hung himself from a tree in his garden.'

'A genuine suicide; or has Howard Green been active again?'

'Try not to see conspiracy beneath every stone, Finlay. Local police are dealing with it ... there's a report being completed by the local CID that their Special Branch are overseeing due to Armstrong's weapons-inspection role. But it looks to be a genuine suicide, yes.'

It was Finlay's turn to pause, his impassive reaction intriguing her for a moment before the reason dawned on her.

'So Kevin's document is lost?' he asked finally.

'There's been no mention of it being found at the house ... you knew didn't you?'

'Knew what?' said Finlay.

'That Armstrong is dead.'

'Kevin told me. His mate went to see him in Wales only to find the place crawling with local uniforms.'

'Who probably seized the document the friend had left to be trans-lated,' she suggested, thinking that was the most likely thing to have happened.

'Not necessarily. Kevin suggested that, as the Armstrong house was littered with paperwork, that particular document might not stick out from anything else.'

'So, it might still be there?'

'Possibly; who knows?' he answered. 'If you're thinking the same as me, that would be along the lines of making sure it's recovered before it falls into the wrong hands.'

'You could do that.'

'How exactly?'

'You're a cop. Ring the locals and find out if anything matching the description was found.'

'That might ring alarms with them,' he suggested.

'Be discreet.'

'Isn't there a better way?'

Toni grinned. 'You could burgle the local police station? Nothing that should trouble a former SAS officer, I would have thought?'

'That was years ago. And what if the locals don't have it?'

'I think you're right to say that calling them might ring alarms bells. So, the best answer has to be to search the Armstrong house, and soon.'

'I agree.'

'So, what happened when you went back to see Shabat?'

⊹

Stuart and Nell returned to the office a few minutes after Finlay had left. In the interim period, Toni had been thinking about what Finlay had said.

Shabat had been more forthcoming once Finlay revealed he knew it was Howard Green who had made the demand of him. But, despite keeping a diary, Shabat had been unable to specify exactly when Howard had approached him. He was able to confirm that Howard hadn't come back to him again though, suggesting that Howard had given up, something which seemed consistent with the Director's warning to him many months previously.

But it was an off-the-cuff remark Finlay made that had really aroused her interest. Something had been said during the conversation with Shabat about Howard Green and his marriage into a well-moneyed family. Shabat had been quite dismissive of the idea, convinced that Howard had his own business interests that seemed to be sufficiently lucrative to mean the MI6 officer was not as beholding to his wife as Toni thought. That had reminded her, quite vividly, of Bill Grahamslaw's questions about Howard, about his motive, what drove him and whether he had something going on in the background that she was best knowing about. And she had made a decision. It was time to get her team to start some real digging.

As soon as she sat down at her desk, Nell tried to continue the conversation about the gun found in Kevin's car but was soon stunned into silence when Toni interrupted her with the first of her requests.

'Both houses?' Nell asked.

'Yes,' said Toni. 'I want you to sweep Kevin Jones' house for any more listening devices and I want you to do the same at his girlfriend's place.'

'It's a crime scene,' Stuart commented. 'It might have a guard on it.'

'I've checked – it hasn't. There's "Do Not Cross" tape on the doors and a regular uniform drive-by, but the local nick were only asked to guard it until the forensic exam was finished. I want you to get Nell inside so she can check for bugs while you do a thorough search for any interesting documents you can find.'

'Anything specific?'

'Anything that looks suspect. Weapons manuals, military stuff, anything with Arabic on it – you know the kind of thing. Nell should have an idea of the kind of thing you're looking for. If it looks interesting then bag it.'

Nell nodded knowingly. She'd clearly guessed what Toni was after. 'When do you need this done?' she asked.

'Tomorrow morning, and in daylight, so make it early. I want both buildings swept before the local murder squad feel any need to go taking another look.'

'And what if we're caught?' said Stuart.

Toni smiled as Nell started to laugh. 'Stuart, you're bloody MI5. Talk your way out of it.'

Chapter 36

Thames House, London. MI5 HQ

'Right people, settle down and we'll make a start.'

T2/0, the Assistant Director – actual name Alexander Dyer – called the meeting to order. Present were fourteen of his section and departmental heads, some of whom drew an unsettling glare when they responded a little slowly to his request.

Like Toni, Dyer was a former Royal Navy officer. Also like her, he was new in post. What was interesting, and what seemed to be having an unsettling effect on some of the more traditional officers, was the fact he seemed to have adopted a far more inclusive policy than his forerunners with regards to keeping his subordinates in the information loop. Soon after taking up his post, he had identified the 'Long Room' – so called because of its shape – as a suitable venue for meetings and had installed a series of paintings, a coffee percolator and a kettle to provide some creature comforts. At the head of the table, a rather shabby and ancient chair had been replaced by a large leather one of the kind so often favoured by a ship's captain. The Long Room had now taken on the style and appearance of an officer's wardroom, similar to those found in all naval vessels, both at sea and ashore.

Toni approved of the changes – she found them reassuringly comfortable and familiar, and suspected the new Assistant Director did likewise.

The previous month's Long Room meeting had discussed, without reaching any real conclusion, the progress of an enquiry into the murder of William Stobie, a former Special Branch detective from the Royal Ulster Constabulary. Stobie had been shot dead two weeks after being acquitted of involvement in the murder of a solicitor in 1989. The Assistant Director wanted to discuss recent press speculation that Stobie was an asset. He'd met a wall of silence from those in attendance that had surprised Toni and angered Dyer. He ended that meeting with a clear warning to all that such a response would not be tolerated in the future.

As the recently appointed head of T1/B department, Toni was now on the official list of expected attendees. Although she had been looking forward to the meeting, she noticed – as the Assistant Director must have – the slumped shoulders and glum faces that now all turned in unison toward the head of the table. It was clear many of her peers would rather have been elsewhere.

On the agenda for today were a number of reports from T2/2 (Research and Threat Assessment) and T5B (Arms Trafficking) and, of particular note, they were to discuss the recent acquittal of Sulayman Zainulabidin on charges of preparing for acts of terrorism. Zainulabidin – who had changed his name and converted from Catholicism in 1979 – had been accused of planning a terror-training camp that he called 'Ultimate Jihad Challenge'. Toni suspected this planned discussion to be the reason for the solemn faces; nobody was likely to relish the prospect of analysing their failings.

She was right, and being so new in post, she remained little more than an interested observer as her peers ducked and dived the questions Alex Dyer wanted answered.

'Why had the prosecution failed?' he asked. A simple enough question which Toni expected would generate a discussion on the standard of the evidence and the defence that Zainulabidin put forward. Instead, the two officers closest to the enquiry simply blamed the jury for swallowing the explanation offered by the defence. 'Not our fault,' they said, almost in unison. Toni smiled inwardly at the backtracking and outright deflection of blame. More like 'don't try and pin the failure on me Mr

Assistant Director', she mused. Spooks well versed in the art of covering their arses.

But Dyer was on a mission. He reminded everyone present – as if they needed reminding – that two other trials had also collapsed earlier in the year. Lotfi Raissi – an Algerian pilot accused of training the 9/11 pilots; and Yassir al-Sirri – who provided the press accreditation to the assassins of Ahmed Shah Massoud in Afghanistan just two days before the 9/11 attacks. Both had been acquitted.

'Three trials since 9/11. Three failures.' The Assistant Director was tight-lipped, his voice low and demanding attention. 'This isn't a witch hunt,' he added, 'but this cannot continue. I want answers.'

Nobody spoke.

Dyed-in-the-wool spooks, thought Toni, as she also remained silent. Entrenched in the doctrine of secrecy. They were all being careful what they chose to divulge, keeping their heads down until the flack died down. Not one of them was prepared to stick their head above the parapet.

It was only when they reached the point of 'any other business' that, for the first time, Toni learned not to feel quite so smug at the discomfort of her peers. Dyer raised a late item, not on the agenda: the recent death of Iraq weapons inspector Julian Armstrong and a report from the local police Special Branch on the circumstances of his demise. They'd all heard about the death, of course. It wasn't every day that a weapons inspector committed suicide. But, to the best of Toni's knowledge, although Armstrong had a PF – a Personal File – he wasn't an asset or considered a security risk.

It was as the Assistant Director reached below the table to retrieve a thick bundle of papers from his briefcase that Toni started to feel her world going awry. He placed a loose pile of A4-sized paper on the table in front of him and, as he did, she noticed him carefully scanning the faces of those present. She saw that the top sheet bore Arabic writing, and wondered, *Could it be?*

A cold shiver ran up her spine. If it was, Finlay needn't bother to go and look for it.

'Bring me up to speed on this, people,' Dyer asked, looking around the room once more as he appeared to search for a reaction. The less experienced looked confused. Others, certainly those more practised in the dark arts of the service, remained impassive.

'What do we know about Julian Armstrong?' he added.

Miles Chadbourne from T5C spoke up. 'An eccentric former weapons inspector living, or perhaps I should say, who lived in Wales. There's a PF on him, I believe.'

Toni wondered what that file might contain, whether it might flag up her interest in Armstrong were she to now take a look at it.

'Was he an agent?' asked Dyer.

'Not to my knowledge,' replied Chadbourne.

'Anyone else?' The question was abrupt, impatient, and hinted strongly that the Assistant Director didn't believe those present were being open with him.

Silence. Dyer waited for several seconds. A pen clicked at the far end of the table.

Toni hesitated to say anything. He could find out about Armstrong without her contribution. There would be plenty on file about the doctor. And, if the document now sat before him on the table was what she thought it was, it may be best she remain quiet.

'And what about this?' he asked, finally, as his gaze returned to the document.

Toni studied Chadbourne's face as the Assistant Director flicked through the pages. He knew something, she could smell it.

'Is there anyone amongst you who might be able to fill me in on what this document is?'

No reaction.

'Is there anyone who can tell me what "Al Anfal" is?'

Chadbourne's face twitched very slightly. For a moment Toni doubted what her own eyes were telling her but it had been there, she'd seen it. Chadbourne recognised the name.

'OK,' the Assistant Director continued, sounding increasingly angry. 'If nobody is going to help me out here, I guess I'm going to have to start the ball rolling. Armstrong was found by his housekeeper. His last conversation with her was a telephone call during which he asked her to delay calling by as he had company. At this moment in time we have no idea who he was referring to, and I find it a little surprising his mind-set could have changed so markedly in the hour following that call that he reached a point where he decided to top himself!'

Several in the room jumped as Dyer slammed his clenched fist on the document in front of him.

'Could we ask the local Special Branch to organise a full forensic search?' The question came from Sian Phillips, who was sat at the far end of the table and seemed unaffected by her Assistant Director's outburst. Sian was T2/1, Deputy Head of Section, responsible for investigations. Hers were shoes that Toni hoped to one day fill.

'Already in hand,' said Dyer, his voice, once again, calm. 'What I want to know, people, is if any of you know how Armstrong came to be in possession of this document?' He tapped the papers firmly with his pen.

No further hands were raised or contributions forthcoming. But Toni felt the almost palpable tension in the room.

And the Assistant Director also appeared to sense it.

But he remained silent. Returning the document to his briefcase, he slid back in his chair and, making no further comment, he walked the short distance to the closed door. And then he was gone, the door closing firmly behind him, leaving those present wondering exactly what had just happened.

Chapter 37

Toni bore down on Miles Chadbourne like a guided missile.

His office, below ground and devoid of natural light, was where she knew he would be headed and where she expected to find him alone. She wasn't disappointed. His door was slightly ajar and, as she pushed it fully open, she found he was already back at his desk, hunched over, nose in what looked like a lengthy report.

'I half expected to see you,' he said, without lifting his gaze from the papers in front of him.

'May I sit down?' Toni asked politely. Catch more flies with honey, she thought, than you ever would with salt. It was an expression her mother had often used when she was young, normally with reference to persuading her father to do something around the house. It had been good advice.

Miles was old school. An Oxford graduate – Balliol, if Toni remembered correctly. Recruited straight from university and now with more than fifteen years in the Service under his belt, it was said he was on first-name terms with several very senior politicians. But now Miles was ensconced in the basement of Thames House. His progress up through the ranks had come to a sudden and rather mysterious halt. There were rumours about what had happened, of course. His liking for alcohol, his bachelor status and his reputed interest in 'the ladies' were all possible reasons why he'd been black-balled. Truth was, nobody outside of Miles and the need-to-know few had any idea. All his peers and subordinates knew was that Miles remained in T5 department, where he was left, very much on his own, to get on with handling whatever report was sent his way.

He extended a puffy hand, indicating Toni could make use of the single wooden seat opposite him. She sat and waited, taking the opportunity to cast an eye around her. Everything looked temporary. A large number of dusty box files sat three-high in one corner and in another a grey two-drawer filing cabinet stood with its bottom section open. There were no pictures, no books, not even a pen holder – nothing to give the room any sense of personal investment.

It looked like Miles had been using the floor to study a selection of documents, which still lay where he had left them. Her guess was that it wouldn't take long for his pretence at being rather too busy to give way to curiosity.

She was right. Fifteen seconds was all it took. He leaned back in his chair and placed his reading glasses on the paperwork.

She smiled warmly. 'You were expecting me?' she asked, with exaggerated curiosity.

'You're new,' Miles answered. 'And I saw the way you were studying us all as the Assistant Director spoke. You were looking for a reaction.'

'Is that how it appeared? I'm sorry. It's only my second such meeting and I guess I'm still learning the etiquette.'

Miles huffed. 'So, I presume you want to talk about what was going on in there?'

'That would be nice, yes … if you didn't mind. I'm feeling slightly out of my depth and, well, I hoped I might reach out to a friend, so to speak.'

'Drink?' he asked.

'A tea would be nice, I don't mind making.'

'I was thinking of something a little stronger.'

Toni frowned slightly. 'Perhaps a little early for me.' She cast around the office, looking for any sign of a kettle or percolator. There was none. Miles might just be toying with her, she thought.

'Yes, it probably is. Anyway, when I saw you looking at me in the Long Room meeting – I wondered if that might bring you down to the dungeon.'

'The dungeon?'

Miles smirked. 'It's what we call the lower levels. Rumour has it that many years ago, some of these rather shabby offices were actually used as cells and interrogation rooms. Nice and quiet, you see, away from prying ears and eyes.'

'Just a rumour?'

'Who knows?' Miles eased his heavy frame out of his chair, then walked around the desk and behind Toni. She had left the door slightly ajar. 'Best keep this between us,' he added, as he pushed it closed.

For a moment Toni felt vulnerable. Miles was behind her, the door now shut. And, to the best of her knowledge, none of the offices in the immediate vicinity were occupied. She brushed the feeling aside.

'They listen in on us, you know,' he continued. 'Monitor phone calls, bug offices. Spying on the spies.'

'Should we be surprised?' Toni replied, as Miles returned to his chair, the frame creaking. 'After all, who better to be targeted by a foreign power than the very people charged with keeping a country's secrets?'

Miles scowled. 'You're comfortable with the idea of being spied on?'

'In some ways I find it reassuring. For example, I know you are someone I can trust as I'm aware that, if you weren't, the watchers would have found you out. So, yes, I'm fairly comfortable with it.'

'I see your point, but I'm not sure if everyone upstairs would agree with you. Anyway, what I can tell you is that I sweep this office every day. So far as I'm able to tell, the watchers are happy with me for now.'

'You do have a pretty good reputation.'

'I see.' Miles paused, as if assimilating what Toni had said, making an assessment of her, weighing up if she could be trusted. 'What, in particular, piqued your interest at the meeting?' he asked, finally.

'The death of the weapons inspector.'

'Ah … Dr Armstrong. I should have guessed.'

'I wondered why he should have a PF?'

'That's easy enough to answer. He travels to countries that interest us, mixes with people we're interested in and gets to see things we want to know about. Each time people like him return from an inspection, we debrief them fully.'

'To good end?'

'I've no idea, Toni; it's not something I've been privy to. But, I expect so. Armstrong was in Iraq, so I'd be pretty confident that, despite Saddam's best efforts, he would have seen and heard things.'

'We spied on him?'

'Likely as not, he was an asset, either formally or through monitoring. His demise will have to be looked at to make sure nothing has been going on that we ought to know about.'

'So why would Dyer be asking us about him?'

'He's fishing. He's new to this branch of the service and he's trying to get up to speed. I'd be fairly sure there were people in the Long Room who know more about Doctor Armstrong than they wanted to say at that time. It wouldn't surprise me if one or two rather more intimate conversations were taking place, perhaps even now as we speak.'

'And what about that report? He mentioned it was called Al Anfal. Is that an Al Q'aeda affiliated group?'

Miles paused, his brow furrowed.

'Did I say something out of turn?' Toni asked.

Again, there was hesitation. For a moment, Miles went to speak and then stopped himself. Toni waited, silently urging him to say what he was thinking.

'You can't say?' she finally asked.

'I … I can say … and I think perhaps I should. But Toni, I do this as a favour that, one day, I hope you will return.'

'We all need friends in this world, Miles. And I'm not the kind who turns her back on a mate or forgets a favour.'

Miles picked up his reading glasses and spun them slowly between his thumb and forefinger. 'Very well … I'll tell you this. Al Anfal is a name you'd best steer clear of. To the best of my understanding it's the focus of a clandestine operation run by Six. I stumbled across it a few months ago and started asking questions. Next thing, I'm grounded, given the warning formula and assigned to my new office for a period "to be determined".'

'Given the warning formula?'

'Told to forget what I knew. The threat was quite clear, Toni. I keep quiet, serve my penance or I end up black-bagged.'

She was stunned. 'You … you mean killed?'

'As I'm sure you've noticed, the Service tends to use rather more sensitive words than "killed" to describe its darker arts. But yes, that is what I mean.'

'You're saying there are people who threatened to kill you?'

'Not so much people, as a particular person. But there were others and I have no doubt it went to a high level. I'm not without connections, believe me, but, despite all my very best efforts, my security grading was downgraded – as I was warned would happen – and I was royally shafted. Some would argue that a few years in the dungeon…'

'…was a lot better than what could have happened?'

'Exactly,' he continued. 'And you still want to be a friend to me?'

'To be honest, I could do with a friend, someone I can trust to discuss things honestly and openly with.'

'Trust? Ha, that's something the Service plays lip service to but … well, when it comes to substance, I fear our seniors show very little faith in us.'

'I know what you mean. But surely mistrust is something inherent in a world full of secrets.'

'Yes, I'm sure,' he continued. 'And it seems I may already be sharing things with you that require a level of trust verging on a kind of friendship, yes?'

'I agree, and I'm flattered, truly. So, maybe can we start here and now? If I show some trust in you, will you continue to return the compliment?' Toni crossed her legs, easing her discomfort on the chair, and, as she did so, she caught the flicker of movement in Miles' eyes as he glanced downwards. He was studying her.

'We can try,' he suggested. 'What specifically was it that interested you about Dyer's questions?'

Toni cleared her throat. 'It was just what we were talking about. The request for information about Al Anfal. I had the impression you weren't the only one in the room who'd been warned to stay quiet on that topic.'

Miles breathed deeply then clasped his hands together, almost as if praying. 'Possibly,' he said, thoughtfully. 'We may never know as it's not something we would discuss. And for obvious reasons, if others have received similar warnings.'

'Do you mind if I ask who it was that warned you off?'

'That I can't say, again for obvious reasons.'

'Did you get any further than just learning about the name?'

Miles glanced over her shoulder towards the door. It was as if he feared someone may be listening outside. Then his lips curled as a smile of realisation began to form. 'You've also heard of it, haven't you?'

Toni was silent for a moment. To learn more she was going to need to give a little. 'Last year. I was researching that book that blew the lid on the Afghan operation to support the Mujahideen.'

'Cyclone. When we were trying to beat the CIA in the race to find the author?'

'Exactly. I stumbled across the name and then followed it up as a line of enquiry.'

'Did it get you anywhere?'

'A call to see Dir'T' and a warning to drop it.'

'Which you did?'

'Immediately, yes.'

'The very thing I should have done. Unfortunately, for me it wasn't the Director of T Section who warned me, otherwise I should have certainly heeded it, as you did. No … I continued to dig and that's when things went tits up.'

'That's when you were threatened?' Toni prodded, hoping she was getting closer to the answer she sought.

Miles nodded.

'And now,' Toni continued, 'given that Dyer is asking questions about the very thing you were grounded for, surely that means it must be less sensitive?'

He raised an eyebrow. 'Who knows, I can only hope. Don't imagine that very thought hasn't been going through my mind as we speak. So, for all the good it will do you, I've decided to give you the name you're after.'

'What's changed your mind?' she asked.

'The realisation that, if something happened to me, at least someone should know who was responsible.'

'So who is it?'

'Not one of us. In fact, it's someone who is not even a member of this Service.'

'He or she is outside MI5?' Toni felt the hairs on her neck rise.

'Yes, but not too far outside. The man I'm referring…' Miles hesitated. As if weighing up, once again, the pros and cons of revealing what Toni wanted to know. 'Did you ever find that author chap?' he continued. 'The one who wrote the Cyclone book.'

'Gone into hiding,' said Toni. 'Last heard of in Brussels, we believe. So … the name of the man who warned you off Al Anfal?'

'Ah, yes, the man I'm referring to,' said Miles. 'It's Howard Green.'

Chapter 38

The Black Mountains, Mid Wales

I knew I should have been watching the house, but it wasn't every day you got to see a sparrowhawk hunt. It looked to me like a female. Not that I was particularly expert, but I remembered being told by an old twitcher who knew a thrush from a fieldfare that the males were too small to hunt anything larger than a blackbird. This one was targeting a small covey of grouse that had been scratching around in the grass upwind of me, unaware of my presence. As I kept a lookout for any movement in Ty Eira – the Armstrong home – I'd become entranced by the family group and had been pleased to see how they reacted quickly to the appearance of the hawk in the sky above them.

The drive down to Wales had taken me nearly three hours and then there had been the challenge of finding an Ordnance Survey map of the local area to enable me to plan a safe approach. The local town had a decent selection of newsagents where I found every map you could want … except the one I needed. They were sold out and, it was only after several blanks and one long but ultimately unsuccessful hunt through old cardboard boxes with a rather sweet young girl on work experience from the local school that I eventually found a shop that had what I needed.

I located a quiet car park near to the Offa's Dyke trail walk, about two miles north-west of my target, worked out what looked like a reasonably safe approach route to Ty Eira, and then used the natural contours of the surrounding hills to conceal my movements. I dressed as if I were hill-walking, with the map hung around my neck in a plastic pouch. If spotted, I doubted anyone would pay me much attention given the number of ramblers and walkers who explored the mountains. Later on though, I'd need to be a lot more careful. One thing I certainly didn't want was to run into the local police and have to explain why I was searching through the home of a recently deceased weapons inspector.

It was a hot day, unseasonably so, the pale-blue sky criss-crossed with just the odd wisps of cloud. In the distance, the peak of Waun Fach dominated the skyline. I was now tucked in to a pretty decent vantage point on the edge of the heather, my prostrate form nicely concealed by the green bracken. I'd made use of an old dry-stone wall to get as close to my target as I needed – far enough away that I wouldn't be seen or heard, but close enough that I could observe movement at both the house and the single approach lane.

It looked quiet. I'd come prepared for a wait, and just in case, I'd packed a small backpack on which I rested my chin. It contained two water bottles, a compass and some high-protein snack bars. I'd decided against bringing binoculars, figuring I could get close enough to the house to see what I needed to. The phone Toni had given me was on silent – a precaution in case it picked up a signal, although that was something of a rarity in these parts.

I gave it twenty minutes, guessing that, if the house had any occu-pants, they would reveal their presence in some way during that amount of time. As I waited, I was grateful for the cushioning effect of the short mountain grass. Rapid and unexpected movement drew attention so I kept everything slow, moving my eyes first, and then my head. It was habit drilled into me many years previously, and had now become so automatic I did it without thinking. I'd spent many a long hour in hides watching caches of concealed weapons that had been discovered by the local police; afterwards, we would wait for someone to try and recover them. Twenty minutes watching a house was child's play. It also gave me time to put together a plan to deal with the kit that lay hidden beneath Kevin's allotment shed. I was going to need to move it, and soon, before Mellor stumbled across it and we were all in the mire.

The sparrowhawk appeared again, then dived and jinked as it narrowed its wings on an attack run. Three, four times, it struck as the covey of grouse dispersed, some on the wing, others on foot into the nearby gorse and heather. The early alarm of one observant bird together with the instant reaction of its pals was sufficient to save their lives. The hawk moved on, and I returned my gaze to the house. It was time to move in for a closer look.

✝

The search wasn't going well. And when I say that, I really mean I was getting frustrated because I hadn't found what I was looking for. And now, that sense of disappointment was beginning to build into a feeling of having been sent on a fool's errand.

I knew there was every possibility, of course, that Kevin's copy of the document had already been seized by the local lads and, as I stood rubbing at an insect bite I'd picked up in the bracken, I was beginning to lose heart.

I'd tried everywhere obvious; desk, drawers, cupboards, boxes, the kind of places where people normally stored paperwork. I'd even looked around the outbuildings, but this had revealed little apart from an ancient, rusty motorcycle and a collection of antique tools that looked like they'd seen much better days. I'd reached the conclusion that the document either wasn't here or it was hidden somewhere I wasn't going to find. Time was now moving on and the longer I stayed, the more likely it was I would be disturbed.

I settled down on the same settee I'd used on the day Dr Armstrong had told me how dangerous possession of the Al Anfal document might be. I was sweating – something that always seemed to make bites all the more irritating – and I was thirsty. I'd left the backpack hidden behind a wall that marked the boundary between the yard and the adjacent moorland so I scanned the room for something to quench my thirst. There was nothing of any use, just a small drinks cabinet containing two half-finished bottles of wine and a barely touched bottle of the same Penderyn whisky Matt Miller in the trafficking office was so partial too.

Whisky wasn't quite what I needed though, so I headed for the kitchen. Just as I was about to run the cold tap for a drink, I heard a car door close. It was time to leave.

Moving quickly, I headed through the back door, eased it shut and, using the building to hide my movement, sprinted for the cover of the low wall I'd first used when checking the house was empty. I'd planned for such an eventuality and, as I had already checked that none of the front windows allowed a view all the way through to the rear yard, I knew I had time to escape. Inside of a few seconds, I was out of sight but close enough to keep a watch on the visitors.

A male voice reached my ears. It sounded like he was giving instructions. At least two of them, then. I crawled to a position slightly further away, using the cover of another dry-stone wall.

More noise. What sounded like internal doors being slammed. Whoever it was, they weren't worried about being disturbed or overheard. Then a crash, heavy, like something wooden hitting the floor.

The sound of splintering wood suggested a search was going on and that they were being thorough. I wondered whether the visitors were from the local Special Branch office, back to conduct a second search. Two more voices caught my ear, one shouting. They were different from the one who'd been giving the initial orders. Possibly three men, then? If they were looking under floorboards, it was possible that, like me, they were now checking places not previously searched.

It was nearly an hour before they finished and for the whole time the focus seemed to be on tearing apart places not previously investigated. Whether they were looking for something specific – possibly the same thing as me – or whether they were simply looking everywhere for anything of interest, I wasn't able to tell. But as I watched them head back to their car, I confirmed three men, and I noticed the way they all moved. They were fit and light on their feet. And there was no joviality to be heard, no jokes or ribbing of the kind cops habitually subject each other to; and they didn't appear to have found anything. In fact,

I thought as I watched, if they'd been plucked from a movie and given American accents, they would have made perfect FBI or Secret Service caricatures.

Not cops then. But if not, who? Intelligence services was my best guess. I waited for ten minutes after their car disappeared from view down the lane before returning to the house. They'd been busy. The house looked more like it had been robbed than searched and it crossed my mind that may have been the intention.

I wandered around, surveying the damage. Floors were up, cupboards and chests of drawers broken up in what appeared to be an effort to locate hidden compartments. They seemed to have quit only when everything had been checked. I thought back to the time when Dr Armstrong had shown me around the place and I tried to imagine where he might hide something he didn't want anyone to find but which he could readily access should he need to. Once again, I returned to the settee in the living room to think for a moment. It was torn open, so I contented myself with a perch on the armrest.

The doctor had experience in both Iraq and Northern Ireland, so he'd told me, and he would have seen some of the ingenious methods used in those places to conceal not just documents, but weapons and explosives. I wondered if he had copied something previously seen.

I noticed the whisky was gone. I smiled. Cheeky bastards couldn't resist taking it, I guessed. Perhaps they'd decided their trip shouldn't be a complete waste of time and had thought they'd help themselves to a little token for their efforts.

I headed upstairs. They really had been thorough. Mattresses in all three bedrooms were ripped open, as were the pillows on the beds and in a store cupboard. The attic hatch was removed – so they'd checked there – and the content of each and every drawer was now spilled on the floor. It was a real mess. But the effort they'd gone to was telling. If they thought there was something to find it was worth me having another look as well.

The only place left for me to look through again was the outbuildings. A small shed produced nothing useful so I decided on one last check through the barn. The old motorcycle was undisturbed but I saw that a rug on the floor had now been pulled to one side. The visitors had been looking for a hidden trapdoor, I surmised. The tools had been moved and an old door that had been leaning against the wall now lay on the floor. I stepped gingerly on it and, rather unexpectedly, I saw that the surface gave way to the pressure of my weight.

'You clever old bugger,' I said, under my breath.

A solid wooden door wouldn't have that much give in it. I tried again, this time pressing harder with my foot. Once more, the wood gave way more than it ought to have done. It was hollowed out.

I lifted the door up and checked the ends. The top was sealed with a narrow edging strip of timber, stained to match the remainder. To the casual glance, it looked like part of the door. I rummaged through the tools, found a chisel and levered the edging free.

Bingo.

Chapter 39

Toni swirled the wine in her glass as Bill finished the washing up. It had occurred to her as they talked that, quite possibly, she had revealed too much. She reconciled herself, however, to the reassuring thought that if you couldn't confide in a lover who also happened to be Head of the Anti-Terrorist Squad, who could you talk to?

He was thinking. She knew that because he always hummed to himself if he was mulling things over. In the few short months they had been seeing each other she occasionally wondered what had gone wrong with his marriage. He was great company, intelligent and attentive. And, as a lover, he was very caring and imaginative. But she had also begun to realise what his employers might see as positive qualities, a wife might have some difficulty adjusting to. He lived for his job, pure and simple. If he wasn't sleeping, Bill Grahamslaw was either at work or thinking about work.

As the tuneless hum came to a halt, he appeared in the doorway to the living room. 'Top-up?' he asked.

She smiled, and nodded. He turned his back for a moment and then reappeared with the bottle and a second glass.

'I've been thinking about this Miles Chadbourne chap,' he said.

'What exactly?' she asked as he poured the wine and sat beside her.

'I was wondering why he opened up so easily? As you say, you don't really know him that well and it's hard to see how he might regard friendship with you as being in his long-term interest.'

'Actually, it would seem he currently has no friends at all in the Service. Ever since he was sent to the dungeon he's been persona non grata, so maybe it was worth a punt.'

'Maybe he fancies you?' Bill grinned mischievously. 'Male lust has seen better men than Miles make errors of judgement.'

'Well he was certainly leering at me,' she said, settling down onto her chair. 'You think speaking to me was an error of judgement?'

'Don't you? He revealed he was under threat of death to keep a secret.'

'Only because it's a secret I know as well.'

Bill sipped at his wine before replying. 'If the order of conversation went as you describe, he didn't know that when he chose to share it with you.'

'But he did know it was out in the open … after our new Assistant Director produced the report on it.'

'And you think that's what it is, a report?'

'Possibly, or a manual of some kind,' she suggested. 'I think Miles is fairly confident that so many people will know about Al Anfal in the near future that there will be no justification in continuing his exile.'

'And the Service would welcome him back with open arms?'

'I don't really know. But he may well be thinking the more people who know the reason he is in the dungeon, the better. Or he may simply think of me as a temporary friend, to be used or cast to one side depending on what happens.'

Bill pursed his lips as he went quiet for a moment. 'So, why weren't you treated in a similar way? How come you get a promotion while he was shafted?'

'I've been thinking about that too. It was Howard Green who was responsible for warning both of us off, but the strings were pulled within Five. I can only conclude it was somebody very senior, maybe the Director, who mothballed Miles' career? Maybe Miles is so well connected that eliminating him wasn't an option?'

'Don't forget you're talking about the same man who promoted you.'

'I could ask him?'

Bill laughed, and flecks of wine sprayed onto the table. 'Now you're being ridiculous.'

She felt her hackles rise. Sometimes he was just a little bit too blunt.

'It has to be something more than that,' he continued.

'I made a video recording of him that he would rather I hadn't.'

Bill smiled as he seemed to contemplate what she had just said. 'What kind of film?' he asked, slowly and deliberately.

'He was with a prostitute, doing things that, well … you can guess, I'm sure.'

'And he knows you have that recording?'

'He does. It's what we used to get him to tell us about Al Anfal in the first place.'

'We?'

'My old Section Head was with me. He arranged the surveillance that found him out.'

'Christ, Toni, you play a wicked game. It's for certain you won't be on Howard Green's Christmas card list.' Bill supped again at his glass and then lifted the wine bottle in a gesture that suggested they open another.

'No, thanks,' said Toni. 'I need a clear head. I'm meeting early with Nell and Stuart. We're making a start on your ideas about looking at Howard Green in more depth and … Oh hell. I forgot to call Finlay.'

'Something urgent?' said Bill, as he headed off to the kitchen. Despite her abstinence, it looked like he was intent on extending their session.

'He was going to check an address to try and recover the copy of the document that Dyer produced at today's meeting. I'd better ring him now.'

Bill called out something unintelligible as she flicked through the address book on her mobile for Finlay's new number. She pressed the listing, waited for it to connect and listened as the automated response from the service provider told her the recipient phone was turned off.

'Damn,' she said, under her breath. 'I told him to keep it turned on.'

'No joy?' Bill asked, emerging with a fresh bottle of wine. 'Sure you won't?'

Thoughts elsewhere, she shook her head to again decline the offer. 'His phone is turned off,' she replied.

'Complaints have seized it. I thought I told you?'

'You did. If you recall, I said I'd give him a burner to use in the meantime.'

'Ah, sorry, I do remember. Is it one of the new type?'

'The latest,' Toni smiled. 'And he knows about the "help me" facility it has.'

'And the fact that you can use it to follow him?'

'I may have omitted to mention that, Bill.'

He laughed. 'Naughty … but I can't claim to be surprised. Go easy with Finlay won't you? He doesn't talk about it but I can tell you with some certainty that he's still having some issues.'

'I know. I've seen it in his face. He's feeling pressured.'

'The point I'm making is that you ought not to be asking him to do little jobs for MI5 as well as his day job.'

'I'm not,' Toni protested. 'He was doing it for Kevin Jones. We wanted to prevent him trying to sell the Al Anfal document to the newspapers.'

'Could Jones do that?'

'Absolutely not. It would get him killed. Anyway, it's academic now that the Assistant Director has their copy.'

'I suppose so.' Bill topped up his glass again. 'You quite sure you won't?' he asked.

'No, thanks … and you should be taking it easy as well. What if you get a call-out?'

'I'll have a driver come pick me up. Promise me something Toni?'

'What exactly?'

'Don't take any risks. Howard Green wasn't bluffing when he threatened you.'

Toni reached out and squeezed his hand 'I'll be careful,' she said.

Bill smiled but she saw doubt in his eyes. He wasn't reassured.

Chapter 40

MI5 Headquarters, Thames House

The phone was ringing as Toni opened the door to her tiny office. She dropped her bag on the floor near her desk and picked up the receiver.

It was Nell, with a request. Could Toni pop over to New Scotland Yard to see her and Stuart? 'We found something,' was all her researcher would say. No detail.

'This early?' Toni asked. 'I was planning to come over at about nine.'

'How about right away?'

She was just about to reply when the office door sprung open. Suze Bickerton, Department Head at T5B, arms trafficking, leaned in. She looked flustered. 'Long Room, five minutes, Toni. Headshed have called an emergency meeting.'

Toni nodded and Suze headed off along the corridor. Ending the call to Nell with an apology, she explained that things would have to wait. 'Headshed' was a colloquial term to describe the bosses, but it wasn't used that often. In fact, the last time Toni had heard the term used was in the immediate aftermath of 9/11 when the Deputy Director-General herself had addressed a meeting of departmental and section leaders.

Certainly, something was up. Before heading upstairs, she glanced in the mirror, tidied her hair and flicked away a speck of mascara she spotted beneath her left eye. A quick check of her in tray revealed nothing so urgent that might give an indication as to the reason for the meeting.

In the Long Room, the atmosphere was alive with gossip. Toni noticed that Suze Bickerton was standing at the far end on her own. Ignoring the nervous smiles of her peers, she negotiated the narrow gap between the walls and the empty chairs until she was close enough to speak without being overheard.

'What's going on?' she asked, as Suze glanced over her shoulder.

'I've no idea. All I can say is that Mr Dyer rang me and said to get everyone who was at yesterday's meeting up here straight away.'

'Dyer called this? It must be about the poor response he received.'

'That's what I thought. Hey up … he's here.'

Toni turned on her heel towards the door and noticed there were two people waiting outside in the corridor. The room fell quiet as Alex Dyer entered, followed by the Deputy Director-General.

☦

Sometimes, Toni wondered if Stuart could actually function without a mug of tea on the go.

For once, she declined the offer to join him. The tiny listening device that sat nestled between her thumb and forefinger held her full attention.

'Just this one, Nell?'

'Yes … although I would have liked a little longer to conduct a full sweep but *he* said we had to leave.' Nell nodded her head towards where Stuart stood near the kettle.

Toni smiled. The mischievous grin on her researcher's face suggested she was having a little joke at her new supervisor's expense.

'I heard that,' called Stuart. 'Having found what we were looking for I decided discretion got the better of valour.'

A few moments later, all three were huddled together, all eyes on the bug. 'And it's the same manufacturer as the one found at Kevin Jones's house?' Toni asked.

'Same model,' replied Nell.

'But there was nothing else in the house to interest us?'

It was Stuart's turn to speak. 'The forensic teams were thorough … as you'd expect, really. We only found this as we had an idea where to look.'

'Behind the plug sockets?'

'Exactly. Nell found it in one of the main sockets in the living room, near to where PC Jones had collapsed.'

'After taking an overdose that in normal circumstances would have killed him,' said Toni.

'So they say. Although ketamine seems a pretty odd choice and not something you'd expect the average PC to have so readily available.'

'Jones isn't your average PC, Stuart,' Nell interrupted.

'Sure, but you know what I mean,' he replied. 'Ketamine isn't like … like paracetamol or one of the stronger pain killers. It's a horse tranquiliser, from what I've read.'

'It's an anaesthetic,' said Toni. 'And it's becoming popular as a recreational drug. So it's quite possible a cop could have had come into possession of it.'

'Illegally?'

'Yes. I do understand the point you're making, and I also doubt very much if Jones was in the habit of anaesthetising horses, Stuart. So, almost certainly he shouldn't have had it. The question is, did he take it, or did someone pour it down his throat, like Robert Finlay is suggesting? Now let's get back to this bug as it's the best lead we have to help us answer that question.' She held the device up to the light.

'What can we do with it, Nell?'

'This one is working. I may be able to use that to trace the receiver.'

'It's a transmitter?' said Toni, her hopes raised.

'Yes, but before I disconnected it, whoever was listening in could relay it using a mobile device to send the signal anywhere. They wouldn't have needed to be nearby.'

Toni leaned back in her chair, now feeling slightly despondent. 'So, we're really no closer.'

'Unless I can find out who planted it. If I can find a record of some kind?'

'Which we've already tried.'

'There might be a paper record,' Stuart piped up.

'Where though?'

'Like we talked about before, the police stores,' he continued. 'I'd start there as that's where they seem to have come from. Everything goes through them at some point, whatever the source.'

Toni thought for a moment as she weighed up the options. 'OK,' she said. 'Go for it.'

She was just about to continue the conversation when her phone started to vibrate. It was Finlay. She answered and asked him to wait for a moment.

'Sorry guys…'

'We know,' said Nell. 'Time for a break.'

As soon as the office was empty, Toni returned to the call.

'I've been trying to get hold of you,' she said.

'Likewise,' said Finlay. 'I found what I was looking for.'

Toni frowned, hesitant in case she had misheard what he'd said. 'What did you find exactly?'

'Can you speak?'

'Of course. You mean you managed to get into the house?'

'Yes. And I found what I was looking for.'

Toni was perplexed, wondering if she was misunderstanding what he was saying. 'The document Kevin Jones had given him?' she asked, to try and make sure she was hearing him right.

'Yes, yes. Is everything OK, Toni? That is what we agreed I would do.'

'But you can't have.'

'Can't what? What's going on here?' It was Finlay's turn to sound confused.

'You can't have found Kevin's copy of the Al Anfal document,' she explained. 'You can't have. Only yesterday I saw our Assistant Director produce it at a meeting. Special Branch seized it and sent it to us.'

'Well, I'm telling you I have. In fact, it's sitting in my briefcase next to my feet as we speak.'

'So, if that's the case, what was it the Assistant Director waved in front of us and asked us about, if it wasn't the Al Anfal document?'

'Your Assistant Director has another copy?'

'Yes, like I said. And we're told it came from Dr Armstrong's house.'

'What did he say about it?'

'He was asking everyone what we knew about it.'

'What did you say?'

'Nothing. For pretty obvious reasons I kept quiet.'

'Maybe the doctor made a copy?'

'Maybe … I'm really not sure what to think now. But I'm pretty sure it was the genuine article I saw in the Director's hands.'

'What makes you so sure?'

'Because of what happened after the meeting when it was produced.'

'Which was?'

'I met with a colleague who seemed to know something about it. He told me he had been black-balled, passed over for promotion, just because he'd stumbled across the existence of Al Anfal. Yesterday he seemed to be buoyed up because the document – the one we think Kevin left with Dr Armstrong – had fallen into the hands of Special Branch and now isn't such a secret.'

'Did they say if they've had it translated?'

'They didn't, but quite possibly they have, because, with one notable exception, every single person at that meeting was given a warning by our Deputy Director-General not to discuss the document with anyone. And you want to know who the notable exception was? Well, I'll tell you. It was the very same man who told me all he knew. He wasn't there.'

'Where was he?'

'I've no idea, Finlay,' she answered, impatiently.

'You were all warned off – all of you? I would have thought that doing that would have raised everyone's interest, got them talking about it?'

'That's not how things work here, believe me. When a Director-General puts the frighteners on, people stay shtum'

'It's … it's just like last year,' said Finlay, his voice becoming more subdued. 'With Howard Green.'

'Trust me, you're not the only one to notice that his name keeps popping up at the moment.'

'Toni, something has just occurred to me.'

'What?' she asked.

'This document I have sitting at my feet. It has what looks like a complete translation with it.'

'Done by Armstrong?'

'Looks like it.'

'He didn't hang about.'

'That's just what I thought. So, there's another possibility.'

'Go on.'

'That what I have here isn't the copy Kevin gave him. Last year, I agreed with him that the copy I gave him would be destroyed. What if he kept it, what if the one I have here is that one?'

Toni hesitated as she caught her breath. Finlay had to be right. She recalled him saying that he'd not actually seen the document destroyed, despite agreeing that would be its fate.

'Is there any way to tell?' she asked.

'Not that I can think of. Shall I bring it to you?'

'No need. Now that she knows about it, I've decided to ask Nell to give it the once-over. I'm here at the Yard, with her and Stuart so I'll come downstairs to collect it from you. Have you given any thought as to what you're going to tell Kevin?'

'Nothing … at, least not at this stage. To be honest, what does or doesn't happen with this document is the last thing Kevin needs to worry about.'

'How did it go?' Toni asked. 'The entry into the Armstrong house, I mean?'

'Well, I wasn't arrested, if that's what you mean. But I did have visitors. A three-man search team turned up. Thing is, they definitely weren't police. Cops have a way of working and moving. These guys were military by my guess.'

'Were they looking for the same thing as you, do you think? Maybe they weren't aware Special Branch had already found it?'

'No way to be certain, but they were looking for something and they were very thorough.'

'Not thorough enough if you found it, though … Makes you wonder, if they were Security Services, just what else they may have been looking for?'

'Armstrong was still a weapons inspector wasn't he?' Finlay asked.

'I'm not sure. Still on the list, I think. We were told this morning he'd been doing some work on the planned Iraq invasion for the government,' said Toni.

'What kind of work?'

'We weren't told.'

'Perhaps somebody making sure the good Doctor hadn't left anything embarrassing behind?'

'I guess.' Toni wasn't sure though. Once again, the name Howard Green was foremost in her thoughts. And she wondered if – like the Increment soldiers before him – Dr Julian Armstrong had been silenced.

Chapter 41

Toni noticed the post-it note on her desk the instant she opened the door to her office.

'Call me. SB.'

The writing looked rushed.

Sensing there was some urgency to the request she immediately hurried along the corridor, tapped on her colleague's door and opened it.

A very startled Suze Bickerton almost fell from the chair she was standing on while she fiddled with the ceiling light fitting.

'What are you doing?' Toni asked.

Suze pressed a finger to her lips, eased herself down and beckoned Toni to follow her. They headed along the corridor and ran up two flights of stairs. Soon, they were outside the door to the Long Room. Suze eased it open and peered in.

'OK, we'll be fine in here,' she said, between deep breaths.

'Were you checking your office for a bug?' Tony asked.

'As should you. Something's afoot, can't you tell?'

'I don't know … I've only just got back from Scotland Yard. I came the moment I saw your note.'

'Well I can tell you that lecture from the ADG has got everyone on edge.'

'He made himself pretty clear. National Security, reputation of the Service, that kind of thing.'

'Indeed. Look, I left that note because you were asking about Miles Chadbourne before the meeting. I just wondered what your interest in him was.'

'Was? Surely you mean "is"?'

Suze paused and glanced to the now closed Long Room doors. 'Come with me, I want to show you something.'

Again, they took the stairs, but this time headed down. Every so often, Suze glanced behind them and, as they entered the dungeon-floor level, where Miles' office lay, she glanced in both directions along the empty corridor before proceeding.

She's nervous, Toni thought, *but why?*

Outside Miles' office, they stopped. 'After you,' said Suze.

Toni frowned. Was this some kind of set-up? She tried the door. It opened easily.

Into an empty office.

'Christ.'

'My words exactly,' said Suze. 'I came down to find out why Miles hadn't responded to my all-ports warning to attend the Long Room meeting this morning. I figured he must have been late in or something. This is what I found.'

'It's like he was never here,' Toni mumbled.

╬

'Oh, for God's sake.' Toni fumbled hurriedly through her handbag in her effort to locate her phone. It had now rung three times in the last few minutes.

At first, she'd ignored it, needing some time to herself to think through the implications of what she and Suze Bickerton had seen.

Others had to be aware, of that there was no doubt – colleagues that Miles had worked with in the past; some of whom had been his friends, and all of whom would have noticed his absence from the meeting. But if they all knew he wasn't around, why was nobody saying anything? Nobody was trusted, so nobody asked … nobody was that brave, or that foolish.

The ADG's warning had therefore had the desired effect. They were all afraid – afraid of the unknown, afraid that whatever had happened to Miles could happen to them too. Suze had been curious to know why Toni had been asking about Miles. She seemed to accept the explanation that Toni had simply felt sorry for him, and that, as a newcomer to the supervisory ranks, she'd seen Miles as possibly receptive to a friendly voice.

The phone went silent just as her fingers wrapped around it.

'Why does that always happen?' she muttered to herself as she read the screen: caller identity withheld.

Slipping the phone back into her bag, she glanced up and down the street. It was busy with cars, vans and people on foot, all going about their daily business. She found herself scanning the faces, looking for anyone familiar or even the slightest indication she was being followed. She'd come out for some fresh air, to the same small square where she'd recently met up with Finlay. Here she could be alone with her thoughts; at least the watchers hadn't mastered how to read those, she mused.

She stopped herself. 'Get a grip, Toni,' she said, quietly. Miles' disappearance had rattled her. Even though it wasn't particularly unusual for an officer to move at very short notice, the fact that it had happened the very day after they had been talking about Al Anfal meant she now needed to be very cautious.

Above the sound of the fountain, she once more caught the sound of her ring tone. It was Nell. She sounded excited.

'I've found which stores the listening device was issued to. It was CIB, the police complaints unit.'

'That's really great, Nell, thanks. But couldn't that have waited until tomorrow?'

'Ah, sorry. But that wasn't the main reason I called. Have you heard the news?'

'Prime Minister Blair has resigned?' Toni said, a little flippantly, immediately regretting her words and the fact that her researcher wouldn't be likely to see the joke.

'Er … no. Has he?' said Nell.

'Probably not, Nell. I'm out at the moment, should I ring you from the office?'

'No need. It's nothing Service related. I just thought you'd want to know there's been a breakout from Barkingside Magistrates' Court this morning. It's just come through on the wire and the news channels are already onto it. Kevin Jones has escaped from custody.'

Chapter 42

'Is that Robert Finlay?'

The voice on the telephone was familiar but I couldn't place it. I was still transfixed by what I was watching on the television in the main

Anti-Terrorist Squad office. Bill Grahamslaw had called me up there to watch the coverage being transmitted from Barkingside. And he wanted me in his private office immediately afterwards.

I wasn't surprised he'd summoned me upstairs, given the subject matter. It was live from the local Magistrates' Court where armed men were said to have helped the escape of a defendant who had been appearing to face a charge of murder. The reporter, quoting a reliable source, was saying that the escaped suspect was a police officer.

It was Kevin, of that I had no doubt. I racked my brains to see if he'd given me any clue that this had been about to happen. He'd said the solicitor I'd seen him with had 'everything in hand' – perhaps that was it. I also thought about his kit, still safely hidden beneath his allotment shed. I'd assumed he'd asked me to move it simply to prevent it being discovered. I now wondered if he'd known all along what was going to happen and if he might attempt contact to try and recover it.

A departmental telephone had interrupted our viewing. The detective who'd answered it had called across that they were asking for me personally.

'Who is this?' I asked.

'It's Sue Corfield, guv. Do you feel ready to save a life today?'

✝

Ten minutes after receiving the call, I was once again in the back of a police traffic car, sirens and blue lights on, headed north. Grahamslaw had agreed to postpone our talk, on the solemn promise he was the first person I'd come to see on my return. Once again, I was on my way to Kentish Town.

This time I was heading to a section house – an accommodation tower block immediately adjacent to the main police building, where single officers lived in individual rooms. I'd lived in a similar one myself. MacNaghton House it had been called, situated just south of Euston, where it provided very convenient housing for officers, new out of training school, who were posted to the nearby areas of Holborn, Tottenham Court Road and Kings Cross.

Sue had given me a very quick briefing on what I was facing. It was Doug Powell again, the very same PC I had spent an hour with in the police station toilets. Apparently he had turned up at the front counter to the police station in a distressed state, asking to speak to John Southern, the Chief Superintendent.

Southern hadn't been available, and before anyone had realised what was happening, Doug had run off. A few minutes later, the warden from the section house next door had dialled 999 to report someone standing out on the top-floor ledge.

The local duty officer was, apparently, talking to him, so far without persuading him to climb back to safety. The crisis negotiation team had been contacted and, as soon as they realised who the 'jumper' was, they'd made the immediate decision to call me.

From my limited view in the back of the traffic car, everything appeared a blur as we sped past. I was long enough in the tooth not to experience the adrenalin rush my first experiences of 'blues and twos' shouts had triggered, but I still enjoyed the thrill of racing along the London streets in the safe hands of one of the best drivers the Met had to offer. Faces turned to watch us, follow our progress for a moment and then turn away as, seconds later, they were left behind.

Once in a while, I caught our reflection in a shop window and saw my own pale face staring out from the rear of the police car. I looked isolated, lonely. The image brought to mind the face of another man, the tortured soul depicted in *The Scream*, the haunting figure created by Edvard Munch so many years previously, and I worried whether I was up to what was being asked of me. I worried that my preoccupation with Kevin's situation would distract me, and I worried I might lose focus, let my colleagues down, and that a young man might die because I'd failed him.

✝

Camden Town tube station appeared.

'Nearly there, guv,' said the PC in the front passenger seat, bringing my thoughts back to the here and now. He was the radio operator and acted as a second set of eyes to the driver. Probably as highly trained as his colleague, it was his turn to 'ride shotgun'.

'Can you kill the siren, please lads?' I said, straining to be heard above the din.

As the electronic wailing stopped, I told myself to relax. I wanted to get to the scene as quickly as possible, but I didn't want to turn up like Jack Regan in a scene from *The Sweeney*. A silent approach, even if it cost us a few seconds, was infinitely preferable to startling a nervous man stood on a ledge and then causing him to either make a decision I was going to try and talk him out of, or worse still, to have him distracted to a point where he lost his footing and slipped.

'Can you find out which side of the building he's standing on?' I asked.

A moment later, the reply came over the radio. West side, overlooking the yard to the police station. That was good news. It meant we could approach from the High Street and our arrival would be concealed by the building. And, it also meant the local press would find it harder to find a vantage point from where they could watch what was happening.

As we slowed to a halt, I saw that blue-and-white tape had been strung across Holmes Road, the side street that gave access to both the police station and section house. On one corner, a McDonald's restaurant looked to have been closed to allow the area to be cordoned off.

Two PCs, posted at the junction, raised the tape so we could get through. I estimated that only thirty to forty minutes could have passed since the 999 call had been made to alert police. Already, the street was chock-a-block with parked response vehicles including a 'forward control' van, complete with satellite phones and a small briefing room, a fire engine and ambulance.

As we came to a halt and I stepped out onto the street, two senior

officers in yellow reflective jackets approached me. I recognised both
and remembered the name of the most senior, John Southern.

Their greeting was friendly – I might even describe it as warm – but
there was no denying the sombreness of the moment and the looks of
concern on both men's faces. I followed them through the foyer of the
section house and into the lift.

My briefing started as soon as the door closed.

'Local uniform inspector has established dialogue and is still talking
to the PC,' said Southern. He asked if I recalled much about him. I said
that I did, everything, including his name – Doug Powell.

'Good. He's out on the ledge which is concrete and about eight
inches in depth. There's a breeze but, at the moment, it's not so bad that
we fear him being blown off. But he's very distressed and, from what
we've managed to glean so far, this is not a cry for help.'

'Did he ask for me again?' I asked.

'No, not this time. He actually asked for Superintendent Mellor from
the Complaints Unit.'

'Did you contact Mr Mellor?'

'We didn't. Mike Rogers is leading the negotiation again and he
was of the opinion that PC Powell might hold Superintendent Mellor
responsible and be intending to commit suicide in a way that shows
him he is the cause.'

'I think I agree with him.'

As the lift doors opened at the top floor, we were met by Peter Hesp,
the technician from the negotiation team who I'd first shown the listening device Kevin had found in his home.

'We meet again, Inspector,' he whispered as he continued to roll out
a length of cable along the corridor. 'Third door on the left for Mike.
Radios off please gents, and no talking in the corridor.'

As we moved silently to the small room where Mike, the Negotiation Coordinator would be waiting for us, I realised I could actually feel
my heart beating in my chest. I clenched my fists, stroking my palms
with the tips of my fingers. My hands were damp with sweat. I felt completely out of my depth and afraid. Somewhere near me, a young man

was standing outside with the serious intention of ending his life. And I was going to be expected to talk to him and to try and persuade him not to.

And I didn't have the first idea how I was going to do that.

Chapter 43

'When someone jumps from a high building, it's very public. We find that most times we get a trained negotiator to them before they decide to leap, we get them down safely.'

I knew Mike Rogers was doing his level best to reassure me, but the very moment he used the word 'trained' he may as well not have bothered.

'So why not use someone more experienced?' I demanded, as the harness Mike was attaching to my waist was pulled tight.

'Feel OK?' he asked. I nodded, and he continued. 'We are. The Inspector out there at this very moment did his training course a couple of years ago. But you'll maybe remember that we use every tool in our armoury to bring about a successful resolution. And my call is that Doug Powell will respond well to your appearance.'

'He asked for Mellor though, not me.'

'Like I said a moment ago, Mellor is the person he holds responsible for the fact that he wants to end it. Getting Mellor here is intended to punish him, to make him watch the result.'

'So, what do I say if he gets angry because you've sent me instead?'

'I don't think he will. And, if he does, remember what you were taught...'

'I can't remember any of it just now. My mind is a blank.'

'Trust me, that's very normal. These things aren't scripted so you just have to play it by ear. Just remember – dignity and respect. Doug doesn't want to die, he wants to end the pain that his life is currently causing him. Your job is to persuade him there's an alternative to death as a way of doing that.'

'Talk as if it were *your* life depending on it, Finlay,' said Southern.

I turned to him, but the best I could manage in response to the helpful suggestion was a half-smile that wouldn't have filled anyone with confidence.

'What Mike says is right,' he added. 'If Doug Powell was set on killing himself, all he would have needed to do was jump off. He's up here because he wants to be talked out of it, I believe. And, for what it's worth, I completely agree with the decision to call you in to help.'

I thought back to both courses I'd attended. In over twenty years I'd only ever been present at two negotiations – the previous one with Doug Powell and as an observer with Max Vernon – the lead police negotiator at the Iranian Embassy siege in 1980. I'd learned more from watching Vernon in real life than I'd taken in during any of the mock-ups the training staff on the course had prepared for us. And even now, I had serious doubts as to whether I would have been able to have done what he did.

But, despite those thoughts, I knew my two colleagues were right. And ten minutes later I found myself standing just behind the local Inspector Mike had referred to, as he pulled away from a large sliding window to allow me access to the ledge. I'd waited as he spoke to Doug Powell, informed him of my presence and sought agreement for me to enter the conversation. The last thing he would want to do was to surprise Doug when he was in such a precarious place, both physically and emotionally. In my right ear, discreetly hidden from Doug Powell, nestled my communication link to the negotiation room, where I knew they would be listening to every word Doug and I were about to say to each other. Around my chest I now wore an abseiling harness with a strong rope that had been secured to a form of brace which sat nestled in the hands of two burly SO19 firearms officers at the back of the room. Their job was to make sure I didn't fall. I lifted the rope, pulled on it gently and was about to step outside onto the ledge when I saw one of the SO19 lads wink.

Bastard, I thought, *easy for you.*

Don't look down, I told myself as I called out through the open window. 'Doug, it's Bob Finlay. I'm here to help.'

✝

I'd given a lot of thought as to what my first words were going to be, my opening gambit, the fail-safe, guaranteed conversation-instigator that would persuade a man on the verge of suicide that I was worth spending his last moments on earth talking to.

Nature took over. I looked down, felt giddy and reached out quickly to hold onto the window frame.

'Sorry, mate,' I said. 'I've never been much good with heights.'

Doug laughed. 'Jesus. I would have thought you the last person to suffer vertigo.'

I grinned, doing my best to mask the sense of panic I was experiencing and the almost irresistible urge to step back into the room, to terra firma, to safety.

And then it sank in, Doug had laughed. And if he could laugh, he could live.

Chapter 44

John Southern offered to arrange a lift back to the Yard for me, but I declined. I needed a walk. The Chief Superintendent didn't press me. I had a feeling, a sense that everyone present was aware of how it felt, that first time you fear a momentary error in something you do or say is going to rob a family of their father.

Mike Rogers, of course, had been through it many times. And, although we'd secured the result we wanted, as Doug Powell was led away to safety, he'd suggested I take a few minutes to myself.

I did as he suggested. An adjacent room was open. I closed the door behind me and, as my legs seemed incapable of supporting me for much longer, I sat down on the edge of the bed. Only then did the emotion of the previous hour begin to hit me. Fortunately, as I stared through the window at the cloudless sky, the door opened behind me and someone shoved a tea into my hand. I took just one sip, and then gripped the mug between my hands in a vain attempt to stop my hands from trembling.

'It's the adrenalin, Bob,' came a voice from behind me. It was Mike.

I went to reply, but stopped myself as tears welled up in my eyes.

'I hope you like sugar in your tea,' he continued. 'Just take your time and when you're ready we'll need to do a post-incident chat.'

A hand rested on my shoulder, reassuring, comforting. 'Just remember … any job that gets them down alive is a success.'

I nodded, and, as the emotions began to ease off, I continued to stare at the sky.

Mike was right, and by the time I had finished the tea, the strength was returning to my limbs. But time had pressed on, and by the time we finished the debrief it was the late-afternoon rush hour and I knew the tube system was going to be experiencing the daily commuter crush.

Before leaving the police station, I rang Jenny. I needed to hear the reassuring comfort of her voice.

'Is he going to be OK?' she asked, after I'd explained what had happened.

'I think so. I promised to speak to the Complaints Unit Commander to see what can be done to help him. He needs help rather than having to face a disciplinary board.'

'You don't think the police will prosecute him then?'

'I would hope not. He's ill, and he needs help.'

It was time to head back to the Yard to see what Grahamslaw wanted and after that, home. I promised Jenny I'd be on my way as soon as the rush hour period had died down. That would give me time to get back to New Scotland Yard, pick up my stuff and then catch a quieter train. She said dinner and a beer would be waiting for me. She reckoned I deserved it.

As I'd been talking to Doug, I'd spent some time looking out across the London skyline. I'd remembered the back streets of Kentish Town and the walk through Chalk Farm and Camden through to Regent's Park. I'd not done it in a very long time, since the days when, as a uniform PC, I'd patrolled those streets on foot and then in a panda car.

Now seemed like a good time to walk that route again. I sought out John Southern, found him in his office, said my farewells and then headed west along Holmes Road. Soon the hum of traffic began to fade into the distance. Just the once I stopped and glanced back, to look at the section house, high above the police station, now deserted and showing no sign at all of what had been happening that afternoon. I wondered where Doug Powell was now. I hoped, prayed, that he was being treated sympathetically. If it was left to John Southern, I had every confidence that would be the case. But sometimes, even the powers of a Divisional Commander were limited. A sense of foreboding took hold of me as I remembered my final words to Doug – 'That's a promise, mate, whatever it takes' – and I repeated them under my breath as a reminder to keep my word. But I also remembered Mike's words as I'd first stepped out onto the ledge – 'Just get him down' – I wondered if I'd just achieved a temporary fix, a life saved but a man still with his future uncertain. And, I wondered if I truly had the power to deliver on my promise.

Avoiding the main roads, I made steady progress and was soon at the north-east entrance to Regent's Park near London Zoo. Commuters in their hundreds were heading towards the Camden tube stations and waiting for buses held up in the traffic. One or two looked at me, but only in passing. None would have even the vaguest concept of what I had been doing less than an hour previously.

As the park opened out before me, I saw fewer people. I walked briskly, enjoying the sensation of freedom and the opportunity to be alone with my thoughts. Worries about Doug Powell were soon displaced by recent memories and more pressing needs. It was here, near the wolf enclosure, that I'd last seen Nial Monaghan, my former Commanding Officer in the SAS. Monaghan was a man I had once called 'friend' and yet he had turned out to be an instrument of the chaos, death and destruction that had so unexpectedly come back to wreck any hope I'd had of a simple life with my family.

Howard Green had been behind that murderous campaign. Howard Green had tasked Monaghan with making sure nobody talked about the highly secretive Al Anfal organisation, about the coordinated and very long-term plan to infiltrate and undermine governments throughout Europe, the Middle East and Africa. I had no doubt that Kevin and I were only alive as Green had believed us both to be in ignorance of Al Anfal. And now, I wondered if that had changed.

I sat down on a bench and stared back in the direction from whence I had walked. A tall man in a dark wind-cheater caught my eye and, for a moment, I felt a hollow sensation of fear. But then he turned off without so much as a sideways glance and headed south along the tarmac path towards Euston Road and the exit from the park. I watched him go, and I smiled to myself at the reason for my insecurity. It was the way he walked, the steady, rhythmic movement of his legs that was more akin to a march than an amble. He moved like a soldier, or more likely a former soldier, long since retired, but still retaining that walk, the way ex-soldiers often do, just like the men I'd seen at the Armstrong home.

That reminder sent my thoughts back to what I had seen in Wales just the previous day. Julian Armstrong, weapons specialist and member of the Defence Intelligence Staff was dead, apparently at his own hand. To some extent, I understood why Armstrong may have wanted his life to end. I recalled with sadness the day I'd visited him and the way he had talked so lovingly of his late wife, and I recalled seeing the plethora of photographs of her he kept in his home, a number that had greatly increased by the time of my second visit. And I wondered if the document I had found was what the others I'd seen had actually been looking for.

None of which was going to help my most pressing problem. Finding and helping Kevin.

Chapter 45

'Nell?' Toni called across the office.

Her researcher rolled her chair away from her work station, stood and arched her back. It had been a long afternoon.

'Are you quite sure this can't be monitored?' Toni asked, the scepticism in her voice clear.

Nell smiled nonchalantly. 'Only if things have moved on considerably since I last checked … about an hour ago. So long as we stay on the dark web and keep off the intranet, we'll be below the Service radar.'

Toni nodded. 'So, how exactly does this "dark web" stop us from being caught Googling the name of the document?'

Nell laughed. 'Mostly because you don't use Google. You get to the dark web by using one of the web browsers that can access it. I'm using one called TOR. The original one was called the Onion Router but TOR, the third-generation Onion Router came out last month.'

'It's something hackers use then?'

'I guess they might, but they didn't design it. It was created during the nineties by the US Naval Research Laboratory to protect their online intelligence communication.'

'It's a US government programme?'

'It was. It leaked out into the cyber world, got adapted and improved, and now virtually anyone can use it.'

'How does it work?'

'It encrypts and then randomly transmits a signal through a network of relays around the world. These are called onion routers and they employ further encryption in a multi-layered…'

Toni instantly regretted asking the question as Nell launched in to the technical detail of what she knew. Interruption seemed the best option to stop her in full flight.

'Hence the name Onion Router,' Toni said. 'I get the picture. Did you get any further with identifying where that bug came from?'

'The Complaints Branch store isn't computerised, but I'm on it, trust me. And the dark web isn't just emailing and chat rooms, you know. You can buy virtually anything on the auction sites.'

'Anything?'

'You name it. You can buy drugs, stolen property, sex … whatever you want.'

'And what about the sellers? Surely they're exposing themselves?'

'That's the beauty of it. As a seller you're completely anonymous.'

'A pity the Increment soldiers didn't know about it then. They could have sold the documents without anyone ever knowing it was them.'

'I've finished reading Finlay's translation of the document,' Nell said.

'Already? So, what do you think?'

'I think it's the real deal. Do you recall the Europol raid a little while ago on Yousef Nada's villa – the banker Swiss police were targeting for money-laundering? That seems to have only produced a strategy document. This Al Anfal thing is far more comprehensive.'

Toni did remember what Nell was referring to. 'Yes,' she replied. 'The document they found was called "The Project", wasn't it?'

'Correct.'

'So do you think this might also be a Muslim Brotherhood document?'

'It might be,' said Nell. 'And, if it's genuine, we have in our possession the detailed plans and objectives of Al Q'aeda, Hamas, the Muslim Brotherhood and any number of other extremist groups. We know their leaders, their operators, how to identify their agents. Perhaps even more important than that, we know their goals, their strategies and have a better understanding of their timelines.'

'So, it is the kind of thing that would be kept very secret indeed?'

'Golly, yes, and to be honest, it reads something like the old IRA *Green Book*, only in much more depth.'

'Their volunteer instruction manual?'

'Yes. But the *Green Book* was much more than just a manual. It was a philosophy … a plan. This Al Anfal document is the same kind of thing, and it's the first indication we've seen that there is now an organisation in the background effectively coordinating many of the extremist groups in the Middle East.'

'A frightening possibility.'

'Indeed,' said Nell. 'Is this what Stuart is looking into as well?'

Toni paused before replying. 'Sort of,' she replied, finally. 'I'm having him follow up on something that might be relevant.'

'Anyone who was connected to this seems to have ended up dead.'

'It looks that way doesn't it?' said Toni.

'Killed to keep them from talking…' said Nell, '…presumably by those who wanted knowledge of Al Anfal kept secret.'

'Which puts us in a very difficult position, doesn't it?'

'Only if it comes out that we know. What if it were no longer secret? We could leak it ourselves?'

For a moment, Toni thought her researcher was serious. 'To the newspapers?' she asked. 'Are you serious?'

Nell shrugged in response. 'It would solve a problem. At the moment, anyone who knows about this is a target to be silenced. Does this have anything to do with the checks I'm doing on Howard Green?'

'Possibly. Have you found anything juicy?'

'Not so far. But Al Anfal isn't such a secret now, after what happened?'

'Everyone at the Long Room meeting heard about it.'

'But none of them have any idea as to its content. If they knew that…'

'Miles Chadbourne had an idea, and now he's disappeared.'

Nell didn't reply. She didn't need to. They both understood the possibilities. As the telephone on the desk in front of Toni began ringing, she picked it up. It was Stuart.

'Can you speak?' he asked.

'Yes. There's only me and Nell here.'

'OK, I'll be quick. First thing, I bumped into a mate of mine from the lab who works on firearms forensics. We got chatting about the PC who's escaped custody.'

'Learn anything useful?' said Toni.

'Not about the escape, no. But I thought you said they'd tied a gun found in the PC's car to another murder?'

'No, I said they were hoping to. Finlay's claim is that Jones is being stitched up and that if the gun found in the boot of his car is the murder weapon used to kill the drug dealer then that would prove it. And he reckoned that to think Jones would put the gun back there rather than using it to shoot himself was just plain daft – I tend to agree with him.'

'OK, well, I guess I got the wrong end of the stick. Anyway, I thought you'd like to know that the Glock they found hasn't been tested yet. The lab has such a backlog of work that it's not likely to be looked at for a week or so.'

Mellor was bluffing, Toni mused; he didn't yet have any evidence. 'How did you get on with the vice squad?' she asked.

'I'm there now. I thought you'd want to know straight away. No arrests or cautions recorded for Martina Proctor since that day we saw her performing on the roof with Howard Green.'

Toni ended the call with a warning to Stuart not to mention what he had learned to anyone. As she replaced the receiver, Nell interrupted her thoughts.

'You think Green's prostitute was another victim?'

Toni allowed herself a smile. Nell was always ahead of everyone else.

'I'm not sure, Nell,' she replied. 'Like I said, I'm just checking.'

'It's just like *I* said: anybody connected with this ends up dead.'

Chapter 46

New Scotland Yard

'He's back. They're bringing him up the stairs.'

Grahamslaw scowled. There were aspects to this job that he hated and this was one of them. As Mellor returned his mobile phone to his jacket pocket, the Commander caught a momentary look of satisfaction on the Superintendent's face.

Bastard's enjoying this, Grahamslaw thought.

With command comes responsibility. With responsibility comes duty, a duty to do what's right, no matter how distasteful or how uncomfortable you may consider that to be. He remembered those words from his Senior Command Course at Bramshill Police College and he recalled the young man who had spoken them. They were delivered in the context of a lecture on leadership, and the young man who spoke them had been an army officer, a veteran of the Iraq War, who had been recounting his experiences of sending young soldiers into situations where they might be killed. Not that Finlay was going to suffer such a fate, but the next few minutes might easily decide his future in the police, and possibly even his liberty.

Mellor wanted to interview Finlay about the escape of his mate from custody, and he wanted to catch him off guard. It went against many of the safeguards that rank-and-file cops expected to be allowed when they were to be interviewed about their suspected involvement in a crime. But he understood Mellor's reasoning, even if he didn't necessarily agree with his methods.

Two men, both masked and wearing identical grey boiler suits, had entered the court room as Jones had been produced from the underground cells to appear before a District Judge. The men had thrown several smoke canisters around the building and, in the resulting confusion, had overpowered several guards, together with a number of uniform and plain-clothes officers who had been in the court room and in nearby corridors. As the escaping group had exited the building, any potential pursuit had been effectively prevented when the officers giving chase had been threatened with handguns.

Grahamslaw had grown to like Finlay, and he trusted him, but only in so far as he knew the Inspector to be honest. The former soldier's predisposition to bend the rules and occasionally act outside the law in pursuit of justice was something that had made him difficult to predict. Mellor claimed to have circumstantial evidence Finlay was involved in the breakout and, the Commander had to accept, the slick operation was exactly the kind of thing the former soldier would have been capable of organising.

The escape was already the subject of an official press release and was all over the news channels. One intrepid member of the public had even managed to record the fleeing men on her mobile telephone, although the detail was poor. What hadn't been mentioned to the press was what had happened afterwards, when the resources of the Met should have been utilised in its effort to apprehend the escapees. Local radio traffic and telephones had, inexplicably, gone down. For several vital minutes people in the court, the next-door police station and officers in radio contact nearby had been frustrated in their attempts to alert others as to what had happened. By the time communication came back online, the van used by the gang had disappeared.

And all this had happened just forty-eight hours after Robert Finlay had been logged as a visitor to the court cells before Jones had been produced before the Judge for an authority to extend his detention. Finlay had disobeyed an order from a senior officer – Mellor – that Grahamslaw had heard himself. Stay away from the enquiry, Mellor had said. He couldn't have made it clearer. And Finlay had fully understood, of that there was no doubt.

So, yes, Mellor was right when he said there was circumstantial evidence and some questions that needed asking.

Finlay was in the shit, the only unanswered question was how deep.

†

'I'll answer your bloody questions when you tell me what you're going to do about Doug Powell.'

Grahamslaw saw Finlay's hands clench into tight fists and, for a second, he thought the Inspector was about to hit his interrogator. 'OK, OK,' he said, trying to ease the tension. 'I think we should all take a moment to calm down.'

The moment Finlay had appeared in the doorway with Mellor's Sergeant close behind, Grahamslaw sensed the Inspector was spoiling for an argument. Mellor had requested the interview but it was soon apparent that Finlay was as keen to speak to his accuser as the Superintendent was to him. All that differed was their agenda.

Mellor got in first. But what followed was more akin to a verbal jousting match than an interview. And then, when Mellor laughed in response to Finlay revealing his promise to speak to the Superintendent about Doug Powell's mental health, any hope of an effective interrogation about the court breakout went swiftly out of the window. Mellor asked his questions – 'Why visit the cells? Why disobey my order? What did you know about the escape plan?' – but Finlay was not at all interested in that topic and refused to engage.

But Mellor hadn't finished. 'The trouble with all you ex-squaddies is you think the world owes you a favour...'

'Enough!' It was time to call a halt to this debacle, Grahamslaw decided. The room fell silent. The Commander waited for a moment, until he was certain that order was restored, then spoke again.

'Thank you,' he continued. 'Now let's all remember who and where we are. Everyone here, regardless of their role in this interview is entitled to be treated with respect, is that clear?'

Finlay nodded and then stared hard at the scowling face of Jim Mellor.

'Very well,' said the Superintendent.

Mellor's Sergeant looked up from where he had been making notes on a pad. 'You OK, Mr Finlay?' he asked.

Good cop, bad cop, the Commander mused. Sergeant shows sympathy for the apparent overzealousness of his senior officer. Different tack, both equally deadly.

'Can I just say something?' said Finlay, his voice now calm.

Mellor raised his open hands, as if in defeat and frustration at the impossibility of his task. Grahamslaw simply nodded in response.

'See that paper on the desk there?' the Inspector continued, pointing to the evening newspaper sitting on the Commander's desk. 'See the headlines? It's about troop deployments and weapons of mass destruction that the Iraqis apparently have access to.'

'What's that got to do with here and now?' Mellor demanded.

'It's about cause and effect, sir.' Finlay seemed to have regained his composure, although Grahamslaw could still sense an underlying anger.

The Commander picked up the newspaper. There was a report from the Defence Intelligence Committee headlined as Finlay described. 'Do go on, Finlay,' he added, calmly.

'When I read headlines like that I see things between my eyes and the page that you could never imagine. Smells return to my nostrils, of dusty heat, the fresh blood of my fellow men and of burning cordite, and I hear as clear as if I were there, the rattle of gunfire and the crash of explosions. I hear the curses of men who are in fear for their lives and of others, who scream through injury or as they struggle to take command. This suburban life that we live here and now … it bears no comparison.'

'I repeat … what has that to do with us?' said Mellor.

'As you damn well know,' Finlay continued, 'I've just come back from talking Doug Powell out of throwing himself to his death. I'm not the best negotiator the Met will ever have, but the team called me because they understand, unlike you, that Powell has seen similar things to me. They asked me to talk to him because they knew he would relate to me and that I would understand where he was coming from.'

'And you did a great job, of that there's no doubt. But set that aside, we need to talk about some very serious crimes and the evidence that links you to them.'

Finlay didn't register Mellor's comment and, if he did, he didn't waver from the point he appeared determined to make. 'You might want to try living Powell's life, Superintendent Mellor,' he continued. 'When you try to sleep you can't. You have nightmares, repeated dreams, waking you up every night in a cold sweat. Just try it. Lack of sleep makes you irritable, angry. You get flashbacks. What that man saw in Northern Ireland is beyond the comprehension of everyday people. Then, in the light of that experience, just ask yourself how you would have reacted to having your uniform torn off so a group of people who you thought to be your friends could station-stamp the cheeks of your arse. I'll tell you how Powell felt … humiliated, in danger, under attack. He needs help, not prosecution.'

'It was a wind-up. If he couldn't take it, he should never have joined.'

'I think you're missing Mr Finlay's point, Jim,' said Grahamslaw. 'He's suggesting PC Powell needs help, not dragging through the courts.'

'And I think we need to get back to why I'm here – to ask Mr Finlay about his involvement in the escape of PC Kevin Jones from lawful custody.'

'It had nothing to do with me,' spat Finlay.

Mellor took an exaggerated deep breath. 'Finally, the Inspector answers. So, what were you doing disobeying a lawful order not to visit Jones?'

'With respect, sir. You ordered me not to get involved in your enquiry. I went to see a friend to offer to arrange for him to get good legal help.'

Grahamslaw replayed the conversation through in his mind, as he imagined that at the very same moment, Mellor was doing the same.

'Don't get clever with me, Finlay,' Mellor replied. 'You knew very well what I meant when I gave you that order.'

'If you meant something other than the words you used—'

'Bollocks. And if you continue to take the piss then, mark my words, you'll bloody regret it. Now, let's move on to what you said.'

The sergeant taking notes coughed, as if wanting to say something. Mellor turned toward him and glared. He was silent for several seconds before saying quietly, 'Maybe time for a formal caution, sir. If we're to ask further questions about—'

'Fuck that,' said Mellor. 'I just want answers.' He turned to face Finlay again. 'If you want a brief and we have to put this to you again then so be it. Just tell me what you and Jones talked about.'

Finlay shrugged. 'Like I said, we talked about him needing a good lawyer. He told me it was all in place and there was a solicitor with him when I arrived.'

'What did he tell you about the plan to escape?'

'Nothing.'

'Did you arrange it?'

'No, it came as a complete surprise to me. And, for what it's worth, I think he is crazy to have gone on the run.'

'What makes you say that?'

'Because of what happened. Your case is that he killed Sandi either deliberately or accidentally and then tried to kill himself using ketamine.'

'And you've got a different theory?'

'You found a gun in Kevin's car...'

'Who the hell told you that?'

Finlay ignored the question. 'So why take a drug that would lead to a slow death rather than use the pistol?' he demanded. 'If he knew it was there then he'd surely have used it on himself. I've been in that dark place myself and, believe me, us blokes don't take pills, we're too impulsive. Taking pills requires planning and thought. Kevin didn't have a lot of that, especially as he knew Sandi's two sons would be home from school that afternoon.'

'That's more bollocks. If he was expecting them home why was he having sex with his girlfriend in the bedroom? He knew the gun was there and he took enough ketamine to send himself to sleep very quickly. Maybe he wanted to avoid making a mess?'

'It still doesn't make sense.'

'It does to me. Jones and his girlfriend meet up for a little fun which involved using the ketamine. She was a nurse and according to enquiries I've made at the hospital where she worked, she could have got hold of it there. Anyway, something goes wrong during their afternoon session. Maybe an accident, maybe Jones lost his temper over something, I don't know. But what I do think is he killed her and then tried to kill himself.'

'He told me somebody jumped him when he arrived at the house and that he never made it to the bedroom.'

'He spun us that load of pony as well,' Mellor replied, dismissively. 'But we found forensics that questions that version. And, come on now, how many juries do you think would swallow a story like that? Somebody breaks in to the house, kills the girlfriend and then pours drugs down the boyfriend's throat. Bloody fantasy...'

'Unless it was true?' said Finlay.

Mellor didn't respond. The Sergeant had now stopped making notes and was fidgeting awkwardly in his seat.

And Grahamslaw remembered Toni, that mind map, and the man whose name lay at its hub. And he wondered.

Chapter 47

A considerable time passed before I noticed the rain on my face.

I felt numb as I stared up at the faceless windows of New Scotland Yard and, as I stood silently, I reflected on what I feared might be the last time I would walk the corridors of the best-known police headquarters in the world. To my left, the familiar revolving sign that had been in place for more years than I cared to recall now taunted me. One face had been changed to show the words 'Working together for a safer London'. What had just happened to me didn't feel much like togetherness.

The meeting with Mellor had started just as I'd hoped for and, in many ways, exactly as I had rehearsed on the walk back into central London. But then, as things had become increasingly heated, the Superintendent had abruptly ended the interview by demanding I hand over my warrant card. He had then pushed a form that I had no opportunity to read into the top pocket of my jacket and ordered his Sergeant to escort me from the building. That I hadn't expected. I had been allowed just one concession – to return to the trafficking office and collect some personal things from my desk. That proved to be something of a poisoned chalice as I'd suffered the shame of bumping into Nina Brasov, who was heading to the gym. Nina had started to chat to me only for the Complaints Unit Sergeant to cut her dead by telling her I'd been suspended from duty and was in the process of being ejected from the building.

Nina was embarrassed, and I felt humiliated, like a naughty schoolboy about to be expelled from class, his friends watching on with a sense of both disbelief and amazement at what they were witnessing. I also felt a growing sense of injustice and anger at Mellor and his bigoted view on Kevin Jones's guilt. Despite my pointing out aspects of the case that should have made any detective doubtful, this particular investigator seemed far more interested in building a case than getting to the truth.

I touched the breast pocket of my jacket and, alongside Mellor's scrunched-up form, I felt the reassuring presence of the burner phone. I pulled it out, checked the screen and saw that the record voice application was still running. I was lucky Mellor hadn't spotted it as he pushed what I now saw was a formal notice of my suspension, into my pocket. I glanced around, fearful of being watched and then, carefully, I switched the device off. Slipping the phone back into my side pocket, I smiled and then gave it a warm pat. Sometimes, I thought, even the simplest things can bring you comfort. Now secure, I just hoped what the phone contained might soon help Kevin's case.

As I headed to St James's Park tube station, I ran through Mellor's words again, wondering if he had a point. He was right, of course. Kevin's claim did seem almost too fantastic to be true.

Heading towards the down escalator, I came across a familiar face on duty at the ticket barrier. A man who seemed to really enjoy his job, I had often exchanged a few words with the guard who now made to wave me through and onto the platform. This time though, as I automatically reached for the warrant card that would allow me free travel on the underground train system, I was reminded that I no longer had that privilege. I was suspended, my ID was in a Complaints Sergeant's briefcase and I would have to pay for a ticket.

'Forgot my card,' I mumbled, apologetically.

'No worries, mate,' he answered. 'Go on through, I'll vouch for you.'

I hesitated, and thought better of taking him up on the offer. It would be just my luck that this would be the very evening I'd run into a ticket inspector on the journey or at my destination when I left the train. Then, any plea for clemency due to a forgotten warrant card would likely as not fall on deaf ears and I would be fined. Far easier, I thought, to buy a ticket.

Far easier, of course, if you had enough money or a credit card. I'd never worried about the cost of underground rail travel, given that it was always free, and I very nearly found myself embarrassed at the ticket office when I discovered how much fare prices had increased. It was only thanks to a pound coin found deeply buried in a forgotten pocket that I managed to scrape together sufficient change to put together the required amount.

'Don't say I didn't offer,' quipped the guard, with a broad grin, as I headed to the platform. I didn't stop to chat, not this time. I had too much on my mind. Not least of which, what I was going to tell Jenny.

Wrapped up in my thoughts, feeling alone and confused by events, I guess I had a pretty reasonable excuse for being distracted. As it was, I hardly noticed my surroundings, let alone the people that came and went nearby. If I had, I may have registered the man walking down the steps about twenty-five yards behind me and the military bearing to his walk. And I might have noticed the dark windcheater jacket, the same jacket I'd seen a stranger wearing as I sat on a bench in Regent's Park not two hours previously.

But I didn't. I didn't register anything.

Chapter 48

The evening was quickly drawing in and, as I walked into the car park at Cockfosters train station, I saw it was now almost empty, most of my fellow commuters having headed home somewhat earlier than I had.

A single amber street light illuminating the exit and entry had very little effect in the further recesses of the expansive tarmac. On its own in the dark, face into the fence adjoining the railway track, the Citroen sat looking rather lonely.

I pulled the phone Toni had given me from my pocket and brought up Kevin's mobile number. I tapped the 'call' button in the vain hope that I might get through to him but, not too surprisingly, there was no response. I glanced at the sky, a slight damp smell in the air suggesting the rain affecting central London was on the way. Not any time soon though, I hoped.

The train journey had given me time to think about what I was going to tell Jenny and what I was going to do next. The more I'd considered what had happened, what had been said during the interview and what I knew to be fact, the more confident I became that Mellor had no real evidence to justify my suspension and, given time, he'd have to concede that fact and I would be able to return to work.

For Kevin though, things were very different. Until he'd decided to escape custody, I would have been reasonably hopeful that my friend might have had a chance. Now though, he was finished, of that there was no doubt. And, while I thought I understood why he had decided to escape, I knew that any chance he might have had of convincing a jury effectively went out the window the moment the first smoke grenade was thrown. Now, all the pieces came together to create a picture of a man who was more gangster than cop, more guilty than innocent.

I had just turned the key in the driver's door of the car when I sensed someone close behind me. I hadn't noticed anyone else enter the car park from the train and, as I checked reflections in the glass of the car, I saw nothing. No movement, no sign of anyone nearby but still the sensation persisted. I turned slightly and picked up my briefcase, all the while scanning the shadows for any sign of danger.

A movement in the rear passenger window caught my eye, the outline of a figure … and then I saw him. Instantly, I knew I was in trouble. Dark windcheater jacket, tall. The words 'Regent's Park' had barely formed in my brain when he lunged toward me.

Fear lent speed and strength to my reactions. I swung the briefcase hard to buy time and space. It connected, somewhere in the upper body area and that was all I needed.

I ran, back to the light, back to the station.

But not for long. My attempt to buy time hadn't worked. Although adrenalin drove my leg muscles hard, I hadn't covered more than a few yards when I felt my trailing leg held in a firm grip. I tumbled forwards, crashing heavily onto the tarmac, my elbow and right shoulder taking the full force of my fall. A burning, searing pain in my shoulder stunned me for a moment as the breath was forced from my lungs. I rolled. My body was hurting but I wasn't done yet, not by a long chalk.

My attacker was powerful, but I was scared, and that fear lent me strength. Although my senses told me this wasn't a mugging, I hoped I was wrong. I wasn't – I learned that in the seconds that followed, as I struggled to free myself from the skilled moves he demonstrated. Everything I tried, every twist, every dig, every attempt at a bite, all proved fruitless. He knew what he was doing.

And then I realised. He wasn't trying to hurt, just to restrain. Not once had he done anything to actually injure me. I stopped fighting, and his grip lessened.

He spoke. 'Are you done?' The voice was strong, the accent that of a Scot, a Glaswegian.

'Who are you?' I demanded.

'If ye'd stop fightin' ya fuckin' dobber, I'll tell ye.'

'OK, OK ... just let me up.'

'Nae chance, pal. You stay right where you are, dae ye ken?'

I understood. I was face down, nose to the dirt, one arm pinned beneath my chest and the other held firmly by a skilled adversary who now sat atop of me. I knew when I was beaten. I did my best to nod.

'Now ... are ye listening?' he continued.

I nodded again.

'OK ... I'm McNeil. Taff Jones says you'll know the name.'

'Teacup McNeil?'

'The same. But I'll nae have a Rupert use that nickname, ye hear?'

'OK, sorry ... is Kevin with you?'

'Don't you worry about him. He's safe enough. I'm here because we need something from you.'

'Where is he?' I asked. 'I have to speak to him.'

'All in good time. Now, seeing as ye now know who I am, I'm going tae let go of your arm but, any funny business and you'll be back on your face, ye ken?'

I did, and true to his word, as I made clear my realisation that my life and good health was no longer under threat, McNeil pulled away from me and stood up.

I stayed sitting as I checked my elbow and shoulder. It was sore but nothing appeared broken.

'You'll heal soon enough,' he said.

I brushed off my jacket, stopping almost immediately as a sharp pain ran up my arm. I checked my hands. The knuckles of my right hand were deeply grazed and, in the half-light from the station, I could make out what looked like fragments of grit lodged in the skin. My fingers were stiff. I flexed them, the resulting pain making me wince.

'We need the document,' McNeil said.

'I guessed as much. Kevin asked me to try and recover it for him.'

'Did you get it?'

'I saw you …'

'At Regent's Park? Aye, I thought ye did. I was with you all the way from Kentish Town. Why did ye walk rather than catch the bus?'

'I needed some space.'

'Aye … I guess you did. I saw what ye did at that tower block and I spoke to a couple of the PCs who were manning the check point. The lad you talked down is a friend of mine.'

'I know, he told me,' I said. 'He's Barry Powell's kid brother.'

'That's right. I remembered what ye did for Barry and told Doug you would help him if he ever found hisself in a jam.'

'So you turning up at Kentish Town wasn't a coincidence?'

'Correct. Dougie told me what had happened with the WPC and how you came to his help. So, when I heard from his missus what he was intending to do this time, I knew they'd likely call you out to talk him down. I just waited till ye finished and then followed you.'

'Doug is a good lad.'

'Aye, he is. But right now we've a rather pressing problem. I want the document you recovered from Dr Armstrong's house.'

'It's gone,' I said. 'The local lads found it before I got there and handed it to Special Branch. They passed it on to MI5.'

McNeil's shoulders slumped. 'Bollocks,' he said, quietly. 'You're sure?'

I maintained the lie. 'Completely. I checked Armstrong's house and couldn't find it. And then I heard from the MI5 woman who looks after Kevin and me that her boss had produced it at a meeting.'

'Ach shit. That's nae good news.'

'Mind telling me what's so damn important about that document?' I probed, hoping to find out what McNeil already knew.

'I'd have thought you'd know. Lots have heard it's a treasure and, to some extent it is. It's what the document reveals that gives it value.'

'Details of a terrorist group?'

McNeil smirked. 'Maybe … maybe not. Some say it's far more than that.'

'Like what?'

'Like I have no bloody idea, Mr Finlay,' he said, angrily. 'And if I did, would I have asked Kevin to have gotten it translated fae us?'

Surmising that the conversation was over, I pulled my legs up and rolled onto my side.

'Stay where you are a minute.' McNeil raised his left hand to me and with his right removed a small phone from his pocket. He pressed in a number and was answered almost instantly.

I heard a tinny voice asking if I had 'it'. McNeil explained briefly that I didn't, and my explanation as to why. He then leaned toward me and handed me the phone.

A voice greeted me. 'Hello, boss.' I recognised it immediately.

It was Kevin.

Chapter 49

'Hope he didn't scare you too much,' Kevin said.

I looked up at McNeil, who appeared to be checking the car park in case anyone had seen the irregular way our get-together had started. He looked relaxed, as if what was happening was all in a day's work.

'I've had better days,' I replied. 'So, do you want to tell me what the hell is going on? I've just been dragged over the coals by Mellor because he thinks I must have been involved in your escape.'

Kevin laughed. 'That man's a first-class prat and if he thinks he can stitch me up with Sandi's murder he's gonna be sadly disappointed.'

I asked how the escape had been organised and how Kevin had managed it, but he wouldn't be drawn. It could wait until later, he said. For now, he needed another favour. He asked about his hide and the weapons and kit it had concealed. When I confirmed they remained undiscovered, he asked me to bring them to him.

'Where?' I asked.

'Moel Prysgau.'

'The house near the Brecon Beacons? That's crazy. You'll be spotted there.'

'No, not the house. The bothy up in the forest. The one we used that time before heading out to Peshawar.'

I remembered it. Bothies were a form of mountain refuge that I'd made use of during several training exercises. Less like a house, more like a tent with walls and a roof, bothies had no beds, sinks, lighting or even a tap. They represented the most basic of living conditions. But what they lacked in luxury, they more than made up for in terms of privacy. Seldom, if ever, visited, bothies only attracted that rare breed of person looking for hermit-like living in an environment where man seldom went. And Moel Prysgau, set in a remote valley in the Brecon Beacons, had the additional advantage that it commanded an excellent view of the only track available to approach it. So, if unwelcome visitors appeared, a quick escape into the mountains could be made. For Kevin, it looked an excellent choice.

'I'm suspended, Kev,' I added.

'I'm not surprised. Mellor made it clear in my interview that he was after both of us. We've been on his radar for quite a while it seems. How soon can you get here?'

'If I can square things with Jenny, I should be able to get to you tomorrow.'

'That would be handy. The lads that exfilled me are suggesting a move to Spain in a day or so.'

'Not on a commercial flight, I presume.'

'One of them has a boat.'

'Who are they?'

'All in good time, boss. I'll tell all tomorrow.'

McNeil had moved to stand over me. I handed the phone back to him and, after making a quick arrangement to join Kevin the day after me, he ended the call.

'How did Kevin get a phone?' I asked, as he pulled me to my feet.

'No idea. It wasn't his, that I can tell you. He told me that he had your new number from when you gave it to him at the court but he'd forgotten it. He remembered mine, so we arranged for me to intercept you.'

'Intercept? Is that what you call it? I thought you were going to kill me.'

McNeil leaned close to me and smiled sadistically. 'Trust me when I say this, boss. If I'd been intending to kill you, you would nae be standing here talking to me.'

Chapter 50

'No trace at all, you say?' Bill stopped chewing and stared toward the restaurant door.

It wasn't often they got together more than twice in a week, but these weren't ordinary times. There was a lot to go through, a lot to discuss.

Toni sprinkled some extra Parmesan onto her half-finished pasta. It looked like her choice of meal had been a better one than her dining partner's. He had picked the steak and, from the look of the faces he was now pulling, it wasn't the best one he'd ever experienced.

'None,' she replied. 'Stuart tells me, according to the vice squad, Martina Proctor is no longer active. Steak a bit chewy?' she asked.

Bill leaned back in his chair, gently placed his knife and fork on his plate and then reached for the glass of red wine near his right hand. 'You noticed?'

'I couldn't help it. Do you want me to call the waiter?'

He sniffed. 'No, leave it. I'll manage. Bit of a coincidence, you think? About Proctor.'

Toni scooped the last of her pasta onto a spoon. 'I'm not sure what to think. He could have bought her off but, given what else has happened you can't blame me for thinking the worst.'

Bill drained his glass and glanced around the almost deserted restaurant. It looked like he was ready to leave. 'Get your man to dig deeper, I'd suggest.' He waved politely to the waiter. 'I'll get this, Toni,' he said.

She smiled and was about to drain her glass as her handbag started to buzz. Her phone was ringing. She glanced down to the seat next to her where the illuminated screen told her it was Nell. She pressed the button to reject the call.

The flat was just a few minutes' walk and, as they strolled arm-in-arm, Toni thought about what Bill had said. He was right, even if it turned up an innocent explanation, finding out the fate of Howard's prostitute would answer a question.

The phone started buzzing again.

'I'd better take this,' she said. 'Nell seems to want me for something and you know what she's like.'

They stopped outside the gated entrance to a block of newly built flats. As Toni pressed the 'answer' button, Bill moved a short distance away, allowing her to speak freely.

Nell dispensed with any pleasantries. 'It was that Superintendent from police complaints who you said has it in for Jones and Finlay.'

'Superintendent Mellor? And what is it you think he's done?' Toni asked.

'You asked me to find out more about the listening device we found in Sandi Beattie's home? Well we did. Stuart helped me get entry to the Police Complaints Unit records.'

'How did he do that? I thought you said they were stored in their offices?'

'They are. We broke in this evening.'

'You did what?' Toni exclaimed.

'Oh, don't worry. It was quite fun, really. And nobody saw us. I took pictures of the records using my phone. Both the devices – the one in Kevin Jones house and the one in the Beattie house – were shown as still being in the stores.'

'So we don't know who took them out?'

'Superintendent Mellor had access to them. It has to have been him.'

'But he didn't sign for them?' Toni insisted.

'No, but there are too many coincidences for it not to have been him.'

Toni sighed. They were getting close, but they weren't there.

'There's something else,' Nell continued. 'But I need your help with that.'

'What is it?'

'The document Finlay brought back from Wales, the one that was connected to the deaths of all those soldiers. I think I may have found something, but I'd need to take a proper look to compare the original with the translation, if that's possible? Could I have a copy?'

Toni thought for a moment – about all the people connected with the Al Anfal document; about how many people who knew about it who were now dead or missing and she made a decision. 'No, Nell. I'm sorry. Whatever it is, you can explain it to me in the morning.'

Nell didn't reply before the line went dead.

'She hung up,' said Toni.

'Problem?' said Bill.

'Nothing I can't handle. I'll speak to her in the morning.'

They started walking again. 'Did I hear Nell mention Robert Finlay?' Bill asked.

'I'll have to tell Nell to speak more quietly. Yes, she wants to have a copy of the document I told you about – the Al Anfal thing – so she can work on it in her own time.'

'The poisoned chalice.'

'She hung up when I said no.'

'I ask because I had Finlay in my office today. He was being interviewed by our complaints branch.'

'About the court escape, no doubt?'

'Yes. They're not sure if he's a suspect or a witness at the moment. They wanted to know if he had any idea where Jones may have headed.'

'What did he say?'

'It was actually quite odd. He'd just got back from Kentish Town where he'd been talking to a lad who been planning to throw himself off a roof and yet, it was almost as if he was expecting that Complaints would be ready and waiting for him.'

'Maybe he was. Perhaps somebody tipped him off, or maybe he just worked out that with Jones breaking out of the court building then he was bound to get a visit sooner or later.'

'Maybe, yes. But he wound the Complaints Superintendent up a treat. It was almost as if he wanted to goad him. He's up to something, that's for certain.'

'So, what's Finlay going to do next?' Toni asked.

'They suspended him and took his warrant card – there's not a lot he can do.'

'Unless he already knows where Jones is, or he was actually behind the escape?'

'I pray he wasn't.'

'I hope you didn't mention the burner phone?'

'Of course not. If Complaints want to have Finlay followed in the hope he will lead them to Jones then they can arrange it themselves.'

'Thank you. That Complaints officer, is he the same bad penny who seems to keep popping up?' said Toni, as Bill reached for the keys to the flat.

'You guessed it,' he replied. 'Superintendent James Mellor.'

Chapter 51

Next morning, Nell was already at her desk.

Toni looked around the office. It looked like her researcher was working alone.

'Where's Stuart?' she asked.

Nell turned away from her screen. 'He's nipped out for a bacon sarnie and said something about calling in on the Missing Persons Bureau.'

'I asked him to run some more checks on that prostitute we caught Howard Green with.'

'Yes, he did mention something about that. He wanted me to check if she's been making any benefit claims.'

'Has she?'

'None, there's no record of a claim anywhere. Any particular reason you're suddenly interested in her?'

'Just another idea I'm following up. So...' Toni paused to make sure she had her researcher's full attention '... how did you get into the Police Complaints offices, Nell?'

'It was surprisingly easy. I don't think they ever expected anyone to burglarise them. Their electronic entry system operates on a key card. I made one and it worked first time.'

'And you're sure nobody saw you?'

'Absolutely. Stuart was brilliant. He strolled around liked he owned the place and worked out where to go to find what we were looking for. I really think he's developing a taste for that kind of work.'

'After his reservations about breaking into the Jones and Beattie homes?'

'Yes, I think he got a bit of a buzz out of it.'

'OK ... let's talk.' Toni placed her briefcase gently on the floor, sat close to Nell and lowered her voice. 'We're sure Superintendent Mellor planted those bugs?'

Before replying, Nell turned off her PC screen. 'As much as we can be,' she said, the tone of her voice considered and serious. 'According to their register they should still be in the Complaints Branch stores, which they're clearly not.'

'So, if it was Mellor, it's possible he was listening in on what happened when Sandra Beattie was killed?'

'Quite possible, although the statistical probability of him having heard things live isn't high. But there has to be the very real possibility that a recording exists of what exactly went on in that house at the key time.'

'So, if we could recover that recording, we might find the evidence that either proves Jones innocence or confirms his guilt?'

'A chance we take if I try and locate it.'

'You could do that?'

'Yes. I could make an attempt to locate it by hacking into the Complaints Unit intranet. If the recording is on a standalone device I'd not find it, but if he plugged that device into their net or he's made a backup, then I might.'

'Give it a try, and keep Stuart in the loop at all times. If you find anything I want to know immediately.'

'Can I repeat my request about that document Finlay brought from Dr Armstrong's house?'

'I don't think it's a good idea, Nell. The more copies, the greater the risk.'

'Could I borrow yours?'

Toni paused before replying. Nell was being persistent. There had to be a reason. 'What did you want to know?' she asked.

'We discussed its similarity to "The Project" papers that were found in Switzerland last year, but I couldn't help noticing it's much thicker.'

'Don't forget it's doubled in size due to the attached translation.'

'Yes, I know, but it's still much bigger. "The Project" is something we knew about but I've heard it said several times that it is more of a philosophy than a plan. It had no detail. I know I've only had the briefest of look through it but, like I said earlier, I'm convinced the extra material on the Al Anfal document Finlay found is that missing information.'

'You're probably right…'

'So, I think you should allow me to study it further.'

'It's toxic, Nell. Those soldiers were all killed to stop them talking about it. I've been warned off, Miles Chadbourne knew about it and now he's gone missing.'

'Don't you think I know that? It's too late now to say we're not all at some kind of risk, so I think we should know exactly what we are dealing with.'

'I thought you said last night that you'd learned something about it?'

'I may have exaggerated slightly.'

Toni stood and walked to the security door. It was firmly closed and yet, without thinking, she still tested it. Nell was right in what she was saying. And she made the valid points that they were already exposed and only a detailed analysis of the document would answer questions they both wanted answering. 'I've been wondering something...' she began.

'Why Doctor Armstrong changed his mind about destroying it?' Nell interrupted.

Toni's lips curved into a broad smile. 'You've been reading my thoughts as well?'

Nell didn't respond to the joke. 'You told me Finlay had agreed it would be destroyed because it was so dangerous.'

'That was what Armstrong recommended to him.'

'And subsequent to that, he changed his mind. I'd like to know what he read that caused that to happen.'

Toni reached down, opened her briefcase and pulled out the two-inch-thick document. She was persuaded. And she knew very well that Nell wouldn't give up until she gave in.

She placed the papers on the desk, straightened them neatly, and sighed. 'So would I, Nell. So would I.'

Chapter 52

The burner phone started ringing for the third time. If it was Toni, she was trying hard to get hold of me.

'Are you going to answer that,' spat Jenny.

I didn't answer. I wasn't really in the mood to talk to anyone and, if I was going to deliver on my promise to get Kevin's kit to him, I needed to be on the road soon.

The previous evening had been a disaster, possibly the worst time Jenny and I had experienced in the whole of our life together. I'd stumbled clumsily over my choice of words when I sat her down and explained what had happened during the interview with Mellor. And then, as we'd talked and I tried to put a positive spin on things, she'd asked questions I couldn't answer. The grazes on my hands had only served to make things worse. Circumstances created suspicions. Her questions became more hostile and I reacted by becoming defensive. It wasn't long before tempers became frayed, things were said in the heat of the moment and, finally, she had stormed out of the house.

I'd gone after her, my thoughts a confused mixture of fear and anger. Drawn by the sound of her sobs, I'd found her sitting on the pavement, feet in the gutter, seemingly not caring who might see her. My attempts at reassurance were brushed aside as I stood accused of being unfit as a father and as a husband. Her words cut into me like a knife.

And then came the silence.

Which, in many ways was worse. At least when we were arguing, I had an idea where I stood and I had a chance to express my views and to defend myself. The silent treatment was new. But it told me something; it told me just how bad things had got if my wife felt unable to speak to me.

Neither of us slept much. Although we shared a bed, Jenny kept her distance and her back toward me. I dozed, but every time she moved I was aware of it. I simply lay there, brooding, wondering if I was a pawn in a game being played by forces beyond my understanding, and torn between my desire to help a friend who needed me and a family I was responsible for.

I felt I could I could handle it, I could juggle the pieces until they fell into place, and that was what frustrated me when Jenny challenged that belief. All I wanted to do at the moment was to try and persuade Kevin not to keep running.

'If I stay there is no chance ... none,' I'd pleaded. 'If I go, there is a chance I can persuade him to return to clear his name.'

But Jenny was having none of it. We'd eaten breakfast in relative silence, each of us talking to Becky and baby Charlotte but not to each other. It was only when she had returned from the school run and the phone had started ringing that she opted to speak.

I'd put a small shovel in the boot of the 2CV while she was out. I estimated it would take at least an hour to recover Kevin's kit and then at least another four hours to get to the bothy in Wales. I was pretty sure I could remember how to find it, but I knew I was going to have to take a circuitous route in case Mellor was minded to have me watched. If I had been him, it's what I would have done. But I also knew that surveillance operations took time to organise, which was why I had tried to impress on Jenny the need to act without delay. With less than twenty-four hours having passed since Kevin's escape from custody, I knew the enquiry team focus would be on trying to locate him. His haunts, relatives, friends and associates would all be checked. That would tie up a lot of manpower, so putting together another team to follow me would be a significant task.

The phone started ringing again. This time, Jenny just looked at me, as if challenging me to answer it.

'I need to move today, Jen,' I said, once more. 'Before the might of the Met can swing into action.'

As I pressed the button to answer the call, she turned her back on me and walked off towards the kitchen. I felt alone, very alone.

It was Toni. 'Where are you?' she asked.

I explained I was at home and, so as not to give anything away, added that I wasn't likely to be going anywhere soon.

'Have you seen the news?' she said. 'The Commissioner has been on saying that no stone will be left unturned in the search for PC Jones.'

'That was to be expected. Nobody likes to have that kind of egg on their face for long.'

'I have news.'

'So do I. Mellor pulled me for an interview yesterday. I'm suspended – and banned from entering any police premises without his permission. And he suspects I was involved in Kevin's escape.'

'Were you?' she asked.

'Of course not, I had no idea. I only went to see him about getting a decent barrister to represent him. Mellor thinks we were hatching an escape plot.'

'Commander Grahamslaw told me this morning. The news I have is that I asked Nell and Stuart to check Sandra Beattie's house. They found another listening device like the one from Kevin's.'

'Where was it?' I asked.

'Behind a plug socket, like the first one. And that's not the half of it. Both devices were part of a batch provided to the Met for evaluation. Guess which department of the Met they were issued to?'

'I'm not in the mood for games, Toni. Just spell it out.'

'OK, sorry. I guess now isn't the best of times for you. Both devices were supposed to be in the stores belonging to the police Complaints Branch.'

'Mellor's department? How did you find out?'

'Stuart and Nell did some digging.'

'CIB should have a log – a register to sign them out?'

'They do. According to the log they should still be in the store.'

'So Mellor or someone in his office might have been doing something he doesn't want a record of?'

'Yes. That's the conclusion we came to as well. Maybe he was fishing for something on Kevin? Commander Grahamslaw tells me that CIB sometimes do that if they think an officer is bent and they're looking for the evidence.'

'Kevin isn't bent, and even CIB have rules about that kind of thing.'

'But you know as well as I do that the decision to give you immunity from prosecution last year wasn't agreed by everyone.'

'So Mellor has been looking to put that right? You know what this means, don't you?'

'What's that?' Toni asked.

'Mellor may have overheard or even recorded what happened the day Sandra Beattie was killed.' A crash from the kitchen told me that Jenny was nearby, probably listening, or possibly just making me aware that she was there.

'Yes … again, that was what Nell and I thought.'

'But he couldn't admit to having placed an illegal listening device in the home of a fellow cop as that could really weaken his case.'

'It might. Grahamslaw thinks, in terms of legal arguments, it might be more complicated than that.'

'But if he has a recording that exonerates Kevin, what would that matter if the bug was legal or not. Kevin would be off the hook.'

'But Mellor would be in deep shit. Something like that could cost him his career.'

'I really don't give a damn about Mellor's career. If there's a recording, we need to get hold of it, and I need to tell Kevin about it.'

'Can you get a message to him?'

'I think so. There may be a way through a mutual contact.'

'Well, I suggest you do that. In the meantime, Nell is already trying to trace the transmission route for the bug and the recipient receiver. If we can, we'll try and find that recording.'

As I ended the call, Jenny appeared in the doorway behind me. 'You'd better go and give Charlie a kiss,' she said, softly.

I frowned, confused by the apparent change in her mood. 'I was listening,' she said, before pausing for several seconds, appearing to search for the right words. 'One of the things I prize about you, Bob, is your loyalty. I can't ask you not to be loyal to your oldest friend, can I? If there's hope for Kevin, then maybe you should try and talk him round.'

I reached for her hand and squeezed it tight. 'I won't take any risks, I promise.'

'You'd better not. Where is he hiding out?' she asked.

'Best I don't say, but it's a long drive. I'll probably be away overnight.'

Jenny sighed deeply. 'Just remember, it's not just me you need to be thinking of. There are two little girls here who are depending on their dad being around as they grow up. We don't want to be visiting you in some prison somewhere.'

Chapter 53

Howard scowled as Petre's fist connected once more with his victim's face. This wasn't going to be as straightforward as he'd expected.

His telephone began to ring. He lifted it from his jacket pocket, checked the screen and recognised Grady's number.

'Enough,' he said, raising a hand to indicate that the beating should cease. 'Get him into the car.'

He pressed the phone's answer button. 'Where are you?' he demanded.

'Getting supplies from the local town.'

'Jones is at the bothy?'

'Making his plans to sort out some Superintendent from the Met Complaints Unit.'

'Let him, it will keep him busy. Is Finlay on his way?'

'Apparently so. He's taken the bait and should be here within the hour.'

'Excellent.' Howard allowed himself a smile. Borrowing Petre Gavrić from the Cristea clan had proved to be a good decision. The Serbian was ruthless as well as resourceful, and his limited English had not proved to be a problem. The way he had worked with Grady and Cathy at the Magistrates' Court had been testament to his considerable experience.

They now had Jones where Howard wanted him; Finlay was about to be the same, and in the back of the Range Rover was the only other loose end. At last things were coming together. Finally he could end this time-consuming game. Finally the clean-up operation would be brought to its conclusion.

'How long before you get here?' Grady asked.

'Tomorrow morning. We need to pick up some kit and I still have a few questions to ask of Miles Chadbourne.'

'How's he holding up?'

'He's surprised me. For an overweight, flatulent desk jockey, he's proving to be a reluctant nut to crack.'

'Put him on the board, that'll make him talk.'

'I plan to,' said Howard. 'We just need to pick up the necessary kit. As you know, there's no running water at the bothy.'

'That's right. You'll need quite a bit if you plan to board Jones and Finlay as well.'

'I'm aware of that, Grady. In the meantime, can I suggest you get some drink down their throats and make sure they wake up tomorrow feeling the worse for wear. It may make the interrogation more efficient.'

'No problem. I'll be waiting.'

Howard ended the call, opened the front passenger door of the car and climbed in. In the rear, he could see Cathy was holding the muzzle of her pistol hard into the ribs of their now-hooded prisoner. Petre was in the driving seat.

As the Serbian started the engine, Howard leaned across to him. 'Call Gheorghe,' he said. 'It looks like he may get his wish after all.'

Chapter 54

Two hours later I was on the A5 heading north towards Birmingham. Hidden beneath the rear seat of the car were the contents of the weapons hide that had lain beneath Kevin's allotment shed, a collection I estimated would see me facing a holiday of at least twenty years, courtesy of Her Majesty's Prison Service.

Jenny and I talked long and hard about what I was intending to do and what I might say to Kevin to get him to see sense. I thought it best not to mention the kit and the weapons to her but, as we spoke and came to an understanding we were both comfortable with, I made a decision. I was going to leave the whole lot with him. My contribution to the collection was no longer something I wished to be part of my life. Its existence may have saved my bacon when my past life came a-knocking, but the longer I retained weapons and kit that could see me sent to prison, the greater the risk. It was time to move on and really put that section of my life behind me.

I was sticking to minor roads as far as I could, avoiding motorway cameras and the regular police patrols that cruised those routes. Every so often, I would dive off into a side street, take a detour, or stop and watch the traffic. Anyone following me would have recognised what I was doing as an anti-surveillance technique, but that didn't bother me. All that mattered was that either I wasn't being tailed or I saw them before they stopped me. I just needed to keep ahead of the game.

As I passed through Birmingham, I was pretty confident there was no tail but, to be safe, I pulled into a multi-storey car park. From the time I'd spent on operations in Northern Ireland, I remembered the challenges such places represented to a surveillance team. With many cars coming and going, a target could easily be out of sight in a few seconds or another car could block your way while manoeuvring or parking. I knew of many operations that had been blown when operatives had either failed to get close enough to avoid losing their target, or their presence had been noticed as they did just that.

As I entered the car park, I collected my ticket and took the opportunity to take a close look at all the queuing vehicles nearby. I made eye contact with all drivers I could see, looked for those containing young children – an indication they could be discounted, but no guarantee – and then headed for the top floor.

My plan was simple. Most car drivers entering would be looking for either the nearest space they could find or one near to the pedestrian exits. Not many head to the roof, so any vehicle that did the same as me would be suspect. Nothing did, but to be doubly sure I then headed straight for the exit and managed to find one driver in the process of reversing into a space on the second floor. I swerved, and timed my move so the lane behind me would be blocked. An irate BMW driver wasn't impressed as I came close to taking off his front bumper. But, as the little Citroen weaved around him to the sound of a blaring horn and an expletive through an open window, I smiled. It was time to switch direction and head west towards Wales.

Evening was drawing in and, as the lanes narrowed and became devoid of other cars, I began the climb from Brecon and up into the mountains. I noticed the slope tipped the car fuel gauge into the red. I didn't panic though, experience had taught me it was one of the little car's quirks on hilly roads. I knew I still had enough for quite a considerable distance.

The main house at Moel Prysgau was deserted. I figured Kevin would have given it the once-over but, to be safe, I took a look around. A sense of nostalgia gave me some comfort as I took in the almost forgotten smell of the place. Damp, stale but relatively clean, it had provided me and many of my peers with shelter when we sought refuge from the ravages of the changeable mountain weather.

The track to the bothy was designed to allow Forestry Commission vehicles access to the woodland for tree felling, so it was more suited to a four-wheel drive than my little car. But, true to its reputation, the 2CV coped admirably with the rutted and boulder-strewn drive. Soon, the tiny shack came into sight. It commanded a good view of the approach and, I had no doubt, Kevin would have seen me coming.

I was right. As I pulled up and switched off the engine, he emerged. He looked a little tired and moved stiffly, but as he shut the bothy door behind him and stood waiting for me, I could see he was smiling. That was a good sign. How he would react and whether he would still be happy after hearing my news, only time would tell.

We wasted little time in unloading my car, moving Kevin's gear into the small hut and stashing it beneath one of the two tiny bunks. Before closing the driver door for the final time, I pulled the phone Toni had given me from my pocket. I checked the battery level. It was nearly full. I was about to turn it off when I had second thoughts, a 'just in case' moment of the kind that is hard to explain or justify but, nevertheless, I'd learned to act upon. As a result, I left it turned on, switched it to silent and then tucked it into my pocket. 'You never know,' I said, beneath my breath.

I then removed the final two bags containing my kit and carried them indoors.

'Long time since we were last here, boss,' Kevin called from the doorway, as I kicked the final bag out of sight beneath one of the sleeping cots.

I said a silent goodbye to my kit before replying. 'I wondered if I would find it, given that we only ever seemed to be here when it was dark.'

'Is it all there? Everything from the allotment?'

'Yes, and the few bits and bobs I had left as well. What you do with it is up to you, but I'm done with it.'

'You sure? You never know when stuff like that may come in useful.'

'I've promised Jenny. Family and being a provider has to take priority now.'

'Something might happen; how can you know?'

'Nothing will. Normal people don't need a secret stash of weapons and I plan to be as normal as life will allow. Do you have the makings of a brew? I meant to pick some things up but I forgot.'

'Manc is taking care of that. He's gone into the town to pick up some supplies. I thought you were him coming back when I heard the car.'

'Manc? Who's Manc?'

'Chris Grady. Formerly of D Squadron. He ran the escape plan.'

Kevin saw me react, saw the hesitation and uncertainty as he said the name.

'What's up?' he asked.

It was as well he couldn't read my confused thoughts. Grady and

McNeil, the two surviving members of the Increment Afghanistan patrol, and within twenty-four hours they had both appeared. I wondered what Toni Fellowes might make of the coincidence.

'I'm not sure,' I said. 'Last year, when Toni was looking into the attacks on us, she asked me if I knew Chris Grady. He was one of the lads on Increment with Bridges and the others. Nell Mahoney mentioned his name recently as well.'

'That's right. It was them that broke me out of court. Grady and another guy I didn't recognise.'

'Not McNeil? I assumed it was him who helped you.'

'He wasn't in on it – he only learned I was out when I called him.'

'How did you do that? I wouldn't have expected you to have had a phone.'

'Grady suggested I call you ... to get my kit. He lent me his phone, but I couldn't remember the number you gave me in the cell at Barkingside so I called McNeil instead and asked him to get in touch with you.'

'Well, he did that alright.' I rubbed at the bruises on my arm as I recalled the car park. 'So, how did you arrange the breakout?'

'It was the solicitor you met.'

'In the cell?'

'That's him. He delivered the message to me. I just needed to be ready when they came. I wasn't actually sure who was getting me out, so it was a relief to see a friendly face like Grady's.'

'I need to talk to you about that breakout ...'

'Not until we've talked some more about this Al Anfal document.'

'Like I said on the phone, it's fallen into the hands of MI5.'

'Yeah, you said. Kinda scuppered my plans that did.'

'What plans?'

'Sandi's kids. I was going to sell it to the press and use the proceeds to set up a trust fund for them.'

'And what about *your* future? Escaping from custody doesn't sound like the actions of an innocent man.'

'I thought you might say that. But I couldn't fight my corner from a prison cell, now could I?'

'Maybe … listen to this.' I took the burner phone from my pocket, turned the volume to full, located the Mellor recording and pressed 'play'. Kevin made to interrupt until he heard Mellor's voice. The device then had his full attention.

'He didn't caution you,' he said, as the recording ended. 'Schoolboy error…'

'I'd wound him up. Maybe that's also how he let slip his take on what happened…'

He breathed deeply. 'He's right, of course. No jury would ever have believed me. They were trying to have me admit it was some kind of sex game gone wrong. Bastards. But why plant a gun in my car?'

'Best I can come up with is that Mellor wants to make something stick. I had hoped that by recording him I'd catch him admitting to stitching you up. Just imagine what could happen if we'd played that in court.'

Kevin frowned. 'Oh, believe me, he's framing me alright … or someone is.'

And as he explained the line of questioning Mellor had taken, it became very clear the Complaints Superintendent was determined to get him, one way or another. And not only that, it was apparent I was also in his sights. He'd been biding his time, watching us and waiting, looking for his chance. It made me angry to think that a cop would plant evidence on a colleague but Mellor was no ordinary man. He was on a mission and, to him, the end justified the means.

I was silenced. The argument was lost.

'And another thing—' But Kevin stopped mid-sentence. Once again, he looked up towards the track, checking the approach track, I guessed, for Grady's return. I sensed something was troubling him.

'Would it be about that document?' I replied. 'You said you wanted to talk some more about it?'

'Yeah, I did. Listen now: McNeil has been doing some more research on the missing Increment lads. Over the last couple of years they've all been murdered or died in accidents. His theory, and I agree with him, is that somebody was eliminating anyone and everyone who had a claim to that document.'

'To what end?' I asked, feigning ignorance.

'To keep the proceeds of selling it for themselves, of course. They would have known that all the lads would want a slice of the pie so they made sure there were fewer mouths needed feeding.'

'So, is McNeil after a slice of the pie as well?'

Kevin shook his head, as if even the very notion of my suggestion offended him. I knew him, though; he would think about what I had said, mull it over and, in his own sweet time, he would come back to me with his opinion.

'Are you ready for the biggie?' I asked, anxious to get Kevin back to focussing on the need to prove his innocence.

'Like what?'

'Like the news that Nell Mahoney found another bug … and it was in Sandi's place.'

'They were recording her?'

'Not *they*, Kev. Toni has found out *who* planted it.'

'I've a feeling I'm not going to like this.' Kevin looked anxious, even nervous as he began to walk up and down the tiny floor space.

'It was Mellor,' I said. 'There's every chance he has a recording of what really happened the day Sandi died.'

Chapter 55

The rumble of an approaching car brought an end to our conversation.

Kevin raised a finger to his lips as he stood and peered through a small window overlooking the approach. 'It's Grady,' he said.

'Does he know about the document?' I asked.

'If he does, he hasn't said anything. McNeil had said we'd run it past him soon to see what he thinks but now it's lost there doesn't seem much point in that.'

I opened the front door in time to watch a rather ancient grey Ford pull up next to my Citroen. It was now getting dark and, in the dim light, I struggled to see who was in the car. Then, as the interior light came on in response to a door opening, I saw the driver – a lean, shaven-headed man in his late forties. He raised a hand in acknowledgement of my presence. Even as he stepped out onto the track and I saw him more clearly, I didn't recognise him. If this was Chris Grady, I would have expected him to be more familiar. The man I now saw could have walked past me in the street without drawing a second glance.

'Captain Finlay?' the stranger enquired of me as he lifted a heavy-looking cardboard box from the back seat of the Ford.

'Are you Chris Grady?' I replied.

'That's right. Can you give me a hand with this?'

I stepped closer and took hold of the box. A quick inspection revealed a selection of dried food, a small gas burner, some vegetables, a container of orange juice and a selection of canned beers. 'You're planning on being here a while?' I asked.

'A day or so. You don't remember me, I'd guess, from the look on your face?'

'Yes, sorry. I expected to.'

'Might be different if I still had my hair,' he quipped, and I smiled at the joke. 'Has Taff told you the plan?'

'He hasn't,' I said 'I'll be honest – I think he should go back and fight the case.'

Grady shut the car door. In his hand he held a bottle of whisky. 'For later,' he grinned as he showed it to me. 'He said you'd say that but, if you ask me, it's already too late.'

Kevin appeared in the light now coming from the doorway of the bothy. 'You two talking about me?'

I managed a smile. 'Chris reckons it's too late for you to go back to clear your name.'

He nodded. 'I agree. In a day or so I'll be out of the country anyway. There's nothing here for me now.'

I turned to Grady. 'Is that the plan you mentioned?' I said, lowering my voice so that Kevin wouldn't hear me.

'I've a friend in Italy; he can hole up there for a while and decide on what to do long term,' he said. 'For now, the important thing is to get him somewhere that your lot can't find him.'

'Running and hiding for the rest of his life is no way to exist.'

'Better than being banged up, wouldn't you say? Especially for a copper.'

Checkmate. I'd lost the argument. Grady knew it, I knew it. With no immediate family to think of, it would need to have been a far more persuasive argument than I could come up with.

With darkness closing in, Kevin suggested we open the beers immediately, while they were still cold. There was no electricity or water supply to the bothy. All it provided was basic shelter. Light was provided by two kerosene lamps that threw eerie shadows across the interior of the tiny building as we moved around. Grady offered us use of the two berths, although as I tried the one Kevin had previously decided was what he termed 'officer standard', I honestly wondered if the floor might have been more comfortable. In the morning, we agreed, I'd head back to London.

While the other two were preparing supper I slipped out to the car, tucked the burner phone under the driver seat and then returned to put some logs I'd found onto the fire. I began to relax as we laughed together, exchanging jokes and old stories as the beers started to flow. We talked about providing a watch, in case anyone should come looking for us, but Kevin and Grady were both of a mind not to worry about it. It was clear they thought we were safe and they were definitely far more interested in enjoying a good drinking session than taking turns on 'stag' outside while the others stayed in the warm.

Although more than twenty years had passed, I was reminded of many occasions when I had hunkered down with soldiers in similar situations that only varied in their degrees of unpleasantness. And yet, it never seemed to bother us so long as we had the company of men with whom the experience was shared. I'd sat through monsoons in the jungle, bitten to buggery by leeches and insects and so wet that our bivouacs lay under water; and I had lain on my bunk in the Afghan mountains where the skies seemed so close you felt you could reach out and touch the stars, yet where it was so cold that men had been known to freeze to death in their sleep and where it was necessary for those awake to check on their mates to ensure they had not slipped into oblivion. There were times – quieter moments when I allowed myself the indulgence of remembering, or like this when I got into conversation with other ex-soldiers – when I'd thought about those places and the camaraderie of shared discomfort and admitted, privately, that I missed it.

Grady cooked using the small gas stove he'd brought with him in the car. Perhaps due to the degree of my hunger or perhaps triggered by the effect of the alcohol, I found myself tucking into the fry-up with gusto.

'Texas hash,' he commented, seeing the speed at which I was eating. 'It was a D Squadron special.'

'Delicious,' I replied, between mouthfuls. 'So, what are you doing with yourself these days, Chris?'

'PMC is what they call it. Private military contractor. I do the circuit and travel wherever the work takes me.'

'Good money?' Kevin asked.

'Yes, if you're thinking of it. But age and being on Scotland Yard's most-wanted list might limit your options a bit.'

Kevin didn't answer. I knew he'd be mulling things over, thinking through ideas on how he was going to continue to make a living. I didn't envy him.

Grady took our plates and spoons and offered to wash up while he went outside for a cigarette. 'Bothy rules – no smoking,' he quipped.

As Grady slipped out the door, Kevin looked at me quizzically. 'I never did understand why you applied for selection, Finlay.'

'To be an SAS officer, you mean?'

'Yes. I remember that first time we met at the end of the Fan dance exercise. You were done in.' Kevin's speech slurred slightly. In the half-light I couldn't see clearly, but my guess was the beer was having an effect.

I was halfway through my explanation of how a bully of a Colour Sergeant at Sandhurst had been the motivation for my application when Kevin opened the whisky bottle and thrust a plastic tumbler into my hand.

'I was bullied too,' he said, his words now drawn out and deliberate. 'Local lad who was a bit of a boxer liked to pick on people at the church disco. Paul fuckin' Slater … I remember that bastard alright. He failed to get in the Marines so I decided to prove myself better than him. Well, I got a taste for it, didn't I, see? And so I decided I wanted to go back to our village wearing SAS wings so I could find him and show him.'

'Did you?' I asked.

'Nah … bastard was in jail for assaulting his ex-girlfriend. I made sure she promised to tell him I'd been looking for him though.'

I resumed my story and finished just as Grady reappeared. He found a third beaker in a store cupboard, wiped the dust away and poured himself a large slug from the bottle. Before long, it was empty and our host returned to the car where he claimed to have another. He was true to his word, but on his return, I had fallen asleep.

Had I not been, things may have turned out very differently. A taste from the new bottle or just a glimpse of its label may have given me enough of a clue as to what Chris Grady was up to and the real reason he'd asked Kevin to persuade me to join them.

But I was asleep. And by the time I realised, it was too late.

Chapter 56

South London

'Quick as you can, Stuart.' Toni glanced behind her. The street was deserted. There was no response as he continued to jiggle the front door lock.

Breaking in to people's houses was always easier in the summer months, she mused. With all the windows now closed due to the cold weather, it would only be Stuart's skills with the lock tools that decided whether they gained entry that night.

All at once, the door gave way. 'We're in,' he whispered.

Stuart stepped forward carefully, scanning the hallway of the terraced Victorian house for any indication of occupation or an alarm system. There was none. He pulled a set of night vision goggles from a bag that hung across his shoulder, flicked a switch near his temple and gave the 'OK' sign. He was ready. Toni had stressed that, until the house was cleared, they would not speak.

They checked downstairs first. Stuart took the lead, listening and then moving. No lights, nothing touched. No clues to be left that they had been there.

Next came the stairs. Two bedrooms and a bathroom on the first floor left to check. Toni could see Stuart treading carefully, making sure to apply his weight to the edges of the stairs rather than the centre. Use the strong points, avoid the creaks that wooden treads under stress would make and reveal your presence. On each step he applied pressure to test it and, only once satisfied it was safe, did he move forward. Carefully, and without rushing, they reached the landing. All the doors were slightly ajar. There was no sound, no movement – no indication of life.

The nearest door looked to be the bathroom. Stuart pushed it open very, very slowly. Just as with the front door, the hinges stayed silent. Toni watched as he leaned around into the room, paused for a moment and then stepped back. As he'd done with the previous parts of the house, he gave a thumbs-up with his right hand to indicate the all-clear.

Toni had figured that, if Miles was at home, he would be using the front bedroom to sleep in. It looked to be the largest and, as she'd suggested to Stuart before leaving the car, what kind of a person buys a house only to sleep in one of the smaller rooms? They'd agreed, therefore, to check the master bedroom last.

The final door creaked very quietly as it opened and, for a moment, Toni wondered if it might be sufficient to wake someone. They needn't have worried. As they crept into the large but unusually tidy bedroom, it was clear Miles wasn't at home. The house was deserted.

Twenty minutes later, electronic sweep and a cursory search complete, they returned to Stuart's car. Only once the doors were closed did Toni speak.

'He's left the hot water system on but, apart from that, I'd say he hasn't been here for several days at least.'

'What makes you say that?'

'The waste bins. They were clean and had fresh bags in them. If someone from the Service had been here they might have emptied the bins but we never put fresh empty bags in place afterwards. No, I think it's more likely Miles is in hiding somewhere. He's left things nice and neat with nothing that would rot or make the place smell ready for when he makes a reappearance.'

'You don't think he's been taken out like everyone else who knows about this document?'

Toni paused for a moment, and then shrugged. 'I'm sorry you had to hear that.'

'No need to apologise. I was starting to piece things together anyway. In a small office like ours, it's hard to keep secrets for long.'

'Yes, I'm aware of that. But I did tell Nell to be discreet.'

'No worries. What's done is done. And now that I do know there's really no undoing it.'

'Mark my words though, Stuart. Do *not* talk to anyone apart from me about it. If Miles turns up in the Thames having suffered the same fate as everyone else involved with Al Anfal then…'

'It's a reminder of what happens to those that talk?'

'Exactly,' said Toni.

'So what did you think of Nell's theory?'

'About Miles?'

'About the document – that it's the full version of the Muslim Brotherhood "Project" document?'

'I think she could be right. She's working on it now, even as we speak. Shall we call her to see if there's any news?'

Stuart agreed. Even though it was gone midnight, they both knew Nell would still be at her desk. Given sufficient incentive and enough caffeine to keep her going, she would work through the night if needs be. They were right, and she had news.

☩

'I hope you don't mind,' Nell said, apologetically.

Toni was livid, and handed the phone to Stuart to give herself a few minutes to think. Frustrated by what she had seen as inconsistencies in Dr Armstrong's translations, Nell had contacted one of her friends through their dark-web connection to see if she could give her a second opinion.

'Tell me what you learned, Nell,' said Stuart. He turned on the speaker to the phone so they could both hear the response.

'About the listening device or the document?'

'Let's start with the bug.'

Nell spoke quickly. 'OK. I didn't get too far with it other than to confirm there is a receiver and that it seems to be linked to a personal computer. Maybe a laptop or something similar. But it's switched off at the moment so I can't trace it.'

'Will you able to if the user switches it on?'

'Definitely. I've set up an activation warning in case that happens but … well, let's just say that if the user never turns it on again, we'll never know who it was.'

'We're pretty sure we know who it was, Nell. We just need to know what he has. What about the document?'

'Slightly better. It was the reference to the word "currency" that didn't seem to make sense. In several places the word is used in regard to banking arrangements and I was cool with that. But, in other places where Armstrong translated sections as "currency exchanges" it was more confused. I thought the translation may be close but not quite right and that's what Melissa confirmed.'

'So, who is this Melissa?' Stuart asked.

'A friend of mine from uni. Is Toni cross?' Nell sounded confused. 'Is that why she passed the phone to you? Tell her don't worry, Melissa has no idea what I do and she thinks it was for a thesis I'm writing.'

'You're sure?'

'Yes, I *am* sure.' Nell said angrily, at what Toni sensed was a reaction to having her judgement questioned.

'OK, OK,' said Stuart. 'Let's keep cool. What exactly did she say?'

'The word was meant to be "trade", as in an exchange of goods rather than currency or money, as Armstrong thought.'

'Did it make a difference?'

'Yes, very much so. The goods they were talking about are people – people who they send on trade routes that they've established between countries.'

'People? … You mean terrorists they send to do jobs?'

'Sometimes, yes; they seem to use the routes they describe for that purpose, but the main reason they use the routes is to generate currency in exchange for those people.'

Toni snatched the phone from Stuart's fist. 'Get to the point, Nell,' she said, impatiently. 'We haven't got all night'.

Nell didn't bite. 'OK. Well, I'm sure I'll be able to tell you more in the morning but what I can tell you now is that one of Al Anfal's principal cash-generators is people. They trade in slaves.'

Chapter 57

Grady looked like shit but it hadn't affected his skills.

'What the fuck,' grunted Kevin. A hand slid sluggishly from the bunk as he opened his eyes and then rolled noisily onto his side.

I didn't reply. I was focussing on the finger now resting on the trigger of the Glock that was pointing at my face. The hand that held it was steady, calm. No fear or sign of adrenalin, a man in control.

I'd woken first and, as the other two slept, I'd nipped out into the adjacent woodland to answer a call of nature that had been nagging at me since I had first started to stir. I scraped a shallow pit, did what I needed to do and then covered it over with the pine needles that littered the ground. I wasn't too thorough and, as I fastened my trousers I thought back to times when operational necessity had meant that even using a scrape in the dirt was banned in case it might reveal your presence to a potential enemy. Taking a dump in a plastic bag, learning how to mask the scent of Western-European urine, all were things you needed to learn to do if you were to survive. But those were days long since passed. I now preferred my creature comforts.

Grady had been awake and was at the door to the bothy as I returned. He held a black bin liner in his hand and seemed to be in the process of clearing away the empty cans of beer.

'You going to get back to London?' he'd asked, quietly, as I followed him inside.

I'd then checked my watch. A quarter to eight. We'd slept late. 'I think so,' I'd replied. 'Soon as Kevin wakes up I'll put on a brew and then be away.'

It was as Grady had reached for the two whisky bottles that things suddenly went awry. I wasn't really paying attention as the first one went into the bag, but as he picked up the second I saw the label, and I recognised it. Penderyn, the rare Welsh make I'd only ever seen drunk by two men. One, a fellow detective. The other, a recently deceased weapons inspector. And just two days earlier, I'd seen three men, who I'd deduced were from the Security Services, searching the home of that weapons inspector and I'd seen one of those men take a bottle of that same rare whisky from the house.

In that instant I thought back to where I had lain hidden in the gorse, watching the men searching Armstrong's cottage, not close enough to see their faces or hear them speak, but near enough to recognise the practised skill with which they worked and the athletic way they moved on their feet.

And in that same moment in time, Grady must have seen the change in my demeanour and realised he was rumbled. And then he moved very, very fast.

✝

'My thoughts exactly, Kev,' I said, focussing on Grady's trigger finger. 'I think our friend here isn't quite who we thought.'

'Keep still, both of you,' Grady barked. 'Finlay, get on all fours, you know the drill. Any funny business and I'll put a round in your foot.'

'I need a piss,' said Kevin, from his bunk.

'Hold onto it.'

I did as ordered, sensing that I needed to discover exactly what was going on before thinking how we were going to get out of it. Old lessons came back to me on how to handle being captured. Grady was as professional as it was possible to be, so we weren't likely to be shot by accident or out of temper. But he might be prepared to wound us if that was needed to maintain control. And he hadn't killed us, which meant he had a reason for keeping us alive. A fact that, at least in the short term, could work in our favour.

Kevin eased himself from the cot and onto the floor of the bothy. I looked up to where Grady had stepped back towards the doorway. He was pulling a phone from his pocket.

I looked across towards my friend. Two of us, both on the floor, both suffering the effects of a night on the grog. There was no chance of jumping our captor, not yet.

'Where are you?' Grady said into the phone. A voice responded. 'OK … as quick as you can. Things haven't quite gone to plan but I've got them both covered.'

…Them *both* covered. Someone at the other end of that call knew that Kevin and I were both here and were now secured. Someone who didn't need to be told who we were and who was now on his or her way to see us.

'Who was that on the phone, Chris?' I asked.

'Shut the fuck up. Now, both of you – crawl out front onto the grass.'

Kevin made hard work of it. Several times he lay flat on his face. I wondered if he was genuinely ill or trying to get Grady close enough to give us a chance. If so, it was a wasted effort. We were dealing with someone who'd been taught the same tricks as us.

It didn't take long before we were where Grady wanted us, both on the grass, on all fours and facing up the track towards the cars.

'Now, we wait,' he said.

'I need to take a leak,' Kevin repeated, this time with some urgency.

'I'm not stopping you,' came the reply.

Kevin turned his face toward me. 'Sorry, boss.' With that, he unzipped his fly and began to empty his bladder where he was. A smell of strong, early-morning urine hit my nostrils, and then he farted. And it was no ordinary fart. This one roared into the world with a force I suspected was helped by some considerable internal effort. He laughed. And that was the trick to get me to look across at him. As I turned, in mind to somehow register my frustration at his failure to recognise our predicament, I glanced to his groin, and I saw the grip of a 9mm pistol that was hidden down the front of his trousers. And I knew what I had to do. One chance, and don't waste it.

As our eyes met, I nodded. Then, dropping my right arm, I rolled fast to my right and away from him and kept rolling. *Keep moving,* I thought. *Don't think, just move.*

Behind me I knew Kevin would have stayed still, allowing Grady to be distracted by and focussed on me. Grady wouldn't want to kill us, so he'd be looking to secure a safe shot that disabled. We had one chance.

A shot discharged. Just one, and behind me I heard a thud as the round hit the earth.

'Forget it, Taff. You wankers must think I was born yesterday.'

Grady had been one step ahead of us. Far from being in the same position we thought, covering us from in front of the bothy, he had moved. Kevin now lay on his back, a Browning pointed at where I would have also expected our captor to be standing. I couldn't see him, and I guessed neither could Kevin. And it's pretty hard to shoot at what you can't see.

'Throw it towards the hut or the next one takes your leg.'

Our chance was gone. And in more ways than one, for I now heard the sound of an approaching car. As Kevin threw the weapon, Grady appeared from behind a log pile. I lay on my back, craning my neck to see who was about to join us. I didn't have to wait long. A black Range Rover pulled up. Inside, I thought I could see four occupants.

As the driver's door opened and a figure appeared, I rolled onto my chest to get a better look. What I saw horrified me, and at the same time answered the question as to why Grady had lured me to this spot.

Then, if it were possible to make a bad situation worse, the front-seat passenger also came into view.

'What the fuck,' I heard Kevin utter the same words he had spoken on wakening to the sight of Grady's pistol aimed at my head.

In front of us stood Howard Green, and beside him someone I had never in my wildest dreams expected to ever see again.

And some words came back to me; words I had heard a government Minister say not so very long ago – words of warning: 'He asked me to arrange the deaths of two people, Mr Finlay.'

And I knew – knew the warning wasn't history, as Toni had assured me. It was current, and the means of its delivery was now staring silently at me.

Petre Gavrić.

Chapter 58

New Scotland Yard

'Thank you, Bill,' Toni said, rolling her eyes, her voice flat and emotionless as she stared at the name on the screen. Too late, she realised, her use of his name had shown a familiarity she would have preferred not to.

'Do you mean Commander Grahamslaw?' said Nell.

'Er … yes. Sorry, Nell. It was something he said that prompted me to ask you to look into Howard's background.'

'Not too much of a surprise then?'

Toni detected an irony in Nell's choice of words and tone that she sensed was deliberate. 'I had a feeling we'd find his mucky hands on this somewhere,' she answered.

'You did ask me to include his finances in my searches,' Nell continued. 'And there's something else I need to show you.'

'Where's Stuart?' Toni asked.

'He must be late in. Can I show you the something else?'

'In a minute, Nell, this is important,' Toni replied. 'Did he find out anything about that prostitute?'

'The one we caught with Mr Green?'

'Nothing much gets past you, does it, Nell?'

'I'm not sure. I hope not. I was curious why you asked him to look into her background?'

'Another hunch I'm exploring.' Toni smiled at her. 'Like you, Stuart seems to have a knack for finding things out.'

The report they had just gone through was thorough and up to Nell's usual standards. By focussing on the additional material the Al Anfal document contained – compared to the Muslim Brotherhood 'Project' report – she had highlighted a selection of the monetary trans-actions and routes used to launder cash and had traced those back to their original sources. In an imaginative move, she had then produced a map of illegal arms smuggling, heroin and slave trafficking routes, and compared them to the financial transactions. The similarities were remarkable. One series of routes had become the focus of her attention when she noticed how they all ended up in one place: Romania. And more specifically, at the door of the Cristea family, the very same people she had been researching less than a year previously.

And, for any normal researcher, that may have been where the trail ended. But Nell wasn't just any researcher. She kept digging, check-ing and cross-referencing until she noticed another coincidence. A file relating to a mercenary soldier: a Serbian called Petre Gavrić who was last seen in Romania, and whose name she recognised from the 'police-wanted' circulations. A man who had escaped a swoop on traffickers that had resulted in the closure of the UK-based Cristea prostitution and pornography operation. Access to his file was blocked but Nell had been determined not to give up until she found out by whom.

And when she did, she had realised it was time to tell her boss.

'So what else did you find out about Howard Green?' Toni asked.

'That he spends well beyond his means.'

'Using money from his wife?'

'No corresponding or equivalent movement of funds that I could find. Wherever Howard Green gets his money from, it isn't her.'

The familiar buzzing of the security door release distracted Toni from the screen. Glancing over her shoulder, she caught a glimpse of Stuart in the doorway. Great timing, she thought, wondering what he would think of Nell's discovery.

'Martina Proctor, the prostitute,' said Stuart, without being asked as he dropped his coat onto an empty desk. 'Not surprisingly, that wasn't her real name. She was, or is, from Romania. Is there a brew on?'

'We were just talking about her,' replied Toni. 'What did you find out? I thought she was a Londoner?'

Stuart headed to the cubby hole and flicked on the kettle as he called back to them. 'Well, she isn't, but I remember her voice too and, yes, she had me fooled as well. Anyway, the upshot is she's disappeared. She had a criminal record for street prostitution as long as your arm. Hardly a week seemed to go by without her being pulled in and either cautioned or charged with soliciting. But a week after we saw her with Howard Green was the last time she came to notice. Since then, nothing. No arrests, not even a benefits claim.'

'Like so many of the other girls that fall into that world and never seem to go home,' said Nell, her voice tinged with sadness.

'Exactly,' said Toni. 'And I can't help but think how convenient it would be for Howard Green if Martina Proctor was no longer in existence.'

'There's more,' said Stuart, from the doorway. 'I ran her prints through the Interpol database and it came up with her original name.

Maria something … I wrote it down so I wouldn't forget it. Anyway, I did some more checking with the Immigration Service and the Home Office and I managed to find out when she came to the UK. She travelled on a scheduled flight from Bucharest in 1999.'

'A flight? You might have thought she'd have come over in the back of a lorry or something?'

'No, she flew. And it gets better.' Stuart was now grinning, as if looking forward to seeing the reactions as he divulged what he had learned. His smile turned to a look of mild disappointment as his two colleagues simply waited silently for him to continue.

'OK,' he continued. 'Get this. I checked the flight list with one of my old mates at Heathrow to confirm what I'd been told.'

'Typical copper,' said Nell, mischievously.

'Just being thorough. And I was glad I did. I found her name on the manifest and you'll never guess who was in the seat next to her?'

Toni frowned. She hated games and was beginning to wish Stuart would stop beating around the bush and get to the point. 'Do tell,' she said, as patiently as she was able.

'Remember Constantin Macovei?'

'The trafficker that was shot by the police last year?' said Toni.

'A Cristea man supplied Howard Green's pet prostitute,' said Nell, as she turned to face the others.

'So, Macovei brought Martina – or Maria, as she was called then – into the country?' said Toni. 'Martina was a Cristea trafficking victim? Are you guys thinking what I am?'

'I can trump that,' said Nell, the frustration in her voice apparent. 'If you'd only just let me.'

Stuart laughed. 'Nell's been trawling the auction sites on the dark web.'

'I'm sorry, Nell,' said Toni. 'You said you wanted to show me something else.'

'At last,' her researcher answered as she clicked the screen of her computer to a new window. 'I found this for sale on a Pakistani auction site. I thought you'd want to know.'

Toni leaned across her to look at what Nell had found. 'What the hell,' she exclaimed.

As Stuart also went to speak, his gaze turned towards the security door. At the same time, a confused look appeared on Nell's face as she too looked across. Toni spun in her chair to see what had distracted them.

Alex Dyer, the new Deputy Director was standing in the office doorway. Stuart must have left the door open. Behind him was Suze Bickerton from Thames House. Dyer looked stern, businesslike, on a mission. Suze looked embarrassed, awkward. As if she didn't want to be here, or something was about to happen that she wasn't looking forward to.

For a moment, Toni was distracted by what Nell had just discovered. She hoped – prayed – her assistant would think quickly enough to kill her screen.

'Fellowes, I believe you know Mrs Bickerton?' Dyer said, sternly.

Fellowes? People like Dyer tended to use the surnames of their officers at meetings and similar formal occasions, but here, in the office, it would normally be first names for them, 'sir' to address him. This clearly wasn't a social call.

Toni nodded politely to Suze. She returned the compliment but avoided eye contact. Stuart was also looking rather sheepish; possibly concerned their conversation had been overheard.

'Good. Fellowes, if you'd like to get your coat and come with me, please. Nell and Stuart, you will remain here with Mrs Bickerton. Make sure you give her your utmost cooperation.'

Nell and Stuart? First names for them but not for me? Toni thought. Things were not looking good. It looked like the shit had hit the fan, big time.

Her hands trembled as she reached for her handbag beneath the desk. She could feel every pair of eyes in the tiny office staring at her, watching her move, looking to see her reaction. *Don't give them the satisfaction,* she told herself; *just keep calm.*

Just keep calm.

Chapter 59

'Want to tell me what the fuck is going on?' Kevin eased himself closer to me as he spoke.

My mind was racing with theories. Howard Green with Petre? What did it mean? Why was an enforcer from the Cristea slave-trafficking family working with an MI6 officer? What was the connection? I ran through what Toni had told me about the Al Anfal document; her warning about it and about Howard's clean-up mission, and the words of Omar Shabat, the Minister. There had to be a common denominator.

I didn't reply, for even if I'd had an answer to the question Kevin had posed, Grady immediately ordered us to stay quiet.

'Well, well,' said Howard, as he stepped close enough to converse without raising his voice. 'A long time since I've seen you two.'

'Nearly twenty years, I'd say,' Kevin answered. 'And I was looking up at you then as well.'

Howard laughed. 'Yes, I do believe you were. I confess, I thought you'd never get out of that little scrape.'

Twenty years? My mind returned to Afghanistan, and to the last time I had seen Howard there. He'd been working out of the MI6 office at Peshawar in Pakistan and had been responsible for much of the reception and analysis of Russian hardware that Beaky had written about in his book, *Cyclone*.

'Your lies nearly got me killed, and you never as much as said sorry or even a little thanks,' Kevin spat.

I heard the bitterness in the words, the rage of a man who held a grudge, and I remembered. I remembered how Kevin had been tasked with covering an extraction of equipment by Howard and his team and how the promise of help to fight off a large Russian force had failed to materialise. I remembered how I'd finally found my friend, wounded and bleeding, in hiding and kept going by a mixture of anger and adrenalin. All bar three of the Mujahideen Kevin had fought along-side had been killed, and every man that escaped had been injured, no exceptions. And I also remembered why, after Toni had told me what had really been going on to hide the real nature of the Al Anfal document, I'd decided not to tell Kevin the truth. I knew my friend well, knew how he'd react to the news that a man who had abandoned him to his fate was also responsible for the deaths of so many of his friends. As old wounds were opened, good sense would have gone out the window as an all-consuming desire for revenge took over. And Kevin would have let that happen; he would have gone after Howard, and he wouldn't have stopped until the man had suffered for what he'd done. And what would have been the benefit? Another man dead and Kevin's life ruined. And for what?

Howard ignored him. 'And what of you, Robert Finlay?' he asked. 'You seem rather less surprised to see me than Kevin. You've become something of a pariah in the policing world, I'm told.'

'What's Petre doing here?' I asked.

'Ah, yes. Well, I'm sure that will all become clear in due course.'

'Do you mind if we stand up?' I replied. Howard was close now, not so close that we could reach him – he wasn't that foolish – but craning my neck to see him wasn't something I wanted to continue. I needed to be on my feet.

'Mr Grady. Would you please cover these gentlemen as Petre secures them?'

I watched as Petre walked to the back of the Range Rover and began unloading something. My view was obscured but, whatever it was, it looked heavy. He then walked to the passenger side of the car, removing a small laptop and what looked like a satellite phone. He placed both items on the bonnet before reaching back inside and emerging with two sets of plasticuffs. As the internal light came on, I also saw what appeared to be the silhouettes of two figures in the back seat. They sat still, apparently watching what was going on.

I lowered my head as Petre took hold of my arms and applied the cuffs. Unarmed and outnumbered, I didn't resist. There would have been little point and, at the moment, I was in one piece, a situation I planned to maintain for as long as I could.

As Petre tied Kevin's wrists, Grady loomed large in front of us. 'You're into that kind of thing, eh, Kev?' he said.

'Just fuck off, Grady.' Kevin lunged forward but Petre moved quickly to counter his adrenalin-fuelled reaction. The Serbian kicked his legs apart and sent him sprawling onto the dirt, his face glaring angrily at the implication of what Grady was saying. He stopped struggling and lay quiet, but I could already see red weals appearing around his wrists as he strained against the cuffs.

Petre quickly turned us both around and sat us down on the grass. He didn't speak and, satisfied we were both secure, he stepped toward the Range Rover.

'Search them then bring them inside,' Howard barked.

Grady placed the pistol he was holding into his belt and then lifted me to my feet. A few feet away, I could see Kevin receiving similar treatment from Petre. All the while, Grady and Kevin stared at each other, their previous friendship now replaced by open hatred. The search was thorough and methodical, and quickly produced the digital recorder that had been sitting in my pocket, a back-up that I'd been planning on using to record the interview with Mellor if I'd been unable to work the burner phone.

Petre opened the bothy door to allow us to follow him in. Howard had pulled one of the chairs to a position against the far wall and was now sitting facing the door. The remaining furniture, a table and two more chairs, he had pushed to one corner to keep the floor area clear.

Grady came in last, made sure we stood facing Howard and then handed him the recorder. Howard turned it on.

'Planning on recording something, Finlay?' he asked.

I didn't answer.

A look of uncertainty flashed across his face. He pressed 'play' and seemed pleased when he discovered the device was clean. 'Bring me the gun,' he said, addressing Grady and Petre. He turned to Kevin and me. 'You two, sit down again.'

As Grady left, we did as instructed. Petre watched from just behind us.

'I don't have long,' began Howard. 'So, to avoid any unpleasantness, I'll be asking for your full cooperation.

For a few moments we waited, with no further conversation taking place until Grady returned and handed Howard a small, brown paper bag. Howard peered inside, grunted approvingly and then, with a toss of his head, indicated for Grady and Petre to leave.

'OK, let's begin,' he said, as the door closed. 'The sooner you answer my questions, the sooner we can all be on our way home. What do you two know about Al Anfal?'

'I should have bloody guessed,' said Kevin. 'You always did have a nose for a quick buck.'

'So, where is the document you were planning on selling?'

'From what I'm told, you lot have it.'

'My lot?'

'The Security Services – MI6, MI5 … whatever name you want to use. You have it.'

Howard appeared about to respond before checking himself and turning to me. 'And what might you have to say, Finlay? What happened to the version you obtained from Bob Bridges widow?'

'I don't know what you're talking about,' I said.

Kevin turned to me. 'Don't be an idiot, boss. If you'd seen what that bloke took from the back of the car, you'd know it was a waste of time bullshitting.'

Howard grinned. 'Ah, yes. What I would call my back-up plan.'

'Well, you didn't bring that water container because you're thirsty, did you?'

Petre had lifted something heavy from the boot of the car. I'd not seen what it was but now, I realised Kevin was right. A large water container meant one thing, and not for washing or drinking. It was to make sure we talked. If Howard didn't get the answers he sought, we were to be tortured. Waterboarding was well known to be both speedy and effective. And Howard had mentioned he was in a hurry.

'Let's move on shall we, gentlemen?' he replied.

Kevin's willingness to talk surprised me, but as the conversation continued in what might almost have been described as a meeting of old friends – bar the fact that one of them was holding the other two prisoner – we made good progress. Howard wanted to know who else we had spoken to about the document. Kevin kept quiet about McNeil.

'You never discussed it with Toni Fellowes from MI5, then?' Howard demanded.

'Would you have wanted to share its value with the Security Services?' I bluffed, hoping he might accept the notion we both believed the document to simply be something we could sell.

Kevin decided to support me. 'We agreed it. Nobody was to know apart from the translator and, as we all know, he's now dead.'

'Yes, quite regrettable. For an old man, he showed remarkable inner strength … until he gave me your names, of course.'

'You killed him?' I said.

'I did my duty, Finlay. I plugged a leak. Don't try and convince me that former Special Forces soldiers like you two wouldn't understand that?'

'So, are we also in need of silencing?'

Howard didn't respond for a moment, as if he were thinking.

'And what about Shabat?' I asked, and from Howard's reaction I saw I had his immediate attention.

'What of him?' he asked.

'I had a meeting with him a few days ago. It was very revealing.' I hoped that by keeping the true nature of the conversation to myself, Howard might give away something useful.

He didn't. He simply shrugged. 'Old news, Finlay and, to be frank, I couldn't give a toss what he shared with you. That lily-livered individual couldn't be relied on and it was a mistake on my part to think otherwise. If he'd done his job as ordered we wouldn't be here now. So, tell me about this document, Jones?'

'I thought we'd come back to that,' Kevin answered. 'I guess you don't want to share? Is that why you sent the others outside because you want to cut a deal to find where I've stashed the copy…'

'It's not a decision I will make,' he replied. 'You need to understand that the men outside work at a lower security clearance level than I do, so there are things I may ask you, answers you may give that I would prefer them not to hear. I can only recommend to those above me as to how you are dealt with, based, as I said earlier, on your cooperation. Right now, you are bargaining for your lives, yes. And it has absolutely nothing to do with whether the document you have is of any value to a potential buyer.'

My heart sank. Kevin was bluffing, buying time, but only I knew that. Howard would now need to know if there was any truth in what he had just said. And there was only one way he was going to get that confirmation. For Kevin that would be a one-way ticket to hell. Unable to reveal a location he didn't actually have, and with Howard unlikely to believe he had been bluffing, torture was never going to work. It would be suffering simply for the sake of it. And, no doubt, I would follow him.

And something else was troubling me. On the floor between Howard's feet sat the paper bag Grady had brought in. It kept calling to me. Howard had said, 'Bring me the gun' – *the* gun. What was it about the gun in that bag that made it the subject of such individual attention?

Then, as I thought more about what Shabat, the Minister, had said, about what he'd been asked to do, about Maggie Price going missing and why on earth someone would kill Sandi and then make Kevin look like the killer; it came to me. And I realised why Petre Gavrić was here.

And I knew we were never going to leave that bothy alive.

Chapter 60

'Where are we going?' Toni asked.

Dyer didn't reply. Instead, he simply marched ahead and out through the revolving doors. She followed, obediently. To one side of the exit, three armed officers from the Diplomatic Protection Group watched the street outside New Scotland Yard and all the people coming and going from the building. Two were armed with what looked like Heckler and Koch carbines. The third, a supervisor it appeared, had his thumbs tucked into the shoulder straps of his body armour. He looked extremely bored.

And long may it stay that way, Toni thought as her Assistant Director approached the rear of a waiting car, opened the door and indicated for her to get in.

She did so, and as Dyer sat down beside her, she asked him again where they were heading.

'Thames House,' he said. Although whether it was in response to her question or as an instruction to the driver, she wasn't sure. In any event, the car pulled way and headed towards the river.

The journey continued in complete silence. 'Make sure you cooperate', she recalled the words of instruction that Dyer had given to Nell and Stuart. What exactly had he meant? Some sort of investigation, it had to be. But what about? The obvious answer was Al Anfal and that cursed document.

The streets were crammed. Taxis, delivery drivers and the ever-growing number of cyclists all contributed to slow their progress. Eventually though, they entered the underground car park beneath Thames House. A security guard waved them through – suggesting they were expected, as even Directors were normally stopped and questioned – and they pulled up adjacent to the lifts.

'With me, Fellows,' said Dyer – his first words since they had set off.

The lift arrived quickly and, as they entered, Toni glanced to see which floor button he pressed. The fourth, Director level. They were heading to his office.

She was wrong. As the lift doors opened, they were greeted by Clare Bowen, the new secretary to Director 'T'. Clare remained impassive as they made eye contact and, like Dyer, who was now stood behind Toni at the rear of the lift, she remained silent as she turned on her heel and headed back to her office. Toni felt the muscles in her thighs twitch and, for a self-conscious moment she fought hard to resist the urge to dive out of the lift and head for the emergency stairs. The Assistant Director used his open hand to indicate they should follow and, as they reached the Director's office, Clare opened the outer door. Standing to one side, she then opened the door to the Director's office itself. He was standing just inside, waiting.

The Director smiled as he thanked Clare. As she retired and then closed the door behind them, Toni felt herself shudder.

┼

'I'm not sure whether to be angry with you or not, Toni.'

Uncertain as to whether she should reply to the Director's leading remark, Toni scanned the papers in front of her for any clues as to what was coming, but the font was too small, and he was being careful not to place them so close that she might be allowed the chance. Two photographs were pinned to the inside front page of one folder he held up for her to see. One was of Chas Collins – the author she had gone to so much trouble to try and locate. The second was Maggie Price, his agent, now the subject of a missing-person's enquiry by the police.

'You do recall our last meeting, I trust?' he continued.

Toni swallowed as she tried to overcome the tension in her jaw. The muscle twitch had stopped, thankfully, but a creeping sense of anxiety was still welling up from her chest. She felt warm, uncomfortably so. 'Yes … of course,' she muttered.

'Then you'll remember I gave you my email together with instructions to keep me personally updated on the Hastings enquiry into Colonel Monaghan and any other developments surrounding it?'

'Of course, I'm sorry. I've been a little wrapped up in it.'

The Director paused, and took a single, deep breath. 'Very well. Perhaps we'll return to that in a moment. For now, we have a very serious situation we need to discuss with you.'

Dyer took the file containing the photographs and placed it in a briefcase at his feet. 'You're aware the agent Maggie Price and her author, Chas Collins, have been of interest to us?' he said.

'I am, yes.'

The Director took over. 'Two weeks ago, we were contacted by our colleagues in Belgium. Chas Collins, as we now know him, was found dead in a dilapidated garage, where he had, apparently, been living rough. At first, they thought he was a simple tramp who had died as a result of carbon monoxide poisoning from a small cooker he had been using. It was only when they ran a precautionary search through Interpol that his fingerprints came up with a match.'

'The CIA will be pleased. That book he brought out last year caused a lot of embarrassment.'

'Indeed it did. Anyway, you'll be aware that the other photograph on that file is his agent, Mrs Price. Mrs Price has also been missing for some time now.'

Toni nodded. Her heart rate was easing as the sensation of panic subsided.

'Good. You're with me so far?'

'Yes.'

'What you won't be aware of – unless you've been discovering things even we don't know about – is that there is strong evidence to believe Mrs Price was killed on the doorstep of her home.'

'Killed? I thought it was a missing-person enquiry.'

'The police have been cooperating with us. We have forensic evidence to link the Price case to an incident nearby on the same night she went missing.'

'An incident?' Toni asked.

'A drug dealer who ended up on the mortuary slab with a bullet in his skull.'

'Yes, I'd heard about that too. I thought the two events were supposed to be unconnected?'

The Director's lips curved upwards, just slightly. Not a smile, more in recognition that Toni was up to speed and paying attention. 'Yes,' he said. 'That is what has been released to the public. In truth, the two events are very much connected. A .22 calibre firearm was used at Mrs Price's house. We know this because a damaged hollow-point bullet of that type was found in the frame of her front door. It was badly damaged but there is every indication it came from the same gun used to kill the drug dealer.'

'A forensic match that couldn't have come from a Glock?'

'A smaller calibre, Toni. It isn't a match good enough for a court, but good enough for us. We have been, shall I say, looking into the circumstances of Mrs Price's disappearance, as we understand that Collins had been working on a new book that exposed the Al Anfal organisation.'

Toni remained silent, trying to recall who knew what. Howard Green had warned her not to talk about it, and yet here was her Director discussing that very same organisation. He had to be testing her, she figured. If she denied any detailed knowledge of Al Anfal, he would recognise the lie. Best to be brave.

'That could be a good reason for discomfort in some quarters,' she replied.

Dyer leaned forwards in his chair. 'Ms Fellowes, we are well aware you made the connection between Howard Green and the former soldiers who first discovered the Al Anfal document. You know, as do we, that he was responsible for silencing any potential leaks.'

'By murdering them, you mean?'

'Murder is a crime. Green's actions were lawfully sanctioned at the highest levels.'

'Well, I'm sure the relatives of those soldiers will be relieved to hear that, sir.' For a moment, Toni had forgotten herself, and the two men clearly heard the bitterness in her voice. That they were minded to forgive the outburst fractionally eased her anxiety levels.

After a short pause, the Director continued. 'And you warned Robert Finlay that any contact he had with the soldiers trying to sell the document could place his own life at risk?'

'As ordered, yes I did. But you know that already, I was given to understand. Finlay told me the document was destroyed.'

'By Dr Armstrong?'

'Yes.'

'Who quite recently came by another copy.'

'Yes, so I'm told. The copy Mr Dyer here produced at a recent Long Room meeting.'

'And after which, you approached Miles Chadbourne?'

'You're well informed, sir.'

'It's my bloody job to be informed, Toni.' The Director spat the words. His lips narrowed, his brow tense, it was the first time he had shown any sign of temper.

Toni's stomach lurched in response to a sudden adrenalin rush. She was sweating now.

'OK, let's carry on,' said Dyer. 'Several months ago we were approached by an agent who informed us he was being put under pressure by one of our officers to arrange the murders of two men.'

Toni felt a feeling of déjà vu as she heard the words 'two men'. 'Does this have anything to do with the Al Anfal clean-up operation?' she asked.

'Yes,' replied the Director. 'The two men are the police officers you have been looking after, Jones and Finlay.'

'Someone wants them dead?'

'Please don't play games, Fellowes. We also know that agent recently passed a warning to Inspector Finlay who I've no doubt told you.'

'Er … yes. He did, sir.'

'Then you'll know the Minister I'm referring to?' The Director looked straight at her, as if he were daring her to lie.

'Of course,' she replied. 'And the officer who wanted Finlay dead is the same man who ran the post-Monaghan clean-up operation – Howard Green.'

'We hoped you might come up with Howard's name without prompting … and it seems you haven't disappointed. Rather helps with confirming we are on the same track.'

'Same track?'

'Stopping Howard Green.'

'From going after Jones and Finlay? I thought you'd specifically warned him off?'

'You are correct. But, as with all such orders, one must ensure they are complied with. So, you see, I've been keeping an eye on Howard for quite some time.'

'I didn't realise,' Toni answered, humbly.

'And not just due to my natural sense of caution, I needed to know if there were others involved with him – others who knew of Al Anfal.'

'Others?'

'Yes, others. Hence my allowing the production of the document at the Long Room meeting. We wanted to see if anyone took the bait.'

'What bait?'

'The bait that you took – Miles Chadbourne. He reacted to the mention of the document and, although you weren't the only person to spot it, you were the only person who followed it up.'

'So, I gave myself away?'

'Not really. As I said, I was already aware of your interest.'

'And Miles is working for you?'

'He is, yes. His posting to the dungeon has been part of our gambit.'

'Did you know his office has been cleared out?' said Toni.

'We were looking for a clue as to his whereabouts. We found nothing.'

'Well, well,' said Toni. 'He certainly fooled me. And would it be too much to conclude that Suze Bickerton is in on this as well?'

'Correct. Which brings us quite neatly onto why we are here now.'

'You want me for something?'

'We do, yes,' replied the Director. 'But before that I should apprise you of the background.'

'The background?' asked Toni.

Alex Dyer reopened his briefcase and placed a file in front of her. 'Take a minute to read this,' he said.

Toni glanced at the Director. He nodded, as if he were reassuring her that she had his blessing to do as was being suggested. She began to read.

A few minutes later, as she began to flick through a series of financial reports appended to the document, Dyer continued where he had left off. 'So, you see you're not the only one to have maintained an interest in Howard Green.'

'I do see,' she replied. 'You've been monitoring his activities for some while?'

'We have,' said the Director. 'It became apparent to me that Howard was working, at least in part, to an agenda not set by us. He pays lip service to orders, but it seems that on occasion he has a predisposition to do his own thing, as it were.'

'A loose cannon,' Toni commented.

'Indeed. I've been concerned that the operation to stop the sale of the Al Anfal document to the press had gone off track and that more was going on than I was privy to. After Finlay and Jones appeared with you on Howard's radar last year, he wanted to have all three of you taken out.'

'Me as well? I was aware of the threat to the policemen, but…'

'And as you're aware. Howard was given clear orders to drop his plans. I wasn't sure about him, though. So I decided to try and get an officer close enough to him that I might be reassured as to his loyalty.'

'So Miles has been undercover, within the Service itself?' Toni asked.

The Director glanced at his number two before replying. 'The tethered-goat trap, to see if Howard would follow correct protocol on discovering another potential leak. Miles was aware of the risk.'

'Quite brave considering his target's track record. Howard didn't do what you expected of him, presumably?'

'Howard Green only does things for his own betterment,' said Dyer.

'Through questionable business interests?' Toni asked, tentatively, all the while wondering if she were taking a step too far. But now that she knew she too was at risk, the game had changed.

'You've discovered something?' he asked, as he leaned forwards in his chair.

'This very day.' Buoyed by the Assistant Director's apparent enthusiasm, she decided to go for it, to say what she knew. 'Howard's interests in the Cristea family seem to extend beyond monitoring them in the interests of the state.'

'In it up to his neck, you might say, Toni.'

'You know?' she asked as she realised it was a statement rather than a question.

Dyer turned to the Director as if seeking approval to answer. The slightest of nods was all Toni saw before he continued. And she'd noticed something else: Dyer had switched to using her first name.

'We've had concerns,' he explained. 'Shall we say … irregularities in Howard's financial dealings have been brought to our notice. It all seems to relate to this Al Anfal organisation he is supposed to be monitoring. Our evidence suggests they pay him, and very handsomely. In return he makes sure we turn a blind eye to what they do, how they generate income and all manner of other activities.'

'Including the trafficking of women?'

'Yes, including the generating of cash through the sale of people.'

'How long have you known?' she asked, avoiding eye contact with the Director and doing her level best not to make her question sound like an accusation that they should have acted more promptly. If the Director took her inference that way, he didn't show it.

Dyer continued. 'For some while now Miles has been putting Howard under pressure,' he said. 'To see if he might make a mistake, expose to us what he is really involved in. We have yet to discover the scale of his operation and whether he is working on his own or with others.'

'Others in the Service? As opposed to what you said a moment ago about others outside who may have known about Al Anfal?'

'Miles's brief was to discover if there are others within the Service, yes.'

'Did it work?' Toni asked.

'We really don't know. Miles Chadbourne's absence from his office isn't our doing. We have no idea where he is and we fear that Howard has grabbed him.'

'And we have no contact method for him?'

Dyer turned once more to the Director. He looked sombre, even a little worried. When he finally spoke, Toni understood why. 'He has a GPS locator in his phone. Two days ago, it stopped transmitting.'

'So, you've lost him?'

'We have. And, as of yesterday, we also lost track of Howard Green. We don't think it's a coincidence.'

'And is Howard still after Jones and Finlay?'

'We believe so. We fear he may already have them as well. Someone with considerable skill was behind the Jones escape from court and we have just learned that a surveillance team the police set up to follow Finlay has reported there is no trace of him anywhere.'

'So, we're too late?' Toni asked.

The Director looked resigned.

'Unless he wants to question them,' she continued. 'To find out what they know and if they've told or involved anyone else?'

Dyer closed the buff folder in front of Toni. 'This file is for you. If you can find our missing officer and the two coppers, then so much the better, but you can still have it.'

'It's pretty damning.'

'It's a copy of what we know about Howard. As you're now aware, it doesn't make for comfortable reading.'

As she reached forward toward the file the Director placed a firm hand on it. 'We know you've been working on this, Toni, and we've been keeping a close eye on where you've been looking, but we don't know all you have discovered. I need you to work on this, officially, and pool even the things you may not think of as important. We need to find them, this has to stop now.'

'To keep Al Anfal secret?' Toni asked.

'For now, yes.'

'Because they don't know that we have this insight into their organisation?'

'Precisely,' said the Director. 'Although, given recent developments, that situation will be subject to review.'

Toni turned to Dyer. 'Did you notice what we were looking at on the computer, sir? When you arrived to collect me.'

'Something on the internet, I believe.'

'It was an auction site, a special one only accessible through the dark web. We were looking at an item that was for sale.'

'Something of interest?' asked Dyer.

'Very much so, it was something that may affect this a great deal. Bids were being invited for a copy of the Al Anfal document.'

Chapter 61

I estimated that maybe an hour had passed since the group had arrived.

Kevin and I were back out on the grass, laid down and watching as Petre fiddled with the cable connections between the satellite phone and the laptop. Howard had opened the rear nearside door to the Range Rover. For some while after our conversation in the bothy, he had left us to ourselves while he and the others formed a huddle in front of their car. Many times they looked across at us, either because we were the subject of their discussion or, likely as not, to make sure we weren't moving.

I was close enough to Kevin to speak to him and, as I watched for any reaction from our captors, I'd quietly explained my theory. 'I'm betting the gun in the bag is dirty,' I said. 'And, if I'm right, it was used to kill the drug dealer near where Beaky's agent went missing.'

'So, what's he brought it here for?' Kevin whispered.

'I think they're planning to use it to shoot me. It'll end up in your hands after they kill you is my guess. So, when we're found, it looks like you shot me when I came to try and talk you into coming back to London.'

Kevin spat onto the grass. 'Maggots. What's the time?' he asked.

'Do I look like I can see my watch?'

'Approximately?'

'About ten, I guess, maybe a bit later. Got any ideas?'

'Not an idea, more of a hope. Three of them, two of us. Not bad odds bar the two in the back of the Range Rover.'

'You'd clocked them then?' I whispered.

'Aye. Been trying to work out who they are. Odd that they're just sitting there.'

'Two against five then? Not the best odds.'

'No drama. I've known worse.'

'Maybe not when they hold most of the aces … not to mention the guns and us being cuffed.'

'*Most* of the aces?' Kevin hissed.

'Yes. I'm not sure but there may be a chink of hope. See the guy fiddling with the computer?'

'Hard to miss him. Sounds Polish or something.'

'I know him – from that trip to Romania last year,' I said. 'He was the bodyguard to the girl I saved from drowning.'

Kevin took a deep breath. 'So, at the moment our best hope is he thinks he owes you a favour?'

'His boss made me a promise … but that was before he found out I was a cop.'

'That made a difference?'

'It was his operation we broke up in that old hospital in the Forest of Dean.'

'Ah … not a big chance you'll be his favourite person, then?' Kevin coughed.

Howard was walking over. He grinned as I looked up. 'Comfortable?' he asked.

'Been worse,' I said.

'Yes, I'm sure you have.' He stepped behind us, leaned down and checked our wrists and pulled us up onto our knees. My restraints were still tight, although I'd had a few vain attempts at testing the plastic, and from the satisfied grunt Howard gave, it looked like Kevin was also secure.

As he appeared in front of us again, I saw that Howard had something small and silver in his hand. It was the digital recorder. He gave a knowing grin as he walked back to the others. As he lifted the device to his ear, I realised he'd been recording us.

At the car, Petre checked his watch. 'It's time,' I heard him say.

Howard walked back to us. 'My congratulations, Finlay. It seems you really have made it as a detective.'

'I was right then?'

'Not entirely. Mrs Price isn't missing, she's dead. Her body is behind the latrine at the rear of this very bothy, in fact. Ready and waiting for the police forensic people to tie her in to Kevin's murderous activities.'

'Killed with the gun in the paper bag, I presume?'

He nodded. 'A nice little .22 Beretta. Small but very effective.' Kevin simply glared.

'So you planted the Glock in Kevin's car?'

'A late arrangement implemented after his unexpected survival.'

'To make sure he was kept in custody?'

Howard smiled. 'You've got it all worked out, it seems.'

'So, who are our voyeurs?' I asked. 'Come to watch have they?'

'In the car?' Howard replied. 'No,' he turned to face Kevin. 'Another of your victims, Jones. An MI5 officer who got too close.'

'Anyone we know?' I asked, hesitantly. I did my best to keep composed, even though I was dreading the answer. An MI5 officer who got too close? It had to be Toni. My stomach reacted as though I had been punched, my breathing shallow and rapid as my chest tightened.

Howard didn't answer for several seconds. I sensed he was enjoying toying with us.

Finally, as he turned to walk away, he replied. 'Who knows, Finlay? Oh … and don't get any ideas about Petre helping you. You're the reason he's here.'

Kevin and I were now on our knees, Howard having placed us in a 'stress position'. It was uncomfortable and intended to be that way. Soon, we would tire and, as our thigh muscles started to shake with the strain then, no doubt we would then be subject to some kind of rebuke, either verbal or physical. It was designed to wear us down, to lower our resistance. Eventually, as our captors moved on to other tried and tested methods, we would talk. That would take time, of course, and I'd developed a feeling that time wasn't something Howard had a whole lot of. He knew we had been through the same type of training he had; how to resist questioning, develop a rapport with your interrogator, give enough to keep them happy, that kind of thing. So, if time was an issue, I figured they were about to up the ante, and to work on us in a way that produced quick results.

Which meant one thing. The water. I'd learned about water boarding during training sessions at Hereford; we'd discussed it and even experimented with it. We'd tried it on each other and, without exception, we'd agreed it was appalling … and effective.

I looked across at Kevin and saw he was watching our captors. Like me, he'd be trying to work out how we were going to overcome them or escape. There was one chance, I figured, not of escape but to buy time. The more we talked, the greater the chance of an opportunity.

Kevin leaned towards me slightly before speaking again. 'He meant that he's planning to kill the MI5 agent and pin it on me?' he said, under his breath.

'It's Toni, Kev. It has to be. She's the only one who knows about it, apart from us.'

His face screwed up as if some awful taste had just hit his tongue, and he spat again. 'End game eh?'

'Yes,' I replied, soberly. 'End game.'

✝

Howard opened the car door, and for the first time I saw the face of the man from MI5. I say man, because at first I wasn't sure and my initial reaction was one of utter horror at what I believed they had done to Toni. It was only when the entire form of their third prisoner fell out onto the stony path that I was able to see it was that of a male. Not Toni then and, for a moment I felt a sense of shame at my relief on discovering it wasn't my friend they had in the car. But, in the same moment, I realised that water wasn't the only technique our captors were prepared to use. Swollen to the point of appearing grossly disfigured, the eyes, nose and lips of the man had moulded together into a single, bloodied mass of bruising and raw flesh.

As Petre stopped what he was doing to watch, a fourth figure dressed all in black and wearing a dark beanie hat appeared from the opposite side of the car.

'Come and help,' Howard called to him.

Grady also approached the figure crumpled in the dirt. He and the new man each grabbed an arm and dragged the poor man to one side, where they then laid him on a large plank of wood with the end that supported his feet uppermost and resting on what looked like a large tree stump. As a series of straps were used to bind him to the plank and restrict movement, I guessed what was about to happen. The water treatment was something that needed the subject to be restrained, either through weight of numbers – a luxury Howard didn't have – or by keeping the person secure. In this case, it looked as if their intended victim was incapable of offering much resistance. If I was next, or if they chose Kevin – which seemed more likely as it was he who had alluded to being in possession of more information – they would not find it so easy.

As the stranger from the rear of the Range Rover went to work with the water container, I saw Howard leaning close to his victim, seemingly talking to him. It wouldn't be long before he began talking, if he hadn't already. There weren't many who could withstand the kind of beating it looked like he had been subjected to.

'Fifteen seconds, they reckon,' said Grady as he came to cover us.

Neither Kevin nor I replied. We knew what he meant. Fifteen seconds was the average time it took for the victim of waterboarding to convince themselves they were drowning. If he continued to resist, Howard and his assistant would stop, wait a few seconds and start again. Three or four repetitions and the man on the plank would be desperate to stop the agony. That is, of course, if he wanted to live. I'd heard tales of people who had held out for incredible amounts of time. It was said, by those who claimed to know, that women often resisted better than men. Something about their higher tolerance to pain, I'd heard. I had no idea if the rumours were true, all I did know was that this wasn't something I'd ever seen myself facing, not even in my worst dreams.

It was as I looked more closely that I caught sound of the voice that came from the black-clad stranger. At first I wasn't sure but as I watched I realised. Howard's third associate was female.

Chapter 62

'Soon as I call "go", we run,' hissed Kevin.

The first session of torture was over and Howard was now asking questions. If he heard what he needed, it was possible things might stop there, but I doubted it. The MI5 officer had kicked and squirmed as his drowning reflex kicked in. His conscious brain could have told him it would be in vain and to preserve his strength, but this was something he had no control over. Try as hard as he might to resist, he did what everyone else who went through the experience did. And as he was probably going through it for the very first time, he panicked, as his survival instinct took over.

I'd been watching, not really because I wanted to see how he fared, for me it was more a case of hoping those who were now questioning him would be distracted. And they were. Petre was still playing with his laptop – God knows what he was doing – as Howard watched his victim suffer. The woman in black poured the water. Grady was the only one paying us attention, and he often glanced away towards the commotion. In those fleeting moments, we had a chance.

'End game' Kevin had said. It was code, well, sort of. Like saying we had one chance left. I'd never put it to the test before, although I was well aware that others had. It was recognition that in a desperate situation, the only option wasn't a good one and was likely to end badly. At all levels within the Regiment there was an acceptance that if being captured by enemy forces was bad enough for ordinary soldiers, for Special Forces it was always worse. And although those times had been the best part of two decades since, I knew all too well what 'end game' meant to them, and what it now meant to us. All or nothing.

Kevin knew I would understand him. One chance, then on our feet and run as fast as we could. Nearest cover was the bothy behind us, but that was a dead end. A log store sat about five yards from me and then, another ten yards further on was the forest, where we would be surrounded by trees. Not only was Grady the only one paying us sufficient attention, he was the only one holding a gun. Kevin would break left, me right. And, if we were lucky, one of us would make it to cover.

I wondered what Jenny was doing. Becky would be in school by now. I pictured our new home, my wife sat downstairs with our new daughter, maybe in front of a breakfast TV programme as she fed her, possibly in the garden if the weather was nice. The house would be quiet. She'd be thinking about me too, worrying, concerned at what I was doing but naively trusting that I would be home eventually, as I always had been in the past.

I was afraid – afraid that this was the time I would fail the people I loved most. I prayed that fear would now give strength to my legs rather than paralysing me. I had been afraid before. That first time you come under fire, hear the zip of a round passing over your head and realise that people are actually trying to kill you, it's a moment that lives forever in your memory. Fear is a knife that twists in your gut but, as many men before me had learned, fear is an illusion. We need it – soldiers, cops, firefighters, anyone who faces danger – for fear is a precursor to bravery. 'There is nothing to fear but fear itself'; I remembered those words, a quote I think, and written by someone who truly understood. Many things are worse than fear, and, as the adrenalin now coursed through my veins and gave me strength, I knew that I had to use it, to master it rather than having it control me.

Across the yard at the front of the bothy, I could just make out what Howard was saying. He held his face close to the man's ear but he was almost shouting. He wanted answers to what sounded like the same questions he had been asking us: Who else knows? Who have you told? What exactly do you know? I caught the sound of a name. Miles. He called their injured prisoner Miles.

As I kept my eyes on Grady and Petre, I flexed my leg muscles to maintain blood flow and, once again, tested the plastic restraints. There was no give and, as I strained my arms, the sharp edges dug painfully into my wrists.

Kevin coughed. *Get ready.*

I looked across at Miles and had to work hard to put the wave of sorrow I felt to one side. We'd be abandoning him to his fate. I was glad I didn't know him. I hoped he wasn't, like me, a man with a family. It would be they who would suffer the most when he didn't come home. Miles, like all members of the Security Services, knew there was a risk associated with that role. He would have been warned, although, like me, he probably thought it could only ever happen to someone else.

Yes, I was sorry. But this was one of those times where survival meant looking after number one. I glanced across at Kevin, waiting on his word, flexing my thighs, preparing myself. Any moment now.

✝

'Comms established,' called out Petre.

Howard stopped what he was doing and turned to face us. 'Not the best timing,' he replied as he studied us. The woman placed the water container she was holding to one side. All eyes were now on us.

'Check their restraints,' Howard ordered.

Grady tucked his pistol into his belt, walked around us and carefully felt the cable ties to make sure we were secure. I had no doubt he saw the marks on my wrists where I had tried to break them but he didn't say anything. As he pulled Kevin's arms up to make a similar check I saw his wrists were also raw.

'Not hurting are they, Taff?' Grady leaned close into Kevin as he hissed the words.

'Not as much as I'm gonna hurt you,' my friend answered.

'Your woman seemed to quite like them.'

'Bastard…' Kevin made to stand but it was a futile attempt. Just as Petre had done earlier, Grady kicked his legs out from beneath him, dumping him winded and powerless on the ground.

Petre turned the screen of the laptop around so that it faced us. It looked like he had set it up for some kind of video call. A large face filled the screen.

'Bring Finlay,' he called.

Grady moved away from Kevin, grabbed hold of my upper arms from behind and dragged me to my feet. Kevin was left where he now lay as I was dragged towards the Range Rover.

And, as the screen of the computer came closer and I was able to recognise the features, I realised what Petre had been doing and why he was here. On the computer, on a live link to somewhere, was a man I knew would gain great pleasure in seeing my demise.

Gheorghe Cristea, father figure to the slave-trafficking gang I had helped to break up, torturer of the women we had rescued, and the very man who had warned me he would not forget.

And, although it now seemed too late to do me any good, the last piece of the jigsaw fell into place. This was Howard's connection, this was his secret. In the days when the Cristeas had run drugs and firearms into Peshawar, Howard, Kevin and I had been deployed there. Howard must have worked with the Cristeas then and had dealings with them ever since.

And Gheorghe Cristea was a man Howard was prepared to help when he needed something done.

Like finding me.

Chapter 63

New Scotland Yard

'Did it work?' Toni called, as she threw her coat towards the rack. It missed its target and fell in a crumpled heap on the floor.

'Would you mind telling us what's going on?' said Nell, her face glued to her screen.

'Did Mrs Bickerton explain?'

'Not a bloomin' word … and she left right after you called.'

'What happened when she was here with you?'

'We sat in silence, mostly,' said Stuart. 'Longest hour I've ever experienced. She only really spoke when I tried to leave.'

'To say what?' Toni asked.

'To tell us both that we had to stay here until she was authorised to release us.'

'I see.' Toni turned her attention back to Nell. 'Did the GPS work?'

'Yes. I have a grid reference for you. It's on the pad on your desk.'

'So where is he?'

'Wales. Near the Brecon Beacons.'

'Wales? Jesus. Is he stationary or on the move?'

'Stationary since I activated the phone's tracker.'

'OK.' Toni glanced at the six-figure number on her pad and then joined Nell at her desk. She beckoned Stuart across from where he stood looking out through the gaps in the blinds that covered the large window. She took a deep breath. This was going to be complicated.

✝

Once Toni had finished summarising what she had read in the report Dyer had handed her, both Nell and Stuart sat quietly for several seconds.

'So … any thoughts?' she asked.

'Does this kind of thing happen often?' asked Stuart. 'Different departments within the Service working on the same thing and our Director knowing about it but not telling us.'

Toni screwed up her face and forced a smile. 'Quite probably. Point is, there now seems to be an officer gone rogue and we need to find him.'

'This Howard Green character?' Stuart asked.

'Yes. According to Assistant Director Dyer, Howard has been turning a blind eye to the traffickers in exchange for information on who they launder money for and where they send it.'

'Like I said,' chipped in Nell.

'And he's dipped his finger in the pie?' said Stuart.

'So it seems. It looks like it started with sexual favours and progressed onto financial stuff.' She smiled at Nell, a look intended to acknowledge that her assistant had been right in her suspicions. 'Last year when we had him in that taxi and threatened to go looking into his bank accounts, he must have shit a brick.'

'Literally,' said Stuart. 'If the look on his face was anything to go by.'

'And the Director's convinced Howard is going after Jones and Finlay?' asked Nell.

'And that the agent he had undercover has been compromised.' Toni replied.

'Miles Chadbourne?' said Nell.

'Yes,' said Toni. 'And now it seems the best hope we have of tracing them is through the burner phone I gave Finlay.'

'They're a good four hours away,' said Stuart, thoughtfully. 'We won't be able to do anything from here and you'd need to do some kind of a recce to try and find out what was going on.'

Toni paused, although her mind was racing. 'How far is the signal from Credenhill Army Base, Nell?' she asked.

'I'm not sure. An hour or so, maybe two hours?'

'No, I mean flight time, or as the crow flies. How long would it take a helicopter to get from Hereford and then overfly that grid reference?'

'Once they were in the air … maybe ten to fifteen minutes?'

'And where is it, a village, out in the open, what?'

Nell tapped her keyboard. A map appeared on her screen showing a mountainous area covered in fir trees. 'Isolated and not easy to make a covert approach, if I might suggest—'

Toni held up her hand to kill any further conversation as she fished in her pocket for a small card the Director had given her not fifteen minutes previously. She picked up the phone and dialled the number. It was answered on the second ring.

'Sir, it's Fellowes here,' she said, her chest tight, her breathing shallow. 'We have a location for Finlay in Wales. I wonder if you might be prepared to put in a call to DSF, Director Special Forces?'

Chapter 64

On my knees, looking up at the screen on the bonnet of the car, I wasn't sure whether to laugh or cry at the irony.

In return for saving the life of his daughter, Gheorghe Cristea – publisher, slave trafficker, arms smuggler and murderer – was planning to grant me a quick and easy death.

'How *is* Marica, Gheorghe?' I asked, enquiring after his daughter in an attempt to remind him I had saved her life. I sensed we were fast approaching the moment when the talking would be over. My fate could prove to be Kevin's good fortune though. With me now the focus of attention, I figured he had a much better chance of making it to the tree line. If I could delay, maybe even create a distraction, some empathy or some doubt, a chance for an escape might happen yet.

On the laptop screen, the face sneered. Sound and vision were out of sync so the heavily accented and angry voice that followed wasn't matched by the lip movements. 'She wishes you dead, as I do, police spy.'

'You'll be a marked man, Gheorghe. If Petre here has told you the truth, you'll know that friends of mine will come after you for this.'

'I doubt that very much Finlay,' called Howard as he stepped closer to me.

From the corner of my eye, I saw Petre smile as he pulled a small pistol from the paper bag he now held.

Gheorghe replied, but I didn't hear it. My ears focussed on the sound of the slide of a small calibre pistol being cocked and the soft click of a round sliding into the breech. My thoughts were elsewhere, a very long way off, in another place, another time.

Then another noise caught my attention. Not close, but familiar. The whump-like beat of helicopter rotor blades slicing through air. And not just any helicopter. The twin rotors of a Chinook.

'Rescue on its way,' I muttered, more in prayer than hope.

Petre glanced skyward as the volume increased. The aircraft was close, but travelling at speed. They were passing through, not landing. But the distraction might provide the opportunity we needed.

Perhaps two or three hundred feet above, the Chinook flew right over us. It didn't deviate course or speed and, within a few seconds, the beat began to fade into the distance as it continued on its journey.

'Seven Squadron from Credenhill,' said Howard, his voice now close. 'Best get this over with in case they're on exercise nearby.'

He was talking to Petre. I figured he was right about the aircraft. 7 Squadron RAF were part of the Special Forces support arm and they often flew routes over the Beacons supporting training exercises and transporting troops here and there.

'Do thy worse for I have lived today,' I said quietly, intended solely for my own ears but overheard by Howard.

From behind me, he misquoted another line from Dryden's poem. 'What has been, has been, and you have had your hour, Finlay.'

I closed my eyes and remembered. 'The joys I have possessed, in spite of fate, are mine,' I said, as I waited. And as the seconds ticked passed I enjoyed them. I could smell the pine scent of the trees, the dampness of the grass, even the aroma of Petre's sweat. I heard the wind, felt it gently stroking my skin and I revelled in the sensation. I thought of Jenny, Becky and Charlie and I felt the warmth of my love for them.

And for the first time in longer than I could recall, I felt at peace.

✝

My ear exploded to the sound of the first shot.

Then there was a second, then more. Rapid firing such that I lost track. Around me I heard cries, the sound of a round hitting the car and, near me, the thud of something heavy hitting the ground.

No pain, I realised. No pain. Either I was dead and was now experiencing my personal answer to a mystery nobody living had ever known an answer to, or I was very much alive and something major had happened. I flung myself to my left, away from Petre and rolled as best I could around towards the driver side of the Range Rover.

Concealed near the wheel arch, I listened for a clue as to what was going on. I was alive, very much so. But what had happened?

Nobody came for me. A second passed, then two, still nothing. The smell of cordite hit my nostrils. I strained at the plastic cuffs around my wrists, ignoring the pain as I pulled on them with every ounce of strength my arms could muster. I rolled onto my side, pulled up my knees and tried to stand. As I struggled, a shadow appeared beside me on the grass. I looked up.

And saw the face of Brian McNeil staring down at me. 'Lie still,' he ordered.

From somewhere nearby the sound of a shot was met by an explosion of glass above us as a window of the Range Rover shattered.

'One x-ray down, three active,' hissed McNeil as he pinned me down.

I felt my arms spring apart and caught a glimpse of a blade in his left hand.

'Take this,' he added, as he shoved a pistol into my hand. 'Mag's full.'

A moment later, he was gone, diving away to my left, away from where I had last seen Kevin. I rolled onto my knees and glanced around me in the hope of finding better protection than the car afforded. The door to the bothy was within a few metres, as was the log store, but both required crossing open ground – exposing myself to unknown threats.

A burning sensation ran up both arms, stinging and raw as the blood started to flow again and feeling returned to my hands. I flexed my fingers as I checked the weapon McNeil had handed me. It was a Browning.

To my right, someone squeezed off two rounds. This time, whoever it was wasn't aiming at me.

I took the chance to take a quick look over the top of the car. In the fraction of a second I allowed myself to be exposed, I saw all that I needed to. Petre was down, face in the dirt near the front bumper, Kevin was away to my right behind a large tree. In front of us, Grady and the woman who'd arrived with him were taking cover behind Grady's car. Of Howard Green, there was no sign. To my left, behind another tree, I caught a glimpse of McNeil.

The only target available to me was Petre. He was lying face down, injured but still alive. Slowly, his right hand was moving towards the pistol he had been intending to use on me. I kept the largest part of me behind the engine bay of the Range Rover and leaned towards him. I could see enough. I raised the pistol, lined the metal sight up with the back of his head and squeezed off two rounds. A scarlet spray of blood and brain tissue flew into the air and his whole body jerked as if a powerful electric surge was passing through it. *End game, Petre*, I said to myself.

I looked across at Kevin, who returned my glance and gave me a thumbs-up. He quickly followed this with a series of hand signals. Two x-rays – suppressing fire – five seconds. I gave him an 'OK' to show that I understood and then began my countdown.

✝

'What happened?' I asked McNeil.

'You didn't know I was coming, did you?' he replied.

I hadn't remembered, but now, as I thought back to the fight in the car park, I recalled the phone conversation with Kevin, and the arrangement they'd made.

I was looking down at Petre. The laptop screen was now dark. Whatever had happened to the connection, I couldn't tell. And I wondered if Gheorghe had been able to witness what had happened before he had disconnected. I hoped he had seen and recognised the prophetic nature of my warning.

Kevin appeared from behind Grady's car. 'The woman's dead,' he said.

'Where's Howard?' I asked.

'He's fine.' Kevin turned away from me and appeared to kick out at something on the floor. A thud followed by a groan caught my ear and, as I approached, I saw Howard Green, uninjured and on the ground. Chris Grady was next to him but looked to be in a poor state. He was on his back, chest heaving, skin pale, and with a mixture of blood and spit spraying from his mouth as he struggled to breathe. In Kevin's hand, I saw he was holding a black bin liner and, as he leaned over Grady, I guessed what he was intending to do.

I was about to say something when McNeil grabbed my arm. I looked at him and saw the warning in his eyes – mind my own business.

By the time I returned my gaze towards Kevin, it was too late. He was on his knees, his lips pressed hard against Grady's left ear as he hissed some form of message. The bag was tight over Grady's face. The hitman's left arm could move, but he was weak from loss of blood and Kevin was strong. Within a few seconds, he abandoned his futile attempt to pull the plastic away from his face and his arm fell away limp by his side. Very soon after that his chest stopped moving as he took his last breath.

I turned to McNeil. 'How long have you been here?' I asked.

'Half an hour or so, while I waited for the right moment. I saw the cars and figured something was up, so I came through the forest on foot. Good job I did, it seems.'

As I listened, I surveyed the scene around us. Miles, the MI5 officer, was still tied to the planks where he had been tortured, the ground around him wet. His face was covered by a grey cloth but I could see he was still breathing.

'We'd best untie him,' I said.

'Leave it to me,' McNeil said. 'I think you and Kevin will be wanting a little chat with Howard over there.'

'You remember him, then?' I said.

'Ach aye, of course. It was him we first handed the Arabic script to. He was the MI6 liaison officer in Afghan back in the eighties.'

'You didn't shoot him? After what he's supposed to have done to all the others on that operation?'

McNeil shrugged, as if what I was suggesting hadn't occurred to him. 'He was nae armed. I took the big guy near you first as he had a weapon drawn.'

'Calm as that?'

'Like we were taught, boss. We're not exactly playing games here, yer ken?'

I understood. McNeil hadn't given our three captors a chance and he'd never intended to. Petre would have been shot before he even realised what had happened to him. Grady and the woman, pinned down by fire from me and Kevin, had been unable to prevent McNeil outflanking them. They hadn't stood a chance, but like McNeil had said, this wasn't a game where you could press a button for a new life. This was kill or be killed.

Kevin was now kneeling beside Howard, whispering something in his ear. The MI6 officer was face down, his arms by his sides, his legs stretched out. As I closed on them I saw his hands, and for the first time I saw the state of his fingertips, chewed and raw, just as Shabat had described.

'There's a phone in the Citroen, Kev,' I said. 'I'll call for help. I think Toni is best to handle this rather than the local cops?'

'Go ahead. Probably best you don't see what I'm going to do to this bastard.'

I thought for a moment. 'What you did to Grady was wrong, Kev,' I said.

'I wanted him to feel what it was like – to go through the same pain as Sandi.'

'OK.' I glanced across at McNeil, who had started to release the MI5 officer from the board he was tied to. McNeil only half acknowledged me. It was clear I'd get no support from him. 'Death is the wrong way to deal with people like Howard, Kev; he needs the humiliation of a public trial...'

'Which we both know won't fuckin' happen,' he hissed. 'If he walks away from here he'll do a deal.'

I was struggling to find the right words. Both morally and professionally I knew the revenge Kevin was intending to inflict was wrong. But at the same time I understood. Like me, though, Kevin was still a serving police officer. I knew the anger he was feeling, I even sympathised with him, but what he was talking about was retribution, not justice.

Then an idea came to me, a way that might get through to him. 'This isn't just about Sandi though, is it Kev?' I asked.

'It's all about Sandi,' he screamed suddenly. Then paused, taking a deep breath before continuing more calmly. 'What Howard did to the others was his job. Everyone who tried to make money out of that document knew they were taking a risk. They just didn't know it was Howard running the show.'

'And what about before that? Toni and I agreed not to tell you about Howard's role because we knew you'd go after him.'

Kevin paused again, as if thinking – or possibly remembering, playing something back in his mind. 'And I understand why,' he said.

'Because of what happened in Afghanistan?' I asked.

'Yes, because of that. He was prepared to let me and the Mujahideen lads die just to get his hands on some Russian kit.'

'And that's why you want to punish him?'

'Summary justice, boss … and in this case, the only way he's ever going to really pay.'

At Kevin's feet, I could see Howard listening as I negotiated for his life. He was keeping very quiet, just as I might have done in his position. I wondered what the instructors on the negotiator course would make of the situation I now found myself in – how they might advise me, what conversation track they might suggest I try. And I realised then that I was losing; for if there is one thing a negotiator has to have as he talks to a perpetrator, it is a determination to succeed and a belief that he can. Without that drive, that will to overcome any issue, he will not prevail. Deep down, I didn't have the will to save Howard. As I had with Petre, I could have put a bullet into the MI6 officer's brain at that very moment and not felt the slightest tinge of sympathy or regret. And Kevin knew it too.

'Make the call, boss,' he said. 'And tell her to hurry up.'

'Tell me you won't touch him.'

'OK, I won't hurt him.'

I returned to my Citroen and made the call. I'd only just connected when I heard a commotion behind me, near the bothy.

I looked across. The MI5 officer was on his knees, slumped forward, his chin resting on his chest. He looked done in. In his place on the wooden planks, Howard Green was struggling to resist Kevin and McNeil as they attempted to restrain him, but he was losing.

Kevin had lied to me. 'I'll call you back,' I said to Toni.

'No, there's something I need to—' she began. As I pressed the button to end the call I just caught her words. There would be time for whatever it was she wanted in a moment. For now, I had to stop Kevin getting in even deeper trouble than he already was.

Chapter 65

'Back off, boss,' Kevin called out.

The anger had returned. McNeil saw me coming and placed his hand on the pistol grip sticking out from the waistband of his trousers. His face deadpan, he placed himself firmly between me and where Howard was now restrained on the wooden planks. Kevin was lifting the end with his feet to replicate the position the MI5 officer, Miles, had been in a few minutes earlier.

The threat stopped me in my tracks, and then a croaky, spluttering sound from my right drew my gaze. Miles was trying to speak. I kneeled down next to him.

'MI5,' he said, weakly. 'Get help ... please.'

With my hand on his I did my best to reassure him. 'Soon as I can ... Miles isn't it?'

'That's right. How did you know?'

'I heard them call you that.' Turning to McNeil and Kevin I could see they were already soaking the same grey cloth Howard had used. 'This guy needs a hospital,' I called.

McNeil barely reacted, just a glance before returning to what he was doing. Kevin ignored me.

'I said, he needs a hospital!'

Kevin went stiff, took a deep breath and then exhaled hard. 'We heard you. You're the one with the phone. Call a bloody ambulance.'

I hesitated. McNeil seemed to sense my concern. 'This man was about to have you executed, boss. What's your fuckin' problem?'

I didn't reply. Truth is, I was torn. Torn between that sense of right and wrong that most of us call conscience, and a lust for revenge that I shared with two men I could see were about to do something I believed I could never bring myself to do. And, I knew that whatever I said to try and dissuade them, at that moment, I wouldn't sound convincing. Even as the wet cloth covered Howard's face and I saw the panic in his eyes, I felt nothing. No sympathy, no hatred, no will to step in.

Through clenched teeth I played my final card. 'Do not kill him,' I said. 'That's a fuckin' order.'

I turned my back. Turned away from what I knew to be right. Something had happened to me. I'd changed, evolved. And I understood. Understood that being a soldier, learning to fight, to kill and to carry on doing so as men fell around you would always come at a cost. The army didn't just turn people like me into men, it turned them into men able to take the lives of others, without feeling, as calmly and professionally as any other job of work. Kevin, McNeil, Grady, Howard Green and me, we were all from the same mould. The only factor that separated us was our moral compass.

It took me several minutes to secure the attendance of an ambulance. Explaining to the emergency operator where I was and the nature of Miles's injuries proved to be a challenge but we eventually got there. The female operator suggested it may be a job more suited to the air ambulance and I agreed.

As I ended the call, I could hear Howard coughing and spluttering as he struggled to answer the questions McNeil and Kevin were asking him. McNeil wanted to know if there was another copy of the Al Anfal document – he hadn't given up on that idea, it seemed – and Kevin wanted answers concerning his arrest, Sandi's murder and the suspicion he seemed to have that Howard and Mellor may have been in cahoots.

I told Miles that an ambulance was on its way to us. He nodded, seemingly relieved. Looking down at Chris Grady I noticed something sticking out from his pocket. As I looked more closely, I saw it was a small leather wallet. I removed it from his jacket and opened it. Inside I found cash, several hundred pounds, at least. There was just one further item, and as I pulled it out for a closer look, I felt a twist to my guts. It was a photograph. Two children, a girl and a boy, both aged about seven or eight. Both in school uniform, both smiling for what looked like their annual class photograph. Two happy kids in a picture carried by their father.

'He had kids,' I said, holding the picture up for the others to see.

'So do you, Finlay,' answered Kevin. 'And that wasn't going to stop him killing you.'

'That's all he had on him. A wallet with cash and a picture of his kids…'

The burner phone began to ring. It was in my pocket and, as I reached to answer it, I saw that my hand was trembling. It was Toni again.

'What's happening?' she asked.

'We're alive, that's what's happening,' I said. 'There's one of your people here, a man called Miles…'

'Is he OK … is he hurt?' she asked, anxiously.

'He's been better, I'm sure, but yes, he's OK. I've called a local ambulance to come and pick him up.'

'A civilian ambulance?'

'Yes,' I said. Toni seemed to want to know everything.

'OK, leave that with me. I'll arrange a heli to pick him up. What about the others the Chinook crew reported, anyone wounded?'

'We're fine … and the other two are Kevin and McNeil.'

'Kevin? Kevin Jones?'

'Yes that's him. Howard was planning on framing him for my murder as well as Sandi and that literary agent, Maggie Price.'

'Jesus … can you give me a minute?'

The phone went quiet as Toni talked to someone on another line. I was glad of the break and took the opportunity to sit down and rest. Her first question on returning to me was to ask after Howard Green.

'OK for now,' I said. 'But, if Kevin does what I think he's planning to do, that situation is going to change.'

'He plans to put things right for the Increment lads?' she asked.

'And for Sandi Beattie. And he also has this notion that Superintendent Mellor was working with Howard.'

'That's not right … Can you put him on the line, let me speak to him?'

I held the phone up and called to Kevin. 'Toni wants to speak to you.'

Waiting with Miles, as we all attempted to listen to what was being said on the telephone, Howard tried speaking to me. I only heard the word 'deal' before McNeil punched him hard in the guts and ordered him to be quiet. Coughing and retching from the blow, Howard took the hint and stayed quiet.

Kevin had walked to a point where he was nearly out of earshot. At first, he and Toni seemed to argue but, as the conversation progressed, I saw his body start to relax and he became less animated. Their discussion gave way to what sounded like a tacit agreement. It seemed Toni had succeeded where I had failed.

'Put the water away, Mac,' Kevin addressed his instruction to McNeil as he handed me the phone. 'MI5 need him intact.'

Less than a minute later, an Apache gunship appeared hovering above us. The noise and downdraft suppressed any further attempt at conversation. Soon after that, a Chinook arrived. I'm not sure if it was the same one we'd seen before but it looked like it. As a team of soldiers wearing a very familiar kit abseiled down and headed up the track towards where we stood with our hands clasped firmly on our heads, I allowed myself a smile.

Kevin had finished untying Howard and was standing watching the Apache as I approached him.

'What did Toni say?' I asked.

'You mean what did she say that you didn't think of?'

'I'm curious…'

'She offered me something you couldn't. A way to clear my name and a fresh start. Bit of a no-brainer, really.'

'And that persuaded you to lay off Howard?' I asked.

'She insisted.'

'We're too old for this,' I said, ruefully.

Kevin smiled sadly as he turned to me. 'We'll see, boss. We'll see.'

Chapter 66

Fleet Street, London, EC4

Kevin pulled the Ford into the side of the road, turned off the wipers and then switched on the hazard lights.

'Wait here,' said Toni. 'I shouldn't be long. And make sure you keep that cap pulled down and your collar up.'

'Yes, boss. Or should I say yes, blondie? That wig suits you by the way.'

'Perhaps we should swap? It itches like the blazes. And remember what I said about eye contact. Avoid it, completely. The eyes are your biggest give away.'

Toni opened the passenger door and stepped onto the pavement. Parking in the City of London was a nightmare. With virtually every street now controlled by double-yellow lines or parking meters she gambled that the awful weather would buy them enough time to avoid the attentions of a traffic warden. 'If someone moves you on, just drive around the block and meet me here,' she called through the open door. Kevin raised a hand to show he understood.

Across the road, a small alleyway led to the pub where her contact had agreed to wait. A large, illuminated glass sign told her she was in the right place: Ye Old Cheshire Cheese.

It looked like the entrance was down the alleyway. On the main road, the three pub windows resembled giant noughts-and-crosses boards, each with nine panes of heavy, opaque glass. Inside, the lighting appeared warm and welcoming. Even though it was late, the pub still seemed to be packed.

Every so often, a customer would either disappear down the alley or emerge to face the rain that was now beating down outside. All the patrons, men and women alike, seemed to be wearing suits. They all looked as she imagined they would – like journalists, winding down at the end of a busy day.

Max Tranter was finishing a pint of beer as she approached. From the look of him, it wasn't his first.

'Mr Tranter,' said Toni, as he drained the glass. Max wiped the sleeve of his sports jacket across his mouth and looked at her reflection in the mirror behind the bar. His eyebrows flicked up as he studied her for a moment. Then he nodded, approvingly.

'Mrs *Smith*, I presume,' Max emphasised the name, his scepticism clear.

'Are you ready?' she asked, ignoring his inference.

'Nearly. My sub-editor on the news desk just called to say that a translator is on her way to meet us.'

'The paper has Arabic translators?'

'No, this lady is freelance, on a daily rate. Expensive but, if what you are offering is genuine, the cost of a translator will be incidental.' He checked his watch. 'She's late. The rain, I guess? Ah … here she is.'

Toni turned around. A woman of Iranian or Persian appearance was letting down her umbrella and shaking the water droplets in the doorway. She was well dressed, elegant even. The coat, the hair, the carefully applied make-up, all suggested someone wealthy.

The woman approached and, appearing to recognise Max, she said hello to him and then introduced herself to Toni. Background voices in the pub meant that Toni didn't quite catch the name but she didn't ask her to repeat it. It probably wouldn't matter. All they needed was her language skills.

Max led the way to the door and out into Wine Office Court. A few yards away was Fleet Street, once home to almost all the national news-papers. Now, thanks to budget cuts and relocations to Wapping and

Southwark, it was only a muted reflection of its past history. The only remaining name on the street was Reuters, and it was widely rumoured that they would be on the move before long.

'Where are we going?' he asked.

'There's a Ford parked across the road on the yellow lines. You climb in the front next to my driver. We'll get in the back. A section of the document is in a folder on the rear seat.'

Breathing in the cool, night air. Max touched his left hand on a polished plate mounted near the door. Toni looked at him quizzically.

'The Sovereigns' Plate,' he explained. 'It bears the names of every King and Queen of England since James the Second in 1685, together with their period of reign. If you look carefully, it may amuse you to note that the most recent entry, that for Queen Elizabeth II, has been inscribed in such a way as to not leave space to record an end to her reign.'

Toni did as suggested, and saw that Max's claim was correct. The translator concentrated on positioning her umbrella to ensure as good a protection from the rain as it might allow.

'I'm something of a royalist,' Max continued. 'It's become my habit to touch the plaque for luck. Shall we go?'

As they reached the main street, Kevin was waiting.

Rain flicked across the seats as they got into the car. Max remembered his instructions and used the front seat. Toni climbed in behind Kevin and sat alongside the translator. Almost immediately, the windows began to mist over.

Kevin started the engine, flicked on the windscreen wipers and started the ventilation blowers. A black taxi flew past, spraying water from the road surface.

'You have the document?' Max asked.

'Like I said in the pub, just some excerpts for now … a taster. The original is well over an inch thick.'

'Can we see what you have?'

Toni handed the folder to the translator. 'I suggest we get moving. I wouldn't want to attract the interest of a passing police car due to us

being on yellow lines.' Max nodded his agreement as Kevin eased the
car out into the traffic.

In the back of the car, the translator quickly got to work. On Max's
instructions, she read out loud in English. She made slow progress –
some of the language was unfamiliar to her – but she was able to explain
most of it. She commented that it was as if it had been written in sections, by different people from varying countries. In the driver's mirror,
Toni saw Kevin smile knowingly as she said it.

They headed east, into the City and then towards the Docklands,
Kevin keeping an eye on the rear-view mirror, in case they were
followed.

They listened in as the translator continued to read. With every
section, Max appeared to focus harder on what was revealed.

Finally, as they passed one of the new Dockland Light Railway stations, Max asked Kevin to stop the car. Politely, he asked the translator
to step out of the car and wait in the cover of the station foyer. She did
as she was asked without replying.

'We never allow them to hear us talk money,' said Max.

'So, you're interested?'

'How much more of this is there?' he asked.

'Like I said, the full thing is over an inch thick.'

Max paused for a moment. 'So how much are we talking ... Mrs
Smith, or whatever your name is?'

Toni ignored the comment. 'Two hundred and fifty K was your
bid, so that's the price,' she said, tersely. 'I imagine your newspaper can
afford it or you wouldn't have gone that high.'

'How would you like payment? Cash, I assume?'

'Half in cash, half into this account.' Toni passed Max a slip of paper
across his shoulder.

He read it. 'A trustee account in the names of Paul and John Beattie?'

'Once the money appears in that account I will be in touch to arrange
to collect the cash and deliver the full document.'

'I know the name Beattie, don't I?' Max asked. 'These names, they're
the sons of the woman who was killed by her cop lover, I believe? The

one who escaped from court and was killed in a drug war shooting in Wales a couple of days later?'

'A tragedy that should be compensated for, don't you think?'

Max sat for a moment. It was clear he sensed a follow-up to the stories he had been pursuing, but it seemed he had taken the warning. 'OK,' he said, finally. 'Let's get back to the document. From what our translator read out, it reminds me very much of "The Project", the report that the Muslim Brotherhood supposedly produced.'

'It should. "The Project" is small beer compared to what I will be handing over to you.'

'Very well,' said Max as he went to open the car door. 'I'm satisfied it's genuine. I'll speak to my editor but the final decision will come from our owner. I don't expect there'll be a problem, though.'

'We have an agreement then?'

'Yes. So, who are you? MI6, perhaps?'

Toni ignored the question. 'I'll be in touch, Mr Tranter.' Then, as the two figures huddled together beneath the translator's umbrella and trotted through the rain and up the stairs towards the station concourse area, she climbed over into the front seat.

'Happy?' she asked Kevin.

'Very,' he answered. 'You asked for two or three times what I would have ... and he didn't bat an eyelid. McNeil will think all his Christmases have come at once.'

'And what about you?'

'I'm good, but that bastard journalist smelled a story, I could tell. He was watching you for a reaction when he said MI6.'

'I thought the same. What about the amount?'

'The money was never a big issue to me, to be honest. I just wanted Sandi's boys to be ok.'

'Good. Now ... let's get back to Camden. We have an appointment with an old friend of yours.'

Chapter 67

'I wasn't aware this building existed.' Superintendent Mellor looked out the window and across the North London skyline towards Chalk Farm as he spoke.

'Not many people are, for obvious reasons,' said Toni.

'In better weather, I'd bet you can see Hampstead Heath from here.'

'And beyond. Although the glass is one way, so people can't see us.'

'Sensible. Now, do you mind if I ask why you invited me over here?'

Toni had laid out the office to achieve the effect she desired. Two chairs, one with its back to the door, a second, larger chair facing it with a desk in between. Formal, and not too cosy. She invited Mellor to sit, and indicated he should use the smaller chair. He accepted and, as she relaxed into her seat, she smiled warmly.

The Superintendent remained expressionless. *Cold fish*, she thought. *Let's see if he stays that way*.

'We need to discuss a few things with you.'

'We … I can only see one of you Miss … er Fellowes, you said?'

'Yes. That's right, *Ms* Fellowes. And when I say "we", I mean we as a Service.'

'Well, what have I done to earn this honour, I wonder?'

'It's with regard to a recent enquiry of yours. The investigation into the death of a Mrs Sandra Beattie.'

Mellor scowled. 'What would that have to do with the Security Service? It was an internal matter involving an allegation against a serving police officer.'

'PC Jones?'

'Correct. His escape from custody only served to confirm his guilt, in my opinion. We would have caught up with him in due course … Ah, I've just figured out why you want to speak about it.'

'Do enlighten me, Superintendent.'

'Well, it's obvious. Everyone knows that you people were in on the steps taken to protect Jones and Robert Finlay from being prosecuted last year.'

'A decision you have an opinion on?'

'Of course. No copper is above the law and those two got away with some serious transgressions. I knew they'd fall into my hands one day. It was just a question of time.'

'So you say that no copper is above the law?'

'Absolutely. And it's the job of people like me to ensure that when they break it they are called to account.'

'You take that job very seriously, it would appear.'

'Damn right I do.'

'Seriously enough to frame an innocent man?'

'Never.'

'Cops do though, don't they? Noble cause corruption I believe it's called, making sure the guilty get their comeuppance.'

'You might very well think that, Ms Fellowes. I couldn't possibly comment.'

Toni smiled at the Superintendent's use of fictional politician Francis Urquhart's words. She paused as she did so, to give the impression she was contemplating something he'd had said or the skill of his response. It was a ruse, as she was about to play her ace.

'Do you mind if I ask someone to join us?' she asked. 'I'd like you to meet them.'

Mellor shrugged and glanced over his shoulder towards the door. 'Sure, but I'm still not entirely sure why you wanted to discuss the Jones case. It's dead and buried now after he was killed.'

'Yes, that's true. Bear with me a moment.' Toni picked up the telephone and dialled the extension number of the next-door office. From her seat, she could hear the phone ringing through the thin wall. It was answered after two rings. 'Could you join us,' she said, before hanging up.

The jaw-dropped expression on Mellor's face as he turned on his seat to face the door was something she knew would remain with her, possibly for life. For a fleeting second she almost laughed. As Kevin came and stood behind her, it even looked as if the Superintendent was in danger of passing out.

'Superintendent Mellor … meet Harry Cole.'

Mellor appeared to compose himself quickly as he responded without hesitation. 'Just what the hell is going on here?' he demanded. 'Jones, I thought you were dead?'

'PC Jones is no more,' said Toni. 'In fact, he never really was. Mr Cole is one of us, a long-serving and very loyal member of the Security Service.'

'I … I'm not sure I follow. Are you saying there is no such…?'

Toni interrupted him. 'I'm saying that the man you tried to pin a murder on is actually a member of MI5, Superintendent. I'm *saying* that the gun you found in his car was his and that he was authorised to have it in his possession. I'm *saying* – and listen to this very carefully as I spell it out for you in as simple terms as my patience will allow – our officer using the name Kevin Jones did not kill Mrs Beattie.'

'But the evidence pointed very clearly—'

'The evidence?'

'Yes. It was clear that you…' He looked accusingly at Kevin. 'It was clear you killed her.'

'But you *knew* he hadn't, Superintendent. You knew that our officer had been jumped by other men, rendered unconscious and that evidence had then been planted by others to implicate him.'

'I knew nothing of the kind. There was no evidence at all to suggest anyone else was involved.'

Kevin turned and walked towards the window. He was listening but knew to stay quiet. He was to leave the talking to Toni.

'You knew, but you were happy to frame PC Jones for the murder.'

Mellor started to stand. 'This is ridiculous. I don't know what kind of a game you're playing here but I'm taking this straight to my superiors. Jones, Cole … whatever your name is. You killed that woman.'

Toni pulled the top drawer of the desk open and withdrew a thin buff folder. 'Would you do me the courtesy of looking at this before you leave us, Superintendent?' She placed the top sheet from the folder on the far side of the desk so Mellor could read it easily.

'What's this?' he demanded, angrily.

'It's a copy of a Complaints Branch register showing the issue of listening devices that were on trial this year. If you look carefully, you will see that two of the bugs are listed as being in your departmental stores.'

Mellor leaned over the desk as he studied the document. Toni caught a whiff of stale breath and tobacco. 'And your point is what?'

'We found one of those devices in the house being used by our officer and the second in Mrs Beattie's home.'

'Ridiculous, I know nothing of that.'

Toni took a deep breath. 'Perhaps you should sit down?' As Mellor returned to his seat, she reached further into the desk drawer and withdrew a small laptop computer. It was already turned on, and as she opened the screen it flickered into life.

'Do you recognise this?' she asked.

Mellor looked confused. 'Possibly … it's a fairly common make and model.'

'This particular one was found in the bedroom of your home – underneath the bed.'

'You've been in my home? You've no right.'

'We've every right, Superintendent. There are a number of statutory instruments – laws – giving us the authority we need when gathering evidence.' Toni tapped the keyboard to trigger a recording to replay. 'How long would you like to listen to this for? I'm certain you've heard it before. We were able to trace this laptop as the recipient of the transmitted signals from both the listening devices.'

Mellor held up a hand. 'OK, OK. What do you want?'

Toni shrugged. 'Perhaps an admission that no copper is above the law might be a good start?'

'Very funny.' Mellor shook his head. 'We have an expression in the job: What goes around comes around. Jones got away with other crimes so I was having him for this one.'

'Even if it meant ignoring evidence you knew exonerated him? Noble cause corruption I think we agreed it is called?'

There was no response.

'You heard the other voices in the recording. You heard the struggle and the sounds of a Taser. And you chose to ignore it because it didn't fit with the case you were building.'

'I'm leaving now.'

'I think it best you hear me out, Superintendent,' Toni continued. 'And I'll tell you what we're going to do.'

'You want a deal?'

'You need a favour,' Toni said, forcefully. 'I have enough here to send you to prison for a long time. In return for keeping this under wraps I will require you to do a number of things.'

'You want me as your pawn?'

'I want you to appreciate the very serious position you find your-self in and how the Security Service is about to make you an offer you would be wise to consider. Now … shall we continue?'

Mellor remained silent as she laid out her terms. Firstly, he would ensure the enquiry into Sandra Beattie would be closed with Chris Grady named as the killer. To that, he agreed quite easily, even though she noticed a look of some discomfort in his eyes on the one occasion Kevin turned away from the window. The second requirement, Toni explained, was regarding Robert Finlay. Mellor was to ensure Finlay was reinstated to full duties with immediate effect and he was to be served with the necessary paperwork stating he was cleared of all suspicion of involvement in PC Jones's escape and was no longer under investigation. Again, Mellor agreed.

Finally, Toni outlined her third condition, which concerned PC Doug Powell from Kentish Town. 'I want you to make sure Finlay's promises to him are met in full,' Toni said, firmly.

'But he held a fellow officer at knife point, and then wasted all our time with that ridiculous demonstration on the roof of the section house.'

Toni stared hard at Mellor, and within a few seconds he took a deep breath and then shook his head from side to side. 'Very well,' he said, submissively. 'What do you need me to do?'

'We don't expect you to have him return to work, I think even we would agree that might be somewhat excessive. No, what we want you to do is make sure Powell isn't prosecuted and he gets to retire on an ill-health pension.'

'I'll never get that past my bosses.'

'I'm sure you'll find a way, Superintendent.'

Mellor huffed. He was beaten, and he knew it.

Interview concluded, Toni arranged for one of the security team to see Mellor to the exit. Having Kevin do it was too much like rubbing salt into the wounds. He went quietly, without further argument and she noticed as he left the office that the spring in his step was now defi- nitely missing.

'Think he'll cooperate,' said Kevin, a few seconds after closing the door.

'He will,' said Toni, 'Nell will be watching to make sure he does.'

☩

An hour later, Toni sat down, once again at her former work station at New Scotland Yard. Nell had been waiting for her and was anxious to know how the interview with Mellor had gone.

'Really well, I think. He bluffed at first but when I pulled out his laptop that clinched it. He rolled over fairly easily. You did a great job.'

'It was nothing. When he turned it on the tracking system did the work for me. It's Stuart you should really thank, he went and retrieved it from under Mellor's bed.'

'Yes. Tell him thanks when you see him won't you?'

'Sure. To be honest, I think he got a bit of a thrill breaking into the home of a Complaints Branch Superintendent.'

Toni laughed. 'Yes, I bet he did.'

'If I'm right, I think you also enjoyed putting Mellor through the ringer?'

'Yes,' she replied. 'Yes, I did. We spend so much time reacting to events, it was nice to do something pro-active for a change. Did you manage to record it OK?'

Her researcher winked and gave a thumbs-up. Job done.

Chapter 68

Bill headed back to the sofa and then sat quietly for several seconds as he ran his fingers up and down the stem of his wine glass. It seemed he needed a few moments to consider what Toni had been saying.

'You think it's for the best?' he asked, finally.

'Tonight really should be the last time, Bill. People are already talking.'

'This flat will be empty without you.'

'It will, but it's not as if we'll never see each other again.' How many times had the ending of an affair seen those words used, she wondered?

He half smiled. 'One for the road,' he said, ruefully.

'Yes. One last evening together. Shall we enjoy the rest of the wine?'

'And celebrate the end of this Howard Green chap?'

'And the end of a year I would prefer to forget.' Toni raised her glass and clinked it against his.

'That saw you promoted and…'

'Us getting together,' she said, finishing his sentence.

'You know, for all the awful things that have happened to Robert Finlay, I find myself envying him.'

'How's that?' she asked.

'For the life he's had. He's seen more things, lived far more, experienced the kind of adventure … more than many of us could even imagine.'

'At a price, though?'

'True. But look at him now. He's settled, two kids and a wife he loves … and who clearly feels just as strongly for him. And look at me: no kids; failed marriage; and now you're giving me my marching orders.'

There was sadness in Bill's voice, a sense of resignation she hadn't detected before. As if the fire had gone from within him. 'He'll be OK now?' she asked, tentatively, although her concerns were now less about Finlay than for the sad figure in front of her, sipping at his wine.

'Men like Finlay are survivors,' said Bill.

'Howard Green's game has ended reasonably well then?' she said, a deliberately feigned hint of pride in her tone.

'It has, I guess. Although maybe not for him, if what you were saying earlier is correct?'

'It is. Green is history. With the exception of the Cristeas, all the agents and contacts he was responsible for handling have been reallocated.'

'The Cristeas are an exception?' said Bill.

'An open sore that we hope to cauterise fairly soon, once we've figured out whether Howard was their only asset.'

'Were the Cristeas the reason Maggie Price was killed?'

'No, that was down to Howard. Her author, Chas Collins, was working on a sequel to the book he brought out last year which was going to blow the lid off Al Anfal. Mrs Price had the only copy of the manuscript.'

'So another woman died to keep a secret? And what about the author?'

'Dead. Howard's people found him in Belgium, in a lock-up garage. I'll spare you the details.'

'And the MI5 officer who exposed Howard?'

'Miles is already back at work,' she replied, as a smile returned to her face. 'He's looking a bit worse for wear but he tells me that Occupational Health have given him a clean bill of health.'

'All very tidy … So, tell me more about this dark web thing you used to sell the Al Anfal document.'

'It was something Nell showed me. It's the underworld of the internet and, not too surprisingly, it has auction sites that can be used to sell things in a way that don't identify the seller.'

'You're confident nobody will ever know it was you that sold it? I'm rather too fond of you to contemplate the idea of you turning up in a body bag one day.'

Toni felt a sudden rush of regret at what she had said earlier. Was it too late, she wondered? She loved his wit, his intellect, how she felt so at ease in his company. And he cared for her, in a way that she found comforting. 'That's nice of you, but don't worry. The strategic value of the document was severely compromised the moment we found another copy for sale. A decision was made to leak it in a way that, at least, did some good for those two young boys. And yes,' she added, 'I'm certain I can't be traced.'

'And Nell says these sites are starting to be used by terrorists, even here in the UK?' he asked.

'She's certain. She only used to see things like recreational drugs and stolen gear for sale, but, from what she tells me, the sites are now seeing weapons being listed.'

'Firearms?'

'Everything you can imagine, from guns to grenades.'

'That's really quite scary,' he said. 'I'm amazed our techie boys have never mentioned it to us.'

'Perhaps they don't know about it yet? Nell has done a report that will be on its way to you soon.'

'Good, thanks. So, where does this leave us?'

'Friends.' She raised her glass again, as if to toast her proposal.

Bill looked defeated, in need of a lift. In many ways, exactly as she was. And he was here, he was now, and he wanted her. She felt another rush of warmth toward him, affection of the kind that she'd felt for no one outside of her family. And, in that moment, she realised that if she went through with her decision, she would miss him terribly.

'With a shared secret,' he answered. 'And both as lonely as we were before this all started.'

'People like us struggle to maintain relationships.'

'Yes … I guess you're right'. He emptied his glass in one. 'One for the road, you said?'

She took his hand, held it firmly and sighed. 'I think we may need to be more careful in future.'

A confused look crossed his face as she changed her grip, stood and led him toward the bedroom.

'Woman's prerogative, William Grahamslaw,' she said, with a mischievous wink. 'This may take a while to explain.'

Epilogue

Double tap, double tap. I smiled, it was Kevin. He always announced his arrival in exactly the same way, by rapping four times on the door knocker.

'Will you get that?' Jenny called from the top of the stairs.

Guessing he'd want a brew, I flicked the kettle on and headed to the door.

'You took your time,' Kevin said, as he stepped into the hallway. 'I thought you two were expecting me?'

'Get away with you.'

'Brew on?'

I smiled. 'Of course.'

I closed the door firmly, but not before I'd checked the drive. Old habits ran deep.

Kevin had called a couple of days previously to set up the visit. We were overdue a catch-up and I had a lot of questions about what had happened since our return from Wales in the rear of an MI5 car – me to be dropped off at home, Kevin headed to a meeting with Toni Fellowes. His timing had been good, just a few hours after he'd phoned I'd also heard from Bill Grahamslaw to tell me my suspension had been lifted and that he was expecting me back at work the following Monday.

Toni had called me twice. First, to tell me what was happening with regard to the bothy. Some rather protracted negotiation had apparently occurred between the Chief Constable of the local force, Dyfed-Powys, and the Director-General at MI5. The day after Kevin, McNeil, Howard Green and I were whisked discreetly away, the body of Maggie Price was located in a shallow grave behind the bothy log store. An initial forensic examination at the scene confirmed she'd been shot and had been dead for some while, but tests on all the weapons recovered had yet to be completed.

Toni was confident that, just as he'd boasted, the pistol I had seen Howard produce from a paper bag had been used to kill Maggie Price and the unfortunate drug dealer who, she'd learned from Howard Green, had crossed Grady's path while leaving Maggie Price's home. She also had no doubt that Howard's intention had been to frame Kevin for the deaths with mine and Miles, her fellow agent, to be added to the list.

There would be an official inquest, she'd explained. The police had insisted on it, but they'd also confirmed the incident was being investigated as a drug-dealer turf war that Maggie Price had inadvertently become involved in.

So, for us, the game was over. For Howard Green, I suspected that whatever life he had remaining wasn't going to be anywhere near as comfortable as he'd been used to. Toni's second call had been to tell me that Howard had been handed over to a group she called the 'sharks'. By that, she meant the men and women within the Security Service charged with monitoring and investigating the Service itself. The deal Kevin had predicted hadn't happened. I'd asked what would happen to Howard. Toni had replied by suggesting I didn't give it any thought.

It had been at the end of that conversation when I'd asked about Kevin and how she planned to bring the accusations against him to a close. Howard's admissions had exonerated him from involvement in Sandi's death, but there was still the question of the gun found in the boot of his car and his escape from custody. 'I'll let him tell you, himself,' she'd said.

A day or so later, he'd called, and he'd said he wanted to talk to Jenny as well. And now he was here. I dropped three tea bags into mugs and, as I made the tea, he waited at the back door, surveying the garden.

'Tidy,' he commented. 'Nice to see you've made use of your time off.'

'Just don't ask me to do yours.'

'Yes … that's one of the reasons I've come to see you.'

'You want me to do your garden?'

He laughed. 'No, in fact the house won't be mine for much longer.'

'You're selling it?' I asked, my curiosity piqued.

'Will Jenny be long?' He turned away from the window without answering my question and then pulled one of the kitchen chairs away from the table so he could sit down. The legs dragged noisily on the wooden floor.

'You two talking about me?' Jenny's voice called from the hall. I turned and, in doing so, missed the second cup as I poured the milk. It spilled onto the counter.

'Shall I do that?' she asked.

Kevin stood up as she walked in. It was my turn to smile at his display of good manners.

Jenny also reacted, albeit a little more warmly, as she placed her hands on his shoulders and planted a noisy peck on each of his cheeks. 'Hello, stranger,' she said. 'To what do we owe this honour?'

I sensed a slight barb to the tone in her voice, a slight emphasis on the word 'honour' that hinted at an underlying concern. I wasn't quite sure if I was being oversensitive, so I decided to ignore it. The reason for it, I figured, was rather obvious. I'd told Jenny the detail of my conversation with Toni and about what had happened in Wales, at least up to a point. The part where Petre had held a gun to my head ready for Gheorghe Cristea to witness my execution was, I thought, a detail too far. During the car journey back to London, Kevin had agreed, and when I'd also sought Toni's advice, she shared our opinion. Explaining that several people had died, that Kevin had been an intended framing victim and that an MI6 officer had been behind it was more than enough for any wife to have to hear. How close we'd actually come to being killed and the luck that had resulted in our survival would only have served to make matters worse.

Jenny finished making the tea as I joined Kevin at the kitchen table. He asked me how I'd been – good; how I'd been filling my time – the garden – as he'd just seen; and he then asked the same of Jenny. It was small talk, a nicety, before getting around to the real reason for the visit. We talked about the girls and Jenny told him how disappointed Becky had been to learn that she would have to wait for another time before she got to see her favourite 'uncle' once more.

'OK…' Kevin took a deep breath, as if he had a rehearsed speech prepared that he wanted us to listen to without interruption. Jenny sat next to me, took my hand and squeezed it tight.

'So, where to begin?' he continued. 'Let's start with Sandi's death.'

'Toni explained,' I said.

'That I'm off the hook?'

'Yes. That Grady is now confirmed as the killer.'

'OK, good. Has she told you about Mellor?'

'No,' I answered. 'She hasn't.'

As Kevin explained, we listened. And I must admit that I felt a smug sense of satisfaction to learn how the Superintendent had been caught out and how his mistake had been used to bring him to heel. I pictured the scene, the office Kevin described, and how the smile must have disappeared from Mellor's face as he was confronted with what Toni Fellowes knew he had been up to. Satisfaction turned to emotion as Kevin went on to explain how Toni had applied the screws to ensure that Mellor adopted a more sympathetic approach to dealing with Doug Powell.

'An ill-health retirement?' I said, my voice croaking a little.

'Effective immediately,' said Kevin.

'I wonder if I should speak to him.'

Jenny leaned in close and with her free hand she stroked my arm. 'I think you should,' she said. 'It might be good for both of you.'

'And what about you, Kev?' I asked.

'Ah…' He paused. 'That's where things get complicated and why I needed to speak to both of you.'

I felt Jenny stiffen beside me. 'You're not staying in the Met are you?' she asked, quietly.

'I'm not, no. In fact, the reason I'm here is to explain that, if we are to continue to be friends, you're going to have to get used to calling me by a different name.'

'They're putting you into a witness protection programme?' I asked.

'No … at least not exactly. I'm dead.'

'You're … dead?'

'PC Kevin Jones, as we know him, died in Wales alongside Chris Grady and the others.'

'How have they squared that?'

'Using the body of Petre, I'm told.'

'You're serious?'

'Couldn't be more so. When Toni first took me in to see her Director I was pretty dumbstruck by the idea, I'll tell you. But the more we talked, the more it made sense.'

'So MI5 are giving you a new identity somewhere … a fresh start?'

'Not somewhere, no. Here, in London. I'm now actually in MI5. They've given me a job and a new name.'

'Which is what?' said Jenny.

'Harry Davies.'

'Harry … Davies?' I said. 'Well, at least they picked a Welsh surname to go with your accent.'

'Yeah, it was going to be Harry Cole but, in the end, I said I preferred Davies.'

Upstairs, I heard Charlie start to cry. 'She's hungry,' said Jenny. 'I'll give her a feed and then see if she'll settle.'

I glanced back towards the hallway as Jenny disappeared upstairs. 'So, what exactly do MI5 have in mind for you, er … Harry.'

'Something that may make you smile.'

And as he explained, I did more than that. I laughed, so much so that Jenny came down the stairs, our daughter firmly attached to her left breast, to discover what was going on. In her hand, she held a letter that she'd picked up from the mat near the front door. The postman must have called while we'd been talking.

'Kevin … I mean Harry is going to be in charge of the ROSE office,' I said, in answer to her quizzical look. 'He's being given Monaghan's old job.'

'But I thought that was the preserve of senior officers?' she replied.

'So did we,' said Kevin. 'But they think a middle-aged former Sergeant can do it provided he's under the supervision of a certain Ms Toni Fellowes.'

'They'll take anyone these days,' I quipped.

Kevin laughed. 'I had to do a two-day familiarisation and then another longer course in a week or so.'

'So, Toni's going to be your boss?'

'Already is. I started yesterday.'

'So, what will you be doing?'

'Would you believe following up on the Al Anfal document?'

'You're kidding me?' I said. 'I thought that was dead in the water now that the press have hold of it?'

'They got most of it, but not all. Toni found that a copy was being sold over the dark web. As it was just about to hit the public domain, the Director-General decided to get in first, sell a copy and cash in before anyone else could. The list of agent's names was redacted though. MI5 have suffered a few prosecution setbacks this last year so I'm joining up with a team who are going to be knocking on a few doors over the next few weeks and months to see if we can't redress that imbalance.'

'They'll know you're coming, now that it's been leaked.'

'We don't think so. Opinion is that the agents don't know how detailed the document is.'

I caught sight of Jenny out of the corner of my eye. She was shaking her head from side to side and, I guessed, was thinking the same as me. The Security Service worked in mysterious ways. I glanced at the letter she'd dropped onto the kitchen table. 'Addressed to you, Robert,' she said. 'Looks official.'

As Kevin and Jenny continued chatting, I picked up the envelope and looked at the writing. She was right. It looked like the official notification of my reinstatement. The Federation rep had said it would be with me soon. I placed it back on the table, thinking I could look at it later after our visitor had gone.

'Why don't you open it?' said Kevin.

'It can wait,' I said

'Go on,' he answered. 'Let's confirm the good news together.'

I looked toward Jenny who just shrugged.

Picking up the envelope, I peeled back the opening and removed a single sheet of folded A4 paper. It bore the logo and address of the Met Commissioner.

'What is it?' Jenny asked.

'It's a letter from the Commissioner … I'm reinstated.'

'Nice one,' mumbled Kevin. 'This is for you as well.' He dropped a small, cardboard CD wallet onto the table.

'What's that?' I asked.

'Let's just call it an insurance policy shall we? It contains recordings of interviews we've done with Howard Green and Jim Mellor. They're both quite long so I wouldn't trouble yourself to listen to them now, but I think you'll find them interesting.'

'Game over?' I asked.

He nodded. 'Let's hope so, boss.'

Acknowledgments

Without a publisher prepared to invest in an author, where would people like me be? Thank you to all the folks at Orenda Books for doing just that and to editor, West Camel who has guided me, challenged me and taught me so much over the last three years.

To my agents, James Wills of Watson-Little Ltd and Kaye Freeman at Andromeda Talent, I extend thanks for always being there when I've needed you and for your wisdom.

To all you marvellous book bloggers who read, review and do such a great job in helping authors like me build a readership.

To those serving and retired members of the emergency and armed services who have advised me, put me right, jogged my memory and corrected my errors, I extend a sincere thanks.

Thanks to my partner, Heather, who has read, checked and critiqued my drafts. Without you, *Wicked*, *Deadly* and *End Game* would never have been written.

And finally, thank you for giving up your time to read my work. I hope you enjoyed the unexpected result of a life spent keeping 'the monsters from the weak'.

Matt Johnson
February 2018

'Terse, tense and vivid writing. Matt Johnson is
a brilliant new name in the world of thrillers'
PETER JAMES

WICKED GAME

MATT JOHNSON

DEADLY GAME

MATT JOHNSON